"A hero to steal your heart!"

—**Elizabeth Boyle,** *New York Times* **bestselling author**

"An immensely satisfying and sophisticated blend of history and romance. I loved every gorgeous, breathtaking page!"

—**Julianne MacLean,** *USA Today* **bestselling author of** *When a Stranger Loves Me*

"*Countess of Scandal* delivers on all fronts. The story raced along, zigging and zagging from Dublin to the countryside, from uneasy peace to all-out war. And the romance...very satisfying!"

—**MyShelf.com**

"A vivid historical tale with breathtaking characters."

—**Michelle Willingham, author of** *Taming Her Irish Warrior*

"Captivating and poignant! Laurel McKee wields her pen with grace and magic."

—**Lorraine Heath,** *New York Times* **bestselling author of** *Midnight Pleasures with a Scoundrel*

"Rich, vivid, and passionate."

—**Nicola Cornick, author of** *The Undoing of a Lady*

Also by Laurel McKee

Countess of Scandal

"Hush, Anna." Conlan's arms slid around her, drawing her tight against him just as she had wanted. "For once in your life, just hush."

His mouth came down on hers. He was not harsh, but he *was* insistent, his lips opening over hers, his tongue seeking entrance. She opened for him, letting him in, meeting him eagerly.

Oh, yes, *this* was what she longed for. That sensation of every rational thought flying out of her, of falling down into pure, hot need.

His hand slid down her back as their kiss deepened, and his coat fell away from her shoulders. The cold air washed over her, but she only felt it for an instant before it was replaced with his heat. He wanted *her*. Not the image of her, the earl's fine, pretty daughter, but *her*.

"I don't want to need you," he said fiercely.

"I don't want to need you, either," she whispered. Her head fell back against the wall. She closed her eyes tightly, reveling in the glorious pleasure of his touch. "But I fear I do. Oh curse it, Conlan, if you don't touch me I'll scream."

"4 Stars! McKee sets the stage for a romantic adventure that captures the spirit of Ireland and a pair of star-crossed lovers to perfection."

—*RT Book Reviews* on *Countess of Scandal*

Please turn this page for more praise for Laurel McKee . . .

Praise for Laurel McKee and
Countess of Scandal

"I am completely hooked on this series already—and I was from nearly the first page of this book! Ms. McKee tells a masterful story of love, rebellion, and beneath it all, devotion to a land and people...Elizabeth and Will's emotional attachment, as well as the obvious physical chemistry they share, leaps from the page."

—RomanceReaderatHeart.com

"Ms. Laurel McKee's magical pen captivates you instantaneously! She has fashioned blistering sensual romantic scenes and a love story that will be forever etched in your mind."

—TheRomanceReadersConnection.com

"Laurel McKee captures the excitement and magic of romance."

—Cathy Maxwell, *New York Times* **bestselling author of** *The Earl Claims His Wife*

"Eliza's and Will's happy-ever-after, once reached, is both powerfully satisfying and forever engraved on the reader's mind and heart. Every word sings with unyielding intensity...Beautifully written, *Countess of Scandal* reads like a captivating love story of epic proportions. The ultimate page-turner."

—RomanceJunkies.com on
Countess of Scandal

Duchess of Sin

LAUREL McKEE

FOREVER

NEW YORK   BOSTON

Copyright © 2010 by Laurel McKee
Excerpt from *Lady of Seduction* copyright © 2010 by Laurel McKee
All rights reserved. Except as permitted under the U.S. Copyright Act of 1976, no part of this publication may be reproduced, distributed, or transmitted in any form or by any means, or stored in a database or retrieval system, without the prior written permission of the publisher.

Forever
Hachette Book Group
237 Park Avenue
New York, NY 10017
Visit our website at www.HachetteBookGroup.com.

Forever is an imprint of Grand Central Publishing.
The Forever name and logo is a trademark of Hachette Book Group, Inc.

Printed in the United States of America

First Printing: December 2010

10 9 8 7 6 5 4 3 2 1

To Mrs. Harold, my high school AP History teacher, and all the wonderful teachers I had over the years who encouraged me in my writing. Teachers rock!

Chapter One

Dublin, December 1799

She really should not be doing this. It was a terrible, imprudent idea.

But that had never stopped her before.

Lady Anna Blacknall drew the hood of her black cloak closer over her pale gold hair, which would shimmer like a beacon in the night and attract unwanted attention. She pressed her back tighter to the stone wall, peering out at the world through the eyeholes of her satin mask. Her endeavor to become invisible seemed to be working as everyone hurried past her without even a glance.

But where was Jane? If she turned coward and refused to appear, Anna couldn't get into the Olympian Club on her own. Jane was the one who was a member, and the club had a strictly enforced "guests of members only" policy. It wasn't likely Jane would abandon her, though. Jane, the widowed but still young Lady Cannondale, was the most daring woman in Dublin, always up for a lark or a dare. She was also Anna's new bosom bow—much to her mother's chagrin. Katherine Blacknall, Lady Killinan, feared Lady Cannondale would land Anna in scandal and ruin.

It was fortunate Katherine didn't realize that most of their pranks were Anna's idea, just like the one tonight.

Anna pressed her hands tightly to her stomach where a nervous excitement fluttered like a hundred demented butterflies. This seemed like such a fine idea when she first heard about the exclusive, secretive, scandalous Olympian Club and found out Jane was a member. Tonight the club was holding a masked ball, the rare opportunity for non-members to see what went on inside its hidden environs. Surely something so secretive must be worth exploring.

Strangely, though, Jane had tried to put her off, to laugh away the invitation to the ball. "It is sure to be quite dull," she insisted, taking the engraved card from Anna's hand after she found it hidden in Jane's sitting room. "The club has such a reputation only because it restricts its membership. There's just cards and a little dancing, like everywhere else in Dublin."

Anna snatched the invitation right back. "How can a masked ball at a secret club possibly be dull? I've been so bored of late. Surely this is just the excitement I need!"

Jane had laughed. "You have been to parties every night this month. How can you be bored?"

"All anyone talks about are the Union debates in Parliament," Anna said. Those endless quarrels for and against Ireland's Union with England, rumors of who had been bribed with titles and money to switch sides, and who had come to fisticuffs over the matter in St. Stephen's Green. She was so vastly tired of it, tired of everything.

It did not distract her from memories of the Uprising, either—from the old, terrible nightmares of blood and death in battle. Only dancing and wine and noise could do that, for a few hours, anyway.

She had finally persuaded Jane to take her to the Olympian Club's masked ball. Anna crept out of her house at the appointed hour, in disguise, to wait on this street corner. But where was Jane?

She tapped her foot under the hem of her gown, a borrowed frock of Jane's made of garnet-red satin embroidered with jet beads and trimmed with black lace. Her own gowns were all the insipid whites and pastels of a debutante, but this gown was much better. The beads clicked and sang at the movement, as if they, too, longed to dance, to drown in the sweet forgetfulness of music and motion. But if Jane did not hurry, they would have to leave the ball before it even started! Anna had to be home before dawn if she didn't want to get caught.

At last, Jane's carriage came rattling around the corner. The door opened, and Anna rushed inside, barely falling onto the velvet seat before they went flying off again. Her nervous butterflies beat their wings faster as they careened through the night, and Anna laughed at the rush of excitement.

"I thought you changed your mind," she said, straightening her skirt.

"Of course not, A.," Jane answered, tying on her own mask around her piled-up auburn hair. "I promised you an adventure tonight. Though I do fear you may be disappointed once you see how dull the club really is."

"I'm sure it can't be as dull as another ball at Dublin Castle," Anna said with a shudder. "Terrible music, endless minuets with stuffy lordlings. And Mama watching to see if I will marry one of them and cease my wild ways at last."

Jane laughed. "You *ought* to let her marry you off to one of them."

"Jane! Never. Just the thought of one of them touching me—that way. No."

"It only lasts a moment or two, A., I promise. And then you have freedom you can't even imagine now. My Harry was a terrible old goat, but now I have his money *and* my Gianni, who is quite luscious." Jane sighed happily. "It is a marvelous life, truly."

"But you are Harry's widow, Jane. You no longer have to endure his—attentions." Anna stared out the window at the city streets flashing by, a blur of gray-white marble, austere columns and black-painted doors. She thought of old Lord Cannondale before he popped off last spring, his yellow-tinged eyes that watched Jane so greedily, his spotted, twisted hands. And she thought of someone else, too, that crazed soldier who had grabbed her in the midst of battle . . . "Not even for freedom could I endure sharing my bed with someone like that."

"Well, what of Grant Dunmore then? He is young and so very handsome. All the young ladies are in love with him, yet he wanted to dance only with you at Lady Overton's ball last week. He would not be so bad."

Yes, there was Sir Grant Dunmore. Not so very old at all, and the most handsome man in Dublin, or so everyone said. Surely if she had to marry someone, he would make a fine enough choice.

"He's all right," she said neutrally.

"Oh, A.! Is there no one in all of Dublin who catches your eye?"

Anna frowned. Yes, once there had been a man who caught her eye. It felt like a hundred years ago, though in fact it had not even been two. When she closed her eyes she could still see him there. The carved lines of his dark, harshly elegant face, and the glow of his green eyes. The way his rough, powerful hands felt as he reached for her in that stable...

The Duke of Adair. Yes, she did still think of him, dreamed of him at night, even though they had not met since those fearsome days of the Uprising. She was on the run with her family, and he was intent on his own unknown, dangerous mission. He would not want to see *her* again, not after what she had done to him.

She shook her head hard, trying to dislodge him from her memories—to shake free any memories at all. The past was gone. She had to keep reminding herself of that. "No, there is no one. I've never met anyone who appealed to me as your Gianni does to you."

"We shall just have to change that then," Jane said. "Oh, look, here we are!"

Desperately glad of the distraction, Anna peered out the window to find a nondescript building. It could have been any other house on Fish Street, a square, harsh, classical structure of white stone. The only glimmer of light came from a leaded, fan-shaped window over the dark blue door. All the other windows were tightly shrouded with dark drapes.

Anna smoothed her black silk gloves over her elbows, taking in a deep, steadying breath as a footman opened the carriage door.

"Are you quite sure this is the place?" she said. "It doesn't look scandalous at all."

"I told you it might be disappointing," Jane answered, stepping down to the pavement. "But then again, the most delicious forbidden places are adept at disguise."

Just like herself? Anna had found she, like this house, was very good at putting up façades and pretending to be what she was not. Or maybe trying on different masks to see which was really her, to hide the terrible hollowness inside. But that would require far too much introspection, and that she did not have time for.

She followed Jane up the front steps, waiting just behind as her friend gave the unsmiling butler her invitation.

"Follow me, if you please, madame," he said, letting them in after examining them carefully. As two masked footmen stepped forward to take their cloaks, the door swung shut with an ominous, echoing clang. Now that they were really in that strange, cold, silent house, Anna wondered if Jane was right—maybe they should not be there.

She caught a glimpse of herself in a mirror as the butler led them up the winding marble staircase, and she scarcely recognized the woman who stared back. In that sophisticated red gown, with her face covered by a black satin mask and a beaded black lace net over her blond hair, she looked older than her eighteen years.

That was good. Sometimes she did not want to be herself at all, didn't want to be Anna Blacknall, with all those duties and expectations and memories.

And she didn't want anyone else to recognize her,

either. If anyone discovered she was here, she would be quite ruined. She would disappoint her mother and family yet again, in the worst way. But on nights like this, it was as if a terrible compulsion, almost an illness, came over her, and she had to run away.

They turned on the landing at the top of the stairs, making their way down a long, silent corridor. Medieval-looking torches set in metal sconces flickered, casting bronze-red shadows over the bare walls. At first, the only sound was the click of their shoes on the flagstone floor. But as they hurried farther along, a soft humming noise expanded and grew, becoming a roar.

The butler threw open a pair of tall double doors at the end of the corridor, and Anna stepped into a wild fantasy.

It was a ballroom, of course, but quite unlike any other she had ever seen. The floor-to-ceiling windows were draped in black velvet; streamers of red and black satin fell from the high ceiling, where a fresco of cavorting Olympian gods at an Underworld banquet stared down at them. More gods, stone and marble, stood in naked splendor against the silk-papered walls. The air was heavy with the scent of wax candles and exotic orchids and lilies, tumbling over the statues in drifts of purple and black and creamy white.

A hidden orchestra played a wild Austrian waltz, a sound strange and almost discordant to Anna's ears after the staid minuets and country dances of Society balls, but also gorgeous and stirring. Masked couples swirled around the dance floor, a kaleidoscope of whites, reds, blacks, and greens. It was a primal scene, bizarre and full of such raw energy.

That nervous feeling faded, replaced by a deeper stirring of excitement. Yes, this Dionysian place was exactly what she needed tonight.

Jane took two glasses of champagne from the proffered tray of another masked footman, handing one to Anna. "Cheers, A.," she said, clicking their glasses together. "Is this more like what you expected?"

Anna sipped at the sharp, bubbling liquid, studying the dancers over the golden rim. "Indeed so."

"Well, then, enjoy, my friend. The card room is over there, dining room that way. They have the most delectable lobster tarts. I think I will just find myself a dance partner."

"Have fun," Anna said. As Jane disappeared into the crowd, Anna finished her champagne and took another glass, making her way around the edge of the room. It was decidedly *not* a place her mother would approve of. It was too strange, too dark—the dancing much too close. One man leaned over his partner, kissing her neck as she laughed. Anna turned away from them, peeking into the card room where roulette and faro went on along with more intimate card games. There seemed to be a great deal of money, as well as piles of credit notes, on the tables.

No, the Olympian Club was assuredly not Dublin Castle, the seat of the British government, and not some stuffy Society drawing room, either. And that was what she wanted. There was no forgetfulness in staid reels and penny-ante whist.

She took another glass of champagne. The golden froth of it along with the rich scent of the flowers was a heady combination. For a moment, the room swayed before her, a gilded mélange of red and black and laughing couples, and she laughed too.

"You shouldn't be here, *beag peata*," a deep voice said behind her, rough and rich, touched at the edges by a musical Irish accent. Though the words were low, they seemed to rise above the cacophony of the party like an oracle's pronouncement.

Anna shivered at the sound, the twirling room slowing around her as if in a dream. Her gloved fingers tightened on the glass as she glanced over her shoulder. And, for the first time since she stepped into the alternate world of the club, she felt a cold frisson of fear trickle down her spine.

The man stood far enough away that it would be easy for her to run and melt into the crowd. Yet something in his eyes, a fathomless, burning dark green behind the plain white mask, held her frozen in place as his captive.

He was tall and strongly built, with his broad shoulders and muscled chest barely contained in stark black and white evening clothes. And he was so dark—bronzed, almost shimmering skin set off by close-cropped raven-colored hair and a shadow of beard along his sharp jaw. Dark and hard, a Hades in his Underworld realm, yet his lips seemed strangely sensual and soft.

They curved in a wry smile, as if he read her fascinated thoughts.

"You don't belong here," he said again.

Something in that gravelly voice—the amusement or maybe the hint of tension—made Anna prickle with irritated anger. He did not even know her; how dare he presume to know where she belonged. Especially when she did not even know that herself.

She stiffened her shoulders, tilting back her head to stare up and up into his eyes. He really was cursed tall! She felt delicate and small beside him when she wanted to feel like a powerful goddess.

"On the contrary," she said. "I find this all remarkably amusing."

"Amusing?" His gaze swept over the room before landing on her again, pinning her as if she were some helpless butterfly. "You have strange taste in amusement, *beag peata*."

"You should not call me that. I am not *that* small."

One dark brow arched over his mask. "You know Gaelic?"

"Not a great deal. But enough to know when I am insulted."

He laughed, a harsh, rusty sound, as if he did not use it very often. "It is hardly an insult. Merely the truth—little one."

Before Anna could tell what he was doing, he grabbed her wrist, holding it between his strong, callused fingers. Though his touch was light, she sensed she could not easily break away. That eerie fascination, that hypnosis he seemed to cast around her, tightened like a glittering web.

Unable to breathe or to think, she watched as he unfastened the tiny black pearl buttons at her wrist, peeling back the silk. A sliver of her pale skin was revealed, her pulse pounding just along the fragile bone.

"You see," he said quietly. "You *are* small and delicate, trembling like a bird."

He lifted her wrist to his lips, pressing a soft kiss to that thrumming pulse. Anna gasped at the heat of that kiss, at the touch of his tongue to her skin, hot and damp. She tried to snatch her hand away, but his fingers tightened, holding her fast.

"You should not be here among the hawks," he muttered, his gaze meeting hers in a steady burn.

There was something about those eyes. . . .

Anna had a sudden flash of memory. A man on a windswept hill, his long, black hair wild. A man who held her close in a dark, deserted stable, who kissed her in the midst of danger and uncertain fates. A man all tangled up in her blood-soaked memories.

A man with dark green eyes.

"Is—is it you?" she whispered without thinking.

His eyes narrowed, a muscle in his jaw clenching. "I told you, *beag peata*. You should not be here."

"I go where I please," she said, an attempt at defiance even as her head spun.

"Then you are a fool. Everyone should be most careful these days. You never know who is your friend and who your foe."

"Insults again?" Angry and confused and, she feared, aroused by him, she tried again to twist away.

He would not let her go. Instead, he drew her closer, his other arm coming around her waist and pulling her up against him. His body pressed against hers, warm and hard through the slippery satin of her gown.

"Since you insist on staying then," he said, "you should have a dance."

Before she could protest or even draw a breath, he lifted her up, carrying her into the whirling press of the dance floor.

She stared up into his eyes, mesmerized as he slowly

slid her back down to her feet. He twirled her about, her hand held over her head in an arch.

"I don't know the steps," she gasped.

"We're not at a castle assembly," he said roughly, dipping her back in his arms. "No one cares about the steps here."

As he spun her around again, Anna stared into a dizzy haze. He was quite right—everyone seemed to use the dance merely as an excuse to be close to each other. *Very* close. The couples around them were pressed together as they twirled in wild circles, bodies entwined.

She looked back into his eyes, those green eyes that saw so very much. He seemed to see everything she tried so hard to keep hidden—all her fear and guilt. That mesmerizing light in his eyes reeled her closer and closer....

She suddenly laughed, feeling reckless and giddy with the champagne, the music, and being so close to him, to the heat and light of him. Well, she had come here to forget, had she not? To leave herself behind and drown in the night. She might as well throw all caution to the wind and go down spectacularly.

Anna looped her arms around his neck, leaning into the hard, lean strength of his muscled body. "Show me how *you* dance then," she said.

His jaw tightened, and his eyes never wavered from hers. "You should go home now."

"The night is young. And you said I should dance."

In answer, he dragged her tight against him, his hands unclasping hers from around his neck as he led her deeper into the shifting patterns of the dance. Even as the crowd closed around them, pressing in on her, she could see no one but him. The rest of the vast room faded to a golden blur; only he was thrown into sharp relief. He held her safe in his arms, spinning and spinning until she threw back her head, laughing as she closed her eyes.

It was like flying! Surely any danger was worth this. For one instant, she could forget and soar free.

But then he lifted her from her feet again, twirling her through an open door and into sudden silence and darkness. She opened her eyes to see they were in a conservatory, an exotic space of towering potted palms and arching windows that let in the cold, moonlit night. The air smelled of damp earth, of rich flowers, and of the clean salt of his warm skin.

There were a few whispers from unseen trysts behind the palms and the ghostly echo of music. But mostly she heard his breath, harsh in her ear. She felt the warm rush of it against the bare skin of her throat. Her heart pounded, an erratic drumbeat that clouded all her thoughts and obscured any glimmer of sense.

For the first time since they started dancing, she felt truly afraid. She was afraid of herself, of the wild creature inside that clamored to be free. Afraid of him, of his raw strength and strange magnetism that would not let her go, and of who she suspected he was. Afraid he would vanish again.

He set her down on a wide windowsill. The stone was cold through her skirts, and his hands hard as he held her by the waist. Anna braced herself against his shoulders, certain she would fall if he let go. Falling down and down into that darkness that always waited, so she could never find her way out again.

"You should listen to me, *beag peata*," he said, his

accent heavy and rich like whiskey. "This is no place for someone like you."

"Someone like me?" she whispered. "And what do you know of me?"

"You are too young and innocent for the likes of these people."

"*These* people? Are you not one of them?"

His lips curved in a humorless smile that was somehow more disquieting than all his scowls. "Assuredly so."

"And so am I—tonight. I am not so innocent as all that." Innocents did not do what she had done, seen what she had seen. They did not commit murder.

"Oh, but you are," he whispered. "I can see it in those blue eyes of yours. You are an innocent here."

She laughed bitterly. "But I can be a fierce innocent when I need to be."

"You're very brave." He took her hand in his, sliding his fingers over the silk of her glove.

She gasped. His hold wasn't painful, but she was all too aware that she could not break free from him, could not escape. The pulse at the base of her throat fluttered, and she couldn't speak. She just shook her head—she was not brave at all.

"Brave, and very foolish," he said hoarsely, as if he was in pain. "Don't do this to me."

"What…" She swallowed hard, her throat dry. "Do what to you?"

"Look at me the way you do." He leaned into the soft curve of her body, resting his forehead against hers. She closed her eyes, feeling the essence of him wrap all around her. She felt safe, safer than she had in so very long, and yet more frightened than ever. This had to be a dream. He could not be real.

He let go of her wrist, bracing his hands on the windowsill behind her. Slowly, she felt his head tilt and his lips lower toward hers—the merest light brush, a tantalizing taste of wine and man. His tongue swept across her lower lip, making her gasp at the hot sensations. The damp heat of it was like a drug, sweetly alluring like laudanum in wine, pulling her down into a fantasy world. He bit lightly at her lip, soothing it again with his tongue.

She felt his hands slide over her shoulders, bared by the daring gown, trailing a ribbon of fire over her collarbone, the hollow at the base of her throat, and the sensitive skin just at the top of her breasts....

But then he was gone, pulling back from her, and his arms dropping away. She cried out involuntarily, her eyes flying open. He stood across from her with his back turned and his shoulders stiff.

She would wager that was not the only part of him that was *stiff*, either, but he would not turn to her again.

"Go home now," he growled, his hands tightening into fists.

Anna was sure she might be foolish, but she certainly knew when to cut her losses and retreat. She leaped down from the ledge, her legs trembling so that she could hardly walk. But she forced herself to turn toward the door, taking one careful step after another.

"And don't ever come here again!" he shouted after her.

She broke into a run, hardly stopping until she was safely bundled into a hackney carriage, racing toward home. She ripped off her mask and buried her face in her gloved hands. But that did not help at all; she could smell him on the silk, on herself, taste him on her lips.

Damn him! How could he do this to her again? Or rather, how could she do this to herself? He had drawn her into his strange world once before—she couldn't let him do it again. She *wouldn't* let him.

Chapter Two

"Aigh se," Conlan McTeer, Duke of Adair, muttered. He rubbed his hands hard over his face, resisting the urge to drive his fist into the stone ledge where *she* had just sat. Even though she had finally shown a glimmer of sense and fled, her presence lingered—a whiff of lilac perfume, a drift of warmth and softness in the air. He flexed his hand, trying to shake away the imprint of her skin there.

It *was* her, Anna Blacknall. He knew as soon as he saw her there in the ballroom with the candlelight shining on her pale gold hair. Despite the risqué red gown and the satin mask, she could not hide her ladylike bearing or the wonder in her blue eyes as she watched the dancers.

Yet even then he could scarcely believe it. Lady Anna, daughter of Protestant aristocracy and the toast of the Society Season, sneaking into the scandalous Olympian Club? Wandering alone amid hardened rakes and roués in her risqué scarlet dress? For one instant, he was sure it must be a trap, something meant to lure him and his work out into the open.

But even as the thought flashed through his mind, he dismissed it. No one knew he owned the Olympian Club. And especially no one knew his connection to Anna, of what happened between them two years ago in the midst of the violent upheaval of the United Irish uprising.

Sometimes in the bleak hours of night nothing could ease the memory of her beautiful face or her fierce anger and fiery spirit. No woman could substitute, no amount of whiskey could drown her out. She stubbornly refused to leave him.

Come the light of morning it was easy enough to push her memory away, because their paths seldom crossed. He occasionally glimpsed her riding in St. Stephen's Green or on her way to the visitors' gallery at Parliament with her friends during Union debates. And he certainly heard gossip about her. But he never went to Society balls, and she never came to *his* sort of parties. Until tonight.

Conlan braced his palms against the ledge. It was mere hard, cold stone now, with no vestige of her heat. He could think now without her intoxicating presence so close. The party whirled on beyond the glass conservatory doors— louder, wilder—but he was removed from all that revelry, as he always was.

He tried to think coldly and rationally. If Anna was not here at the behest of someone trying to ruin him, why *was* she here? He had heard rumors that she was a most daring young lady, the toast but also the talk of Dublin for her exploits—card playing, horse racing in the park, lines of suitors trailing behind her. Perhaps she had slipped into the Olympian Club on some kind of dare.

But how could she get in? His staff was well-trained to scrutinize invitations and to only let in members and a very limited number of their guests. The exclusive nature of the club was one factor in its great success. People always wanted to be in where others were out, and they were willing to pay a great deal for that.

Someone, then, had brought her as their guest. And he intended to find out who that was, to make sure Anna had found out nothing at all on her little visit. She wasn't stupid. She might be able to convince all of Dublin into thinking her a fluff-brained Society beauty, concerned with nothing but ballgowns and games of chance, but he knew better.

He rubbed at the scar just beneath the cropped hair at the back of his neck, feeling the raised ridge that was a constant reminder of just how quick-witted and brave Anna Blacknall could be. And how he had once played the fool for her. She was the only person who managed to slide past his defenses during the dangerous days of the Uprising, the only one who brought him down.

That would *not* happen again.

Conlan frowned as he stared at the faint shadow on the window where her head had pressed. *Is it you?* she had whispered. Did she remember, too?

A moan echoed through the conservatory followed by a rustle of silk. He was not the only one to lose his wits in passion amid the plants then. *Good*—that was what the Olympian Club was designed for, to wrap people up in hedonistic delights, make them forget everything else in pleasure so they gave up all their power. All their secrets.

Its allure was not meant to work on *him*, though. Pleasure could hold no snares for him any longer; he learned his lesson when he was a careless young man and nearly lost everything for it.

Silently, he pushed away from the ledge and crept around the banks of towering palms and heavily scented flowers. There were a few couples hidden amid the shadows, engrossed in each other, but one pair lay entwined on a wrought-iron chaise just under the moonglow of a skylight. The woman's head was thrown back, her gown slipping from her white shoulders. The distinctive auburn hair identified her as Lady Cannondale.

The man who knelt over her, kissing the curve of her neck as his hand slid beneath her skirt, was Sir Grant Dunmore, Conlan's cousin—and most bitter enemy. Once, years ago, Grant tried to use the Penal Laws that allowed a Protestant to claim a Catholic relative's property. Conlan's ancient title saved his estate, but it was a hard-fought battle and not one he would ever forget or forgive.

Conlan smiled. It had been a long road trying to lure Grant into the web of the Olympian Club. And yet in the end, all it had taken was Lady Cannondale's charms.

"Oh," she moaned, hooking her bare leg around his hips, tugging him closer against her. "You *are* being terribly naughty tonight, Sir Grant."

He laughed hoarsely, bracing himself on his forearms to gaze down at her. "Not nearly as naughty as I can be, my dear Jane."

"Then why are you holding back?" She threaded her fingers through his bronze-colored hair. "Tell me again about how cleverly you persuaded Lord Ross to vote for the Union...."

Conlan had a sudden vision of Anna sighing as he kissed her, her mouth opening to him. What would she have done if he laid her back on one of those chaises, spreading her legs and tugging up her dress as Grant did with Lady Cannondale? A little daredevil Anna might be, but he doubted she would welcome him with moans and sighs, her lithe legs wrapping around him tightly.

But a man could always dream.

He backed away, leaving Lady Cannondale and her lover to their business. He hurried out of the humid darkness of the conservatory and back into the whirling brightness of the ballroom. The music had reached an even faster pitch, the dance more frantic, and the laughter even louder.

He peered into the card room, making sure Anna hadn't retreated there. He had heard she enjoyed a hand of whist almost too much. But all was well there. The roulette wheel spun with abandon, notes of credit no doubt piling up. Sarah, one of the pretty faro bankers, noticed him watching and gave him a little nod. Another most successful evening at the Olympian Club.

The buffet in the dining room had just been replenished and footmen now hurried to and fro with trays laden with fresh glasses of champagne. Conlan wouldn't be needed for a little while longer. So he hurried down the stairs into the austere marble silence of the foyer. McIntire, who had long been the butler at Conlan's family estate of Adair Court in County Kildare, had come out of retirement for this job and was calmly sorting invitations at the front door. No one else was around.

"How did we do tonight, McIntire?" Conlan asked, leaning on the gilded balustrade. The cool quiet was delicious after the bacchanalia of the ball.

"Quite well, Your Grace," McIntire answered. Conlan had told him several times not to do all that "Your Grace"-ing at the club, but McIntire was set in his ways. "Every invitation that was sent was redeemed, and most members brought guests of their own. Shall we be expanding the membership list soon?"

"That all depends on who applies." Conlan tapped his fingertips on the gilded marble, thinking of Grant Dunmore and Lady Cannondale entwined on the chaise upstairs. If his cousin applied, they could assuredly add one more member. "Tell me, McIntire, do you remember a lady in a red and black gown arriving this evening? With blond hair?"

McIntire looked affronted. "I remember *everyone* who arrives here, Your Grace. That is my job."

Conlan grinned. "And you are extraordinarily good at it. Who did she come with? A man?"

Suddenly, he had the strangest urge to punch whoever dared bring Anna here tonight. The man who held her arm, leading her through the door to the questionable delights of the Olympian Club...

"She came here with Lady Cannondale, Your Grace. In fact, she left a note for her ladyship before she departed."

Conlan laughed aloud. With Lady Cannondale—of course. He had vowed he wouldn't be a fool over Anna Blacknall, and yet there he was wanting to fight her imaginary escort like a pub brawler. "Did she leave? Alone?"

"Yes, Your Grace. She ran out of here so very quickly she left this." McIntire picked up a black satin cloak from where it was draped on a chair.

Conlan frowned as he reached for the slippery fabric. It still smelled faintly of lilacs, its springtime sweetness strange and unexpected in the lurid midst of the club. "Did she go in Lady Cannondale's carriage?" If she walked, alone and unprotected in the cold night, he would have to rescue her.

"One of the footmen found her a hackney." McIntire hesitated before he went on, shuffling the invitations in his wrinkled hands. "She seemed rather upset, Your Grace."

And well she should be, the little *cailleach*. Sneaking into a masked ball—being dragged away and kissed by a barbaric Irishman. Hopefully she had learned her lesson.

And hopefully *he* had learned his, too.

"She shouldn't have come here," he said roughly. "Lady Cannondale should have more care with the people she chooses as her guests."

McIntire watched him thoughtfully. "I beg your pardon, Your Grace, but do you know her?"

"I know she's a young lady who has no business here. If she tries to come into the club again, McIntire, let me know at once."

"Of course, Your Grace."

"Sir!" one of the footmen called down the stairs. "Sarah sent me to tell you Lord Overton is asking for more credit in the card room."

"Tell her to meet me in my office; I'll deal with it there." Conlan folded Anna's cloak over his arm and turned back up the stairs.

Sarah waited for him in his small office, sitting on the edge of the desk, her long legs crossed under her black silk skirts. She smiled at him, leaning back on her palms as he closed the door behind him.

"Took you long enough to get here, Conlan," she said.

Conlan tore off his mask, running his hand through his rumpled hair. "It's a busy evening."

"Oh, yes, I know. Lots of dancing..."

He ignored that. "There's a problem with Overton?"

"Not a *problem*. He just wants yet more credit. He used it all at the faro table tonight, the naughty man."

"Hmm." Overton was one of the most vocal proponents of the Union of Ireland and England, thanks to the massive bribes he received from London. Had he gone through that money already, burying himself in gaming debts again? Interesting.

But not as interesting as the appearance of Lady Anna Blacknall tonight. She stayed in his mind, like the *cailleach* he called her, refusing to depart and leave him in peace. He kept hearing her voice, feeling the softness of her skin under his touch and her breath on his lips.

He tossed aside her cloak, the shimmering fabric sliding to the floor. If only *she* could be tossed aside so easily. He had the terrible suspicion that he had not seen the last of her, though. Something had bound them together since those secret moments in the deserted stable, and those bonds tightened now, reeling him closer to the mysterious golden witch.

"*Aigh se*." He didn't *want* her in his head again; he couldn't afford the distraction, not now when all his hard work was so close to completion. He just had to drive her out. She was just a woman, after all, and an Ascendancy woman at that. A pampered lady of the Protestant aristocracy.

He smiled at Sarah, moving closer to the desk. He planted his hands on either side of her, feeling the warmth of her voluptuous body, breathing in the familiar scent of her perfume. A musky French blend, not fresh lilacs like Anna Blacknall.

She laughed, throwing back her head as he pressed an openmouthed kiss to her shoulder, bared by the low-cut gown. Her brown hair gleamed in the lamplight and her tall body wrapped boldly around his as she pulled him against her. Sarah had none of the golden litheness of Anna, which was exactly what he needed to drive the *cailleach* away.

"Do we have time?" Sarah whispered, her hands reaching eagerly for the front of his breeches.

Her desire fueled his, as it always did. His old friendship with Sarah was uncomplicated, enjoyable, born of mutual need and mutual hatred of the English. But tonight, even as he kissed her, he kept seeing Anna's face in his head. Heard her voice in his ear, calling out his name.

"There's always time," he muttered, forcing Anna's image away as he pressed Sarah back onto the desk and eased into her welcoming body.

Chapter Three

"Yeow!"

The piercing shriek split the quiet night on aristocratic Henrietta Street. At its sudden clamor, Anna tripped and crashed to the pavement.

"Blast!" she cried, her knees stinging under the skirts of her borrowed gown. But the pain was nothing to the certainty that she had been found out. She was caught sneaking back into the house, and there would be no freedom ever again.

She knelt there, the wind cold on her bare arms and her heart pounding like thunder in her ears, as she waited for doom to fall. Instead there was the soft brush of something fluffy and feathery against her skin.

"Yeow." Quieter now, not so much the scream of wrath. A cat's bright green eyes peered up at her in the dark before it stalked off into the night.

Anna's breath left her lungs in a great whoosh, and she hung her head to laugh. Just a stray cat. She wasn't about to be raked over the coals after all, although surely she would be if she didn't get in the house soon.

But her legs still trembled, too weak to let her stand up just yet. She sat back to assess the damage. Her gloves were torn where her hands had hit the pavement. Her palms were scraped, but luckily the dress was intact. She had left behind her beaded hair net along with her cloak, and now her hair fell from its pins to straggle down her neck.

So much for sophisticated elegance. One kiss, and she went dashing home like a coward, turning into a ragamuffin as she went. One *fiery* kiss, unlike any she had ever known since . . .

Since the last time he kissed her, in that deserted stable. The Duke of Adair—yes, it had to be him. She was sure of it despite the mask. Even though they had not met for two years, she remembered every brief second of their encounters. She especially remembered the way his touch made her feel so very *alive*, as if she had been asleep all her life and only awakened when he touched her.

She stripped off her ruined gloves, scowling. She did not know exactly what part Adair played in the ambush on her brother-in-law Will's regiment, but she wasn't entirely a fool. He was an Irish nobleman, whose estate had been nearly taken away by the Penal Laws against Irish Catholics. He had not been strolling away from a tea party when she found him hiding in that stable. She was a masochistic fool, swooning for a man like that. It was stupid, dangerous—and horribly alluring.

"Damn it all," she muttered, balling up the silk gloves in her fist. She would just have to stay away from him in the future, which shouldn't be too difficult. They hardly moved in the same circles. And she had to hope he had not recognized *her*, although she had the sinking suspicion he had.

But she couldn't worry about that now. She had to get into the house before she got caught.

She grabbed onto the iron railings, hauling herself to her feet even as her knees screamed in protest. Once she had her balance again, she dashed down the stone steps to the servants' entrance below the street level.

It was usually locked once everyone retired, but she had had a new key made and easily let herself back in. The cool corridors were quiet, still smelling faintly of the roast and boiled vegetables from dinner and the smoke from the banked fireplaces. All the servants were upstairs in their quarters asleep, but soon enough they would be down here to start the day all over again. She had to hurry.

Not even daring to breathe, Anna ran up the back stairs and down the carpeted hall to her chamber. Her door, along with those of her mother and sister, were closed. The house was silent. Success was within her sight!

But all that triumph collapsed when she slipped into her room, only to find she was not alone after all.

Her younger sister, Caroline, lay on her stomach across Anna's bed, a book open before her. The flickering light of one candle glinted on her spectacles.

"So you're back at last," she said calmly, turning over a page. "You were gone a very long time."

"Caroline!" Anna cried in a whole new rush of panic. She crossed her arms over her midriff, wishing she still had her cloak to cover the scarlet gown. Surely even Caroline, who cared nothing for fashion, would notice such a thing. "What are you doing here? Are you spying on me?"

"Certainly not. I merely happened to glance out the

library window earlier tonight and saw you leaving. I was rather curious because you claimed to have a headache after dinner."

"Did Mama see?"

"No, she had already retired." Caroline closed her book, *Great Battles of Ancient Ireland*, and sat up on the bed. Her brown eyes were bright with inquisitiveness.

"Are you going to tell her?" Anna asked warily.

"That depends. Where were you?"

She could hardly tell Caroline the truth—that she had run off for a night of dancing and gaming at the notorious Olympian Club and ended up kissing a wild Irishman in a dark conservatory. To buy herself a moment to think, she ducked behind her dressing screen to struggle out of the gown. Luckily, Jane's garments were made to get out of fairly easily. Her Gianni must be so happy.

"I just needed a breath of fresh air," Anna said, draping the slippery red fabric over a chair and kicking off her heeled slippers. "This house is so stuffy sometimes."

"So it is," Caroline answered. Anna heard her climb down from the bed, the sound of pouring water. "No wonder Eliza always hated it. But why did you need a ballgown to go for a stroll?"

Anna froze as she rolled down her stockings. She had a sudden flashing image of Adair dragging up her skirts, his dark hand on her pale thigh, warm and strong and delicious....

"Blast," she whispered, shivering at the thought. She tore off her light stays and chemise, pulling her nightgown over her naked skin before she could have any more such fantasies.

"What did you say, Anna?"

"I said—what else would I wear for a midnight stroll?"

Caroline suddenly poked her head behind the screen, holding out a damp washcloth. "You have rouge on your lips still."

Anna took the cloth in silence, scrubbing at her rouged lips and powdered cheeks. She wished she could wipe away Adair and the burning intoxication of his touch so easily.

"Were you meeting Sir Grant Dunmore?" Caroline asked.

Now *that* Anna did not expect. "Grant Dunmore? Why would you think that?"

"He sent you flowers again today." Caroline gestured to a basket of deep purple violets. "And you brought them up here and left all the other bouquets in the drawing room. Everyone says he is courting you, but then again so is every man in Dublin."

"I brought those in here because I happen to like violets." Anna made herself laugh, pushing past her sister to sit down at her dressing table. Her hair was still a mess, falling down around her shoulders, and her cheeks were red from excitement and fear. Surely she couldn't fool anyone. Guilt was written all over her face.

She snatched up her hairbrush, yanking it through the tangled waves of hair. "Out of every man in Dublin, why do you think I was meeting Grant Dunmore? He is hardly courting me—we've only danced a few times and gone for a ride in the park once."

But then again, Jane had also thought he was courting her. Was that what everyone in Dublin thought?

"He is very handsome," Caroline said. She took the

brush from Anna's shaking hand. "Here, let me do that. You'll pull your hair out by the roots and then no one will want to marry you."

"Least of all a man as handsome as Grant Dunmore?" Anna asked, suddenly curious. Caroline never seemed to notice men at all; she cared mostly for her books on Irish history.

Yet Sir Grant *was* handsome enough to catch even Caroline's distracted eye. He would make a fine match, and then everyone would cease gossiping about her after all the offers she had turned away.

But Grant did not make her blood sing when he touched her hand in the dance or when he smiled at her. It seemed only mysterious, dark, elusive Irishmen could do *that*. Maybe her soul was so blackened that Conlan was what she deserved.

"The two of you would look well together," Caroline said, gently drawing the brush through Anna's hair.

Anna laughed. "You only want me out of the way so *you* can marry next! Will you find a handsome beau like Sir Grant?"

"Not at all," Caroline said. "I already have a plan."

"What sort of plan?"

"I shall marry Lord Hartley. Then I won't have to bother with debutante balls at Dublin Castle at all."

"Hartley!" Anna cried. "Caro, he is quite ancient. He's already been married twice and has three children, plus very little hair."

"I admit he is not as handsome as Sir Grant, but he is a scholar and has a marvelous library. He's also a member of the Hibernian Society and could allow me access to *their* library," Caroline said matter-of-factly. She was the only girl Anna knew who would marry someone for their library. "And he is hardly ancient, only forty-five. Hardly older than Mama."

"And you are only just sixteen. You shouldn't rush into such things, Caro."

Caroline laughed as she neatly plaited the now smooth strands of golden hair. "You are scarcely one to lecture me on *caution*, Anna! You never did tell me where you were tonight."

"I was not with Grant Dunmore."

"Then who were you with?"

"I went to a party with Jane," Anna said cautiously. And that was true, as far as it went. Caroline certainly didn't need to know about Adair or the Olympian Club.

Anna had the sudden urge to confide in someone about all her confused emotions. Caroline was too young and her mother was out of the question. If only Eliza were here and not living in Switzerland with her husband, Will. Her older sister certainly understood ungovernable passion.

But Eliza was not there, and Anna just had to ignore those feelings until they vanished.

"Mama won't like that," Caroline said. "She quite disapproves of Lady Cannondale."

"That's why I didn't tell her. And you won't, either, will you, Caro?"

Caroline tied off the end of the braid, her eyes narrowed in a most ominous manner. "I might not—if you help me with something."

"Help you with what? I don't have any pin money left for you to spend at the bookshop."

"I suppose you lost it all at whist. But I don't need money."

Anna was deeply wary now. "What *do* you need?"

"Mama is interviewing drawing tutors for me tomorrow. You are so persuasive with her; surely you could get her to let me stop all these infernal lessons. Dancing, music, deportment—it's all such a vast waste of time."

"Because you mean to skip debutante balls and marry Lord Hartley?"

"Because it gets in the way of my studies. Persuade her to not hire a drawing teacher, and I won't tell her you were sneaking out with Lady Cannondale."

"I'm sure she would not listen to me."

"And I'm sure she would!" Caroline knelt down beside Anna's stool, staring up at her with beseeching eyes. "Please, Anna darling, talk to her for me."

"Just talk to her?" Anna said doubtfully. "That's all you want?"

"That is all. Except maybe you could also loan me that gown sometime. . . ."

Chapter Four

It was the crowded hour at St. Stephen's Green. The wide, graveled lanes and walkways, lined with neatly clipped box hedges, were filled with people on horseback and foot and in fine carriages. Everyone went there every afternoon after Parliament adjourned and before the evening's theatres and assemblies opened, to see and be seen. They wanted to hear the latest gossip, to criticize the fashions of everyone else, and find out the latest in the saga of the Union. The chatter was nearly deafening.

But Anna was bored with it all. She saw it every day, and it never changed. The gossip was always the same; no one ever did anything truly shocking or exciting. Only the partners changed. And no one different ever showed up at the park.

She perched on her prized mare, Psyche, leading the horse at a sedate pace alongside her mother's open carriage. Even Psyche seemed restless today, shifting uneasily as if she wanted to run free. Usually at this time of year, they were home at Killinan Castle, joining in the hunt and going for morning rides over the rolling countryside. They could gallop and jump, the wind tearing through their hair as if they were flying.

But there were no free, wild spaces in the city. No dirt lanes or fences to leap over. And Anna's mother refused to leave Dublin while everyone else stayed there, waiting for the Union question to be resolved one way or another and indulging in Christmas festivities. Or perhaps she refused to leave until Anna was married off.

Anna tightened her gloved hands on the reins and forced Psyche to settle down to a slow walk. She studied the faces around her, friends and acquaintances she had known all her life, and wondered who had been hidden under masks at the Olympian Club. Who had been there losing all their money at faro, dancing lasciviously with people not their spouses?

It added some interest to the gray, chilly day. But it made her remember her own lascivious dance all too well.

"Anna," her mother said. "Are you listening to me at all?"

Anna glanced at her mother from under the lacy veil of her riding hat. Katherine Blacknall, Lady Killinan, sat in her fine carriage, her fur-trimmed dark blue gown and black parasol striking against the pale yellow velvet upholstery. Her ribbon-trimmed hat was the latest fashion as always. Anna wondered why she could not turn her considerable matchmaking skills from her daughter to herself. She was still very lovely, with the golden hair Anna had inherited, smooth ivory skin, and large blue eyes. But Katherine claimed to be very content in her widowhood—and looking forward to grandchildren.

She would have to look to Eliza and Will then, for Anna was not quite finished with her freedom.

Anna smiled at her. "Of course I am listening, Mama. I'm merely a bit tired today."

Katherine's eyes narrowed. "Too many late nights, I fear. Perhaps you should stay home more often."

"And turn down all those kind invitations? Surely we don't want to offend anyone."

"Yet these outings seem to achieve nothing," Katherine murmured. She nodded at a passing carriage, her serene smile masking the concern in her eyes.

"Of course they achieve something," Anna said. They brought her sweet, sweet forgetfulness, even if only for a few hours. When she was dancing, flirting, playing cards, she thought only of that present moment. Yet Society balls were nothing like the Olympian Club. Now, *there* was real forgetfulness.

Not that she could ever get in there again. She had not heard from Jane all day, and she feared her friend was angry at her for running away like that. Or worse, thought her an easily shocked ninny.

"Oh, yes?" said Katherine. "And what is that, my dear?"

"They introduce me to eligible *partis,* of course. Isn't that why we stay in Dublin?"

Katherine laughed ruefully. "It does not seem to matter how many fine young men you meet, Anna, as none suit you."

"I just want to be happy in my marriage, Mama. As Eliza is with Will, as you were with Papa."

Her mother's lips tightened. "And I want that for you, of course. But soon you will have refused every eligible man in Dublin."

"Then we can go to London, or Milan. Or I could go

stay with Eliza in Switzerland." That would not be so bad, Anna thought. Eliza's life had always seemed so exciting, so full of importance and purpose. Perhaps she could show Anna how to find that purpose, too. Show her how to be useful.

"I hardly think it has come to that yet," said Katherine. She waved at a carriage full of friends across the way. "Lord and Lady Connemara have invited us to a country house party for Christmas. The fresh air will surely do you some good—you *have* been looking a bit tired lately, my dear. And they have a fine library, which should keep Caroline occupied. Some days I am not sure what to do with her. She is too clever for me. She doesn't enjoy the things other young girls do."

Anna laughed. "So I am too social, and Caro is not social enough?"

"I did not say that."

She did not have to. Anna was quite sure all three of her daughters were a disappointment to Katherine, who was so good, kind, and beautiful that she was called the Angel of Kildare. One daughter was exiled for her political beliefs, her support of the United Irishmen in the Uprising two years ago. One was wild and wayward. And one cared only to study and marry old men for their fine libraries.

And that made Anna remember her promise to Caroline. She would speak to their mother about all those hated ladylike lessons, and Caroline would keep her mouth shut about Anna sneaking out.

"Speaking of Caro, Mama..."

Katherine sighed, as if she knew she would not like what Anna said. "Yes, my dear? What about your sister?"

"She says you are interviewing drawing teachers."

"As soon as we return home today, as a matter of fact. I have found several that come highly recommended, including one from France."

"I think Caro feels drawing lessons would—well, would take up so much time," Anna said carefully. "What with music, dancing, and deportment, which she is already studying every day already."

"And doing very poorly at, I'm sorry to say," said Katherine. That tightness was back around her lips, but she still smiled and nodded at all her many friends. "I thought she might at least find drawing useful for copying illustrations from those old books she's always poring over."

"Perhaps if you put it to her that way, instead of presenting it as one more feminine accomplishment. I think she fears you mean for her to sit and do watercolors of flowers."

"There is much to be said for feminine accomplishments! Every lady must be graceful and elegant if she is to be noticed, to take her place in our world. I know Caroline hates me for taking her away from her books, but she must see reality. She must come out of her dreams and see life as it truly is, not as she wishes it to be. If lessons are needed to accomplish that, then so be it."

Her mother sounded uncharacteristically grim, fierce even. Anna looked at her in surprise, but Katherine went on smiling. "I think—well, I think Caro has her own plans, Mama."

"A plan, is it? Oh, yes, my girls always have their own plans. But matters do not often turn out as we think they should." She suddenly waved her gloved hand. "Look, there is Lady Connemara. I must go and tell her we accept her kind invitation for Christmas."

"I..." Anna glanced desperately around the park, searching for some excuse to escape. She was suddenly very confused and strangely sad, although she did not know why. She glimpsed Jane in the distance, a glimmer of her bright green gown against her distinctive yellow phaeton.

"I should go say hello to Lady Cannondale, Mama," Anna said. She waved to her friend, who was surrounded by a flock of admirers, and Jane waved back.

"Lady Cannondale," Katherine said coolly. "You seem to spend a great deal of time with her lately, Anna."

"She is fun," Anna said. "And I think I can learn a great deal from her."

"Learn what exactly, my dear? I am not sure..."

"She is respectable, surely! There can be nothing untoward in my friendship with her. She is a countess, like you. Her husband was a member of Parliament."

"Like me?" Katherine murmured. "Fine, go speak to her. But be quick. You need to greet Lady Connemara, as well."

"I will, I promise. I always do my duty."

As Katherine gestured to the coachman to turn the carriage toward Lady Connemara's, Anna tugged at Psyche's reins and led the mare along another path. The crowd still pressed in close on all sides, a tangle of laughter and empty chatter that sounded like tinkling glass in the frosty wind. Her head ached from the champagne of the night before, a dull throb behind her eyes that only added to her restlessness. She still had that wild urge to run away, but as usual, there was no place to run.

At last, she reached Jane's phaeton, and the throng of admirers parted to make way for her as they called out jovial greetings. The handsome, dark-eyed Gianni sat by Jane on the carriage seat, his arm protectively near her shoulders.

"Lady Anna! You are looking very well today," Jane said, giving her a questioning smile.

"I feel well, thank you. Quite looking forward to the Fitzwalters' ball tomorrow."

"Are you indeed?" said Lord James Melton, one of Jane's eager suitors. "Dull as tombs, I would say. Since Lord Fitzwalter has gone on his penny-pinching ways they serve nothing but vile watered wine and dry cake!"

"A sin indeed," said Anna, and in a city where lavish hospitality ruled, it was. "But they don't stint on their orchestra, and the ballroom at Fitzwalter House is as enormous as ever. The dancing should be quite fine."

"It will be if *you* will partner with me for the supper dance, Lady Anna," Lord James said quickly.

"Not fair, Jimmy!" one of his friends protested. "You already engaged Lady Cannondale for the opening quadrille. You will monopolize all the loveliest ladies."

Jane laughed. "I am sure there will be plenty of dances to go around! Don't you agree, Anna?"

"I hope you have each saved one for me," said a deep, smooth voice, full of wry amusement and the silk of a posh accent.

Anna twisted around in her saddle to see that Grant Dunmore had stopped near their little group. He tipped his hat to her, and she was reminded of what Caro said. *He is so very handsome.*

He was certainly that. Anna thought of a book in her father's library at Killinan Castle, a volume of Greek myths that called Apollo the "Ever-Bright." The golden god of the sun had nothing at all on Sir Grant Dunmore. He sat easily on his horse: tall, elegantly lazy, his dark green riding jacket perfectly tailored over his broad shoulders, his cravat tied in a stylishly elaborate loop and fastened with a pearl pin. His hair, a bit long for the fashion and brushing his collar, was a glossy bronze-brown, his eyes an otherworldly amber color that seemed to glow in the hazy sunlight.

Those eyes focused on her and a faint smile was on his perfectly shaped lips. It made her cheeks feel too warm in the cold breeze, made her want to laugh and turn away. Looking at him was like looking at the sun—too fine and heady for every day.

A vision flashed through her mind, erasing for a split second the handsome man before her and the laughing crowd all around them. She saw a dark man, a Hades rather than an Apollo, his moss-green eyes intense as he reached for her. She felt his warm breath on her face, felt the slide of his hands on her bare skin and the spark of excitement deep inside of her.

Cailleach, he called her. Witch. But he was the one with magical powers, drawing her out of her bright, hectic world into the darkness of his. The terrible thing was, she liked it. Far too much. Something in him called out to her, and she wanted to run back for more.

Anna shook her head hard. She could *not* go back to Adair, to his club and whatever turmoil he fermented there. She had enough of darkness two years ago, and enough of other people's ideals that proved to be ashes and death in the end. Enough of the violence that lay hidden down inside of her. She wanted only sunlight now, frivolity and forgetfulness. At least that was what she told herself, over and over until it was true.

She peeked at Grant Dunmore from under her veil. He was laughing with Jane and Gianni now, the merriment making the elegantly drawn angles of his face seem lit from within. Maybe he *was* what she needed. She had to marry someone, and he was a good choice.

"And what of you, Lady Anna?" he said. Even his voice seemed full of light, like rich summer honey, smooth and sparkling. Not rough, like Adair's. Not touched with the wildness of Ireland. "Your friend says she is brave enough to dance with me. Are you? Or did I trod on your feet last time?"

Anna laughed, remembering the way she glided down the dance floor with him at the Overtons' ball. "Oh, Sir Grant, you are one of the finest dancers in Dublin, and I am sure you know it. I was quite the envy of the ballroom."

"Oh, no, Lady Anna," he said softly, his gaze almost like a gentle caress as it moved over her face. "*I* was the envy of every man there. I know there were many who were aching to call me out for dancing with you twice and taking you away from them."

Anna laughed. "Well, I don't want to be the cause of any violence, Sir Grant. We should only dance once at the Fitzwalters' then."

"I shall count the hours until then," he said, and something in his charming smile made even the trite compliment blush-worthy.

Jane watched them with her own amused smile, twirling the ribbons of her bonnet in her hand. "Perhaps you can fill those hours by telling us the news from Queen's County, Sir Grant, since you have just returned from your estate there. I heard there was some new unrest in the area. Should we all flee for England again, as we did two years ago?"

Anna glanced sharply at Grant. New unrest? But things had seemed so quiet in the last year or so, aside from those silly brawls between pro- and anti-Unionists. At Killinan Castle, the fields were tended again and the house full of parties. The wounds left in the lush, green landscapes by battles and fires were healing. The past was hidden under laughter and pretty clothes. And if there was a strange tension that never quite went away—a wary, shrill anxiety—that could be ignored. Sometimes.

But if true violence burst forth again, real warfare and bloodshed, that could not be ignored. And she feared it could not be healed again.

Grant's jaw tightened, but he just gave his usual charming smile. A smile could hide so much. "I doubt flight will be necessary, Lady Cannondale. It's true there were some small disturbances at my estate I had to look into, but it turned out to be just the usual Irish nonsense. Boys dressed up as ghosts trying to set fire to barns and haystacks. Someone splashing the words 'No Union' across my portico in red paint. A nuisance, to be sure—that marble came all the way from Siena. But it won't happen again."

"Damned Whiteboys," one of the other men muttered. "You'd have thought the Irish would have learned their lesson two years ago."

"They'll never learn," another man said. "They're like monkeys—just keep doing the same things over and over, battering against the bars that are there for their own good."

"Should've hanged the lot of them two years ago," the

first man added. "Pitt was a fool, letting Robert Emmet and Colonel O'Callaghan escape to France to keep spreading their poison. No wonder the peasants here keep acting up. I hope you put a stop to that, Dunmore, before it can grow."

A muscle ticked along Grant's jaw, and his smile turned frosty. "It won't happen again, I can assure you."

Jane suddenly snapped her fingers, cutting off their words. "How bloodthirsty you have all become! It's quite ruining my fine afternoon. I command you to speak of something else, something amusing."

The men laughed ruefully, apologizing and shuffling around as the conversation turned to horse races. But Anna couldn't get rid of the sour, sick feeling in the pit of her stomach. The cruelty wasn't over; it was never over. It was only hidden by a thin layer of glitter and laughter. Violence was always on the edge of erupting, and she couldn't bear to be caught in it again. She had been both its victim and its perpetrator, and she wanted only to be done with it.

Perhaps she *should* go to see Eliza in Lausanne. She heard it was quiet and pretty there among the snowy mountains and meadows. But if United Irish ideas were still spreading, Eliza was surely a part of it, and there could be no real peace there.

"I should find my mother," Anna said softly.

"Will I see you at the Napiers' card party tonight, Anna?" Jane said.

"Of course. If you all will excuse me..."

"Let me go with you to find her, Lady Anna," Grant said. "You look very pale. Are you unwell?"

"I am quite well, thank you, Sir Grant," she answered,

trying to smile at him through that cold feeling. "But I would be glad of the company."

He turned his horse with hers, and they moved back to the wider lane, leaving Jane with Gianni and her other admirers. The crowd had thinned a bit as the light grew pinker and the promenade hour drew to a close, but there were still several carriages rolling slowly along. Anna did not immediately see her mother's equipage among them.

"I am sorry if I upset you, Lady Anna," Grant said. "I should not have spoken of what happened on my estate. It was nothing at all, I assure you. Just a bit of mischief, easily dealt with."

"A bit of mischief," Anna murmured. "Yet is that not how the Uprising began? A bit of mischief that got out of hand?"

"Those were terrible days indeed," he said gently. "And I am more sorry than I can say if you were affected by them, Lady Anna. It can't happen again, though. England has learned not to underestimate the Irish propensity for violence, and the military force here is twice what it was. Control has been tightened, and soon we will be a true part of Great Britain."

Anna smiled at him and nodded, but she had her doubts. Some people thought the Union would erase their troubles in one stroke. Yet how could that be, when the troubles ran so deep? They were not the same nation, no matter how it was worded in the Act of Union.

"I feel quite safe in Dublin, Sir Grant, I assure you," she answered.

"And Dublin could not do without you, Lady Anna," he said. "The ballrooms would be quite desolate if you were not there to brighten them."

Anna laughed. "Oh, Sir Grant, I am sure you say that to all the ladies."

"No, I assure you I do not." He leaned from his saddle to reach for her hand, gently unwinding her fingers from the reins. He raised them to his lips for a lingering kiss. "I think there is no other lady in Dublin quite like you."

She laughed again, but deep inside she felt an odd tinge of disquiet. Though flirtatious, there was nothing improper in his words, nothing Anna had not heard a hundred times before. Men always made such compliments; they were empty little baubles. Yet as Sir Grant gazed at her over their joined hands, she glimpsed a look in his golden brown eyes she could not quite define. A sort of calculation, perhaps, a speculation. Something deeper than most men.

Then it was gone. It vanished in an instant to be replaced by that polite, charming smile.

Anna took her hand back and wrapped the leather reins over her palm. "I am sure my mother would say there is no other lady in Dublin who causes as much trouble as me!"

Sir Grant sat up straight in his saddle. He gave her a rueful half-smile. "Ah, but what is life without trouble, Lady Anna? Very dull."

Anna glanced down one of the pathways in search of her mother's carriage. She wanted nothing more than to go home, to be quiet and alone and not have anyone look at her. Everyone was always watching, watching.

Yet her wish was not to be met just yet. Her gaze collided with that of another horseman halfway down the path—a dark green stare that she remembered very well.

Adair. Her heart thudded in her chest, and she couldn't hold back a shocked gasp. What was he doing here, at the promenade hour when all respectable society was at St. Stephen's Green? She had never seen him here before, though his name was bandied about often enough in political circles.

Was he—could he be here because of her? Had he truly seen through her disguise at the Olympian Club?

But even as that thought flashed through her mind, she knew it was foolish. If he wanted to confront her, blackmail her, he would not choose to do so here. And why would a duke blackmail *her*? Why would he even care what a silly debutante did?

She took a deep, steadying breath, forcing her hands to relax on the reins as her horse shifted restlessly. The fact remained that he *was* here, and he was the least foolish man she had ever met. If he did not yet know that she was the lady in red, which wasn't very likely, he soon would. Especially if he kept staring at her so intently.

She peeked at him again from beneath her veil and found that he *did* still watch her. His face was shadowed now by the brim of his hat, the play of dark and light making the rugged angles of his high cheekbones and jaw even more chiseled. A trace of black beard shadowed his cheeks, and his hair was midnight black along the nape of his neck. He even wore black, fine wool and leather, and Anna thought again of Hades, thundering up from the Underworld to snatch poor, unsuspecting Persephone from the sunlight.

He raised his hat to her in a salute, giving her a little half-bow from his saddle. His lips parted in a grin, and she saw that he did know. He knew, and it seemed he was laughing at her.

A burst of temper flared through her, hot and sharp.

She longed to spur her horse forward, to snatch that crop from his hand and bring it down over his dark Irish head! How dare he laugh at her, after—after...

After that kiss in the conservatory. That wild, primitive kiss that left her so shaken. And, yes, left her longing for more. She had never found such wondrous forgetfulness as she had in those moments in his arms. Maybe after she whipped him for laughing, she would bury her fingers in his hair and drag him against her for another taste.

She touched the tip of her tongue to her dry lips, just under the edge of her veil, and his smile faded. His expression darkened, and his eyes narrowed on her mouth. Slowly, deliberately, she licked her lips again.

"Lady Anna," Grant said, drawing in his horse next to hers. "Shall we..."

His words cut off abruptly as he glanced down the lane to where her attention was focused. She sensed him stiffening, his hands tightening on the reins.

Adair, too, grew tense, the sensual, shimmering haze that seemed to linger between them dissipating in an instant. His stare snapped to Grant, his fist opening and closing as if he clutched a dagger. She would not be surprised if he was quite proficient in a knife fight—or a fight of any sort.

"Do you know my cousin, Lady Anna?" Grant said tightly.

"Your cousin?" Anna said, shocked. If ever there were two men less similar than Adair and Grant Dunmore— less likely to be kinsmen—she had never met them. The sophisticated center of Ascendancy Society that was Sir Grant and the wild black Irishman Adair?

Surely not. Grant had to be speaking of someone else along the pathway. Yet the lane was nearly deserted now.

"The Duke of Adair," Grant said. Ice dripped from every syllable of the grand title. "He is watching you."

Anna looked back to Adair. He seemed to watch not her but Grant, or rather he watched the two of them together. He had relaxed, his black-gloved hands loose on the reins, a strange, humorless smile on his lips. Yet even across the distance, she could feel the heat of those green eyes, glowing with fury.

It was obviously not a happy family connection.

"I have met him once or twice," she said. She could certainly never tell the circumstances of those meetings, in a burned-out stable amid the fury of the Uprising, and in a deserted conservatory at the scandalous Olympian Club. She did not even want to think of them herself, her two darkest, truest moments. "But I would not say I know him. We have not been formally introduced."

"Then we should correct that oversight, Lady Anna, for I believe his ducal estate is not far from Killinan Castle," Grant said, suddenly spurring his horse forward. He reached out to grasp Anna's bridle, as if he would force her to follow.

Anna tugged hard at her reins. "What do you mean?"

He glanced back at her, those golden eyes burning. "I thought every lady longed to make the acquaintance of a duke."

"Not *that* duke," Anna muttered. "And I am not sure why you would want to speak to him, either, Sir Grant. It's obvious you don't care for each other."

He dropped her bridle and laughed wryly, as if he just

realized his strange behavior. "True. The two family branches are not what you would call close."

"Then you should ignore him and help me find my mother," she urged him. "I am suddenly quite tired."

"I would be happy to oblige, Lady Anna," Grant said. "Yet I fear it is too late."

"What do you mean...?" Anna looked past his shoulder to see that Adair was now coming toward them, his face set in grim determination that was quite terrifying.

But she had no time to flee, and she found she did not even want to. That fiery urge to beat Adair about the head, and then leap on him and kiss him, flared up in her again. She lowered her chin, glaring at him in fury—fury at him and at herself for what he made her feel.

Adair turned his horse neatly, blocking her and Grant from making an escape. The two men watched each other with a wary steadiness like two gladiators as they circled before attacking.

"Cousin Grant," Adair said, his voice all genial affability. But Anna heard the roughness of his Irish accent just beneath, and she remembered how that brogue deepened with anger and passion. "An unexpected pleasure to see you here."

"Unexpected indeed," Grant answered, equally polite. "But surely not so unexpected on your end—cousin. I make my home here in Dublin, yet you have not been seen in the city in many months. Not since the last time rebellion raised its bloody Irish head."

"How wrong you are. I often come here to partake of the rare delights of town." Adair's gaze raked slowly over Anna's body in her snug purple velvet habit, making her shiver as if it was his bare hand that touched her. "As do you, I see. There are no beauties to be found like those in Dublin, am I right?"

"You will not dare look at Lady Anna in such a way!" Grant growled. "She is the daughter of Lady Killinan, which you would know if you mixed in proper society at all, instead of wallowing in the mud with your Fenian peasants."

"Is she a lady indeed?" His raven's wing brow arched as he looked again at Anna, giving her a knowing smile. She felt her cheeks turn hot and prayed he wouldn't see the damnable blush under her veil. "And a paragon of English femininity, I'm sure. Meek and modest and biddable, especially to the right man. A man with a strong touch." He held out his crop, touching just the tip of it to Anna's lace collar. "Or for the right price. Have you discovered that price yet, Grant? Or perhaps it is too high for the likes of you...."

He slid that whip lightly down her bodice, his gaze following its path as Grant shouted in fury. But Anna had had quite enough of Adair's game. She grabbed the crop, snatching it out of his hand and throwing it to the ground.

"Enough, both of you!" she cried. "I came here for a pleasant outing, not to find myself a bone between two snarling mongrels. If you must quarrel, then go off and compare the size of your—estates elsewhere. You don't belong among civilized people until you can learn some manners. And I do not care if they're Irish or English manners."

Grant looked at her with temper in his eyes, as if he would turn his anger onto her, but Adair just laughed. He sat back in his saddle, watching her with approval.

"Bravo, Lady Anna," he said. "Well stated. You are

quite right. We don't belong near fine ladies such as your-self. I apologize."

"As do I," Grant said grudgingly. "I should not have allowed you to be exposed to a private family quarrel, Lady Anna."

"Oh, I am sure her ladyship has been *exposed* to far worse," Adair said.

Grant swung back to him angrily. "And what is that supposed to mean?"

"Nothing at all, cousin," Adair said coolly. "What do you think it means? What thoughts lurk in my filthy Fenian mind?"

"I said enough, gentlemen, and I meant it," Anna inter-rupted. She tugged at Psyche's reins, trying to edge around Adair. He stood his ground, watching her.

She stared back at him, unable to look away. The rest of the world—the park, Sir Grant, the distant sound of laughter—faded around her as she looked into Adair's eyes and remembered the feel of his kiss, his touch....

She tore her gaze from his, blinking away those blurry, urgent images. "Fisticuffs might be amusing some other day," she said, trembling as if caught in a buffeting wind, "but I am weary of this now."

Suddenly, a sharp cracking noise split the air, followed by two more. It was a startled instant before she realized it was gunshots, whizzing right past her ear.

Her terrified horse reared up beneath her, and she was too shocked to grasp the reins. She felt herself falling, falling, her heart dropping to her feet. The sky whirled over her head and the wind rushed past her in a shrieking whine.

There was no time to scream, almost no time to realize

what really happened. Anna hit the ground hard, all the breath forced out of her body, and her head collided with the gravel path. Stars spun before her eyes, followed by a hazy gray fog.

Distantly, she felt pain in her shoulder and a dull ache in her hip. Vaguely she could hear shouts and screams, but they were muffled and so far away. She closed her eyes against those reeling stars, and she was back *there* again. Lying helpless in a field as bullets ricocheted overhead and exploded in a deafening roar. The sun was blazing hot, and the coppery smell of blood was thick and sickening in her throat.

Someone touched her arm, and for a moment it was that crazed soldier, forcing her legs apart as he heaved his sweating, stinking body over hers. She screamed and tried to fight, but the pain sharpened, flooding over her with a paralyzing force. Still she pushed at him, sobbing.

"Anna!" a voice called, full of urgent fear and a thick Irish accent. No redcoat then. "Anna, for fuck's sake, quit fighting me. Y'have to lie still, *cailleach,* I beg you."

Anna made herself open her eyes, gasping for air. The sky still swayed, tilting to and fro as if she had drunk far too much wine, but she forced herself to focus on the face above her. It was *not* that soldier intent on rape, but a dark, lean man who looked completely uncivilized with black, rumpled hair and wild green eyes. He didn't belong here at all, but on some ancient Celtic battlefield.

"Adair?" she whispered.

"You recognize me?"

"Of course. I could never mistake you for anyone else. But you should not be here. You were at the stable...." Yes, the abandoned, burned stable. Not the battle.

"I fear you're the one felled this time, *cailleach,* not me. Can you feel this?" He slid his hand over hers, pressing hard on her fingers. "Can you move them?"

She carefully wiggled her fingertips, but it felt like a bolt of lightning shot up her arm at the movement. "It hurts!"

"Better that than numb." He raised her limp hand to his mouth, kissing her wrist just above the edge of her glove. His mouth was warm and strangely soft, soothing. It made her want to press even closer, to curl up in the strength of him. There could be no nightmares there.

"I'm so sorry," he muttered, holding her hand against his cheek. She felt the bristles of his beard on her skin. "You shouldn't have been here."

"No, she should not!" another man shouted. "They were shooting at *you,* you bastard. This is your fault."

Grant Dunmore. He had no place in her old memories. That realization made her remember entirely where she was, what had just happened. St. Stephen's Green, the shots, her horse rearing...

"Psyche!" she cried. "My horse. Is she all right?"

"Shh, lie still," Adair said, gently holding her to the ground. "She is fine; everything is fine now. I won't let anyone hurt you again."

"You're the one who caused this!" Grant yelled.

"I said no more fighting," Anna whispered weakly. "So rude."

Adair smiled down at her. That smile transformed him, making him seem younger, freer. Why did he not smile more often, Anna wondered dazedly.

"Good girl. You must be feeling better," he said.

"Good girl? I thought I was a witch."

"Anna!" her mother screamed. "Oh, dear God, what has happened?"

Anna heard the rustle of silk, smelled the sweetness of lily perfume, and her mother's face swam into view above her, blocking out the shifting sky. Katherine's cheeks were white as chalk, her eyes wide and bright with tears.

For as long as Anna could remember, her mother had been cool and calm, as serene as the angel she was called. She nursed her servants and tenants, all her children's childhood accidents, with a quiet, kind efficiency. She ran the vast corridors and wide acres of Killinan Castle with never a hair out of place. Only once before had Anna seen her reveal her fear so starkly—when they were fleeing Killinan for Dublin during the Uprising and ran into that horrible battle.

She had followed Anna anxiously for months after that, always so watchful. Only recently had Anna found a measure of freedom again. This incident would surely put an end to that.

"Anna, are you hurt?" Katherine said, taking Anna's hand in hers as her gaze frantically scanned for any wounds or blood.

"I am fine, Mama," Anna answered. She made herself laugh, shaking away the last stubborn remnants of her fears and memories. Of her desire for another kiss from Adair, even while bullets flew. "Just a bit startled."

Katherine sat back on her heels, still holding tight to Anna's hand. She glanced around them, from one face to the other, as if she sought answers. Only then did Anna realize that a crowd had gathered around them.

"What happened here?" Katherine demanded.

Anna sought out Adair, who stood just beyond her mother's shoulder. He looked even more disreputable than before. He had lost his hat, and his hair fell over his brow in a windswept tangle. His cravat was raked loose, and there was dust on his coat. He stared back at her, that wildness in his eyes tempered with caution.

She gave her head a small shake, silently begging him to go along with her. "I just fell from my horse, Mama, that is all. Psyche took a fright at the noise, and she reared up. I'm sure it was some idiots shooting at rabbits."

"Psyche? How can that be? You've trained her so well," Katherine said, frowning.

"All horses are unpredictable sometimes, Mama. I am quite well, I promise. Just had the breath knocked out of me for a moment. Luckily, these two gentlemen, Sir Grant Dunmore and the Duke of Adair, were nearby and came to my rescue."

"Adair?" Katherine twisted around to stare at the duke. "Yes, I thought I recognized you."

He gave her a bow, the polite gesture at odds with his rakish dishabille. "Lady Killinan. It has been a long time."

"Indeed. I suppose it is fortunate you decided to show your face in Dublin after all this time to help my daughter."

"I am glad I happened to be nearby, though I'm sorry I was not able to prevent the—accident."

"That is what happened then? You saw it all?" said Katherine.

Adair's eyes narrowed, and Anna gave him another pleading look. "Yes," he said shortly.

"And you, Sir Grant? You saw it, too?" Katherine demanded, her stare moving above Anna's head to where Grant was standing.

"I—yes, Lady Killinan," she heard Grant answer. He did not sound terribly convincing. "It was most unfortunate. Such a relief that Lady Anna is unhurt."

"That remains to be seen," Katherine said crisply. "I must get her home and send for the doctor, then we will be sure."

"Mama, I don't need a doctor," Anna protested.

"You shall have one nonetheless. And no parties until next week at least." Katherine looked back at Adair sternly. "Don't just stand there, Your Grace. Help me get my daughter to the carriage."

"Lady Killinan, let me..." Grant said hastily.

But Katherine shook her head. "One assistant is quite enough, thank you, Sir Grant. Perhaps you would be good enough to fetch Psyche and see her home? She seems to have wandered over to that patch of dry grass, quite unconcerned about all the fuss she has caused."

"Of course, Lady Killinan," he answered, most grudgingly.

Anna heard him move away. One more cool, sweeping glance from her mother dissipated the crowd, but their whispers still echoed. Anna could just imagine their words—*How trouble does seem to follow those Blacknall girls....*

Adair knelt beside her, sliding his arm gently around her shoulders and helping her sit up. Suddenly, she was surrounded by the smell of him, the scent of citrus-scented soap she remembered all too well from their dance at the Olympian Club. The heat of his large, strong body supported her, and it seemed to tie her to him. She leaned against him and rested her cheek on his shoulder. The roughness of his beard scraped against her brow, tickling. It made her laugh, feeling quite reckless.

How could she possibly have such longings—the longing to wrap her arms around his neck and hold him close, the longing to kiss him—after what had happened? It was obvious the trouble that followed *her* around was nothing to the trouble surrounding the Duke of Adair. Secret clubs, shootings in the park—and that was only on the surface, the part she could see. Who knew what darkness he kept concealed?

If she was smart, she would push him away now and run, never looking back. Never think of him again. But she had definitely never been able to resist a puzzle.

"Hold on to me," he murmured close to her ear. The sound of his voice slid over her like fine brandy, deceptively smooth and alluring.

Anna clutched at his shoulders as he lifted her from the ground. The pain in her bruised hip, so distant while she was distracted, shot down her leg. "Ouch!"

"You see, Lady Anna, your mother is right—you need a doctor," he said. He held her as easily as if she were a feather, cradling her against him as he followed her mother toward the carriage.

"You don't know me, Your Grace," Anna protested. "You can't possibly know what I need."

"Oh, I think you would be surprised by what I know." He laid her carefully against the velvet cushions and took her hand in his. He raised it again to his lips, his stare frighteningly solemn above their linked fingers.

She swallowed hard. He let go of her, and she quickly tucked her hand in a fold of her riding habit. "Perhaps we should maintain that sense of mystery then, Your Grace, and stay away from each other."

He laughed and that solemnity vanished. "Oh, Lady Anna, I am sure that would be very prudent. But I have the distinct sense neither of us are prudent people, aye?"

Katherine climbed up into the carriage next to Anna, and Adair stepped back. The laughter was gone, but a smile still lingered on his lips.

"Thank you for your assistance, Your Grace," Katherine said. "However it came about, I am happy you were there to come to my daughter's aid."

"As am I, Lady Killinan," he answered. "Perhaps I might call in the next day or two to make sure Lady Anna suffers no ill effects from her fall?"

Anna stared at him in shock. Just the thought of him calling in Henrietta Street was so—so prosaic. So ordinary. So very unlike him. An Irish rebel, sitting in her mother's drawing room taking tea?

She pressed her hand to her mouth to hold back a laugh. If she started giggling hysterically, her mother would be sure that she injured her head and call in battalions of doctors.

Katherine arched her brow questioningly. She tilted her head, studying Adair with her cool blue eyes. "I suppose you may call, yes, Your Grace. I would like to have more conversation with you. We are practically neighbors in Kildare, are we not?"

She nodded to the coachman, and the carriage lurched into motion. Anna glanced back over her shoulder to see that Adair watched them leave. He lifted his hand in farewell, then they turned the corner onto another lane, and he was gone.

"Oh, my dear," Katherine sighed. "Such a very odd day."

"Oh, yes," Anna whispered. Odd indeed.

Chapter Five

Now, on top of everything else, he had an assassin to track down.

Conlan watched Anna's carriage until it vanished from view. She stared back at him, as if she wanted something, expected something, from him. A puzzled frown creased her brow, but there was no fear in her eyes. Any other young English lady would have been shrieking with panic after being shot at on her afternoon ride. After an initial flash of fear, Anna Blacknall just seemed—curious. Just as she had been at the Olympian Club.

She wasn't a woman to be easily frightened, that was clear. His barbaric behavior as he tried to get a reaction from Grant, being thrown from her horse—being kissed to within an inch of insanity in the conservatory. None of it scared her for long. Yet, in that instant when he first knelt beside her on the ground, he did see fear in her eyes. She didn't seem to be there at all, but someplace far away, plunged into some old nightmare.

Everyone who was in Ireland in '98 had those nightmares, the fears and grief that never quite left. He couldn't afford sympathy for a pampered Society lady like Anna Blacknall. But in that moment, he had the overwhelming urge to hold her close until all the panic was gone. He wanted to keep her safe.

Which was the very last thing he could do. It was his fault that she was in danger today in the first place. And he *would* find out who did it. Find them and make them sorry indeed.

The sound of laughter brought him back to the present moment. He shook away the image of Anna lying on the cold ground and looked over his shoulder. Most of the crowd had dissipated, going home to prepare for their evening parties, but a few people lingered. They watched him curiously. Perhaps they, like Lady Killinan, wondered why someone like him was back in Dublin now, right as the Union issue was boiling toward crisis. Surely they whispered of the way trouble followed him everywhere.

Conlan could have told them the answer. All the McTeer men, back to the days of Brian Boru, were born with the dark mark, the curse of leading a fractious, quarrelsome family who were only united in hatred of each other and the rest of the world. The curse of trying to maintain their people and their ancient lands in a harsh country ruled by an iron-strong foreign power. That had been his calling, his purpose, ever since he was born. It was hard, dangerous, and lonely work, and as Duke of Adair it was his work alone.

But he had never seen *trouble* like Anna Blacknall. Trouble with golden hair, soft skin, and fine blue eyes that saw far too much. He certainly did not need her kind of trouble, now of all times.

And now too much attention was on him. He glared

at the curious onlookers, sending them scattering into the park. Only one man remained: Grant Dunmore, Conlan's long-lost cousin.

If only he had stayed lost. He was the last person Conlan wanted to see now. Well, second to last—he did not especially want to see Anna Blacknall at the moment, either.

He swung his dark glare onto Grant, who stood at the side of the lane holding the bridle of Anna's horse. He didn't flee like the others, but neither did he come closer. Perhaps he remembered the beating Conlan once gave him during that bloody lawsuit of his. The suit that tore the Irish branch of the family from the English once and for all.

Conlan didn't have time to deal with Grant now, not as his cousin deserved. In only a few hours, the Olympian Club would open for another night. And he had to go about catching a would-be murderer, one who wanted Conlan dead so much that they didn't care who else they hurt.

Or maybe the murderer stood before him now, his own kinsman.

Conlan scooped his battered hat from the ground, dusting off the gravel. "What are you doing here, Grant?"

"I could ask you the same thing. Why aren't you skulking at Adair Court, as you have all these years?"

Conlan grinned, enjoying his cousin's obvious pique. Conlan had stayed mostly out of sight since he came to Dublin, concentrating his efforts on the Olympian Club and on meeting with his old contacts. But now his plans had to move forward, and he had to gain more visibility. The Union vote would be soon. To judge by today's dramatic events, he had succeeded too well.

Not that he enjoyed being shot at, even though he had too much experience of such things. And he definitely didn't like Anna Blacknall being caught in the bullet's path. He would have to be even more cautious in the future and even more ruthless in finding his enemies.

Some enemies, though, were obliging enough to appear right in front of him.

"Perhaps I am in Dublin for the very reasons you guessed, cousin," Conlan said. "To enjoy the amenities only town can offer. Such fair ladies in our capital city, wouldn't you agree? And they're so—accommodating."

An angry red flush stained Grant's face, and his fist tightened on the mare's bridle, making her shy away. "You had best stay far away from Lady Anna in the future! I don't even want to hear you speak her name, let alone make your filthy insinuations."

Well, well. There appeared to be something between Lady Anna and Grant after all. That was useful knowledge. "I insinuate nothing about Lady Anna. Any daughter of Lady Killinan must be above reproach, I'm sure." Except when she donned a low-cut red gown and snuck into a masked ball. But that contradiction was only part of Anna's strange allure. "Even one who is with you."

She was too good for Grant. A man like his cousin could never appreciate such a dichotomy in a woman, never tolerate complexity or independence. He could see the world only one way, and his narrowness would crush Anna eventually, no matter how strong or stubborn she was.

It was a shame.

Grant dropped the bridle and took a menacing step across the path. Conlan automatically braced himself for a brawl, planting his feet firmly on the ground and stretching his fingers toward the dagger concealed under his coat. But even as he did so, he knew it wasn't needed. His cousin's methods were much less direct than public brawling, and he never dirtied his pretty hands himself.

"I don't know what you think you understand about me, Adair," Grant said, "but you *will* stay away from Lady Anna."

"Such a storm of fury over the lady. Yet I have heard no betrothal announcements."

Grant's jaw tightened. "Things are different now, Adair. Ireland will soon be a part of Great Britain, a full part, and once I am allied with the Killinan estate I will have as much power as you. More even, than some mere Irish title. You had best watch your back."

"As I had to today?" Conlan said, his tone deceptively bland.

"I had nothing to do with that! But I applaud whoever did."

"Even if it put your fine fiancée in danger? How ruthless of you, Grant."

"That was your fault, Adair!" Grant shouted. His temper obviously burned hotter and hotter under that elegant surface, even as Conlan felt his own emotions covered with a layer of impervious ice. He couldn't afford to give in to anger, to pummel Grant Dunmore as he so deserved. This was a battle that had far too much at stake.

And he definitely could not be distracted by Anna Blacknall.

"You're obviously not fit for decent society, Adair, despite your high-sounding title," Grant said. "Stay away from Lady Anna or . . ."

"Or what?" Conlan took one slow step, then another and another toward Grant, until he stood a mere foot from his cousin. Alarm flared in Grant's eyes, but to his credit he stood his ground. "Or you will challenge me to a duel, perhaps?"

"It would give me great pleasure to call you out."

Conlan laughed coldly. "Don't bother. I am no gentleman, remember? I could just shoot you in some dark alley at night, cousin, with no one the wiser. And I know how much you like to frequent dark alleys."

Grant gave him a sneer. "I am sure I have not a fraction of the knowledge of such places as you do—Your Grace. And I have too much honor to deal with you as you deserve. But if you dare trifle with my future wife…"

Conlan stepped away, reaching for his horse's reins. "I would not be so sure of Lady Anna's intentions if I were you, Grant."

"What do you mean?"

"Just that there seem to be hidden depths to your golden doll that you could never fathom. I doubt she will be an easy pawn in your schemes." He swung up into the saddle and turned away from Grant. "Good day, cousin. I'm sure we will meet again soon. I find Dublin suits me quite well."

Conlan rode out of the near-deserted park, leaving Grant still glaring after him. No, Anna would not be the placid, perfect Society wife, the pawn for ambition, that Grant expected. But could she unwittingly aid Conlan?

It was an intriguing thought, and Conlan had to explore it further. He would do anything, use any tool to keep his people safe. But it was a thought that would have to wait until later. Right now, he had to track down his killer.

Once he turned out of the gilded gates of St. Stephen's Green, he moved away from the wide streets and pale marble mansions of refined Dublin and galloped toward the Liberties. His cousin was right about one thing: Conlan knew a great deal about dark alleyways. It was there, amid the narrow, fetid lanes and squalid nests of burrows and brothels, that his quarry would be found. He hoped that whoever it was enjoyed their ill-gotten coin while they could. Their moments were definitely numbered.

Chapter Six

Y ou're home at last! You're very late."

Anna glanced up as she stepped through the front door to find Caroline hanging over the banister. She had pushed her spectacles atop her head, and the glass glinted in her untidy brown hair. There was an ink stain on her pale blue bodice.

Anna almost laughed. Her sister looked just as untidy as she did herself! Who knew that such pursuits as riding in the park and studying Irish history could be so perilous?

She stripped off her gloves and unpinned the ragged remains of her hat. Now that the danger was past, and she was out of the intoxicating presence of the Duke of Adair, she felt so weary. Weary and aching. Her hip throbbed where she had landed on the ground, and her head felt heavy. She longed to crawl into bed with a tisane and the newest French romantic novel and forget all about this most bizarre afternoon.

But hiding under the bedclothes would just convince her mother that she was indeed ill, even as she claimed so vehemently to be well. She would be locked away with doctors and cups of beef tea for days when there was so much to do. So many mysteries to unravel.

Katherine studied her closely as she removed her own hat, and her eyes were much too shrewd and discerning. It was always difficult to fool her mother, though Anna could certainly do it when she set her mind to it. She gave her mother a cheerful smile.

"Caroline, I'm afraid your sister took a spill from her horse," Katherine said. "I made the carriage come home very slowly so she would not be jostled."

"Which I said was quite unnecessary," Anna said. "I am perfectly well."

"*Anna* fell from her horse?" Caroline cried. She dashed down the stairs and seized Anna's hands in hers, carefully scanning her for injuries. "How can that be? You never fall! Unlike me; horses hate me."

"Psyche was startled, that's all," said Anna. "I was not paying proper attention."

"Were you flirting with someone?" Caroline asked.

Anna laughed. "Of course! What else is the promenade hour for? I was talking to a *duke*."

"A duke! How fascinating," said Caroline. "You've always said you wanted to be a duchess. Was he terribly handsome? Will you dance with him at the Fitzwalters' ball?"

"She will not," Katherine interrupted, "because Anna must stay home and rest, not go dancing at balls."

"Mama!" Anna protested. But she could say no more, for the butler, Smythe, stepped forward to gain her mother's attention.

"I beg your pardon, my lady," he said, "but the drawing teacher is waiting for you in the library."

"Oh, I had quite forgotten about that appointment in all the excitement," Katherine said, a little frown creasing her pale brow. The Angel of Kildare never kept anyone waiting, not even teachers.

"Shall I ask him to come back tomorrow?" Smythe asked.

"You should ask him to go to perdition," Caroline muttered.

"Caroline, that is quite enough." Katherine glanced at Anna, clearly torn between keeping her appointment and fussing over her daughter.

Anna did not feel like being fussed over. "Go on, Mama. Caro will look after me for a while. This is the *French* drawing teacher, yes? You shouldn't let him get away."

"Very well," Katherine said reluctantly. "Send in some tea please, Smythe, and tell Monsieur Courtois I will be with him shortly. Caroline, take your sister to her chamber and make sure she lies down."

"Yes, Mama," Anna said meekly. Before Caroline could argue again, Anna seized her arm and dragged her along up the stairs. Her maid, Rose, already waited in her chamber with hot water and a clean gown.

As Anna set about tidying up, Caroline flopped down across the bed. Her spectacles flew across the coverlet. "I suppose with all the flirting and such you did not have time to speak to Mama about the lessons."

"I did," Anna said. She winced as Rose dragged the brush through her tangled hair. "And she said she thought you might enjoy improving your drawing. You could use it to copy illustrations for your research or for sketching historical sites."

"That is true, I suppose," Caroline said grudgingly. "But it will still take up so much time. I'm pressed to find spare hours to read as it is, what with dancing and deportment and all that."

"Perhaps if you do very well at drawing, you could persuade Mama to let you drop another lesson," Anna said. Rose buttoned her into a fresh, long-sleeved muslin dress that hid the bruises on her hip and shoulder. "And maybe this French teacher is handsome. That would make the lessons fly by, I'm sure."

Caroline rolled over onto her stomach. "Don't be silly, Anna. What use is a handsome Frenchman to me?"

"Oh, yes, I forgot. You are practically betrothed to Lord Hartley and his library."

Caroline gave an unladylike snort. "Forget Lord Hartley and Frenchmen. Tell me about this duke. He must be terribly attractive to make you lose your seat on a horse. Is he more handsome than Grant Dunmore?"

Anna closed her eyes, picturing Adair in her mind. His black hair and roughly chiseled face, the mocking laughter in his eyes. The anger, and fear, as he knelt beside her on the ground. "He is not nearly as handsome as Sir Grant. Some would say he is not handsome at all. But he is—complicated."

"Complicated?" Caroline propped her chin on her fist and stared at Anna keenly. "That sounds terribly interesting. Most of your suitors are no more complex than their own hunting hounds."

Anna laughed. "Oh, thank you very much, Caro! I know I am far too shallow to attract any men *you* deem interesting, but they are not all that bad. Some are rather sweet."

"It's not your fault. It's just the way they're brought up, like Papa. They aren't taught to think for themselves, I suppose, or imagine a world different than the one they grew up in."

Anna pushed away the rice powder Rose offered and went to sit on the bed with Caroline. "Well, this duke is Irish, with some kind of terribly ancient title, so maybe he was brought up differently than all our Ascendancy suitors."

"An Irish duke? Now that is very interesting. How did he come by this title? Is he Catholic?"

Anna wondered those things herself, and so much more. Adair was an intriguing puzzle, one she longed to decipher, clue by intriguing clue. "I have no idea about his title, though I think his estate is near Killinan Castle. And I suppose he is Catholic, though I don't know for sure."

"However did you meet him?"

Anna could hardly tell her the truth. That would be her own secret, and Adair's, forever. "When he came to my aid today, of course. He was the first to reach me when I fell."

"How romantic. A dashing, not-quite handsome Irish duke coming to your rescue. I'm sure he has many tales that would be so useful for my research. When can I catch a glimpse of him?"

"Soon, maybe. He asked if he could call on us here, and Mama said yes."

"Mama agreed?" Caroline said, her eyes wide with astonishment. "Oh, my. Now I wish I had gone riding with you today."

There was a knock at the door, and a parlor maid came

in with a curtsy. "Lady Cannondale is downstairs, Lady Anna. She says she wants to see if you are well."

Anna nearly laughed aloud. The butler would be quite chagrined at all the activity so late in the day! Smythe was quite proper and anxious to uphold all the proprieties, including calling hours. "Send her up to my sitting room, please, and ask the butler to arrange for some refreshments."

Maybe Jane would know something about Adair. She did seem to know all the gossip, and she was a member of the Olympian Club after all.

"I will leave you to Lady Cannondale's care, Anna," Caroline said as she slid off the bed. She found her lost spectacles and pushed them back on her nose. "I have more reading to do before dinner."

"You're not going to listen at the library door, are you?"

Caroline sniffed. "Of course not. I am not so mischievous as you, sister."

"No one is." Anna hurried next door to her own sitting room where Jane already waited. She still wore her green carriage dress from the park, so obviously she had not yet gone home to prepare for the evening out.

"Oh, Anna my dear!" she cried, and rushed forward to kiss Anna's cheek. "I just heard of your accident. Are you terribly hurt?"

"Only my pride. My fine equestrian reputation will be quite ruined."

"I'm just sorry that I had already left." They were interrupted by the servants bringing in tea, and only once they were settled by the fire did Jane go on. "It sounds so exciting. Tell me, is it true the Duke of Adair came to your rescue?"

Anna nodded as she stirred at her tea. "I happened to be speaking with him when—when it happened." She remembered the pop and whine of the bullets, whizzing past her toward him, and she shivered. They were both very lucky.

"Were you really? Hmm." Jane took a thoughtful sip. "I daresay Grant Dunmore won't like *that*."

"No, he did not. I thought there might be a brawl right there on St. Stephen's Green."

"So he was there, too?"

Anna nodded.

"Oh, my dear." Jane gave a delighted laugh. "How delicious. And to think I missed it all."

"The duke said they were cousins of some sort. I take it there is no family love lost."

"To say the least." Jane set her cup down and leaned forward in her chair, as if settling in for a good coze. "Do you not recall that old business over the estate? Adair Court is not terribly far from Killinan."

Anna also leaned forward so as not to miss a word. Jane did always know the *on dits*. "Unless it happened in the last year or two, I might not have heard. Mama didn't like us listening to neighborhood gossip when we were girls." She didn't like it very much now, either, but she couldn't stop Anna.

"You did not know Adair almost lost the estate, which his family has held on to for centuries, due to the old Penal Laws?"

"Yes, I did hear something of that," Anna said. Under the harsh old Penal Laws against Irish Catholics, which had only been fully revoked in 1793, a Protestant could sue to take possession of a Catholic relative's land if he could prove the Catholic was disloyal to the Crown or misused the property. Since a Catholic was thought by definition to be disloyal, it was not a hard claim to make, but in truth that law was very seldom enforced at all. Most Irish families tended to protect their own, no matter what their disagreements.

But the Adair case had been a spectacular one. Titled lords fighting over thousands of acres and hundreds of tenants, a fine ancient castle. And...

"No!" Anna cried. She slumped back in her seat, feeling like a fool for being so shocked. She should have realized immediately when she saw them together, put together the old stories and their obvious hatred for each other.

"It was Grant Dunmore who brought the suit," she whispered.

Jane nodded. "He never really had a chance, of course. Adair might be many unsavory things, but he *is* a duke. His ancestors held on to that title for centuries through whatever means necessary, and he is quite their ruthless equal. Dunmore was a fool to try it out. But his estate in Queen's County is nothing compared to Adair Court. He wanted property to match his ambitions, and it blinded him to reality. He made a bad enemy of his cousin."

Still stunned by the depth of the poison between Adair and Grant Dunmore, Anna shook her head. "How do you know all this?"

"Everyone knows. But my husband was one of the members of Parliament who heard the case. He was always very chatty, my Harry." Jane gave her a sly smile. "And now they have you to fight over, A. How wonderful."

Anna crossed her arms against a sudden harsh feeling

of anger and foolishness, and a cold understanding. "I am not a bone for two snarling mongrels to fight over."

"I hardly think a duke and a baronet could be called mongrels."

"I don't want to be mixed up in that old business! There is too much hatred and division in this country already. It can't be good to toss fuel on old embers."

"You're quite right, of course. But forgive and forget is hardly the Irish way, is it, my dear? The enmity between those two goes beyond any lawsuit or pretty woman. You do not have to be their pawn, though. *You* can use *them* to your own advantage."

"What do you mean?" Anna asked, now thoroughly confused. "Short of taking a riding crop to both of them, I can't imagine I could ever control them. And I can't see what *advantage* I could find in them, either."

Jane toyed idly with the ribbons of her dress, smiling mysteriously. "Do you not? Well, I must leave you to think about it then. I have to go home and change for that card party. I suppose we won't be seeing you there?"

Anna shook her head. She was only half-listening; her mind still reeled with all this new, fascinating information. "No, but I am sure I can persuade Mama to let me attend the Fitzwalters' ball tomorrow."

"Oh, I so much hope you can. Since I missed the excitement at the park today, I must pray for another show."

"I doubt that will happen. Adair never goes about in Society, does he?"

"Somehow I have the feeling his reclusive habits are about to change." Jane rose to her feet and kissed Anna's cheek again before she smoothed on her gloves. "I am so happy you're unhurt, Anna. You will think of all I've said?"

"Of course, Jane. Good-bye until tomorrow."

After her friend departed, Anna wandered over to the window to stare down at the street. Beyond the ivy-covered portico, Henrietta Street was quiet in the gathering darkness. No one was yet abroad in the darkened streets. They were all preparing for parties or the theater, or perhaps for more daring fare. Perhaps some of them were going to the Olympian Club.

Was Adair there now? She closed her eyes and pictured him tying on a mask, moving through the empty rooms that would soon fill up with laughter and lust, the despair of money lost and the excitement of flirtatious glances and new affairs.

How she wished she were there, too. Despite her tiredness and the ache of her bruises, that old plague of restlessness was even stronger tonight. It was like an imp of mischief deep inside of her, urging her on to new trouble.

She opened her eyes and stared out blindly at the gathering twilight. If she did want trouble, she need look no further than Adair. He was danger come to dark, thrilling life, full of mystery and secret—or not so secret—enmities. He was intriguing; she could not deny it. But it seemed that somewhere in her heart, hidden away, so tiny she could hardly see it, was a kernel of her mother's prudence.

She would not put on her own mask and sneak out tonight, no matter how much she wanted to. She had much to consider. Jane had said there was an "advantage" to be had in the feud between Adair and Grant Dunmore. Anna had no idea what that meant.

But she was certainly going to find out.

Chapter Seven

Katherine paused in front of the mirror in the corridor before she went to attend to her duty in the library. The fading light from the windows fell over her disordered hair and pale face, and she feared it revealed the strain of the day. Once, she could recover from any crisis full of energy and eager to take on the many tasks of a lady with a large estate. Being the chatelaine of Killinan Castle and the mother of her lively girls had been her whole life, and she would do anything for her family and home. She still would.

But how tired she felt! How aged. She knew she was not so old, only in her forties, and she looked younger. Like most girls from good Anglo-Irish families, she married young and had her children quickly. Six of them, though only three lived. But she *felt* as if she was a hundred years old. Seeing Anna crumpled on the ground was terrifying. It brought back so vividly those days when she could do nothing to protect her children, when she had come so close to losing them to war and rebellion.

"Oh, Anna," she whispered. Her beautiful, sweet, wild,

vulnerable girl. She was safe now, but how long would that last?

Katherine's own mother told her that the hardest thing in life was letting one's children fly free. Letting them make their own mistakes. But she had not said just how very many mistakes children could make!

Katherine smoothed her blond curls, mercifully only lightly streaked with silver. She pinched her white, still-smooth cheeks to add a hint of color and straightened the fur-trimmed bodice of her blue gown.

"I am not quite ready to give up and sit knitting by the fireside just yet," she said resolutely. Widow's caps could wait until Anna and Caroline were settled. And Caroline would never be settled without a bit of polish, including drawing skills. She spun around and marched toward the library, swinging open the door.

The lamps in the large room had not yet been lit. Only the pink-gold setting sun lit the dark paneled walls and towering shelves of books and the brown velvet chairs and settees. Though the house actually belonged to Eliza, Katherine had hung her own husband's portrait over the fireplace. Lord Killinan smiled down at her, happily ensconced forever with his beloved hunting dogs at his feet and Killinan Castle in the background.

He could not feel the chill in the air. The fire had died in the grate, and a tea tray sat cooling on one of the marble-topped tables. Katherine rubbed at her arms in the silk sleeves, glancing around for the drawing teacher.

He was half-hidden in the shadows as he stood before one of the shelves, his head tilted to examine the volumes. He seemed quite unaware of her presence, which gave her a stunned moment to study him.

Monsieur Nicolas Courtois was not exactly what she had expected. All Caroline's other teachers were fussy older men in black coats and old-fashioned wigs. Katherine's own art teacher when she was a girl had also been older, a temperamental Italian who had megrims over her paltry watercolor efforts.

Monsieur Courtois had come very highly recommended. Her friends had raved over him, and their daughters had gone into raptures when his name was mentioned. Now she suspected his skills with charcoal pencils, paint, and canvas had little to do with that enthusiasm. Monsieur Courtois was, not to put too fine a point on it, sublimely handsome. A chalky beam of sunlight fell over him, turning his pale hair to shimmering gold. He was tall and elegantly lean in a stylish but not ostentatious dark green coat and ivory cravat. His profile looked like a classical cameo, perfect and pure.

He reached out his hand and slowly, caressingly traced the spine of a book. A smudge of paint on his fingers was the only flaw in his handsome persona. He touched the leather cover with an intense concentration that made Katherine imagine how he might touch a woman's skin....

She caught at the back of a chair, suddenly so dizzy she was sure she would fall. The man seemed like a dream, a vision, caught there in the light of that perfect moment. He was not a real man at all. He could not be, for no real man had ever made her feel like that. She was always impervious to such nonsense, even when she was a girl. She had never giggled over men like her friends.

You are just overly tired, she told herself sternly. Yet she could not look away from him.

She clutched tighter to the chair, and as she swayed, her

skirt rustled. He spun around at the sound, his shoulders tensing and his beautiful hands tightening into fists. No, he was not a dream. He was quite real, and facing her directly, he was even more handsome. His face could have been taken directly from a Hellenistic statue, its proportions and angles were so perfect, yet his skin was a light, sun-kissed gold.

A statue brought to heated, glowing life. *Young* life, she saw with a pang. He had none of the lines and scars of age.

"I am sorry I startled you, monsieur," she said, trying to regain her usual serene calm. *She* was the lady of the house; she was in control of the situation. No matter how good-looking he might be.

"Ah, no, madame, *I* am sorry," he answered, and of course he would have a delicious voice to match his face. His English was perfect, but touched with a French accent like soft velvet. "I became much too distracted by your fine library."

"Not at all. The books deserve to be admired. I fear only Lady Caroline reads them lately. Please, monsieur, do be seated. I should ring for some fresh tea."

"No, my lady, please do not trouble yourself on my account. I did not even notice when they brought the tray in earlier." He gave a rueful laugh.

Katherine wondered why the maids were not still hanging about in here, gawking at him. She certainly would, if she were fifteen years younger and not a countess who was supposed to be dignified. "Well, I could certainly use some myself. It has been a rather trying day."

A concerned frown knit his brow, and he took a step toward her. "My lady, you do look pale. Please, sit. Allow me to ring the bell."

He held out his hand, and automatically Katherine slid her fingers into his grasp. It was entirely strange and untoward, of course, yet it felt entirely natural. His paint-stained fingers closed lightly over hers. She stared down at the contrast of his golden skin with her pale complexion, and warmth shot all the way to her toes. It was utterly enchanting, like a summer's day of clover and sun, and slow, warm laziness.

Her throat tightened, and she feared she would burst into tears. Why these feelings now, with this gorgeous young man she had just met? Now, when it was all too late?

Monsieur Courtois also stared down at their hands, his face as smooth and unreadable as one of those cameos. They both stood perfectly still, as if stunned and frozen in the moment. Finally, he glanced up at her, and she saw that his eyes were brown. Such a dark brown they were nearly black, even deeper and more fathomless against his silvery blond hair.

Slowly, his fingers slipped away from hers, and he offered her his arm. Katherine took it and let him lead her to the settee nearest the empty fireplace. She was not a short woman, yet she barely came to his shoulder.

Once she was seated, he went back to tug on the tasseled bell pull by the window. Away from his warm nearness, she could take in a breath again. She stared hard at the carpet under her feet. *Don't be a fool,* she told herself sternly. Would she be as foolish as Lady Kingsley, who last year found herself banished to a desolate estate in the north over an affair with her children's dancing teacher? It had been the talk of Dublin, the folly of a lady over a handsome young face. It had cost her everything.

But you are not married, as she was, another devilish little voice whispered. She was free, or as much as a titled lady could be. The Duchess of Leinster had married *her* children's tutor. If she, Katherine, were discreet...

She shook her head. That was utter foolishness. Ireland was a small place; everyone always knew everything. She had spent her whole life upholding the reputation of the Angel of Kildare, of her family. It *was* her life. She would not throw it away because of a sudden weakness over a handsome face and a strong pair of shoulders. Besides, a young man like Nicolas Courtois would never look twice at a woman such as her.

Yet he *was* looking at her. He smiled at her as he sat down in the chair across from her, and there was a tiny dimple set in his cheek.

Katherine folded her hands tightly on her lap. "I am Lady Killinan, of course, Monsieur Courtois, and your pupil here would be my youngest daughter, Caroline. She is sixteen and requires a bit of...polish before she makes her formal debut." That dimple deepened, and Katherine twisted her hands tighter together.

"Most sixteen-year-olds are in need of polish, my lady," he said. "But I am sure if she is *your* daughter she needs very little help at all. She is sure to have as many suitors as she likes, quite without the advantage of proficiency at art."

Katherine laughed at his light flattery, and his smile grew as if he took pleasure at making her laugh. "My daughter is pretty, if I do say so myself, monsieur. Yet she is also quite scholarly, and I know she will much enjoy learning more of art. Drawing and painting can make us see the world in new ways, yes?"

Ways that one could never have fathomed, she thought bemusedly as she looked into his dark eyes.

Monsieur Courtois leaned forward, bracing his elbows on his knees as he looked back at her. "It can indeed. To be honest, my lady, I would relish a pupil who was actually interested in my lessons."

"Really? Is that such a rarity then? You came highly recommended. Mrs. McGann told me that you worked wonders with her daughter."

He laughed and said in a soft, confiding voice, "Miss McGann, I fear, could not so much as draw a straight line when I took on her instruction. If, after many long hours of hard work, she could execute a recognizable tree—well, that is more a tribute to my stubbornness than any pedagogical skill I may possess."

Katherine laughed, too. She felt quite sure Miss McGann had been much too distracted by her tutor's good looks, and too happy to have hours of his attention, to be much concerned with the proper perspective of trees.

"However it came about, Mrs. McGann was very happy with your progress," Katherine said. "As were your other past employers. A certain stubbornness will be most useful in working with my Caroline."

"Perhaps you would care to look at some of my work, my lady? Then you can judge my skills for yourself."

Oh, yes, that little devil whispered. That would mean spending more moments in his company, which was too tempting.

She batted the devil away, trying not to blush like a schoolgirl. "Certainly, monsieur."

As he went to fetch his portfolio from the desk, two maidservants brought in the tea tray. Katherine noticed they took far longer than required to set up the cups and pots, sneaking glances at the Frenchman and simpering.

He seemed not to notice them at all, and they scurried away at Katherine's stern glance. Monsieur Courtois handed her the black leather portfolio, drinking his tea as she sorted through the sketches. She wasn't sure what she had expected, but the other drawing teachers she interviewed presented work of careful, correct proficiency. These were something else entirely.

His images were portraits, many of his pupils and their families, as well as landscapes of Irish rolling hills and architectural sketches of buildings around Dublin such as Parliament, the Customs House, and the Crow Street Theatre. But they were more than reflected images. There was a movement and emotion, a *life* to them that was quite extraordinary. He saw the world around them so differently than other people, Katherine thought. He saw past their careful façades to the complex, confusing, beautiful core. To life itself.

What would a drawing of her look like from his pencil?

"These are quite wonderful, monsieur," she said. "You have a great talent. Too great to be teaching distracted debutantes, I think."

"Ah, well, my lady, I do like to eat, and wages greatly help with that." But he seemed pleased with her compliment. "Do you really like them?"

"Very much." Katherine turned to an image of an elegant chateau set near a rippling river, the pencil lines denoting the movement and sparkle. The doors were half-opened, a woman's face was just barely glimpsed in the purplish shadows. Despite the black and gray colors, she had the feeling of warmth and belonging from the house, almost a fairy-tale shimmer. There was an old, settled elegance and comfort to the place. "Have you been to France recently? Surely this can only be in the Loire."

"You know France, my lady?"

"Oh, no, not well. I was there on my wedding trip many years ago. But I thought it was the most beautiful place I had ever seen—except for Killinan, of course."

"It is beautiful, yes. It is heaven on earth. But I have not been there since I was a child."

"You left during the revolution?" Katherine looked up at him over the sketch. A darkness had descended over his countenance, and it was as if he had drawn away from her, though he still sat right there.

"Yes, Lady Killinan. My mother, she was the daughter of a duc. That was her father's house; she loved it above everything else. And my father was one of the hated so-called tax farmers of Paris. He was killed, and my mother fled with me to London."

"Oh." She looked again to the house, which she saw now was a reflection of a life vanished, a lost sweetness remembered. How would she feel if she was run out of Killinan? Her heart ached for what he must have suffered. "I am so sorry, Monsieur Courtois."

"It was a long time ago, my lady," he said, a finality in his voice. Was he sorry for his confidences? She hoped not, for she wanted to know more.

She carefully placed the drawings back in the portfolio and handed it back to him. "Would you be able to begin next week, monsieur?"

He smiled at her. "I believe I could, Lady Killinan."

"Excellent. I'm expecting wonders with Caroline."

He laughed, and the shadows of the past vanished like a wisp of smoke. "I shall certainly endeavor not to disappoint, my lady."

As Katherine looked at him, she was quite sure no lady was ever disappointed spending time with him. She found herself much too intrigued by him, wanting to know more and more. It would take an iron will on her part not to try and find out.

⁊ↄ

Nicolas Courtois shut the door to his room firmly behind him, closing out the shrill arguments of his rowdy neighbors. He could still hear their incoherent shouts, but he knew they wouldn't last long. The quarrels happened every night, and every night they moved into tearful reconciliations and loud lovemaking. His own Crow Street Theatre melodrama for the price of rent.

He tossed his coat and portfolio onto his one table and went to open the window. A rush of cold air washed over him, damp and bracing, and he leaned his palms on the old wooden sill to lean into it. He felt restless tonight, unsettled, and he was afraid he knew the reason why.

Lady Killinan.

He closed his eyes and pictured her face, her soft, wondering smile as she looked at his drawings. She was so beautiful with her golden hair drawn loosely back from her heart-shaped face, pale as an ivory miniature. With her elegant hands and bright blue eyes. He longed to paint her, perhaps as a classical goddess on a summer hillside in Greece, her tall, slender figure draped in diaphanous white robes.

But how could he capture the sadness in those eyes? The aching loneliness that hid there so deeply?

They had only spoken for a brief time, yet he was so moved by her, by all that beauty and sadness. When he heard people speak of the Countess of Killinan, of the goodness and sense of duty that made them call her the Angel of Kildare, he had expected a matron of stolid practicality and kind charity. He had hoped she would be the sort of compassionate lady who would hire him despite the deep suspicions so many English held for the French, especially after the thwarted French invasion of Bantry Bay in '97.

But he had not expected *her*. She did seem to be an angel, an otherworldly creature too lovely for the chaotic world they lived in. Too gentle. She made him think of the noble ladies of France who came to his childhood home, so fine and elegant and delicate. And when she touched his hand—a bolt of burning desire shot through him, shocking and much too real. Her eyes widened, as if she sensed his sudden lust and was startled by it.

"*Connard*," he cursed, pounding his fist against the sill. A splinter drove into his skin, yet he welcomed the sting. It was better than the burn of a desire he had to suppress.

Lady Killinan had hired him at a better wage than he had ever made in Dublin before. She admired his work. He needed the job; yet surely if he was wise he would refuse it and never see her again. She was a complication he did not need, not in his precarious position. She could never discover what he was doing in Dublin.

He threw himself onto his narrow bed and covered his face with his hands. His neighbors were into their reconciliation phase, moaning and setting their cheap bedframe to creaking. He laughed ruefully at the lustful sounds, which only reminded him what he could never have with the beautiful Lady Killinan. But he couldn't help imagining what she would feel like under his touch, what she would taste like. What her body looked like under the layers of fashionable silks and laces, and how she would moan against his mouth.

He had long suspected Dublin was hell. Now he was sure of it.

Chapter Eight

"A nna, dear, is there something amiss with your glove?"

"Hmm?" Anna glanced at her mother, who stood beside her as they perched on the Fitzwalters' grand marble staircase, waiting for their turn to enter the ballroom. Despite the cold winter night outside, the imposing house was steamy-warm due to the crowds packed onto the stairs and jammed into the foyer below. Their high-pitched chatter bounced off the marble floors and ornately plastered walls. Tulle ruffles, tall plumes, and overly starched cravats were everywhere.

But Anna didn't notice it at all. She hadn't even realized she was plucking at the tiny pearl buttons of her silk glove.

"No, nothing is wrong at all," she said and tucked her hands in the satin folds of her white gown.

"Are you sure about that?" Katherine sighed and smoothed her own silver-gray skirts. "I knew it was a mistake to come here. You should be at home resting."

"If I rested any longer I would scream! Caro insists on reading me tales of gruesome old Celtic battles at all hours. They give me nightmares. I had to escape from her, and where better than at a ball?"

Katherine gave a strange little smile, her eyes suddenly the soft, warm blue of a summer stream. "Once she begins her drawing lessons next week, she will have no time to pester you."

"So she has given in to the inevitability of more lessons?"

"Oh, yes. She even seems to be looking forward to them. I am sure she will be even more so when she meets Monsieur Courtois."

"I'm looking forward to it myself. I asked Rose about him, and she started giggling madly. All the maids do that. He must be quite intriguing."

"He is that, for certain. I think he will be a very interesting addition to our household." The smile on Katherine's lips deepened, as if she had a secret.

Anna felt suddenly suspicious. Her mother thought the new teacher "interesting"? What could that mean? And why were her cheeks so pink?

"I can't wait to meet him," Anna said, and meant it. Maybe this small domestic drama would distract her from Adair. He kept popping into her head at the most inconvenient moments. She even dreamed of him at night, the most unsettling visions of him lying next to her in bed, whispering in her ear. His hand sliding slowly up her leg beneath her chemise, hot friction of skin against skin...

She plucked at the glove button again, only to drop it at her mother's glance. She wondered if he could possibly be at the ball tonight. Jane had said he would appear more in Society. But even if he was, if she saw him, what would she do about it?

Just how bold was she feeling?

They finally advanced a few steps, trying not to trod on the elaborate train of the lady ahead of them. "Remember, Anna," her mother said, "the doctor said no dancing tonight."

"I remember," Anna said with a sigh. "I will sit with the chaperones along the wall and behave myself with exemplary decorum."

"Ha! I should like to see *that,* my dear," Katherine said. Anna was sure that if her mother were not Lady Killinan, paragon of all things proper, she would have given a most inelegant snort, as Caroline was prone to do.

At last, they entered the ballroom to find it only marginally less crowded than the stairs. The Fitzwalters possessed one of the largest ballrooms in Dublin, no small feat in a city that prided itself on its hospitality and its capacity for a good time. It was an enormous space, made to feel even larger by the mirrors hung on the cream silk walls and the domed ceiling.

Those mirrors reflected polished parquet floors lined with banks of white hothouse roses arrayed with holly. The gathered crowd glittered, their gowns and jewels sparkling under the lights of a dozen Waterford crystal chandeliers. The dancing had not yet begun, but an orchestra played on a dais surrounded by potted palms. Liveried footmen moved about with trays of wine and claret punch. Through a set of open doors was a well-stocked card room.

Anna took a glass of the punch and sipped at it as she studied the room. It was all the height of splendor, very fashionable and elegant, sure to be talked of for days. Everyone who was anyone was there. And it was absurdly

dull. She was sure she had been here before, and she had.
Or at least places exactly like it, a hundred times before.

*Perhaps it would have been better to stay home with
Caro and her ancient battles,* Anna thought. That strange
old plague of restlessness, which parties were supposed to
distract her from, came back over her, stronger than ever.

She followed her mother across the room, their progress
glacially slow as they stopped to greet all their acquaintances. She was asked about her fall at the park, pressed
to dance again and again, and for once she was glad of the
excuse to refuse a reel or a minuet. She wasn't in much of
a dancing mood. And she did not see Adair anywhere.

Not that she could see much of anything in the crush,
except people's backs. She reached for another glass of
claret punch, but her mother shoved a glass of lemonade
into her hand instead.

"Just because there is no dancing for you tonight,
Anna, doesn't mean you should spend the whole evening
in the card room," Katherine said.

Anna laughed. "No dancing, no cards, no champagne.
What a merry evening."

"I doubt you will be entirely bereft, dear. It looks like
your hordes of admirers are about to sweep you away."

And indeed a group of young men, led by Lord Melton,
descended on her just as she reached the edge of the room.
When she told them she could not dance, they declared
their intention to stay by her side and keep her company
all evening.

"You cannot do that," she said, laughing at them.
"There would be too many disappointed young ladies
who *do* want to dance."

And some of the suitors were soon carried off by their

mamas to do their duty, but some stayed with Anna, bringing her refreshments and chattering on about new carriages, horse races, and of course, the Union. It seemed she had missed a fight in Parliament that very day.

It all made her want to scream, to throw her glass against the wall and run. She closed her eyes, remembering the Olympian Club with its lush banks of black orchids and lilies and the wild, whirling strains of waltz music. The masked figures clinging together in the dance. No one there spent precious moments boring everyone with tales of their new curricle or their latest house party prank. There, it was all pure feeling and emotion, sinking deeper and deeper into velvety darkness until there was only sensation.

A gloved hand lightly touched her arm, a warm caress on the bare skin just below her lace sleeve. Anna opened her eyes and turned to find Adair standing behind her. And the entire miserably dull evening suddenly brightened.

He looked entirely correct for a fine ball, clad in perfectly tailored black-and-white evening dress. His gold-shot white silk waistcoat was very elegant, and his cravat, though simply tied, was fastened with a black pearl pin. He had shaved, the strong angle of his jaw and curve of his high cheekbones starkly revealed. His dark hair was brushed back from his brow. He could certainly pass for a gentleman of fashion.

Except for his eyes. Those deep green eyes watched her with a gleam of roguish, mocking laughter. It was as if he saw right through her party façade to the real longing beneath.

"Lady Anna," he said with a bow. "How lovely you

look tonight. I'm very glad to see you have recovered from your accident."

"Yes, I am quite recovered, thank you, Your Grace," she said. She gave him a curtsy, noting how silent her flock of suitors suddenly became. They glared suspiciously at Adair, but they did not dare say anything to a duke. Especially a duke with a reputation for brawling and secret nefarious deeds.

The silence was most refreshing.

"Do you not dance tonight?" Adair asked.

"Alas, no. The doctor forbade it."

"I'm sorry to hear that. I've been told you're one of the finest dancers in Dublin."

She laughed. "I enjoy the exercise, certainly. But I have more enthusiasm than skill."

His brow arched. "More enthusiasm than skill, eh, Lady Anna? Well, that is easily remedied—with practice." Somehow, she had the feeling he did not entirely speak of dancing.

"We are keeping Lady Anna company this evening," Melton suddenly said, rather pugnaciously.

Adair merely gave him an amused look. "How fortunate for her. But it can't be healthy for you to stay in one place, Lady Anna. Would you take a turn about the room with me?"

He held out his arm, and Anna slid her fingers through the crook of his elbow. Through the silk of her glove, she felt the lean power of his muscles and the heat of his skin. She felt quite compelled to go with him, as if she could no more stay behind than she could cease breathing.

She remembered Hades and Persephone again and wondered if this was how poor Persephone felt when she looked up into those hellish black eyes. He was dangerous, to be sure. But he was also terribly *interesting.* When she was with him, all that numbness went away, and she felt alive. He cast a spell over her, she knew that.

She walked off with an apologetic smile to her suitors. Adair led her along the periphery of the ballroom where the crowds were thinner and the air cooler. She could almost hear herself think there, despite the curious glances and sudden whispers they were attracting.

"Are you really all right?" he said quietly.

"Oh, yes. Just a few bruises. But what of you, Your Grace?"

"Me?"

"I'm quite sure I was not the target there on St. Stephen's Green. I *am* rather envied for my gowns, but I doubt anyone takes a shot at a lady for such things. Except Lady Forest. I do have my suspicions about her."

His jaw tightened. "You needn't worry about me. That will not happen again."

Anna froze. "You found the culprit then?"

He didn't answer. His gaze swept over the packed ballroom, the sparkling display of Ascendancy Society. He did not belong there any more than a jungle panther belonged among chattering monkeys.

Anna wasn't sure that she belonged there, either. There wasn't anyplace that she really belonged.

"Do you feel in need of some air, Lady Anna?" he said.

"I do believe I am, Your Grace," she answered. Never mind that it was threatening to snow outside. She would rather be anyplace than that ballroom with everyone watching. "But where is there to go?"

He gave her an unreadable smile. "I know a place."

"Of course you do."

He led her out of the ballroom and back to the grand staircase. But rather than go down to the foyer, they went up. It was quiet there, almost silent.

"Where are we going?" Anna asked. "To hide in the attics?"

His hand slid down her arm, his fingers intertwining with hers as he led her onward. It got darker the higher they went. Only a few lamps burned from wall sconces, and it was blinding after the dazzle of the chandeliers. Anna held tight to his hand.

"Or maybe there is a conservatory?" she whispered.

He glanced back at her. He seemed made of shadows here, all mystery and puzzles. "Would you like that?"

She wasn't yet sure she could say she *liked* what happened between them in the Olympian Club conservatory. It had been so out of control. But it had awakened something inside of her, something she craved. If she felt it again, she almost feared she couldn't live without it. Couldn't live without him.

"I don't know," she said truthfully.

"Neither do I." He tightened his clasp on her hand, and they continued their ascent. "But there is not a conservatory here."

"What is it then?"

At the top of the stairs, he turned down a narrow corridor lined with closed doors. He opened one of them at the very end and led her out into the night. Anna found herself on a narrow walkway, high above the street. A waist-high iron fence held them back.

"I saw this from the street, and I asked one of the footmen how to access it," he said. "It has been a while since

I attended an affair such as this, so I thought I might need an escape route."

"How clever of you, Your Grace," she said. "I often feel a need to escape them myself. I wouldn't have thought of running across the roofs."

She drifted over to the railing, enchanted by the unexpected vista. Dublin lay before her in the cold gray blackness of the night. The pale marble houses glowed through the mist, their windows bright amber squares. Carriages glided along the street below like toys. And the Liffey was a ribbon of the deepest blue, stars glinting on its surface.

She tilted back her head to take in the stars overhead. The moon was a fat quarter, suspended high above her. "I can breathe here."

She heard a rustle of movement and felt him slide his coat over her shoulders. The fine, thin wool held the heat of his body, and his scent surrounded her. She closed her eyes, inhaling deeply.

"I fear it is cold up here," he said roughly. His hands lingered on her shoulders, and she leaned back against him. She hoped he would not draw away, and he didn't. His arms came around her waist, holding her safe there above the city.

"I don't feel cold at all," she said. "Thank you for bringing me here, Your Grace."

He laughed, and the deep, hoarse sound echoed through her body. It was as if a tie, delicate yet unbreakable, snaked out from him and around her, binding them together. "You have to stop calling me Your Grace. I'm not your usual sort of duke."

Indeed he was not. He wasn't the usual sort of anything. "What should I call you then?"

He hesitated for a moment. "My given name is Conlan."

"Conlan." Anna tested it on her tongue. It felt rich and strange, a name that suited him. "It means 'hero,' does it not?"

"I thought you said you did not know Gaelic."

"I don't, not very much. But my sister Caroline does, and she's taught me a bit. As much as my featherbrain can hold, anyway."

"It must be useful for you, this façade of not knowing much."

Anna reached out and grasped the cold iron railing. She had feared that he could see through her. Now it seemed he really did. "What do you mean?"

"I mean, you are a very intelligent lady. Why else would you not want everyone to see that, unless it serves you in some way?"

"In case you haven't noticed, intelligence is not highly prized in females. Not in my world."

"Are you so concerned with impressing brainless British fops and gossiping matrons then? I don't believe that, Anna. I don't believe you care about impressing anyone at all."

She felt suddenly angry. Angry that he saw so much, more than she wanted anyone to see—even herself. It didn't pay to look too deeply into her soul. She wasn't sure that she would like what she saw there.

She spun around, breaking his hold on her. She leaned back against the railing. "What do you know about it? You don't have to live in this world. You haven't been to a Society ball in—well, ever, as far as I know."

He braced his hands on the railing at either side of

her. "I have too many duties on my estate to waste time waltzing in overdecorated ballrooms," he said. His accent was strong again. "And why would I want to? It's dull as hell."

"Of course it is. So why are you here now?"

"Because it has come to my notice that sometimes a duke has other duties. Duties that might include dancing pumps and gloves."

"But why now?" Anna cried. He was so, so close to her, his large, hot body mere inches from hers. And she longed to arch up into him, pressing herself tight against him. "Why come to Dublin ballrooms now, when you've been lucky enough to avoid them so long?"

He smiled, but there was no mirth in it. It was bitter and self-mocking. "Maybe I came to this ballroom to see you, Anna."

She shook her head. "No, Conlan, I don't believe that. You have some kind of angle playing, and I want to know what it is."

He laughed harshly. "And why would a featherbrain even care?"

"I don't…"

"Hush, Anna." His arms slid around her, drawing her tight against him just as she had wanted. She clutched at his shoulders. "For once in your life, just hush."

He pulled her even closer, and his mouth came down on hers. He was not harsh, but he *was* insistent, his lips opening over hers, and his tongue seeking entrance. She opened for him, letting him in, meeting him eagerly.

Oh, yes, *this* was what she longed for ever since that night at the Olympian Club. That sensation of every rational thought flying out of her, of falling down into pure, hot need. He tasted of wine and mint, of that dark, rich essence she remembered so well.

His hand slid down her back as their kiss deepened, and his coat fell away from her shoulders. The cold air washed over her, but she only felt it for an instant before it was replaced with his heat. He cupped her bottom through the thin silk of her gown, caressing, massaging, until she moaned into his mouth.

He lifted her high against his body and swung her around until she was braced against the stone wall. She wrapped her legs around his waist, tugging him into the curve of her body. She could feel his erection pressing iron-hard through his breeches, and it gave her a primal thrill. He wanted *her.* Not the image of her, the earl's fine, pretty daughter, but *her.*

His lips slid down her arched neck, his tongue dipping into the hollow at the base of her throat. Her pulse pounded there, frantic with need. She wanted him, too. Something deep inside of her, something night-black and primitive, called out to that darkness in him.

He cupped her breast in his palm, stroking it through her lacy bodice. "*Diolain*, Anna, I need..."

"I know," she gasped. She threaded her fingers through his hair and tugged his mouth back to her skin, to the soft curve of her neck. She shivered as his warm breath washed over her and cried out as his hand closed over her breast.

"I don't want to need you," he said fiercely.

"I don't want to need you, either," she whispered. Her head fell back against the wall. She closed her eyes tightly, reveling in the glorious pleasure of his touch. "But I fear I do. Oh, curse it, Conlan, if you don't touch me, I'll scream."

He roughly tugged down her bodice and chemise, baring her breast. He rubbed the rough pad of his thumb over her nipple. It hardened under his caress, pink and erect, aching.

"You are so beautiful," he whispered.

She had been told that before. But not until now, under his gaze, did she almost believe it. She watched, mesmerized, as he bent his head and took her breast into his mouth. He sucked at her hardened nipple, his tongue swirling around it until she cried out. Her legs tightened around his lean hips, and she arched against him.

He drew her deeper into the hot wetness of his mouth, biting down lightly and soothing it with the edge of his tongue. She heard the mingling of their harsh, uneven breaths, the whine of the wind, their soft groans and incoherent words. The city far below was forgotten, the fact that she would be missed, her precarious reputation—she knew only his mouth, his hands. Him.

His hand slid lower, over her hip, down her bent leg, until he grasped her skirt in his fist. He pulled it up, his palm tracing her ribbon garter until he touched the bare skin of her upper thigh. With her breast still in his mouth, he caressed the arch of her hip, tracing her naked, soft skin. He still wore his gloves, and the feel of the leather made her shiver.

Then his hand slid even lower, to her most secret, vulnerable spot. For an instant she froze, stiffened, but he pushed her thighs wider and traced his thumb along her damp opening. She forgot to be afraid, forgot objections—forgot even her own name. He dipped his touch inside her, pressing deep, and she cried out.

His open mouth came over hers as he caught her moans.

He gave her no mercy, his fingers driving into her with a hot, delicious friction.

She reached out for him blindly. Her hand flattened against his chest, where she felt the pounding of his heart and the force of his breath. She slid her touch down, down, over his flat belly, his lean hip. At last, she covered that hardness in his breeches, and she instinctively closed her fingers over him. It pulsed under her touch, and she felt a surge of some new power inside herself.

She pumped herself a bit against his fingers, mimicking the movement on him with her hand. Her head fell back as he groaned.

"Ach, woman, are you trying to kill me?"

Anna laughed. She wrapped her legs tighter around him, pulling him closer to her. "Do you not like it?"

"I like it too well. That's the problem." His hand slid away from her, slowly trailing along her leg as if he couldn't quite let her go. But he lowered her to her feet, and her hand fell away from his erection. He braced his palms to the wall on either side of her. His body was shaking, just as hers was.

She leaned her forehead against his chest and dragged in a shuddering breath. From somewhere in the distance, she heard the chime of church bells.

"I—should go back," she whispered. "My mother will be looking for me."

He nodded. "I'll see you to the ballroom."

"No, I think it's best if I go alone. You should—compose yourself." She nudged her hip against the bulge in his breeches.

He laughed hoarsely. "That might take a while. You cast a powerful spell, *cailleach*."

Anna was quite sure she wasn't the one with the dark magic. She gently kissed his cheek, inhaling deeply of his scent as she reached up to smooth his hair. How gorgeous he was, her Hades, her Celtic warrior. How tempting.

"Anna, I'm sorry..." he began.

"No," she said. "You're not. Neither am I. We both knew this would happen again—and again."

"I should stay away from you then."

She traced her hands lightly over his shoulders. The thin linen of his shirt was damp over his taut muscles. Oh, how she wanted to stay here all night and learn more about him!

"Just try to stay away from me, Conlan," she whispered against his ear. She slid his coat off her shoulders and gave it back to him. "I'll find you. I'm a witch, remember?"

He stepped back from her, and she slipped away from him. Her legs were shaking, but she managed to stumble out of their rooftop walkway into the dark corridor. There she smoothed her hair and her gown, tugging her bodice carefully over her still-aching breasts.

She felt strangely *buoyant* as she made her way back to the ballroom. The light and noise she hated so much earlier now seemed exhilarating. She wanted to laugh, to skip and dance, but she made herself walk sedately as she searched for her mother. She just prayed Katherine hadn't been looking for her for long.

But it seemed her mother wasn't searching for her at all. Katherine stood near the orchestra's dais, talking with a man in a dandyish pale blue silk coat. His back was to Anna. Her mother's lips were pressed tightly together, and her unhappy expression darkened some of Anna's golden mood.

She glanced back over her shoulder and wondered if it was too late to slip away, to run back up those stairs to the enchanted walkway high above the city. But Katherine had glimpsed her standing there and waved her forward.

Anna pasted on a smile and made her way through the crowd to her mother's side. As she came closer, she saw who Katherine spoke to and that urge to bolt grew.

It was George Hayes, her mother's distant cousin, and by far the most annoying member of the whole extended family. Anna remembered all too well the last time they saw him. It was in the early days of the Uprising, when she, Katherine, and Caroline huddled at Killinan Castle waiting for news—or an attack. His regiment had come into the county to root out rebels, and George took a detour to Killinan to scare her mother and bully her into giving up any tenants who might have joined with the United Irishmen.

Anna was sure that he also hoped to catch out her sister Eliza, an ardent United Irish supporter. A catch like the Countess of Mount Clare, as Eliza was then, would have put quite the gloss on his career. But he underestimated Katherine.

They learned later that he helped to brutally clear out a village thought to harbor rebels, burning houses and terrorizing old men and pregnant girls. A village that lay on Adair land. Many of the cruel soldiers later met bad ends, but not George. They heard he was reassigned to a northern regiment, thanks to his unfortunate wife's wealthy family, and they luckily did not see him again.

Until tonight. What was he doing in Dublin? Nothing good, Anna was sure of that.

As Anna came nearer to the little group, she saw that George stood next to his mousy little wife, the sad northern heiress Ellen, and with Grant Dunmore. George seemed to be doing all the talking.

A footman passed by with a tray of champagne glasses, and Anna snatched one up and drained it quickly before she reached her mother's side.

"Anna, there you are," Katherine said. "I was looking for you."

"I'm sorry, Mama. I found some friends I had to speak to, and I quite lost track of time," Anna answered.

"I am sure a young woman as lovely as Lady Anna has no shortage of friends clamoring for her attention," George said heartily. His face was quite red; apparently he had been indulging in the excellent wine, too.

Anna barely managed to hold on to her smile.

"You remember my cousin, Captain Hayes, don't you, dear?" Katherine said.

"Indeed I do. Such a surprise to see you here tonight, George," said Anna. "You're very far from Belfast."

"And thank God for that. The farther from that northern hellhole the better. No culture at all," George said, signaling to a footman for more wine. "Dublin is the place to be these days. Right in the thick of things. This is where the action is—and the prettiest ladies."

Ellen, a native of Belfast, looked steadily at her hem. Despite her stylishly elaborate gown of gold-spangled tulle and silk, she looked wan and tired.

"You look lovely this evening, Mrs. Hayes," Anna said to her, feeling a twinge of pity. It must be terrible being married to George. "I hope you are enjoying your time in Dublin?"

"Oh, yes, I . . ." Ellen began.

"The city is wasted on her," George interrupted. "She

just sits at home all day, won't go to shops or parties to mingle with the wives of important people. No spirit at all. Unlike you, eh, Lady Anna?" His red-rimmed gaze slid down Anna's body, making her feel rather cold and clammy all over. It was amazing how none of the things she did on the walkway with Adair made her feel dirty, but one look from George, and she felt filthy. "Isn't that right, Sir Grant? I'm sure you agree with me about the fiery spirit of these young Dublin ladies."

Grant gave him a cold look. "Lady Anna is everything a lady should be, I am sure, as is Mrs. Hayes. I'm very glad to see you have recovered from the—incident, Lady Anna."

"Thank you, Sir Grant," Anna said. She gave him a grateful smile and stepped closer to his side, away from George. "I am very well. And thank you for returning Psyche home."

"I only wish I could have done more to help," he said. "There are so many undesirable elements in town lately. One can't be too careful."

"No, indeed," Anna said. She thought of Adair's mouth on hers, his hand on her bare breast. If that was an undesirable element, then she wanted more of it!

"Your mother tells me you cannot dance this evening," said Grant. "But perhaps you would care to play a hand of whist with me in the card room?"

She certainly would. Anything to get away from George's avid stare and his wife's obvious misery. But she hated to leave her mother alone with them. She glanced at Katherine uncertainly.

"Go on, my dear," Katherine said. "Just don't lose too much. I see Lady Connemara over there, and I must speak with her."

"Of course," Anna said. "Mrs. Hayes, even if you don't care to go out often, I hope you will take tea with us one day soon at Henrietta Street."

"Thank you, Lady Anna," Ellen whispered. "I would like that."

Anna took Grant's arm and turned with him toward the card room—only to be brought up short by Adair's smoldering stare.

He stood near a bank of roses, away from the dancers and the gaiety of the party. Against the white flowers, his black hair and clothes were even darker. The god of the Underworld, of doom, at the foolish mortals' ball. He watched her and Grant with such intensity she was surprised that she didn't burst into flames. His stare was angry and—and possessive.

Grant's arm tensed under her hand. "I see Adair is here," he muttered.

"Is he?" Anna said. Her throat was tight, her breath trapped in her lungs. She managed to tear her eyes from Adair, but she could still feel him watching her. Her skin burned with the force of it. When Adair looked at her as if he, too, remembered every moment of their kisses...

It gave her a thrill, like a bolt of sizzling lightning. A terrible, naughty thrill. She feared she was *not* the proper lady her mother was. But then, she had known that for a long time. Adair just seemed to bring it out of her even stronger.

"I did not notice," she said.

"He seems to have noticed you," said Grant. "Come, let us go into the card room."

"Of course." She let him lead her through the crowd, trying to ignore the knowing smiles as they passed by. But before they could reach the door, she heard a sudden crash and a woman's scream—not usually sounds to be found in an elegant ballroom.

Anna whirled around, her heart pounding in a sudden burst of fear. The crowd closed in behind her, everyone clamoring for a better view of the commotion, but she caught a glimpse through a small gap. Adair had George by the throat, holding him to the wall beside an over-turned urn of roses. Lady Fitzwalter, aghast at the crude display in the midst of her fine ball, was the screamer, while George's wife hovered nearby.

Adair's genteel appearance of earlier was utterly van-ished. His face was dark with fierce anger, his grip on George implacable as George flailed and fought in vain. It was as if the duke had melted away, and in his place was an ancient Irish warrior who would tear off George's head and hurl it across the floor at any moment. It was primitive and raw, especially in the midst of such a refined party.

The elegant crowd seemed to feel that, too, and it brought out the ancient fighter in all of them. Everyone watched with avid interest to see what might happen next.

"Trust someone like Adair to cause such a scene," a man behind Anna said with a snicker.

"Lady Fitzwalter should know better than to let an Irishman into her ballroom," someone replied. "They're just a lot of dirty bog-dwellers no matter what the title."

Anna longed to turn on them, to slap their smug faces whoever they were, but she seemed frozen in place. She couldn't tear her gaze from Adair and George.

The duke gave George another shake, and Anna heard

him growl, "Say that again, Hayes, and directly this time. None of your cowardly whispers."

"It's only what everyone is saying," George choked out. "Fenian bastard. You shouldn't even look at her."

Adair's fist tightened, and George kicked out as his face turned even more red.

Anna shook her head in disbelief that such a thing was happening. Where was the gentlemanly duke who greeted her in the ballroom? Where was the man who had kissed her and held her so tenderly on the roof only moments ago? In only moments, he had vanished, and her world was shaken up again.

She remembered when they met at the park, his crude words to her as he taunted Sir Grant. Who was the *real* Conlan?

A lady's gloved hand touched Adair's shoulder, gently but firmly drawing him back. Anna saw to her surprise that it was Jane who refused to let him go even as he tried to shake her away. She spoke quietly into his ear. At first Anna was sure he would push Jane away and get on with the business of thrashing George, but then something in Jane's words seemed to reach him.

His grasp loosened on George's throat, and he shoved him away. Adair let Jane take his arm and lead him toward the door. The crowd parted in sudden silence, but George foolishly surged forward again to strike a glancing blow at Adair's jaw. A drop of blood appeared there, bright crimson on his skin, and Adair responded with a fierce uppercut to George's chin, which sent him sprawling at his wife's feet.

Ellen fell back a step as if afraid he would soil her hem. Lady Fitzwalter looked so furious she would surely explode from it. Adair and Jane disappeared through the ballroom door, and the crowd burst into sound again.

Anna felt Sir Grant take her arm again, and she spun toward him, astonished he was still there. She had forgotten everything, stunned by the sudden violence of that moment between Conlan and George.

Sir Grant, unlike everyone else, looked surprisingly calm and composed. The contrast between him and his cousin, between their two different worlds, had never been more striking. She found she craved his calm, his safety, and she swayed toward him. His touch on her arm tightened.

"Are you quite well, Lady Anna?" he asked solicitously. "Such a shocking scene."

But not one he was surprised by, she would wager. "Yes. One doesn't expect such things in a Dublin ballroom. I wonder what George said to cause such a reaction?"

Grant's jaw tightened. "It hardly matters. My cousin has a fearsome temper. Anything could have set him off. Come, let me fetch you a glass of wine. You look quite pale. Perhaps then we can have that card game."

Anna nodded, too confused to make any protest. She *did* need something to calm her nerves, to help her think clearly again. She had never been quite so confused.

Chapter Nine

Conlan remembered Anna going into the card room on Grant's arm. His head bent toward hers as he said something to her, quiet and intimate, and she laughed. They looked as if they belonged together, both so beautiful, so shining with privilege and the ease of belonging. They were the perfect Anglo-Irish pair. Or so Grant liked to think.

Grant had spoken of the power that would come with a connection to Killinan. Surely Anna's beauty and the attention she gathered in Society was in his thoughts as well. Grant had always been very ambitious, even as a schoolboy, the pride of his mother. She was Conlan's aunt on his father's side, and she had left her family behind to marry an English Protestant. She was sure her only son, her golden boy, would go far, not only in Dublin but in London as well.

A perfect wife and hostess was essential for a gentleman's advancement, a lady of beauty and refinement who could charm the stuffy English and convince them not everyone in Ireland was barbaric. Conlan was sure his cousin saw only Anna Blacknall's shining surface, her looks and connections, and thought her perfectly suited to his purposes. But if he did achieve his goal and carry her to the altar, Grant would be unpleasantly surprised by his bride's true nature.

Conlan had the sense Anna would not be a pliable tool to anyone's ambition. She would chafe at the constraints of such a life, no matter how gilded, and one day she would explode with it. What would Grant's perfect life look like then?

Conlan wouldn't mind seeing such a thing, not after the way that Grant worked so assiduously to ruin the lives of everyone on the Adair estate. But the thought of Anna Blacknall's spirit turning hard and bitter as she spent her days with a man who wanted only her name and her pretty face in his drawing room—it made him feel sad, and also guilty. For did he not think to use her as well? Did he not cause her pain every time he saw her—even with that scene tonight?

He reached for a glass of champagne that Jane left on a table and downed it in one swallow, wishing it were something stronger. Now he remembered well why he avoided such gatherings. They were dull and insipid. Their opulence reminded him too sharply of how hard his tenants worked to keep the bare necessities of life, how precarious their existence was, especially after the Uprising. The money Lady Fitzwalter paid for her flowers alone would keep a cottager family for a year.

And that was why he came here, why he endured the balls and promenade hours in the park, the empty chatter and the dark intrigue. Why he put himself out there to be shot at. He had a duty to his people, his home, and he would uphold it no matter what he had to do. Union with Britain would set his cause back decades, and he would fight it, no matter who he had to ally with.

No matter who got hurt.

He was obviously no good at this game, while Anna Blacknall was at the center of this world, no matter how much she might chafe at its restrictions. She would know a great deal, even if she wasn't aware of it. He had to discover what she knew, especially about Grant's activities in support of the Union.

"Sit down and let me see to that cut," Jane said firmly. She pressed him down into a chair in the small, dimly lit sitting room and peered closely at his chin. She had charmed Lady Fitzwalter and persuaded their irate hostess to let them use the chamber until the crowd quieted.

"It's nothing," Conlan insisted. Now that the flash of temper had subsided, he felt weary and sorry for creating yet another scene—and in front of Anna, too.

"I'll be the judge of that." Jane dabbed at the cut with her handkerchief, her eyes narrowed. "What on earth did George Hayes say to you?"

"It doesn't matter."

"I beg to differ. If he suspects anything about our work..."

"He doesn't. He's too sotted to see past his own nose. It was—personal." Conlan remembered Hayes's crude remarks about Anna, and his anger came rushing back. It had gotten the better of him once. He couldn't let that happen again. Jane was right. It jeopardized too much.

"Ah," Jane said with a sage nod. "A woman."

"Something like that. Or maybe I just don't like the man."

Jane sighed and left off dabbing at his cut to sit down beside him. "I know the feeling. I often want to hit someone at parties. Such gatherings are tedious indeed, even with the diversion of a good fight, but they can be so useful. Everyone comes through these parties eventually, and even without whiskey, they can be wonderfully indiscreet. Did you hear anything of interest before you took a punch at George Hayes?"

"Some tips on promising racehorses to look for next season, but beyond that, nothing. You English have no conversation."

"Unlike your Irish gift of gab? Ah, well, take heart, Your Grace. A connection made here in Dublin is never wasted, if you haven't ruined it tonight."

"Speaking of connection, I understand you have become friendly with my cousin."

Jane smiled slyly. "Indeed I have. He is a most interesting person, though not as indiscreet in his conversation as I would like. Not yet."

"He has said nothing of his cohorts?"

"He has said nothing of the Union at all. But I am working on it. We meet again tomorrow night. I will try and discover what he knows about who shot at you in the park. Unless you already know?"

Adair thought of the ex-officer he found at the pub in the Liberties, a wreck of a man stewed in cheap grog that he bought with ill-gotten coin. An army man reduced to a gun for hire. "I know who did the shooting, but not who paid him. He could give me no names even after a most thorough grilling."

"And where is he now?"

Conlan shrugged.

"In the Liffey, I would imagine." Jane fluttered her fan as she studied the sitting room.

"Perhaps, but I did not put him there. His employers would have no use for a hired assassin soused on gin and talkative, no matter how little he knows."

"They will try again. You are too threatening to certain elements."

"Perhaps."

"Of course they will. Union means a great deal of money, titles, and royal favors to fiercely ambitious men. If you stand in their way, they will do all they can to dispose of you. You know that, Adair."

"You stand in their way, as well."

"But they do not know that. Your power is your title and your raw strength; mine is my gift of deception."

"I will watch my back."

"I hope so. We can't do without you." She snapped her fan shut. "But next time someone takes a shot at you, I would prefer that my friend Anna Blacknall not be nearby."

Conlan's fist tightened on his glass, the fragile bowl creaking ominously. He set it down on the table. "I hated that she was in danger, as much as you do."

Jane tilted her head as she studied him. "Or even more so?"

"She is a fine lady. I will not see her hurt."

"Anna is not made of porcelain. She is stronger than people give her credit for, and smarter. She spends a great deal of time with Grant Dunmore and his ilk, and they would not be so careful what they say around her. She could help us—if we kept her away from any danger."

Conlan had thought just that himself. But somehow

when Jane said it, it seemed cold and calculating. Yet wasn't that just how he had to be?

"How could we find out what she knows?" he said.

"We could recruit her to our cause. Her sister is Eliza Denton; I'm sure she shares our views."

Conlan thought of Anna crumpled on the ground at St. Stephen's Green, her eyes closed, face white as death. "No."

Jane pursed her lips. "I'm sure you are right. Subterfuge works best with some people. And I must go practice some of that subterfuge right now, Your Grace. I heard that Lord Ross is here and he is one of the most vocal proponents of the Union. Think about what I've said. I'll be in touch when I have more information."

She sashayed away, her silken skirts rustling, beautiful and flirtatious. Lord Ross didn't stand a chance. The door clicked shut behind her, and Conlan was alone.

Deception indeed. None better at it than Lady Cannondale. In '98, she had worked for the United Irishmen. Now she worked to stop the Union, to keep the dream of an independent Ireland alive. And none suspected, least of all poor Lord Cannondale when he was alive.

Adair had to do the same, to be as discreet as Jane, but his patience with the ballroom was at an end. The cloying scents of roses and French perfume, the artificial laughter, the music—it made him want to roar like the barbarian they thought him. He needed something else, something real. . . .

Conlan closed his eyes. The cut stung a bit now, but the silence around him was calming. Surely his temper was spent for the night, and it was safe to emerge from his lair. He had to apologize to Lady Fitzwalter.

He heard the door open, and his muscles tensed. His eyes flew open and he automatically reached for a dagger that was not there.

But it was no enemy who faced him. It was Anna. She shut the door behind her and leaned against it, watching him warily. What did she think of him now, the barbaric Irishman?

He rose slowly to his feet. "You've lost your escort," he said.

"Yes, to the faro table. It's rather dull to watch someone else gamble. I told him I had to find my mother."

"But you found me instead."

"I saw Jane in the corridor, and she told me you were in here."

"And you dared face the lion in his den?"

She gave him a smile. A reluctant one, but a smile all the same. "You don't seem quite so fearsome now, though I think my cousin George would disagree. He was screaming as they carried him away."

"He seems to have no sense of proportion. That wasn't even the beginning of a real thrashing, though I'll be happy to show him the difference one day."

Anna bit her lip. "Whatever did he say to you in the ballroom?"

Conlan shrugged. He certainly didn't want to tell her. "Nothing too important. I was a fool to lose my temper like that."

"It must have been of *some* importance for you to hit him like that in the middle of a ball. You certainly stirred up this party! No one has seen such excitement in ages. It almost makes me wish you had given him a real thrashing."

Conlan studied her, caught by a sudden gleam of amusement in her eyes. He had a sudden wild idea, one he wasn't sure she would agree to.

"Would you rather go to a *real* party?" he said.

A smile quirked at the corner of her mouth, and he found his stare drawn to those pink lips. Lips that tasted as sweet as they looked, he remembered all too well. "At the club?" she asked.

"That's not a real party, Lady Anna." The Olympian Club was even more artificial than the Fitzwalters' ballroom. It was just darker and more secretive.

"Where then?" she said. She sounded intrigued but still wary.

"Do you trust me?"

She laughed. "After tonight? Not a bit. Sadly, I think that only adds to your attraction."

He found himself grinning like a fool despite the sting of the cut on his chin. Thought him attractive, did she? "That's good, for I'm not in the least bit trustworthy. But I do know how to find a fine time in this town."

"I'm quite sure you do. When?"

"Tonight. Meet me at your servants' entrance at two?"

"Maybe, maybe not," she said lightly. But he would wager that she would do it, the little daredevil. Jane thought Anna was in danger from him, but he saw now it was the other way around. "If I do, what should I wear?"

"Not this," he said, gesturing to her shimmering white gown. "And not red. Something simple, if you have it."

"I have costumes for everything, Your Grace," she said. "Don't be late."

She left the room and her soft laughter floated back to him. And he knew he really was a fool.

Chapter Ten

Anna stepped into the dim, smoky room behind Adair and nearly laughed aloud with startled excitement. She knew that if she was at all sensible, she would back out and run away now. Well, if she was *really* sensible, she would never have come with him at all. She would have never even considered it.

But no one had ever accused her of having a surfeit of good sense. Her restless curiosity always got the better of her. She couldn't be sorry for it, though, for this was all quite fascinating. It seemed to be a tavern of some sort, a long, narrow room barely lit by smoking, guttering tallow candles. The low ceiling was whitewashed, crossed by smoke-encrusted beams, and the floor was sticky, cracked flagstone. The walls, which had once been just as white, were mostly hidden by old, fly-specked mirrors and paintings of scantily clad women and melodramatic historical scenes. A small group of musicians with drums and fiddles and pipes played a lively song of a wild rover who renounced his wild ways for good while people sang and clapped along. A few dancers spun down the middle of the floor.

Anna tugged her knitted shawl closer over her black dress and made sure her mobcap covered her hair as Conlan led her past the dancers. She wanted to watch tonight, to observe everything around her, without being noticed herself.

Though perhaps that would not be possible while she was with Adair. Voices faded as he stepped into the room and heads swiveled toward the door. Even dressed in a plain wool coat and black cap, he attracted attention. Or perhaps he was already known here.

He took her hand in his, his gaze scanning casually over the room. His bland, pleasant expression never altered, yet Anna noticed that everyone immediately turned away, back to their own business. If he was known here, then he had power, for he was obeyed without uttering a word. She remembered how it was at the ball, too. Everyone stared at him, speculated about him, but no one wanted to anger him. Look what happened when someone like George got on his bad side.

And then there was the person who shot at him on St. Stephen's Green. She had no doubt Adair would find the shooter sooner or later, and she didn't much want to know what would happen then.

Yet, strangely, she felt safe with him. She shouldn't, of course. He was probably the least predictable, least *safe* person she had ever met. Yet she sensed that something in them was the same, that he understood the wildness inside of her that she tried to banish or at least hide. With him, she didn't have to hide.

She didn't have to hide *everything,* anyway. There were some things even he should not know.

"All right, Anna?" he said quietly. He glanced over at

her, his eyes that bright, glowing green in the shuddering shadows.

"I'm not sure yet," she answered. "What is this place?"

"Just a tavern. A friend of mine owns it. It's a fine place for a quiet drink and a think."

Anna gave a wry look at a man slumped over the nearest table. He was snoring amid a tangle of empty tankards. "Or a place to get completely foxed?"

"If that's your pleasure. At least here you can be sure no one will see you and kick you into the gutter while you're pissed."

She glanced back at the closed door. The street outside was not one where she had ever been, though neither was it a stinking stew like the notorious Liberties. It was a narrow cobblestone lane lined with tall slivers of houses and cheap inns, which looked as if they housed servants and lower clerks. The people in here were roughly dressed, but they seemed friendly. It wasn't grand, of course, yet it was far preferable to the artificial glitter of the ball. No one stared at her here. No one wanted or expected anything from her. She was free, for the moment. Free to do whatever she wanted.

And she wanted to have a drink with Adair. Perhaps he, too, would feel free, and she could learn more about him, like what he was up to in that burned-out stable two years ago. He intrigued her so much, and yet he was closed to her.

She squeezed his hand. "Are you going to get me a drink then? I'm not in the mood to get, er, pissed, but I am parched after our journey."

He laughed. "I imagine a hackney is rough going after a coach and four, my lady."

"I've been in worse," she said, remembering the rickety cart they used to flee Killinan ahead of the rebels in '98. "And my mother would consider four vulgar."

"Of course. We mustn't be vulgar." He led her across the room to the end of the bar. A burly, bearded man in a stained apron leaned there. He looked up and smiled at Adair.

"Conlan, my lad, you haven't been around in an age," the man said, his gravelly voice heavily accented. His grin revealed broken teeth, and his nose above the tangle of his beard was crooked. Perhaps the tavern was not always so peaceful and merry then.

"I've been busy," Adair said.

"So I've heard."

"Have you indeed?"

"Word gets around."

"Especially to you, Liam. But you look well. I hope Betsy and Amy are, too."

"Aye, and Amy will be glad to see you." Liam the barkeep eyed Anna and her hand in Adair's. "Or maybe not."

"This is my friend Anna," Adair said. "Anna, this disreputable fellow is Liam McMasters, once the most notorious prizefighter in southern Ireland, and now a respectable tavern owner."

Liam snorted. "Not so respectable as all that, or so my Betsy claims. She wants me to stay home more. It's a pleasure to meet you, Miss Anna. We haven't seen such a pretty face here in—well, ever. Conlan is a lucky man."

Anna laughed. "He is that, Mr. McMasters. Born under a lucky star."

Liam gave her an odd look. "And she has a pretty voice, too. What will you have, Miss Anna? Order whatever you like. I'll see this lucky fellow pays up."

Anna leaned her elbows on the scarred bar as she studied the bottles. No champagne, of course, but she was tired of the stuff anyway. "An ale, I think. Your best brew, since Conlan here is paying."

"And a whiskey for me, Liam," Adair said. "Are the boys here tonight?"

"Setting up in the back room, if you want to go through," Liam said as he poured their drinks.

"Have there been any messages lately?"

Liam glanced warily at Anna. "Not yet. Pete's gone to Cork, though, should be back soon."

Conlan nodded and seemed thoughtful as Liam moved away to serve other customers.

"Conlan *is* a fine name," she said and took a swallow of her ale. "It suits you—hero."

"My mother was a fanciful sort," he answered. "She loved the old tales. When I was a child I wished I was called William or Phillip, something less—whimsical."

"And my mother was not fanciful at all. I had to be called plain old Anna, after her mother."

"I doubt anyone could call you plain anything." He reached over and took her hand. He turned it over on his palm, studying the curve of her fingers. She stared, fascinated, as he raised it to his lips, pressing a warm kiss to her wrist. The tip of his tongue touched her pulse, pounding just under her skin.

He held her hand to his cheek and smiled at her. "Do you like it here, not so plain Anna?"

She swallowed hard and tore her stare from that smile to study the dancers. No one paid the least bit of attention to them now, and she had the feeling they wouldn't even if she crawled onto Conlan's lap and tongue-kissed him wildly. It was wonderful. It made her want to throw back her head and laugh.

"Yes," she said. "I like it very much. Though it seems a bit quiet, not really what I expected when you asked if I wanted to go to a real party."

He laughed and sat back in his chair. He still held on to her hand. "It's early yet. I thought it wouldn't be grand enough for you."

"I'm tired of grand." She drank more of her ale and leaned across the table toward him. "Do you come here very often?"

"Not as much as I used to."

"Yes—you've been busy." She turned his hand in hers and examined the calluses and scars along his palm and the tips of his fingers. They were broad, strong, working hands, tanned by the sun. He wasn't like any duke she had ever known or imagined. "Busy doing what?"

His eyes narrowed warily. "I have a great many duties. Surely you know that; your family also owns a large estate."

"Oh, I do know what a place like Killinan or Adair requires. And I daresay you are much more involved in your people's lives than my father ever was." She traced those scars with her fingertip, a light, teasing pattern back and forth. His muscles tensed, but he didn't pull away from her. "Yet you're here in Dublin now."

"Sometimes those duties are in the city, alas, and won't be put off."

"You wish you were back at Adair?"

"It's my home," he said simply. "Where I belong."

Anna felt a sudden wistful pang. "What does that feel like, Conlan? Belonging?"

He turned his wrist to catch her fingers in his again, holding them tightly. "Do you not belong to your family, Anna? To your home?"

"When I was a child I thought I did. I loved nothing better than riding over the fields at Killinan Castle. I would go as far from the gardens as I could, out where it was wild and quiet." She closed her eyes and saw once more her long-forgotten refuges. "There was a place by the river I loved. I would lie there in the cool, green grass and stare up at the sky as I listened to the whisper of the water. It was like the voices of the fairies, telling me tales of the real Ireland that was lost."

"The fairies," he murmured. "Yes, you would hear them."

"I loved my home then," she said. "I wanted to stay there in that place forever."

"What happened?"

She opened her eyes to find him watching her. "I grew up and learned what was expected of me. I was not Irish, not really, and wishing would not make it so. The fairies wouldn't speak to me. Killinan isn't really mine. My mother has her life interest in it, and then it will go to Eliza's son, if she has one. I have to make a proper marriage, an English marriage, and live a proper life. Dreaming about river fairies and green hills, of being useful and needed, does me no good."

He said nothing, just smiled at her sadly in that silence. Yet she feared he could see what she did not say, what she pressed down deep inside.

"I do like it here," she said. "I feel like I can think here. It was good of you to bring me."

He laughed humorlessly. "Ah, Anna me girl. It was not good of me at all."

He reached across the table and wrapped his fingers around the back of her head, dislodging her cap. He drew her close to him and kissed her. His lips were parted but gentle, as if he gave her time to draw away. She didn't want to draw away, though. She wanted to be closer and closer, to forget everything in the passion that rose up in her with his touch. She leaned toward him, opening her mouth under his.

He groaned deep in his throat, the rough sound echoing through her. His fingers tightened in her hair, and his kiss turned hotter. He tugged her head back to give him deeper access, and she held his face in her hands, half afraid she would lose him and the way he made her feel.

His mouth slid from hers, and he turned his head to kiss her palm. "Anna, Anna," he said. "What you do to me."

"What I do to you?" she whispered. He made her head spin, made her want to laugh and sob all at the same time, to run out and throw her arms around life and all its forbidden wonders.

"You're a terrible distraction," he said.

"Good. Come distract me again." She tugged him back toward her lips, but as soon as they touched in another kiss, a louder burst of music broke over them. Anna fell back in her chair, startled, and Conlan tore himself away from her with a soft curse. "Do you want to leave now?"

She nodded and took his hand to let him lead her out of the room. The bar was even more crowded than before, Liam busy pouring out more ale and whiskey for thirsty customers.

"Come back soon, Miss Anna!" he called. "We'll put your ale on Conlan's bill again. He owes me so much already, he won't even notice, the old villain!"

Anna laughed and waved at him. She wished that she *could* come back, whenever she felt like it, but that seemed unlikely. This would probably be just one night that she could remember.

At least it was not quite over yet. Conlan raised his arm to hail a hackney, but she caught his hand in hers. "Let's walk for a while," she said. "I need to clear my head a bit."

He looked down at her. "Are you sure? It's cold."

It *was* chilly after the crowded tavern, but she liked the bracing winter wind. She tugged her shawl up over her shoulders. "Just for a bit. It's so quiet here."

He nodded and offered her his arm as they set off down the street. "We can certainly walk if you like, but I wouldn't call this pretty. Not like your Henrietta Street."

"Henrietta Street is big and dull and overly lit. You can't see the sky there." Anna tilted back her head to stare up at the black velvet sky, dotted with whirls of diamond-dust stars. "There's nothing like an Irish sky in the winter, so clear and bright."

"I can think of a few things even more beautiful," he said. "Such as you—Miss Anna."

Anna laughed happily. His compliment, simple as it was, just added to the glow of the evening. It was strange how excited she felt around him—how happy—even though they always seemed to run into trouble. The numbness of her life and her past faded away when she was with him, and she felt burningly alive again.

It was dangerously addictive.

"I've never been compared to the night sky before," she said.

They turned the corner onto another narrow, quiet street. The river had to be close by, for she could hear the lapping of its tides against the embankment and the faint noise from waterfront taverns. On their street, though, it was dark.

"You must get such compliments all the time," he said.

"Oh, yes. But not even a fraction of them are truly meant." She stopped to lean against a rough stone wall, her head tipped back to look up at the bright stars. "No one ever means what they say, not really. Sometimes I feel like I live in a world whose language I only partly understand. It's like a code, and I haven't entirely learned it."

Conlan leaned his hands against the wall to either side of her. His large, strong body shielded her from the cold wind, and she was surrounded by his heat. He smelled of smoke and whiskey and the citrus soap he used.

She reached up and curled her fingers into the front of his coat. The coarse cloth tickled her bare skin, and she could feel the shift of his body underneath.

"You can believe the truth of this," he whispered close to her ear. "You are so beautiful. But so sad."

"Sad?" She laughed, trying for her usual carelessness, but even to herself she sounded uncertain and shaky. "I am the most fortunate girl in Dublin. What do I have to be sad about?"

"I should like to know." He gently brushed the back of his hand over her cheek, his knuckles softly skimming over her skin. "What do you hide behind those summer eyes, Anna?"

"You are the one who knows about secrets. The things you hide must be legion."

"Me?" His fingers slid slowly down her throat, resting just where her pulse pounded in the vulnerable hollow. "I'm just a simple Irishman."

"I may not be as clever as my sisters, Conlan McTeer, but I know a Banbury tale when I hear one. There is nothing simple about you." Anna wrapped her arms around his shoulders, tugging him closer to her. "What are you really doing in Dublin? What is the Olympian Club all about?"

He stared at her in the darkness, his hand pressed to her throat. "A man has to make money somehow."

"I don't believe that."

"Believe what you will. But know this—it would be best for you to stay away from that place in the future."

"If I cared what was best for me, I wouldn't be here now."

He laughed ruefully. "Nor would I. We're not good for each other, Anna."

She smiled up at him. Suddenly, she felt very naughty. "I think sometimes we are very good for each other indeed." She went on tiptoe, pressing a soft kiss to the hard line of his jaw. The new growth of his beard prickled at her lips, and she laughed. She spread a ribbon of openmouthed kisses along his cheek and caught his earlobe in her teeth, biting down lightly.

He groaned. "Anna..."

"Don't you like that, Your Grace?" she whispered in his ear. She leaned her body against his and felt the heaviness of his erection through their clothes. "I think you do."

"Of course I do, *cailleach*. I like it too much."

"There's no such thing." She slid her hands up over his shoulders. They were tense and hard, as if he struggled to hold himself back. She buried her fingers in his hair, the silken strands wrapping around her skin. "I like this, too. I've never felt the way I do when I'm with you, Conlan.

I know it won't last. I know soon you'll vanish from my world again. But for now—will you kiss me?"

He shook his head, but he did not turn away from her. It was as if he couldn't help himself. His lips captured hers, open and hungry and rough.

She met him eagerly, welcoming the thrust of his tongue into her mouth. He pushed her back against the wall, and her head leaned against the stone as they kissed and kissed. She didn't feel the cold or the hard brick at her back. Whenever they came together like this, she knew only him.

The blood ran hot in her veins, burning her from the inside out. She tasted him in her mouth, mint and whiskey and darkness, and it made her want more. She wanted to fall into him, and she wanted him to want her just as much, a feeling so primal and basic it would not be forced away.

Through the blurry haze of their kiss, she felt him tug down her bodice and touch her breasts through the thin chemise. He covered them with his palms, his fingers wrapped over their soft curves. His thumb circled her nipple, flicking at it until she cried out with the shock of pleasure.

He wasn't gentle, but she did not want him to be. She wanted his touch, his kiss, his body on hers, all of it. He caught that aching nipple between his thumb and finger and pinched lightly, sending a sizzling bolt of lightning all through her.

"Conlan!" she cried, her throat arching back.

"Shh," he whispered. "Someone will hear us." He covered her mouth with his again, and she felt him carry her backward. She opened her eyes to find they were in a recessed doorway, completely wrapped in shadows. Conlan was outlined in the starlight, her Hades of the night.

She kissed him again, reaching out for him hungrily. That was how she felt, *hungry,* starving for his touch, for more of that wild pleasure. He met her willingly, his hands sweeping over her ribs, her hips, pulling her against him.

His lips moved to her cheek, his tongue dipping into her ear as she gasped, then moving down her throat to her shoulder. He nudged the strap of her chemise aside and scraped his tongue over her skin. She arched her back, silently begging, and he gave her what she wanted. He took her nipple into his mouth, sucking her hard through the linen.

Anna drove her hand through his hair and held him to her. He reached down and grasped her skirt, dragging it up and up until it was caught around her waist. Dizzily, she felt his body slide down hers and lean her back hard to the wall.

"What—what are you doing?" she whispered hoarsely as he knelt between her legs.

He looked up at her, and she saw the gleam of his wicked smile. "Your disguise would have fallen away in a second, *cailleach,* if anyone saw these silk stockings. So fine and soft..." His hand slid up the inside of her leg, pushing her thighs apart. He lowered his head, kissing her knee, her silk garter, her trembling skin.

"Not as soft as this, though," he said, and she felt his touch comb through her damp curls and delve inside her. His caress was rough and warm. "And so wet."

Then his mouth replaced his hand. He licked at her seam, making her cry out in shock.

She reached down and tried to drag him back, but he would not be turned away. "What are you doing?"

"Kissing you, of course," he whispered against her. "Don't you like it?"

"I..." His tongue pressed into her, tasting deeply. "Oh, *yes.*"

He laughed, and shockingly she felt the sound deep inside. "I knew you would." His fingers spread her even wider, his tongue sweeping along her aching folds as he tasted her. It was utterly scandalous, completely intimate. Anna knew she should be disgusted, but she couldn't be repelled by something that felt so—so wonderful.

She closed her eyes tightly and let the sensations wash over her. It was like sparks dancing over her skin, burning, shooting the pleasure higher and higher until she couldn't breathe.

His tongue touched one spot, and she cried out, her body taut as a bowstring. "Conlan, I—oh!" she gasped. Those sparks caught into flames, a bonfire of pleasure that soared through her. Her mind flooded with white-hot light, and everything else vanished.

She felt her knees buckle, and she collapsed toward the stone doorstep. Conlan caught her around the waist and lowered her gently. For a moment, all she could do was shiver. The heat of her climax dissipated, and she felt the cold wind again and the hard stone beneath her.

So *that* was what she read about in her romantic novels. That was what her married friends giggled about. They quite underestimated the matter.

Or perhaps they had just never met the Duke of Adair.

Anna slowly opened her eyes and found herself sitting back against the wall. He lay beside her, his head buried in her rumpled skirts. As she watched, he slowly wiped his mouth with the back of his hand. He turned his head to stare up at her.

"That was utterly shocking, Your Grace," she managed to say. "And wonderful."

He laughed. "I am said to be a man of many talents."

"Oh? And what are some more of them?" She leaned down to kiss him, a spasm of pleasure rushing through her when she smelled herself on his lips.

He kissed her back, but only for a moment. Then he grasped her shoulders and held her back from him. "*Le d'thoil,* please, Anna, don't touch me. If you do, I'll explode."

"Oh," she whispered. Suddenly, she understood. She had found release; he had not. Her gaze swept down his body to the hard bulge in his trousers. It strained against the seams. "What you did to me—women do that to men, too, I think."

"Ach, Anna, you're determined to kill me!" he groaned.

She was suddenly overcome with a terrible curiosity. What did he feel like, taste like? Could she make him cry out, make his world disappear as he had for her?

She reached for him, but his hand shot out to grab her wrist in an iron clasp.

"I want to . . ." she began. Her words were cut off by a sudden shout from outside their doorway haven.

In an instant, Conlan was on his feet and dragging her up to hers. He tugged her bodice over her breasts and pushed her rumpled skirts down. The shouts were louder, several coarse voices and then a clatter. And it was coming closer.

"What's going on?" she said.

"Don't say a word," he muttered. He pressed her back to the wall, in the deepest part of the doorway. "Stay here and be very, very still."

He leaned away from her to peer carefully out onto the street. The shouts grew even louder, and she could finally make out a few words. "Down with Union! Down with Lord Ross!"

Conlan shoved her tight against the wall, covering her with his body. Over his shoulder, she watched the protesters surge past. Perhaps two dozen men bearing flickering torches, shouting and banging on cymbals and crude drums. Most frightening, they carried an effigy of Ross with a noose around his neck.

A shutter opened over a window across the street, but was hastily slammed shut again. Not another soul stirred. Perhaps the neighborhood that she had thought so peaceful and quiet was merely fearful and keeping its head down.

Anna clung to Conlan's shoulders, remembering old tales of Paris in the Revolution. Men's heads borne aloft on pikes. Women snatched from their carriages and torn apart by a howling mob. Blood running thick in the gutters.

She also remembered the dead bodies she saw in '98, Irish peasants and British soldiers both, tangled together in a terrible carnage. Burned houses, the summer air foul with smoke and blood. Was it all going to happen again?

She leaned her forehead to his shoulder and closed her eyes until the noise of the mob faded. He had been part of it, too, hiding in that stable on that terrible night.

"They're gone," he said gently. "It's safe to go home now."

"Is it?" Anna opened her eyes to stare up at him. "Oh, Conlan. Someday I think you'll have to kiss me someplace more comfortable. And private."

And she would have to find out just why he was in Dublin. But for now, she was too tired and dizzy from everything that had happened between them to even think straight. He laughed humorlessly and took her hand in his as they ducked out of their doorway back into the night.

They made their way toward the river, out of the narrow streets, and into wider lanes Anna knew better. The more familiar environs didn't instill comfort in her, though, for the city seemed eerily silent. It was very late, but usually even the wee hours of fun-loving Dublin were full of sound and motion. The streets were quiet and darkened now. Even the stars overhead seemed to be sliding toward the horizon, leaving the sky black.

Then it was not so silent anymore. As they came near the river and the large, old brick houses that lined the embankment, built to echo the Customs House, she heard shouts and the crackle of flames. It sounded like the mob that surged past their doorway, only amplified by the silence of the night.

Anna tightened her grasp on Conlan's hand and looked up at him. His jaw was set in a taut line, his head up like a wild animal sensing danger. "What is happening?" she whispered. She had heard so many people warn of such things, at fine balls and tea parties, but she had dismissed their concerns. Were they right in the end?

He didn't answer. "This way," he said abruptly, tugging her down an alley. It was so narrow that they had to go single file. Conlan led her past piles of empty crates lined up along the brick walls. It smelled damp there behind shops that she had probably visited before, thick with rotting produce and the cold threat of freezing rain. The noise was muffled there.

They emerged from the end of the alley into another street, one she recognized well, for Caroline's favorite bookshop was there. It was utterly blank and silent with the shops shuttered. From the distance, there was a plume of silvery smoke spiraling into the black sky like a ghost.

Anna pressed close to Conlan, watching the smoke with a growing sense of horror. It was all happening again! Burnings, battles, the terrible uncertainty of what could happen next. They had all been fools to think themselves safe in the city. Being trapped behind walls was surely even worse—there was nowhere to run.

She barely had time to clutch tightly to his hand before they were caught up in the surging crowd and carried away down the street. In the distance, she could hear the clang of bells, and the acrid tang of smoke was thick in her throat as they were swept closer to the river.

Panic welled up inside of her, and she dug her fingers into Conlan's hand. She had to get away from there!

Conlan drew her closer to his side. "You're not in danger, Anna," he said close to her ear. "Not when you're with me. Stay close, and I'll get us out of here."

And strangely she believed him. They were trapped in a mob, and he was the last person that she should trust because he was so very full of secrets. Yet as she looked up into his steady eyes, she *did* feel safe. A dreamlike calm descended on her, driving away that cold rush of panic.

"But what's happening?" she said, stumbling against him as someone ran into her.

He had no time to answer. The crowd spilled out onto

the river's embankment, which was lined with old houses. One of them, a large old-fashioned structure, was ablaze, red-orange flames licking from the shattered windows and engulfing the brick walls. A boat moored in the river was also aflame. Crates of linens and wool meant for export to England floated in the river, and more crowds stood watching the conflagration.

Any of them could have set the fire, but now they just stood and stared, transfixed. The wind grew sharper and colder there by the water, tinged with the sourness of smoke, but the only sounds were the crackle of flames and a few scattered cheers as another window exploded.

"Conlan, you're here!" a man shouted.

Anna glanced over Conlan's shoulder to see a tall man hurrying toward them. He was clad all in black, his lean face streaked with gray ash.

Conlan let go of her hand to slide his arm around her waist and hold her to his side. "McMann," he said. "What's going on here?"

"Committee business," McMann answered with a humorless grin. "Lord Ross will rue the day he took English bribes, I would wager."

"I don't remember any such business," Conlan said tightly. Anna looked up to see the flare of anger in his eyes, illuminated by the flames. "Where is Foster? Was this his doing?"

"He's in the alley behind the house," McMann said. "He had to supervise the distribution."

"We'll see about that." Conlan took Anna's hand again and said, "McMann, take the lady home while I have a wee word with Foster. It's clear matters have gotten out of hand here."

McMann's face twisted with disappointment, but he said, "Of course. I'll be back quickly."

"You'd best not. Trouble is not far ahead," Conlan said.

"No!" Anna cried as he started to let go of her hand. "I want to stay with you, to help if I can."

He kissed her palm quickly and then gently pushed her away, toward McMann. "You can't help here, Anna; it's too dangerous. Go with McMann now, he'll see you safely home. He may be an impulsive fool about some things, but he can be trusted."

"But..."

"Go on now, *cailleach*. I have to take care of some business now."

Those clanging bells grew closer, louder, and the crowd that had been enthralled by the flames scattered in sudden noisy confusion. The roof of the warehouse caved in with a great roar, sending flames shooting high in the air.

"Go!" Conlan shouted. He pushed her to McMann, who grabbed her firmly by the arm and half-carried her through the roaring crowds. He was too strong for her to break away, and over his shoulder, she saw Conlan's figure disappear along the embankment.

Ireland was in flames yet again, and Conlan was a part of it all. Was she being a damned fool to be so drawn to him? To give up a safe place in the world to go with him?

"Will he be caught?" she said as McMann led her over a bridge and farther and farther from the chaos. Her heart ached at the thought of Conlan in prison.

McMann laughed roughly. "Not him, miss. We need him too much."

Anna wanted to ask who "we" could be, but she was

afraid of the answer, of knowing everything once and for all. Besides, she was sure McMann would not tell her anything.

She was suddenly so weary. All the excitement of the night drained away, leaving her tired and confused. She followed McMann numbly, wrapped in her own thoughts.

"Where do you live, miss?" he said as they left the district of shops and old houses behind for the relative safety of newer, finer townhouses and squares. It was eerily silent there without the flames and bells.

"Henrietta Street," she said automatically.

Surprise flickered over McMann's face at the mention of the fine address. He wondered who she was, to live at such a place and be here with a man like Conlan McTeer. Anna could see that. She often wondered who she really was, too.

"The servant's entrance," she said, and hurried on into the mysterious night.

Chapter Eleven

Well, I suppose Lord Ross is fortunate that no one was home last night, and that he is already building that fine new house on Fish Street," Katherine said. She, Anna, and Caroline rode in their carriage on the way home from the shops, mired in the traffic snarl that formed while everyone stopped to gawk at Lord Ross's partially burned house by the river.

Anna stared out the window at the smoke-stained walls, starkly outlined against the gray sky. So that was the end result of all that ruckus last night, a pro-Unionist's house destroyed. "It's lucky the flames were put out before those warehouses over there caught fire."

Caroline put down her book to peer past Anna's shoulder. "They're full of bales of linen and wool, not to mention whiskey and rope. They would have gone up like a Catherine wheel. Were the culprits caught?"

"Some of them," Katherine said. "But I heard many of them escaped into the night."

"That's a surprise, considering how many extra troops are quartered in Dublin for the Union vote," said Caroline.

"I suppose they were all busy elsewhere, in the taverns and brothels, and couldn't get here until too late."

"Caroline, please," Katherine murmured. "You shouldn't speak of brothels."

"No one can hear me but you and Anna," Caroline said. "I'm sure I can't shock the two of you. Everyone knows that's what soldiers get up to. Brothels, brothels..."

"All right, Caroline, that's enough," Katherine said sternly, but Anna could see she wanted to laugh. Anna pressed her hand to her mouth to hold back her own giggles. She must be hysterical from lack of sleep.

"I'm glad we'll be going to the country soon. Hopefully the Christmas festivities will distract you from such gossip," Katherine added.

The carriage at last lurched forward into a break in the crowd, and they slowly rolled toward home.

"Maybe the mistletoe will finally inspire Anna to choose one of her suitors," Caroline said.

"Maybe Caro is in a hurry to get me out of the way so she can marry," said Anna. She thought of the stark anger on Conlan's face last night as they watched the burning warehouse. Maybe Sir Grant was the right and safe choice after all.

"She can't do that until she finishes her studies and makes her debut," Katherine said. She glanced at the little watch pinned to her pelisse. "Speaking of which, this delay has made us late for Monsieur Courtois's first drawing lesson. He will think us so terribly lax."

"I'm sure that's not what he thinks of us," said Caroline as she opened her book again. "Especially not you, Mama. You are the Angel of Kildare. You can do no wrong."

Katherine laughed. "Angels can be tardy, too, I suppose."

She glanced over at Anna, who still stared blindly out the window. "Are you quite well, Anna dear? You look tired."

Anna tore her gaze from the passing streets to smile at her mother. "I'm fine, Mama. Never better."

"I knew you should not have gone to the ball last night. You are wearing yourself out."

Anna almost laughed to think what her mother would say if she knew the *real* reason why her daughter was so sleepy. Drinking in a tavern; kissing an Irishman in a dark doorway. Letting him kiss her *down there*. And then the fire...

She shivered at the memory of his mouth on her, of that terrible, wondrous pleasure, and the shock of violence that came afterward. She clutched her fists tight in her fox fur muff. "I am fine," she said again. "I just didn't like seeing that burned building. It was too much like—then."

"Of course. I don't like remembering, either," Katherine said quietly. "But it is behind us, my dear. It won't happen again."

Anna nodded, even as she had her grave doubts. Ireland was always like a powder keg set too near a flame; perhaps it always would be. Much like Adair himself.

They arrived back at Henrietta Street at last, only to find the foyer bustling with activity. As footmen took their wraps and saw to the shopping parcels, Smythe handed Anna two boxes and Katherine a stack of cards.

"Monsieur Courtois is waiting for Lady Caroline in the library, my lady. And Lady Anna had two callers while you were out, Sir Grant Dunmore and His Grace the Duke of Adair. They both left flowers."

Anna looked at him in alarm. "They were not here at the same time, Smythe?"

"No, Lady Anna."

Of course not, or surely their furniture would not still be intact. Anna opened the boxes to find Grant's violets and a sheaf of deep red, almost black orchids from Conlan. She buried her nose in them, inhaling the faint, earthy scent of the orchids.

"Sir Grant has invited us to a party at his house," Katherine said as she perused one of the cards. "Supper and whist with a few friends. Shall we go, Anna dear?"

"Of course, if you like, Mama," Anna said. "I don't think Sir Grant has ever opened his house to guests before. How curious."

"It seems his aunt, Lady Thornton, is to play hostess. That should be interesting. The last time I met with her, she had gone quite deaf and liked to converse with the teacups. But we can certainly attend."

She glanced at the card underneath, and her lips pursed. "What is this, Smythe?"

"That, I fear, is the other matter, my lady," Smythe said. "Captain Hayes waits for you in the drawing room. He did insist on waiting for your return."

"Oh, dear," Katherine sighed. "Did you give him tea?"

"He asked for brandy, my lady. Most emphatically."

"Whatever could George want? Besides our liquor, that is," said Katherine. "I suppose I will go in. It gets close to dinnertime; surely he will have to leave soon."

"I must go in for my drawing lesson," Caroline said quickly, backing toward the library. "Mustn't keep monsieur waiting!"

"And I must go upstairs and rest," said Anna. She had no desire to see George, to feel that slimy, speculative sort of look that he always gave her. "I am quite tired after all."

"Cowards," Katherine murmured. She squared her shoulders and marched toward the drawing room, like a martyr going to the scaffold.

As Anna fled up the stairs, she heard George's booming, slurred voice. "Katherine! Took you long enough. What's this I hear about your Frenchie drawing teacher? Most unwise, I would say. The dirty villains are just biding their time before invading again. He's probably a spy...."

Anna ran even faster toward the shelter of her own room.

She had told her mother earlier that she was not tired, but once she was alone in the quiet safety of her chamber, she felt drained. The long nights were catching up with her, she thought as she loosened her gown and lay down on her chaise.

Soon, very soon, she would have to face her future and make a decision once and for all. She could not go on crazy adventures forever, could not go on with dangerous men like Adair. She had her family to think of, her place in Society, and her duty. Grant Dunmore was a good choice. It was what she was born for, to be a wife and mother, and a Society hostess. How could she marry Grant, though, knowing the sort of man he was? A man with no family loyalty.

Anna closed her eyes against the pounding in her head. She couldn't decide the rest of her life right now. She pulled the blanket up over her head and drifted into sleep, letting the thick darkness pull her down.

But she didn't find oblivion in sleep. She only found more restless dreams.

She was back at Killinan Castle, and it was night. Not a

cold, wintry night, though; it was a hot summer, the darkness dusty and heavy. The grand rooms, spaces she had known since she was born, were empty and silent. Everything was filled with an ominous dread.

Anna stood at the top of the sweeping staircase, staring down at the marble floor of the foyer. The blank stone eyes of ancient statues stared back at her, and she suddenly knew when it was. Her dream—and she knew that it was a dream, even as she knew she could not escape it—had catapulted her back to the days of the rebellion. Their neighbors had fled in fear of the advancing rebels, but Anna was trapped in the tomblike silence of Killinan.

She seemed alone there, too, without her mother and sisters. The shadows crept closer and closer. She ran down the corridor to one of the windows, throwing open the casement to try and find a breath of clean air. The gardens, her mother's great pride, were also dark, lit only by faint moonlight. The white gravel drive stretched away toward the road, offering the illusion of escape.

If she fell from the window, Anna wondered, would she tumble out of the dream and back into her Dublin bedroom? Would the danger be gone, or just waiting to return?

She heard a sound, a footstep, a rustle of cloth, a low moan of pain. Her startled glance flew to the doorstep, and a wave of sickness rose up in her at what she saw there. The dream suddenly became all too real.

It was *that* night again. The night the ominous quiet of Killinan was broken by a sudden pounding at the door, rousing them all from their restless sleep. Eliza went down alone to answer it, insisting they all stay hidden, but she didn't know that Anna watched from the upstairs window.

She saw a man, or devil as he seemed then, leave the wounded Will Denton on their white stone steps. The man was tall with broad shoulders, wrapped in a black coat, his long black hair and beard tangled and wild. The blood stood out starkly on Will's torn white shirt, revealed by his open red uniform jacket, and as Anna leaned out of the window to see better, she could smell it, too. That coppery tang of blood, the mustiness of death, blotting out the sweet summer flowers.

She could only hear a few muffled sounds. Eliza's scream as she knelt by her lover. The man's gruff brogue, telling Eliza she should take Will and flee. Then the devil was gone, and Eliza and their mother dragged Will into the house.

The black-haired man had haunted Anna's nightmares for a long time after that. Yet she had never seen him, not really. In her dreams, he usually took on horns and glowing red eyes.

But when he looked up at her now, a ray of moonlight fell across his face, and he took on a very different aspect. It was Conlan. Conlan who had left Will at Killinan. He stared at her for a long moment and vanished into the blood-soaked night.

Anna sat up on her chaise, her heart pounding. For an instant, she had no idea where she was. That hot summer night at Killinan, months and months ago, was so near. The terror was so fresh that she shook with it.

She pulled in a shuddering breath and forced herself to open her eyes and look around. She was in her Dublin chamber, with the fresh, pale, blue-and-white walls and flowered bed hangings, her cloak draped over the dressing screen. The portrait of her with her sisters hung over the carved white mantel. Killinan Castle was far away, and that time was long ago.

It was dark gray outside the window, yet it couldn't be very late, for Rose hadn't come to light the lamps and help her dress for dinner. She could only have been asleep for a short time. But she felt as if she had passed years in her dreams.

Anna pushed back the blanket and rose on shaky legs to go to the window. The winter fog was creeping in, like shreds of silver-gray silk spreading down the street. It was a perfect night for concealment, for nefarious deeds. Just as *that* night had been.

"Was it just a dream?" she whispered. Had her exhaustion made her put Conlan's face onto the devil's in a bizarre twist of her imagination? Or was that what she really saw that night and then forced herself to forget? Could he really have something to do with the ambush of Will's patrol?

"Remember, remember!" she whispered, pressing her forehead to the cold glass. But the dream vanished again, and her memories of those days were hazy with the fear and uncertainty they all felt back then. She had tried to forget for so long that the memories didn't want to be unearthed now.

What would she do if it was Conlan? Demand answers, probably. Eliza and Will deserved them. And Anna needed to know the truth, too. Maybe then she could truly put those days behind her and move on, free of them. Free of Conlan and her obsession with him.

Anna turned away from the window and tiptoed over to open the door a crack. She listened carefully, but the house was quiet. Hopefully odious George was gone and her mother was lying down with a cold compress to recover. Caroline was probably working on her drawing.

She didn't have much time to convince them all that she was having a megrim and needed to be left alone for the night. She spun around and went to remove Jane's red gown from its hiding place in the back of her wardrobe. As she unfastened her day dress, her gaze fell on the open box of dark orchids. She had to make a decision, once and for all.

Chapter Twelve

This Union business makes for strange bedfellows, does it not, Adair?"

Conlan took a long drag on his cheroot, peering through the blue-gray smoke at his friend Mr. Foster. The meeting in the back room of McMaster's tavern had not yet begun so the space was only half-filled, men milling about as they muttered together in low, angry voices. The thick mist rolling in outside seemed to make the atmosphere even more tense. The specter of the fire hung over them.

"Aye," Conlan said. "I never thought I would be in with Ascendancy politicians like Grattan and Ponsonby, but we do what we must. They stand against Union, so I stand with them for now."

"Even though they are not prepared to make common cause with those for Catholic emancipation?"

Conlan inhaled deeply, feeling the bite of the smoke in his lungs. It wasn't as acrid as the taste of religious conflict in his mouth. He had lived with *that* all his life, from the first time he heard his mother complain bitterly of having to marry his father in a Protestant church first to satisfy the law. It would never go away, and he knew that.

"Prime Minister Pitt thinks Union will be an integrative force, make us all one nation united in a common cause," Conlan said. "With the Catholics as a harmless minority enfolded by the majority. Clearly he knows nothing of the nature of this country if he thinks such a thing can ever happen."

"And the pro-Union Catholics believe Pitt when he flirts with emancipation?"

"I cannot speak for all Catholics, Foster," Conlan said with a laugh. "Pitt might think he can push through Catholic emancipation once Ireland is tied firmly to England, but in that, too, he is deluded. I know the Ascendancy—they will riot if forced to let the Catholics into politics and the law and their precious schools. That doesn't concern me right now, anyway."

"Oh?" Foster reached for his whiskey. He had looked more nervous as the night went on, and now his hand shook as he took a long drink. He had been like that since before the warehouse fire.

Conlan didn't know why the man was so jumpy at a simple organizational meeting. They were only planning to talk, not start an armed uprising—yet.

"No," Conlan said.

"Then what does concern you?"

"Taking care of my people, of course. I might not be able to sit in Parliament, but I don't care to see eighty boroughs disenfranchised and thirty-two members whittled down to one. The power of the landowners is my power to protect those who depend on me," Conlan said firmly.

"That sounds like Orange talk," Foster said. "Are you

prepared to join the Loyalist families who would shun you? Shun all of us?"

"While it suits my purpose." Conlan stubbed out his cheroot. "I'm not afraid to get my hands dirty, Foster, nor should you be. Our time grows short, with the vote coming up after Christmas. There's no time to be choosy about our allies."

"And no time to be choosy about our methods!" McMann interrupted. He was a young hothead, unpredictable but useful. "Ross's old house was burned, but it would have been better to burn his new house, with him inside it. Make them listen to us at last."

Conlan shook his head. "Don't be a fool, McMann. What did violence gain us two years ago? Torture, transportation, and the rope. The people are more oppressed than they were before."

McMann slumped back in his seat, his arms crossed. "So we just talk and talk? Talk gets us nowhere!"

"It's hardly just talk," Conlan said. "Is it, Foster?"

Foster swallowed hard. "Wh-what do you mean?" Beads of sweat popped out on his brow despite the cold night.

Conlan had merely suspected Foster was up to something before; now he was sure of it. Was the man a spy? For who? "What do you think I mean, Foster?"

Foster reached again for the whiskey, not meeting Conlan's eyes. "Nothing, of course."

Conlan pushed back from the table and went to ease back the edge of the black curtain and peer out into the gathering night. The fog was thick now, a blue-black miasma that didn't let even a glimpse of starlight shine through. The Olympian Club would be quiet tonight because of the weather, but it was perfect for other, more surreptitious tasks.

He thought of Anna, wondering where she was tonight. Did she venture out in the bone-chilling damp to dance with her admirers? Did she see his cousin, the man who claimed to be her future husband? And did *she* see Grant that way? Perhaps her daring escapades with Conlan were merely a last fling before she settled into life as Lady Dunmore, queen of Ascendancy Society.

He didn't sense that in her, though. She was reckless, to be sure, and impulsive. He felt like she didn't quite know herself, that she wanted more than her life offered but didn't know where to find it. There was something inside her that she fought against, something he wanted so much to know about. He wanted to know *her,* everything about her.

But that meant that he would have to let her know him in return, and that he couldn't do. He had let her too close as it was. She declared herself a frivolous featherbrain, but that was far from the truth. She was one of the smartest women he had ever met, old beyond her years in some ways, and if she could ever find her focus—heaven help them all.

So if she *was* with Grant tonight, being paraded on his arm before Society as his pretty prize, Conlan shouldn't care. He should let her go to that life. Yet Grant was so very unworthy of her.

And he, Conlan, was not much better. He got her involved in fires and rough taverns. That knowledge couldn't stop him wanting her, though.

"What's amiss with Foster tonight?" McMann said quietly at Conlan's shoulder.

"I'm not sure," Conlan answered. He watched as a few of their cohorts emerged from the fog and went into the tavern. "But I think we should be careful of what we say to him. Can you have some of your men follow him for the next few days?"

"Of course!" McMann said, too eagerly.

"Discreetly," Conlan warned. "We don't want anyone to know. And I don't want his body dragged from the Liffey."

"Certainly not. It won't get out of hand, Adair, I promise. They'll just see where he goes, who he talks to. If he's taking English bribes." McMann paused. "Do you want some of the boys as guards for yourself? After what happened at St. Stephen's Green..."

"No. They'll just get in my way. It won't happen again."

"I hope not. We can't do without you, Adair, not so close to the time."

The others came into the room in a flurry of cold wind and shouted greetings, and there wasn't time to say anymore. The meeting was about to begin.

$$\mathcal{BD}$$

"A quiet night, eh, McIntire?" Conlan said as he handed his greatcoat to the butler in the Olympian Club foyer. He could hear only a murmur of sound drifting down the staircase from the club.

"It's a nasty night out there, Your Grace," McIntire answered, shaking out the damp coat. "Sensible people are at home by their fires."

"The Olympian Club doesn't trade in sensible people, McIntire."

"Obviously not. Lord Fitzwalter is here, and Mr. Napier. They were quarreling already. And also..." McIntire hesitated.

"Who else is here then? Grant Dunmore, perhaps?"

"No, Your Grace, not Sir Grant. But you did say to let you know if the lady in the red gown reappeared."

Conlan froze. "She is back?"

"Yes, alone this time. I know we are not to admit guests without a member escorting them, but it seemed better not to send her back out into the night."

"Quite right. I will see to her, McIntire." Conlan dashed up the stairs two at a time. Anna was back at the Olympian Club? What game did she play now? It seemed his imaginings of her evening, parading through Society as the future Lady Dunmore, were quite wrong. Sneaking into his club seemed much more like her.

He strode down the corridor, smoothing back his rumpled hair and straightening his coat. He usually did not go into the club except in evening dress, but it seemed there was no time to change. Where Anna was concerned, there was not a moment to lose. If he failed to keep pace with her, she would leave him behind forever.

At the closed double doors, there was a basket full of masks for those who forgot theirs and preferred to be anonymous, and he grabbed up a scrap of white leather and slid it over his face just before he went inside. The ballroom was dark and silent; there was no dancing tonight. But a few people sat at the small tables in the dining room, partaking of the buffet and the fine wine, and a steady hum of voices flowed from the card room.

Conlan scanned the people gathered there, their heads bent over games of whist and trictrac. It was only the regulars tonight, the ones who showed up to play deep several times a week. Except for the lady who sat at the faro table.

Anna wore her red-and-black gown again, a spot of brilliant, burning color in the cold night. Her golden curls were piled high, fastened with two of the perfect black orchids he had left at her house. She wore a black satin mask over her face, but it couldn't conceal her bright smile. She laughed as the dealer turned up the player's card and clapped her black silk-gloved hands. The dealer said something that made her laugh even more, the two of them chatting like old friends.

Only then did Conlan realize the faro dealer was Sarah, his business partner, friend, and sometime-lover. She and Anna bent their heads together as they talked, almost like they were about to share female confidences. Sarah was very good at eliciting secrets from gamesters, but he certainly didn't want her hearing any secrets from this one.

Sarah's gaze met his, and she smiled in welcome. Anna glanced back over her shoulder, and her smile faded a bit. She waved to him, though, and he hurried across the room to the faro table. Anna had a pile of chips in front of her, and she turned one gracefully between her fingers.

"A quiet evening," he said, watching the slow movement of her hands.

"Not for this lady," Sarah said. "She has the devil's own luck. I'm afraid she'll break the bank."

Anna laughed. She set down the chip and reached for a half-full glass of wine. "Not tonight. I know to quit while I'm ahead."

If only he did, too, Conlan thought. But he feared he never knew when to quit when it came to Anna Blacknall.

"Lucky for us," Sarah said. Her shrewd gaze moved between Conlan and Anna, a small smile on her lips. "We may end the evening in the black after all."

"Perhaps the lady would care for some supper then and leave the table to someone less lucky," said Conlan. He held out his arm to Anna.

She drained her glass before taking it. "Thank you, sir. And thank you, madame, for the conversation. It was most...enlightening."

As Conlan led her from the card room, he leaned down to whisper in her ear. "What are you doing here, Anna?"

She slanted him an unreadable glance. "Are you not happy to see me?"

"I'm always happy to see you." Too happy. He remembered the taste of her female essence on his tongue, the way she moaned and pressed him closer, and his traitorous penis hardened. "I'm just surprised you ventured out in this fog by yourself. It's too dangerous, especially after the fire."

"I need to talk to you."

"And you could not send me a note? I would have called on you tomorrow."

"This isn't the sort of conversation for my mother's drawing room."

"Come with me." He steered her down a dark hallway and into his private office. Sarah had been working on accounts there earlier, it seemed, for a lamp was lit on the desk next to a pile of ledger books. The rest of the room was in shadow.

Conlan shut the door and leaned back against it. He watched as Anna sat down on the leather chaise by the wall and took off her mask. Her ivory face glowed, and he could smell the sweetness of her perfume. Her presence invaded the whole space, making it hers as she did with everything.

"What was so urgent then?" he said.

At first, she didn't answer. She slowly peeled off her gloves, folding them in her lap as she studied the office. "Your faro dealer is quite charming, and I like her gown. If that's the uniform of the Olympian Club, I may have to ask for employment here."

"You'd be good at it. Everyone would be so distracted by you that they would throw their game. But I think your situation in life is not quite so dire yet that you need to seek employment in a gambling club."

"It might be, if I am discovered here in this wicked den of vice."

"Then why risk it?"

"Because I like wicked dens of vice, I suppose. They're far preferable to the Castle and the Rutland Square assembly rooms."

"Anything would be preferable to the Castle, I'm sure."

"Yes. Cold, drafty, dull place."

"I'm glad I'm not invited there then." Conlan sat down on the edge of the desk and took off his mask. Anna's presence, so close in that small, dark space, wreaked havoc with his good sense. "But you did not come here to speak of Dublin Castle, I hope."

"No." She leaned back on her elbows. "You know my sister, Mrs. Denton, I think."

Where was all this going? He was even more baffled by Anna than before. "Of course. Everyone knows of the famous Lady Mount Clare."

"And her husband, Major Denton, as he was before he resigned his commission to go abroad?"

Conlan braced his fists on the edge of the desk. "I have not had the pleasure of meeting Mr. Denton."

"You did not even encounter him during the rebellion? His regiment was in County Kildare, near Adair Court, I would think."

"What are you asking me, Anna?"

She rose slowly to her feet and came toward him. She set her hands to either side of him on the desk, leaning so close that he could feel the brush of her soft hair on his throat. He held himself rigid, not grabbing her and dragging her across his lap as he longed to.

"One night at Killinan," she said softly, "there was a knock at the door. Caro and I were terrified; we had lived with the awful certainty that any day we would be burned out. Mama even had our grandfather's old dueling pistol loaded by her bed. But Eliza went down to open the door, telling us to hide and flee if need be, and she found Will there, wounded and bleeding, unconscious on our doorstep."

Conlan watched her, not saying anything.

"We thought him dead, and Eliza was inconsolable. Will is her great love, you see, and he has been since they were children. But we nursed him back to health, and he took us to Dublin, where it was thought we would be safer. I thought I remembered nothing of that night, though I did go to the window. It was such a black night, and I was so very scared."

Her face looked perfectly white, and her eyes were wide and almost midnight-blue as she remembered what happened. He recalled that night, too, every awful moment of it. He wrapped his arms around her waist and pulled her closer. She went to him, but she stared past his shoulder, as if she was far away.

"But you do remember now?" he said.

"I don't know if it's a memory or a dream." She looked directly at him then, steady and serious. "Was it you? Did you leave Will at Killinan?"

So it had come back. The night that he came across the ambushed patrol, too late. They were all dead except Will Denton, clutching his miniature of Eliza Blacknall as he bled into the Irish earth. "Yes. It was me."

"And did you—were you the one who wounded him?"

"No. I swear on my mother's grave, Anna. I did not hurt your brother-in-law or any of his men. One of my tenants told me about the planned ambush, but I reached them too late to do anything but find Denton."

She studied him closely. She reached up and took his face in her soft hands. "In the Uprising, did you kill? Even if it was not that day, did you kill?"

He could not lie to her, not when she looked at him like that. "Yes."

"So did I. I have blood on my hands, the same as you, Conlan." She let out a ragged breath. "I wanted so much to forget those days. I tried everything—parties, card games, drinking. But it is still with me. What I saw, what I did. Do you feel the same?"

Shocked, Conlan reached up and clasped her hands in his. He held them tight against his chest, feeling her tremble. "Sometimes in life we're forced to do terrible things, *mo chuisle*. Whatever you did, it was only because you had to."

"He tried to rape me, that English soldier," she said

tonelessly. "I panicked, I only wanted his—his hands off me. He pressed me to the ground and pulled my legs apart. I felt his—his *thing* against me. So I stabbed him with his own dagger. I stabbed him over and over until he was dead, and I was covered with his blood."

A hot, wild fury filled Conlan at her words, at the horrible image they drew. Someone dared touch her, violate her, his beautiful Anna. If the *tudan* was not already dead, Conlan would scalp him and cook his heart over a bonfire as his Celtic ancestors had done to their enemies. He would send him to hell.

He held Anna against his chest and pressed a tender kiss to her temple. Her pulse beat frantically under her skin. "You did the right thing, the only thing you *could* do. You should never think of it again."

"I know, but..." She tilted her head back to look up at him. "Do you go to confession, Conlan? I've heard that Catholics do that often."

"I fear I have not been to church in years, *cailleach*." Though he kept a chapel and a hidden school with a priest-teacher for his workers' children, he could not go himself. His soul was too stained. "I went when I was a child sometimes, and my mother would have a priest visit from France."

"And did you feel clean afterward? Forgiven?"

He laughed. "Considering my sins at the time consisted of stealing a pie from the kitchen and disrespecting my mother when she scolded me about it, I don't think I needed much cleansing. It's a different matter now. It would take a century of confessions."

"I would just like to forget, to know myself again as I once did." She flattened her palms against his chest, sliding them down until she reached the bottom button of his waistcoat. She slid it free as she kissed his throat. "You make me forget, Conlan."

And she made him forget, too, God help him. "Anna, you should let me take you home."

"No, I want to be here with you." She kissed his jaw, his cheek. Another button popped free, and another. She went up on tiptoe, whispering against his ear. "Don't you like it when I'm here with you?"

"Aye, I do."

"Then kiss me, Conlan. Please."

With a deep groan, he dragged her against him and covered her lips with his. His tongue slid deep into her mouth, and she greeted him eagerly. Their breath mingled, frantic with a need deeper than any he had ever known.

She spread his waistcoat wide and slid her hands over his thin linen shirt, tugging it out of his waistband. She touched his bare skin, her fingers teasing over his ribs, then his shoulders. The edge of her nail scraped over his flat nipple, and he moaned at the rush of sensation.

"Anna—you really should go," he whispered against her lips.

"I can't," she answered, a sob in her throat. "I want you. I want it to be you, now."

And he wanted her so much he could not see straight. It had nothing to do with his work, with Ireland, with what her family could do for him or with annoying his cousin. It was only her, Anna. She was all he wanted that night. All the beauty and sweetness that he had ever craved and thought could not exist in the world.

In answer, he kissed her again, roughly, nothing held back. He forced her head back as his tongue plunged deep into her mouth. She met him with equal fire, her arms wrapped tightly around him, her nails digging into his bare back.

He slid off the desk and walked her backward until they tumbled onto the chaise. She pushed his coat off and tore his shirt over his head. He tossed them to the floor and leaned back into her to kiss her throat, her shoulder, licking a ribbon of fire over her soft skin.

"You are gorgeous," she whispered, closing her eyes as she held on to him. "My god of the Underworld."

"If you stay with me," he said, "you may never see sunlight again."

"I like the darkness." Her hand slid lower and unfastened his breeches. He sprang free from the fabric confines, hard as iron, and he dared not move or even breathe as her soft, tentative touch slid over him. "Do you like this?"

"*Diolain,* yes," he said hoarsely.

That seemed to embolden her, for her caress grew more certain. She slid down his length, then up again, leaving agonized pleasure in her wake. She shoved his breeches down over his hips and reached around with her other hand to caress his taut buttocks.

If she didn't stop, it would be over before it began. He jerked out of her arms and stood up to strip out of his boots and breeches. He stood before her, naked and hugely aroused.

She didn't run in fear, his witch. She lay back on the cushions and studied him, a smile on her lips. "I feel quite overdressed now."

"I can help you remedy that, *cailleach.*"

"I'm quite sure you can." She sat up and turned her back to him so he could unfasten her gown. As it eased away from her body to reveal her slender back, bare of corset or even chemise, he pressed his lips to the curve of her spine. She was warm and soft as summer cream, smelling of sweet lilies and the earthiness of orchids.

She trembled as he touched her skin with his tongue, tasting her. As her gown fell away and she kicked it to the floor, he slid the pins from her hair and watched the heavy golden mass tumble over her shoulders.

She lay back across the chaise, her bare body very white against the brown cushions, and stared up at him with parted, flushed lips. His avaricious stare took in her bare breasts, high and crowned with erect pink nipples, down to the indentation of her waist, her hips. And the vee of blond curls between her legs, glistening with the moisture of desire.

She still wore her stockings, black silk with red ribbon garters, and that pale hair seemed even more golden against their vividness. He remembered the musky taste of her, the sweet, salty smell, and he slid his hands slowly up her legs as he parted them and drew her to the edge of the chaise. He wanted to erase any of those terrible memories from her mind forever. To make her only remember pleasure.

He knelt between her thighs and softly kissed her bare skin just above her red garter. Her fingers threaded through his hair as she pressed him closer, and he was most happy to oblige. He traced her seam with his tongue before plunging deep into the soft, hot core of her and tasted her intoxicating essence.

Chapter Thirteen

Anna was sure she was dreaming again, but this time it was no nightmare. This time, she floated on a cloud of pleasure and bright joy.

When she ran away from home tonight, she was so terribly confused. She wanted to know the truth, yet she wanted to shut it out as well. To push it back into the dark recesses of the past and forget about it. She knew Conlan could help her forget. Perhaps, being so much a part of it all, he was the only one who really could. The only one who could understand and see past the pretty picture, which was all anyone else wanted to know.

But more than even forgetting, she had to know the truth. There was no moving forward without it. Conlan swore he had not wounded Will that day, and Anna knew that to an Irishman an oath on his mother's grave was sacred. But that did not mean he was innocent of all wrongdoing in those black days. He confessed to killing—just as she had.

When she told him that, said the words she had never uttered aloud before, he hadn't looked at her with disgust and loathing. In his eyes, she saw only understanding and sadness.

That sympathy released something inside of her, like a captive bird soaring free into the sky, and it made her want him with a desperate force she couldn't deny.

Anna tugged at his hair, drawing him up from between her legs until he braced himself over her. He held himself carefully so he wouldn't crush her with his strength, but she wanted him closer and closer. She wanted to lose herself in him and see his very soul.

She wasn't afraid any longer. And she had forgotten how wonderful it felt to be fearless, to not be alone.

She wrapped her legs around his hips and tugged him into the curve of her body. His skin was warm, damp and satin-smooth over his powerful muscles. She traced her fingertips over his taut back and his buttocks, exalting in the feel of him, the strong life force of him.

"How alive you are, Conlan," she whispered. She kissed his shoulder, tasting the salt-sweat beaded there. She craved that life like she craved the sun and the air. She needed him more than she had ever needed anything else.

"Anna," he said roughly. He buried his face in the curve of her neck, and she felt him breathe in deeply of her. He felt a longing that echoed her own. "I tried to fight against this—whatever it is between us."

"I know. So have I. But I can't fight any longer. I know it's wrong, that we can't really be part of each other's lives, but..." She drew in a shuddering breath and smelled him. The clean, dark essence of him—and herself on his lips. "I don't want to fight now. I have no strength left."

"Anna." He kissed her neck, his mouth open and hot,

sliding over her shoulder, the curve of her breast. "You are not like anyone else in all the world."

"Neither are you. So we must be meant for each other—for tonight."

He swept aside her hair to kiss her ear. She felt the rush of his breath and the bite of his teeth on her soft earlobe, and it made her shudder with a lightning rush of lust. She arched into him, rubbing against the iron hardness of his erection.

His mouth touched that sensitive spot just below her ear, nibbling at it as she cried out.

"Do you like that?" he whispered. His accent was thick in his voice, rich with the greenness of Ireland. Her ancient warrior god.

"I—I feel like I'm falling," she gasped. The room twirled around her, and she tightened her arms around him to hold herself on the earth.

"Let yourself fall. I'll catch you."

So she did. She imagined leaping off a precipice into the fog, a thick gray cloud shot through with red and gold sparks. "Anything can be on a night like this," she said.

"You can be anything that you want, Anna," he said, sliding deeper into her caress. "What is it you want to be?"

"I don't even know any longer. I only know I want you now." She traced her hand down his chest, the hair sprinkled over his hot skin rough on her fingers, and then along the sharp curve of his hip. She felt his back stiffen and his breath catch as she touched his penis. It hardened even more under her light touch, and she traced its velvety, hard length in fascination.

He shuddered as she caressed over its head, catching a tiny bead of moisture with the tip of her finger. Overcome with curiosity, she lifted it to her lips and tasted the salty musk, licking it from her own skin.

"Damn, Anna!" he groaned. "You'll kill me yet, I swear it."

"I told you—I want you now. And I think you want me, too."

Conlan's hand touched her between her spread legs, his thumb sliding into the wet core of her. "I've never wanted anything more. But I don't want to hurt you."

"You won't. I trust you." She closed her eyes and spread her legs wider, letting him feel her desire. "Please, Conlan."

She heard his ragged breath as he reached between their bodies and gently parted her folds as he sought entry. Then she felt the stretch and burn as he eased slowly inside of her.

Her years of horseback riding and activity had left her not as tight as she feared, but it still hurt as he entered her, as her womanhood accommodated his thick length. She gasped at the friction, the new sensation of fullness and pressure.

"I'm sorry, *mo chuisle*," he whispered. His body went still, his arms rigid as he held himself balanced above her. His buttocks tightened as if he would withdraw from her.

"No!" Anna cried in protest. Her legs closed around his hips to hold him to her. "It's better now."

And it really was. The ache was fading as her body grew accustomed to his, leaving only that fullness and a glimmer of something she could not quite grasp. Something very—pleasant.

He drew back one slow, tantalizing inch at a time, almost sliding out of her before he flexed his hips and plunged deep.

"Oh," she sighed as he did this again and again, faster and faster. That seed of pleasure grew, flowering and expanding low in her stomach. Every nerve ending in her body seemed to come to fiery life, ignited by the feel of his body in hers, joined to her in every way. She learned his rhythm, arching up to meet him as they moved together, ever faster, more frantic.

The room was hot and humid against the cold night outside, the whole planet narrowed to his body in hers. The two of them together. Behind her closed eyes, she saw sparks, gold and silver, shimmering, and a humming started in her ears, growing louder and louder like a rising chorus of pleasure. Then she realized it was *her*, her making those mews of joy and ecstasy. And she didn't even care. She just wanted more and more. Wanted this to go on forever.

Then all her thoughts and senses, everything she was, flew apart in an explosion of fiery stars. She felt like she was soaring into the sun, her old self burning up until she could emerge, phoenix-like, into a new life.

Above her, Conlan shouted out in a torrent of Gaelic words as his back tightened. He pulled out of her, and she felt the damp warmth of his seed against her hip. He collapsed beside her, to the chaise, their arms and legs entangled.

Anna slowly sank back down to earth, as if on a cloud of feathers. She had never felt so relaxed, her bones soft in her body. So tired, so light, so—confused. And yet also so certain. She didn't know what would happen tomorrow, or even in the next hour. But for now, she was where she should be.

Next to her, she heard his breath, the tremors of his release slowed. She opened her eyes and rolled onto her side, gazing at him in the sputtering lamplight. His eyes were half-closed, and he gave her a lazy smile that made her heart speed up again.

"Are you all right, *cailleach*?" he murmured.

"Oh, yes." Better than all right. She was at peace. Even if it was only for a moment, it was a rare, wondrous gift. She kissed the corner of his mouth in silent thanks.

"I should see you home," he said. "It grows late."

"Not just yet. We have a little time." She hated the thought of leaving this room. Here they were safe; they were together and nothing could touch them. Out there, the whole world and all its troubles and expectations waited.

She sat up on the edge of the chaise and untied her ribbon garters. She rolled down her stockings and cast them away, giving him a long glimpse of her bare leg before she reached for his discarded shirt. She pulled it over her head, and let its soft folds wrap around her. It smelled of him, and of her too, their essences mingled.

"It suits you much better than me," he said. He reached out for her and tugged her back into his arms. She curled up against him, her back to his chest, and closed her eyes with a smile. They were as close as two people could be, she and Conlan, at least for that night.

Chapter Fourteen

Katherine couldn't shake away the feeling that something was wrong. She could not sleep, even though it was far past the hour to retire.

She set aside her book and looked out the drawing room window. Usually there was a view of the grand house across the street, its pillars and portico echoing their own dwelling in lovely symmetry, but tonight everything was concealed by a thick blanket of fog. It muffled the streetlights and even the moon, making it seem much later than it really was. She shivered, and not just from the damp chill.

Drawing her shawl closer around her shoulders, she went to pull the draperies shut. It had been a quiet evening, most unusual in the round of Dublin holiday merrymaking. With Caroline's lesson running long and Anna indisposed with a headache, Katherine took her supper on a tray by the fire. She had thought she missed the quieter life of the country, but now in the long, silent moments filled with her own thoughts, she wondered if the social round didn't have its advantages after all.

It did not always pay to look too deeply into one's own heart; she had discovered that long ago. As long as she did her duty and spent her time looking after others, she could dismiss any doubts or fears, any hint of sadness.

Tonight, though, there was nothing she had to do, no useful task that waited for her. And all those doubts clamored at the edge of her mind.

"Oh, what is wrong with me?" she muttered. She curled her fist into the satin drapery as she stared out at the misty night. Nothing *should* be wrong. Anna was on the verge of being betrothed to Grant Dunmore, a most suitable gentleman, and Caroline seemed to be settling down to her lessons. Her motherly work was nearly done. She should be proud and happy, and planning for the future.

Not restless and worried. She felt like she was on the edge of something, that events she could not control or even understand were rolling toward her like a landslide.

"Don't be ridiculous," she said sternly. Such things did not happen to a person twice in her life. She and her family had survived the Uprising, and she had worked hard to put their world back in order. All was well now. It was just the rumblings over the Union that had her so uneasy.

She pulled the curtains over the window, blotting out the night. If only she could be happy again, carefree like when she was a girl so long ago, before marriage and duty had pressed in on her. Those days were so brief that she could hardly recall them.

She took up a candle and went upstairs to the silent corridor where the bedchambers lay. Perhaps her ominous feelings would disappear if she saw everyone was safe.

Caroline was asleep in her bed, the blankets thrown back haphazardly and her book open next to her. Katherine carefully removed her daughter's spectacles and tucked the coverings around her before she blew out the lamp and tiptoed from the room.

Anna's chamber was dark, her bedcurtains drawn, so Katherine did not come closer. Anna had looked so tired lately, so preoccupied. She needed her sleep. And Katherine had hopes that the country air, and the resolution of the Dunmore engagement, would do her daughter good.

She sighed as she made her way back downstairs. Not that the Dunmore matter seemed quite so certain now, with the advent of the Duke of Adair into their lives. His appearance in town and his attentions to Anna were a puzzle, and not one she was entirely sure she liked. He was handsome, of course, and dashing, and possessed of a fine estate despite his less than stellar background. A ducal title made up for a lot.

Yet he was so mysterious, his life as shadowed as that fog outside. Anna was a high-strung girl, one that had been worrisomely clouded by sadness since the rebellion. A man so complex might not be good for her.

But since when did young ladies want what was good for them? Especially ones as passionate and strong-minded as her daughters.

Katherine turned toward the library with the thought that maybe a lighthearted novel or some poetry would distract her from this strange mood. She pushed open the door and froze at the sight that greeted her.

Nicolas Courtois sat at the desk, bathed in a circle of pink-amber lamplight that turned his skin and hair to molten gold. He had his head bent over an open sketchbook, and the flickering light cast shadows that chiseled his high cheekbones and strong jaw into fine sculpture. His hair fell in an untidy sweep over his brow, which would tempt any woman to smooth it back, to touch its softness and trace her fingertips over his handsome face.

Well, perhaps she *did* understand a bit after all, the foolish rush of feeling over a handsome face. Strange— she had never felt like that before. Why now, with a young Frenchman, her daughter's teacher?

Perhaps this was the sense she had of something amiss out there in the night. Of standing on the brink of her own uncertain future.

Nicolas leaped to his feet at her entrance, running his fingers through his hair to push it back. It just sent the locks into greater disarray.

"Lady Killinan," he said. His lilting French accent seemed heavier tonight. More foreign and exotic. "Forgive me."

Katherine straightened her shoulders as she tried to recover herself. "I did not realize anyone was here."

"I was merely waiting for the fog to lift. It was quite thick when Lady Caroline finished her lesson. We ran too long," he said. Across the shadowed space of the library he stared at her, his eyes so dark and deep they seemed almost black. He, too, seemed very startled. Only by her sudden appearance? "*Je suis desolée,* I am sorry."

"Oh, no, Monsieur Courtois," she said. She stepped into the room and set down her candle on the nearest pier table. Her hand had begun to tremble so she feared she couldn't hold on to it. "You were quite right to stay. It cannot be safe to try and cross the city in such weather. I just wish I had known; you could have dined with me."

"That is kind of you, my lady. One of your maids brought me refreshments." He gestured to a tray of bread and cheese on the desk.

"Of course she did." The maids were all in love with him. And Katherine feared that she was just as foolish as they were, drawn by a godlike face and a sad story. By his great artistic talent. He was not dull like the Society men she knew, not bound to expectations and old ways of thinking. He saw true beauty and goodness in the world.

She tightened her shawl over her shoulders. She should go, but she didn't want to, not at all. She didn't want to go back to her cold, lonely night.

"Then perhaps you would share a brandy with me, monsieur," she said. She hurried over to the small sideboard holding a crystal carafe and etched glasses. "We need something warm on such a dismal night."

"That is very kind of you, Lady Killinan," he said. He sounded cautious.

She should be cautious, too, but she didn't want to. The fog seemed to close the world around her with a sense of unreality. "Not at all," she said as she poured a generous measure of brandy into two of the glasses. "It's quite selfish actually. I'd like the company on such a dismal evening."

"Then I am glad I happen to be here. I'd like the company, too."

She handed him one of the drinks and clicked her glass to his. "*Salut,* monsieur."

"*Salut.*"

Katherine tilted her head toward the sketchbook. "More of your own work?"

"No, it is Lady Caroline's." He turned the drawing so she could see, his hand brushing hers. "She says it is your house in Kildare County."

"Oh, yes!" Katherine could see it now, the old medieval tower of Killinan Castle, the lines uncertain but recognizable. "I think she was holding out on me when she said she has no artistic talent."

"She has very good instincts, a good sense of proportion. She just needs a bit of . . ."

"Refinement?" Katherine laughed. "I fear all my girls need that."

"I cannot believe that, Lady Killinan. They are your daughters, are they not? *Telles meres, telles filles.* Like mothers, like daughters."

"*Meres et filles?* I begin to think that might be true." And she began to think she herself was not so *refined* after all. Not when she stared at him in the lamplight and felt the stirrings of an undeniable desire deep inside. She never thought that she possessed such feelings at all. It was very startling.

She took a long drink of the brandy, letting its fiery smoothness slide down her throat.

"Lady Caroline asked if I could teach her some French," Nicolas said, draining his own glass. She saw the streaks of paint staining his long, elegant fingers. "She thinks it might be . . . useful."

"You are a miracle worker, monsieur. Caroline never wanted to learn French before, only Gaelic. I'd be happy if you could come for extra lessons."

"Then I will tell her I agree."

Katherine refilled her glass and drifted over to sit on a settee by the fireplace. "Have you ever been married, monsieur?"

"I'm afraid not," he said. He sat down in a chair across from her, and she saw that the brandy had erased the caution in his eyes. He gave her an unreadable half-smile. "I hear it is a most—how do you say? Amiable state."

Katherine laughed. She felt her own caution, her usual reserve, ebbing away. She was just a woman enjoying the company of a handsome young man. "I am not sure about that. Sometimes it must be."

"Your own husband looks as if he was a kind man." Nicolas nodded toward Lord Killinan's portrait over the fireplace. "Even though the artist was not of the best quality, he captured something good-natured about the eyes."

"Perhaps the quality was not so fine because the artist was in a hurry," said Katherine. "My husband was always impatient to be in the hunting field, and he had no time to stand still for a portrait. But he *was* kind enough." He never had a harsh word for anyone, and he gave her her daughters, her home. That made the match a success, especially in the eyes of Ascendancy Society, but not one full of excitement and fire, or even true understanding.

"I'm surprised you are not married," she said.

"My life is too unsettled for any lady to bear," he answered. "I move from post to post."

"Oh, I think a woman would put up with a great deal more than that to have you for her husband!"

He tilted his head, laughing. That laughter seemed to light him from within, making him seem even more handsome—if such a thing was possible. "Do you think so?"

"Of course."

"Well, I have not met this very patient lady yet. And I have never been in love, which I would not marry without."

"Neither have I. Been in love, that is," she said without thinking. She wished she could call back the words, especially when his eyes darkened.

"How can that be?" he said, his voice low, richly accented. "You are so very..."

"So very what?"

"Beautiful. In France, you would have been in love many times. Men would throw themselves at your feet just for a smile."

Katherine suddenly couldn't breathe. She wanted to cry at his sweet words, at the intense expression in his dark eyes as he looked at her so intently. "Men in Ireland must be different from men in France," she said.

"Then they are fools," he said fiercely. "If they are too occupied with hunting and cards and drinking to see a marvelous woman like you, then they are *imbeciles*."

She laughed shakily. "I think we have both had too much to drink, monsieur."

"*Non,* I speak only the truth." He sat down next to her on the settee, so close she could smell him and feel the heat from his tall, lean body. He was so handsome, she thought in a daze, so gloriously young and fierce and ardent. He was so very, very tempting. She had spent years being good. She hadn't realized how exhausting it was until now.

"In Paris, you would be a goddess," he said. "You would reign over the whole city, and it would light only for you. I have never seen anyone like you. If I were not who I am..."

"Then don't be." Katherine did something she never, ever thought she would—she dropped her iron control and gave in to temptation. She reached up and touched his face, tracing the line of his cheekbones and brow. He felt so warm and fair, so needful. She had never imagined there could be such a man.

"Don't be yourself, Nicolas, just for this moment," she whispered. "And I won't be Lady Killinan. I am so weary of her, weary of everything."

"What is your given name?" he said softly. He tilted his face into her touch and closed his fingers gently around her wrist.

"Katherine."

"Katherine." He kissed her palm, his open lips caressing each finger, each bit of soft, trembling skin. His eyes closed as he savored her, inhaling deeply of her perfume. In that moment, she did feel like a goddess, like Paris—and all the world—would be at their feet.

She felt such a profound, painful longing sweep over her at his kiss. She had always been puzzled by her friends when they threw themselves into passionate affairs, when they spoke in heated whispers of their rapture over some man. But now—oh, now—she understood. The ice she had spent her whole life trapped in melted away, and she was vulnerable to every emotion in the universe.

He kissed her wrist, the tip of his tongue touching the delicate pulse beating there. She rested her other hand on his head, caressing the golden silk of his hair. Her young, gorgeous god.

He turned his face up to her, and their mouths met in

a passionate kiss. There was nothing tentative or awkward about it. It was as if they had kissed a hundred times before in a dozen lifetimes, and their lips and bodies fit perfectly together. It was like coming home after a long, long journey.

Katherine parted her lips and welcomed the slide of his skillful tongue against hers. He tasted like brandy, and like himself, and she felt his breath mingle with hers, quick with excitement. It had been so long since she was kissed and never like this. Never as if she was a precious, desired being.

Nicolas groaned against her mouth, and his hands grasped her waist to carry her back down to the cushions. His weight was delicious on top of her, his body so strong and warm. She caressed his shoulders and pushed his coat away, impatient with anything that impeded her desperate touch.

"*Belle cherie,*" he muttered. His kiss traced over her cheek, along her throat to the soft skin above her silk bodice. She felt his tongue caress the swell of her breast.

Katherine felt something vital and desperate come alive inside of her. The youth she had lost in duty and motherhood, the womanhood she had denied even to herself, roared into being.

"*Tres belle, tres belle,*" he whispered. He kissed her cheek again, soft and lingering.

She clutched at his shoulders, so dizzy she feared that she would faint. She opened her eyes—and met the painted gaze of her husband. Her stolid, dull, kind husband with their home behind him in the sunny distance. *My angel Kate,* he used to tease her. *That's what they call you, you know—the Angel of Kildare. And they're right.*

Bitter despair rushed through her, colder than any icy fog. Her heedless, wonderful passion, suited to a young girl and not a respected widow, collapsed into ashes. Love belonged to the young.

She pushed frantically at Nicolas's shoulders. She had to flee, to run away and sob in private. No one could see her tears, least of all this man. This young, gorgeous, desperately unsuitable man.

"No," she whispered, pushing at him harder.

He left her immediately, scrambling to his feet. He stared down at her with dark blue eyes, his breath harsh, as if he couldn't believe what had just happened. He spun away from her and caught up his rumpled coat from the floor. His back was rigid with iron control.

Katherine slowly sat up and tugged her own clothes into place. Her hair tumbled over her shoulders like a girl's and she felt even more foolish. She couldn't pretend to be what she wasn't. She couldn't give in to what she wanted like an impulsive child and ruin everything she had created in her life.

"I'm so sorry," Nicolas said in that musical Parisian voice. "I—I will go. You won't have to see me again."

"No, no," Katherine murmured. She swung her legs off the settee and found she trembled so hard she couldn't hope to stand. "It was my fault. I was feeling a bit woeful tonight, and we had too much to drink. Please, monsieur, I don't want you to abandon your job. Caroline needs your help, and I . . ."

And she could not bear the thought of never seeing him again. Despite her foolish behavior, despite the temptation, she didn't want him to vanish into the mist.

"I need your help, too," she said. "I promise, I will not—importune you again."

"Importune?" He laughed harshly. "*Non,* madame, I think I was the one who has importuned *you.* You are so beautiful, and I—but there is no excuse."

He was—what? Katherine longed so much to know. More than anything, she wanted him to sit beside her again, to let her rest her head on his shoulder while he told her the secrets of his heart. Perhaps then the aching loneliness would ebb away, for them both.

But that couldn't be. She had her place in life, and he had his. It would only hurt them both to try and reach across that gulf again.

"Please, monsieur, return for your lesson tomorrow," she said. "I have errands to attend so I won't be here."

"If you wish it, I will come," he answered.

"I do. Please." Katherine closed her eyes and listened as the door closed softly behind him. Only then did she let her breath out, collapsing into herself. He would be back—but she had to stay away from him.

Once she was sure she could stand without falling, she retrieved her shawl from the floor along with their empty glasses. As she went to place them carefully back on the sideboard, she glanced out the window to see that it was still foggy outside. That terrible miasma that made people behave in insane ways. But surely it would be gone by morning, and she would feel like herself again.

As she stared out the window she caught a glimpse of flashing red in the gray. It looked like a running figure, dashing away from the house. A ghost, or just someone else foolish enough to be out in the night? But when she went to look closer, whatever it was had entirely vanished.

Katherine laughed at herself and her strange fancies, which were so unlike herself. "You need to get hold of yourself," she said. People were depending on her, and she could not let them, or herself, down. Never again.

Chapter Fifteen

"Will you wear the pearls, Lady Anna?"

"Hmm?" Anna murmured, startled by her maid's words. Rose had been dressing her hair in silence, leaving her free to daydream. To remember last night with Conlan in every single, burning detail. That small office, bound by the misty night and her desperate desire suddenly set free, seemed like the real world and her familiar bed-chamber the dream.

"Will you wear the pearls, my lady?" Rose repeated as she pushed the last pin into Anna's upswept coiffure. "They go so well with the gown."

Anna glanced in the mirror at the reflection of her gown, freshly pressed and hung on the wardrobe door. White again, of course, silk trimmed with fine lace.

She thought of her red dress, hidden deep under her bed. It was rather rumpled now, the hem torn and the lace damp from her mad dash through the mist. She could never give it back to Jane now.

She closed her eyes and saw Conlan's green eyes watching her as she eased the gown from her body, leaving her completely naked before him. Bare in every way, her body, her secrets, the shame of the past. Then it had seemed so necessary to lay all before him, to seek forgetfulness and refuge in his lovemaking. And she found that, and so much more, in his arms.

Now, in the light of day, in her familiar home, uncertainty crept in. Could she trust him? For she knew very well that she could not trust herself.

"Yes, the pearls," she said. She would look the perfectly respectable debutante for Grant Dunmore's party. No one would imagine that she spent last night playing Adair's doxy.

The door suddenly flew open, and Caroline rushed in. She wore her pale blue muslin evening gown, but her white satin sash was untied and her hair not yet dressed.

"Caro, you will be very late," Anna said.

"I know, and we don't want to make a bad impression on your favorite suitor. But I need to borrow your blue shawl."

"Of course, if you'll let me dress first." As Anna stood to let Rose help her into her gown, Caroline plopped down at the foot of the bed as if she was in no hurry to leave or finish her own toilette. Anna didn't mind. Company kept her from thinking too much.

"Is it true Sir Grant has a large library of old manuscripts?" Caroline asked.

"I have no idea," Anna answered. She smoothed the lacy cap sleeves over her shoulders. "He doesn't seem especially scholarly. Where did you hear that?"

"I saw Lord Hartley in the bookshop a few days ago, and he told me Sir Grant's father was a great collector of works on ancient Ireland. I haven't heard of any sale, so perhaps they are still in his library."

"Ah, yes, your future husband, Lord Hartley," Anna teased. "You'll just have to ask Sir Grant."

"If he does have such a collection, your marriage to him could be most beneficial."

"That's what I live for," murmured Anna. "To be beneficial to you, Caro." She felt a twinge of irritation that everyone seemed to think her engagement to Grant Dunmore was a *fait accompli*. It was far from that, especially since she had made love with Conlan, Grant's cousin and his enemy. But she couldn't forget what a good, safe choice Grant could be. "He has not even made an offer, though."

"He will, I'm sure." Caroline gave her a searching look. "If you want him to, that is."

"Everyone seems sure I should."

"Sure you should do what?" Katherine said. She swept into the room dressed in her bronze-colored satin and lace, a leather box in her hands. "My goodness, it looks as if my girls are having a party in here!"

Anna examined her mother's face as Rose twitched her hem into place and fastened the pearl necklace around her neck. Katherine looked pale today, her smile strained. It wasn't like her usual calm serenity, but perhaps it was just another sign of the uncertainty they all lived with these days. Maybe a wedding would be the distraction Katherine needed, the prospect of one less daughter to worry about.

"Caro thinks I should marry Sir Grant," Anna said. "She heard he possesses a fine collection of manuscripts."

"I'm sure that is not the only thing to recommend him," said Katherine.

Anna laughed. "To Caro it is."

"That will make finding a husband for Caroline much easier then." Katherine set her box on the dressing table and tugged Caroline off the bed. She briskly tied her daughter's sash and smoothed her rumpled sleeves. "Go get your maid to finish your hair, dear, we must leave very soon. The carriage is ordered for eight."

Caroline dashed away, grumbling, and Katherine sent Rose after her, saying she would help Anna finish.

"Is something wrong, Mama?" Anna asked as her mother closed the door.

"Not at all. I just brought you something. A little gift." Katherine took the box from the table and handed it to her.

Anna lifted the lid and exhaled sharply. The diamonds and pearls of her grandmother's tiara sparkled up at her. "Mama! Grandmother's tiara?"

"Yes. You seemed to enjoy it when you wore it to the queen's birthday ball a couple of years ago. I thought it was time it went into your safekeeping."

"I remember that ball," Anna said. It was the last grand occasion at Dublin Castle before the Uprising. A lavish show of British and Ascendancy power, glittering and cold. "But surely this is much too valuable to give into *my* hands. I am the unreliable daughter, am I not?"

Katherine laughed. "You will appreciate its beauty much more than Eliza or Caroline ever could. Besides, soon enough you will be a married lady, a Society hostess in your own right. You will have need of it then."

Anna stared down at the sparkling jewels and felt their full weight bearing down on her. They meant so much more than mere diamonds and pearls. They meant her family name, going back generations, and all it stood for.

The power and expectation of position—and the falseness of it. Everything she had been running from was catching up to her. Soon she would stumble and fall, and that expected life would catch her.

"Mama," she said. "Do you want me to marry Grant Dunmore, if he makes an offer?"

Katherine gently smoothed a curl back from Anna's cheek. Her hand was soft and cool, and she smelled of lily perfume. It made Anna achingly remember childhood, and the illusory safety of the nursery at Killinan Castle. Back then, she was sure nothing could touch her because her mother, an angel, watched over her.

She looked up at her mother and saw that Katherine's face was pale and thin, her eyes shadowed with concern. Perhaps now it was Anna's turn to take care of *her,* and of Caroline, too.

"I want you to be happy and secure," Katherine said. "I want that for all my girls."

"Is Eliza happy and secure?"

Katherine laughed again, shaking her head. "She is most assuredly happy. I am not sure she will ever be secure."

"And you will always worry about her?"

"Of course. She is my daughter." Her palm smoothed over Anna's cheek. "I worry about you, too."

Anna reached up and caught her mother's hand in her own. "There is no need to worry, Mama, for I am quite well. I will make the right decision, and I will make you proud."

"Darling, I *am* proud of you! How could I not be? I just worry at times that perhaps because of—of what happened..."

Anna froze. "With that soldier, you mean?"

Katherine's hand tightened. "Yes. That it might make you frightened of marriage."

"No. It was so long ago. And I know marriage is very—different than that. I saw you and Papa, who were so happy, and Eliza and Will, and I know what it can be." She could never tell her mother the truth—that in Adair's arms, his bed, she had found the joy of sex and left the violence of that long-ago moment behind. That with him, she had been free for one precious night.

Anna closed the lid on the box and gave her mother a smile. "Please, Mama, don't worry about me. I promise I will do as you wish."

"Anna," Katherine said uncertainly, "I fear you might have mistaken my words...."

Anna shook her head. "I haven't. I will be happy and secure. I will marry, and have children, and wear this tiara to grand balls so that everyone will say I am the queen of Ireland, your worthy daughter. I will even help you look after Caroline. I haven't been much use to you, but I will be now, I promise."

"I want you to promise me you will be happy."

"I will."

"Then that is all I need." Katherine kissed her cheek. "Are you ready for the party? I fear we will be late and that will never do."

"Of course." And she was. She was ready, at long last, to face the future.

$\mathcal{B}$

Katherine paused by the window to see if the carriage was ready and was caught by a flash of movement in the gathering darkness. It was Nicolas Courtois, leaving after Caroline's lesson. The collar of his coat was drawn up against the cold wind, but he wore no hat and his pale hair shimmered. He paused before crossing the street, and she saw his perfect profile etched in the gloom, like an ancient prince on a coin. Yet his brow was furrowed as if he concealed dark thoughts. Then he strode across the street and vanished into the night.

Katherine released a breath she hadn't even realized she held. She curled her hands into tight fists, as if she could physically fight away the feelings that took hold of her whenever she saw him. They were such overpowering, unfamiliar emotions—lust, tenderness, need. For a young Frenchman! She hated that terrible sensation of not being in control.

She counseled Anna to be cautious, to seek happiness in security and duty, yet it seemed she could no longer do the same for herself.

She stared at the empty spot where he had stood, seeing again his tall figure and his handsome face. His sad eyes. Each time they met since that crazy interlude in the library, they were painfully polite and correct. He reported on Caroline's progress and she remarked on the weather, and they parted after a few minutes, having barely even looked at each other.

Yet all the time, she remembered the feel of his lips on hers. The music of his voice that made her tremble. Yes, she wanted him, longed for him. When she was a girl, before her dutiful marriage, her staid, faithful years with Lord Killinan where her house and her children were her consolations, she had dreamed of someone like Nicolas Courtois. Someone handsome, tender, artistic, and passionate.

He had never appeared then, and she thought such a man could only live in dreams. And she had given up on dreams long ago.

Why, oh why, did her dreams come to life *now,* when they could never be?

She pounded her fists against the windowsill, glad of the stinging pain that brought her back to herself. She needed a reminder of the costs of being foolishly romantic.

"Mama? Is something wrong?" she heard Caroline say.

Katherine pasted a smile on her lips and turned to see her daughter hurrying down the corridor. Her sash was untied again. "Of course nothing is wrong."

"You were frowning so fiercely. I thought you must have seen something outside that displeased you."

Displeased her? Far from it—unfortunately. "I was just checking on the weather before we set out."

"Is it foggy again?"

Katherine remembered that fog, the thick cloud of gray mist that enclosed her and Nicolas in the library and made them forget everything. "No, thankfully. It should be a pleasant evening for Sir Grant's party."

She drew Caroline to her and set about retying the errant sash. "Caroline, dearest, how are you enjoying your art lessons?"

"Very much, Mama. Monsieur Courtois is showing me the best way to accurately transcribe images from old, faded parchment, and we're studying ancient pigmentation methods," Caroline said enthusiastically. "He knows so very much. It's quite fascinating."

"So you don't want to give them up after all?"

Caroline laughed. "I was very silly to protest against

them. Drawing is very useful, not like dancing and embroidery. And I like Monsieur Courtois. He loves art so much, and he is very good at teaching it without shouting, as the nasty old dancing master does." She paused. "Why? Is something amiss? Is Monsieur Courtois leaving?"

"No, not if you want him to stay." As Katherine wanted him to stay, so desperately much it was almost a physical pain. Even if nothing more could happen, she wanted to see him, to make sure he was well. "I'm glad you enjoy your lessons."

"I do." Caroline turned around, smoothing her unruly hair back into its combs. "Mama, is Anna going to marry Sir Grant?"

"I do not know, dearest. That is up to her—and him. I don't think he has asked her yet. He certainly hasn't come to me to ask permission."

"He will, though. But does she *want* to say yes?"

Katherine sighed. "I don't know," she said again. It seemed she didn't really know anything any longer. Not even herself.

Chapter Sixteen

If there is any house that requires a tiara, it is surely this one, Anna thought as she examined Grant Dunmore's dining room. Whatever had driven him to seek the Adair estate, it was not need of money.

The dining room, and its adjacent drawing room, were vast, pale spaces filled with ornate plasterwork that scrolled around valuable paintings and surrounded ceiling frescoes of classical scenes. Grecian statues reposed in specially fitted niches, and yellow brocade draped the windows in lavish poofs and swirls. The furniture was all matching yellow and white satin, French gilt, and Venetian glasswork. Lush carpets lay thickly over the flagstone and parquet floors.

Anna stared down the length of the polished mahogany table where the lavishness of the cuisine, laid out on silver and porcelain platters, matched the beauty of the furnishings. Candlelight gleamed on the heavy silverware and the vases full of hothouse roses. A sparkling Waterford chandelier swayed overhead, presiding over the loud laughter of the company, laughter surely fueled by the free-flowing fine wines. The distinguished guests, the highest nobility, politicians, churchmen, and famous beauties, partook of all that was offered so generously by their host.

Grant Dunmore himself sat at the head of the table, impossibly handsome in that sparkling light. He belonged in that elegant setting. It was his perfect domain, one he ran so smoothly with a mere nod of his head or a gesture of his hand. Even though his aunt, Lady Thornton, sitting at the foot of the table with her ear trumpet, was nominally the hostess, she did nothing to aid the gaiety and perfection of the night. It was all Grant.

What she could do with such a place, Anna thought, if it was hers. She had been trained all her life to be a fine hostess, to plan soirees and run a household just like this. With a man such as Grant Dunmore, she could lead Society and make an invitation to this house the most sought-after in Ireland.

That seemed to be what her mother wanted for her, what she ought to want for herself. But was it really?

She prodded at her food with her heavy silver fork, noting how carefully its etched pattern matched the hand-painted china. It was all so painstakingly planned, so false—so useless.

Suddenly, she saw Conlan's dark face in her mind, heard his laughter as they sat together in that rough tavern. She longed to be *there,* with him! Even when they were in danger together, when she didn't understand him at all, she felt ten times more alive, more vital, more needed, than she did here.

Where are you, Conlan? she thought. *What are you doing?*

She prayed that wherever he was, he was safe and

taking care of himself. Or maybe the pretty faro dealer at the Olympian Club did that for him?

"My heavens, Anna," she heard Jane say from across the table. "I do hope that chicken fricassee has not mortally offended you."

Anna glanced up at her friend. The candlelight, so soft and mellow-gold on everyone else, seemed to turn Jane to pure fire. Her green satin gown, along with the emerald combs in her red hair and the diamonds dangling from her ears, sparkled blindingly.

Anna wondered idly if she could borrow that beautiful dress. After the mess she made of the red gown, she doubted it. But it was so much finer than boring white.

"It is quite delicious," she said. "I just seem to have no appetite tonight."

"You need more wine then." Jane nodded to one of the footmen who immediately stepped forward to refill Anna's glass. The man's yellow satin livery and powdered wig gleamed, another touch of perfection in Grant's house.

"It *is* very fine," Anna said. She sipped at the dry, golden-white liquid, hoping it would drown her melancholy.

"Only the best for Sir Grant's house," Jane said. "It is beautifully arranged, don't you think? So very fashionable."

"It needs a mistress," Lady Thornton suddenly cried. Her ear trumpet trembled in her hand. "Someone to look after it all."

"Someone to pay the bills?" the man to Anna's left, Lord Melton, whispered.

Anna glanced down the table to Sir Grant, to see if he heard them. He gave her a smile and raised his glass to her in a little toast.

"Is he in some sort of trouble?" Anna whispered back. "He seems quite comfortable."

Lord Melton, who had consumed a great deal of that fine wine, took another deep drink. "Appearances are worth all in our fair city, don't you agree, Lady Anna? And Sir Grant is better than most at upholding them. He has political ambitions, you know, and those do not come cheap."

"Surely he has chosen an auspicious moment for such ambitions," Anna said, thinking of rumors of the immense bribes the British government handed out in exchange for support of the Union.

"If one chooses the correct side," Lord Melton said, taking another drink. "These are uncertain days, Lady Anna. Matters could go either way."

Uncertain days—to say the least. Anna sipped at her own wine, unsure what to say.

"A wife," Lady Thornton announced. "That is exactly what my nephew needs. A rich wife."

ℬ𝒟

Caroline slipped into Grant Dunmore's library, away from the false laughter and brightness of the party and into a silent realm of books and solitude. Only when she inhaled the wondrously familiar scents of paper and leather could she relax again. Anna and their mother were always so good at parties, at being gracious and sociable and charming. To Caroline, soirees were a miserable business.

She straightened her spectacles and examined the room. It was not as large as the library at the Henrietta Street house, but the walls were completely lined with floor-to-ceiling shelves filled with rows and rows of enticing books. Beneath the tall, narrow windows were flat glass cases filled with an array of objects. There was not much furniture, but what there was looked comfortable and inviting, chairs and cassocks upholstered in worn green velvet. Everything was lit by a crackling fire in the grate.

Caroline loved it. It was the perfect refuge from the gossip and card playing. She drifted over to the largest shelf and examined the leather-bound volumes. Plato, Petrarch, Shakespeare.

"Perhaps Sir Grant is not merely a sporting man after all," she murmured as she spotted a thick volume of Herodotus in the original Greek. There were also the works of French *philosophes* and English scientists, treatises on agricultural methods and animal husbandry.

Most intriguingly, there was a row of books on Irish mythology. Caroline slid one from its place and thumbed through it, all those beloved stories of Cuchulain and Maeve and dark gods and goddesses and fairies. The pages were all cut, and it seemed well-read.

Sir Grant pretended to be not at all interested in Ireland, like all his crass Ascendancy cohorts. He seemed to seek only land and rent rolls, and the power they brought. Was it all some kind of act? To what end?

Caroline put the book back in its place. She was better off studying history; it was much easier to understand than men. Especially men like Grant Dunmore.

She went to examine the glass cases. There were bits of Greek and Roman antiquities, small alabaster statues, coins, and gold and amber jewelry, as well as beautifully decorated medieval prayer books. A small antique cross gleamed with old rubies and pearls.

But there were also Irish objects. A brooch in the shape

of a serpent with emerald eyes. A gold goblet etched with an intricate knotwork pattern. And a small book, open to one page.

Caroline leaned closer to make out the faded words scrolled across the vellum between a twisting blue-green dragon. It was in Gaelic, and rather dim, but she made out *"Ne ceart go cur...."* and the words *"Giniuint Mhuire gan Smal 923."*

"Oh, blast," she whispered, staring down at the book in stunned disbelief. *"The Chronicle of Kildare.* It can't be."

"So you found my treasure," Grant Dunmore said from behind her.

Caroline had been so preoccupied with the book that she hadn't even heard the door open. She spun around, her heart pounding in surprise. He leaned in the doorway, all casual grace in his fashionable evening clothes, his arms loosely crossed over his chest. But he watched her closely.

"I'm sorry if I'm not meant to be in here," she said, her mouth suddenly dry. She usually had no trouble talking to men; most of them cared only to natter on about hunting or cards and required only nods and smiles for their monologues. That was convenient, for it gave her time for her own thoughts.

Grant pretended to be just like them, but she had the growing suspicion that he wasn't at all. He was always watching when he thought no one paid attention, always listening. This most erudite collection of books and artifacts confirmed it. There had to be more to that old scandal of the Adair estate than met the eye.

More to *him*.

"I just needed a quiet moment away from the party," she finished.

"I don't blame you a bit, Lady Caroline," he said amiably. "These gatherings can be quite tedious. Always the same people, saying the same things."

"But this is your own party!"

"Even worse. I am aiding and abetting dullness."

Caroline turned back to the glass case, staring down at the beautiful, priceless little book. It was less disturbing than his strange, golden-brown eyes. "You are the host. Surely you could turn them in a more amusing direction?"

She heard him push away from the door, the soft slide of his shoes on the thick carpet. He reminded her of the tiger that she once saw in a menagerie, beautiful, elegant, seemingly lazy, but able to turn deadly in the blink of an eye.

Anna was surely in trouble if she did marry him.

"Have *you* tried to turn Lady Thornton from talking about the fashion in turbans?" he said. He leaned his palms on the edge of the case, right beside her. He gave her an amused little half-smile.

She could see all too well why half the ladies in Dublin were in love with him. That smile did the strangest things to her own thoughts, making them feel all twisted and turned in her mind. Yet she could not shake away those suspicions that it was all some kind of façade.

Dublin was a city of façades, of codes and false words and hidden alliances. Perhaps that was why she preferred the faraway past, when Ireland was a land of clans and warlords, battles and doomed romances. Clear alliances.

"I see what you mean, Sir Grant," she said. "Turning Lady Thornton from turbans would be beyond human endeavor. Even Cuchulain would have been foiled by the perambulations of her conversation."

"You were quite right to take refuge in here," he answered. "I often feel the need to escape myself."

"It is your fault I neglect my social duties now, you know."

"Oh? How so?"

"By creating such a perfect sanctuary as this." She waved her hand around the lovely library. "It's such a wondrous room, Sir Grant."

"I am quite flattered, Lady Caroline, for you are said to be quite the expert on libraries."

"I have found refuge in one or two in my time. You have a fascinating collection." She looked back down at *The Chronicle of Kildare.* "Especially this."

"It is my greatest treasure. You have a very discerning eye."

"*The Chronicle of Kildare,* written by a monk named Brother Michael in the 900s and hidden away from the Vikings with the other treasures of his monastery. I thought there was only one in existence, the copy at Trinity College. And they would never let a mere woman see it. I have had to make do with old translations, and they are so unreliable."

"There are actually three originals that I know of," Grant said. There was none of the usual fashionable ennui in his voice, only a shy sort of pride. Caroline found it dangerously appealing. "The one at Trinity, which is where I first heard of it when I was at school there, and one owned by a French marquis, which vanished in the Revolution. And this one."

"Wherever did you get it?"

"I fear that must remain my secret, Lady Caroline." He took a small silver key from a box on the mantel and unlocked the case. Caroline watched, wonder-struck, as he carefully removed the book and held it out to her. "Would you care to look at it more closely?"

She had never wanted anything more in her life. Her hands trembled with the force of her desire to touch it. "May I really?"

"Of course." He gently took her hand and laid the volume on her palm.

The calfskin cover, dyed green and lettered in gold, was soft and cool on her skin. She drew it toward her, carefully turning over the vellum page. It told the tale of an ancient battle in Kildare, one where the beleaguered forces of the heroic King Connor were saved by the timely intervention of a dragon. Among the fanciful mythology was much real history, long thought lost in the mists of time.

The letters were faded to a reddish-brown, but the carefully detailed illustrations were still bright, touched with bits of gold leaf and precious lapis.

"Oh," Caroline sighed. "It is the most beautiful thing I have ever seen, Sir Grant."

He laughed. "Lady Caroline, I have never seen a woman so happy, even when she has just been given diamonds."

"This is far better than any diamond."

"I agree. Most people wouldn't think so, though. They would say it is only an old book, an Irish one at that."

"Then they are great fools."

"Perhaps. Or perhaps *we* are the fools, giving so much for a bit of leather and paper." He drew out the chair behind the desk. "Here, sit. Take a closer look at it."

Caroline was most happy to oblige. She laid the book

reverently on the smooth wood, reading more of the dragon battle as Grant sat down beside her. "But it is so much more than bits of paper, isn't it? It's history and life. When I think of the man who wrote these words, hundreds of years ago, I feel connected to him and to what happened here so long ago. Connected to anyone who ever read this story and was moved by it. It shows we are part of something bigger than ourselves and this present moment."

"Yes, I know. Perhaps that is why I wanted this book so much. To show myself I am part of this land, just as King Connor and Brother Michael were. That perhaps I have something to contribute to it."

Startled, Caroline looked up at him over the pages. "Who are you and what have you done with Grant Dunmore?"

He laughed and shook his head. When he turned back to her, that shy pride she found so very appealing was gone. The Sir Grant everyone knew—cynical, sophisticated, careless—was back. And she felt the sharp sting of disappointment. Their moment of connection, so brief yet so real, had vanished.

"Perhaps I am just greedy, like everyone else in Dublin," he said. "Perhaps I just like to possess things."

"I wouldn't mind possessing *this*," Caroline murmured. She gently touched the gilt edge of the pages before carefully closing the *Chronicle* and handing it back to him.

His hand closed around hers, his touch cool and strong. Caroline found she wanted to twine her fingers with his, to feel his touch grow tighter and warmer. Despite his changeable nature, all his secrets—or perhaps because of them—she was so intrigued by him.

"Maybe soon we will be family, and then you can read

the *Chronicle,* or any of my books, whenever you like," he said.

At the reminder that he was practically her sister's fiancé, icy water was doused on Caroline's intrigue. She dropped his hand. "That is very kind of you. Thank you for letting me see the *Chronicle.* It's beautiful."

Grant took the volume and placed it back in its case. As Caroline watched in sadness, he locked it up and pocketed the key. "I would show it to your sister if I thought it would impress her."

Caroline laughed. "Anna reads poetry and novels, but she is not much interested in history or mythology. She makes fun of my studies."

"Oh?" He leaned back on the edge of the case, all lazy grace again. "What do you think *would* impress her?"

"Sir Grant, you are one of the most sought-after gentlemen in Dublin," she said bluntly, suddenly impatient with his game playing. She was also angry at herself for being drawn to his scholarly pride, for what she had imagined this collection said about him. "All the ladies are in love with you. Surely she is impressed already."

He arched his brow, which made him look like a quizzical young Celtic warrior from the *Chronicle* itself. "All the ladies?"

"Well, at least half of them."

"But not the so-very-hard-to-impress Blacknall sisters?"

Obviously one of the Blacknall sisters was not so hard to impress. Caroline was drawn in by the mere sight of a rare book. "If she did not like you, she would say so. Anna is very honest." Usually. Though Anna, too, had seemed quiet and secretive lately. Everyone was infected by the uncertainty of the times.

"Then I am glad to hear I may have a chance after all."

"I could put in a good word for you," Caroline teased. "I can easily be bribed with old manuscripts."

"I will remember that for the future," he said with a laugh.

She longed to ask him what his true feelings were for her sister. Did he care for Anna, not just for her dowry and connections and beauty? Did he even know her at all? Would he be a good husband to her, or would they lead their own separate lives, as so many fashionable couples did?

Her sister deserved a good match, a man who knew and appreciated her. And Caroline was sure any man with a library like this deserved the same.

"You should go back to your guests," she said. "You are the host, and I have monopolized your time long enough."

"Of course I should return, Lady Caroline, though I can't remember when I have so enjoyed being—monopolized. Shall I escort you back to the drawing room?"

"No, thank you. Luckily for me, I have no pressing social duties at the moment. I'll just sit here with the books a bit longer."

"Lucky indeed. Please stay as long as you like." He left the room, shutting the door behind him, and Caroline lowered her head to the desk.

She wished she could just stay with books all the time. With careful study, any conundrum could be solved within their pages. People she could never decipher, no matter how long she puzzled over them.

Once she could dismiss Grant Dunmore as a very handsome, very sophisticated, idle man of Society. Now she had no idea what he was. But idle he was not.

After several long, quiet moments she finally felt calm

again. Grant Dunmore was Anna's problem, but the Blacknalls were a close family. They shared each other's problems, which meant Caroline would keep a close watch on Grant in the future.

She straightened her skirts, which always seemed to be rumpled, and her hair, which always seemed to escape its pins. She would never be the elegant beauties her mother and sisters were. Then she left the library, closing the door on all its wondrous treasures.

As she made her way down the corridor toward the drawing room, she thought she heard voices. Low, urgent murmurs from the shadows. She certainly did not want to interrupt some tryst by bumping into the secretive couple. She would just slip quietly into the drawing room.

But she was brought up short by a quick glimpse of the people who hid behind one of the marble pillars. Grant Dunmore's beautiful bronze-brown hair glowed, quite unmistakable. His head was bent toward a woman as he whispered intimately in her ear, and his hand splayed across her back to draw her closer.

The woman was not Anna, but Lady Cannondale in her distinctive green gown. She tilted her head back as she listened to him, a knowing smile on her lips. As Caroline watched, flabbergasted, Lady Cannondale touched his cheek. Her gloved hand slid slowly down his throat to toy with his cravat. It was a familiar, casual caress.

Caroline bit her lip hard to keep from shouting in protest. She might be buried in her books most of the time, but she was not a complete fool about how the world worked. This was certainly no chance meeting between these two, Anna's almost-fiancé and her friend. The way they touched showed they were very intimate indeed.

The bastard, Caroline thought bitterly as she tiptoed away. They were so occupied with each other that they did not even notice anyone else was there. And with Anna in the very next room!

She wanted to scream at them and to beat Grant Dunmore over the head with one of his own books. Such a villain did not deserve a treasure like the *Chronicle of Kildare,* and he certainly did not deserve her sister. Yet such impulsive action would only draw attention and cause embarrassment to her sister. Anna had suffered enough pain in her life already.

The best thing, the only thing, Caroline could do was make sure her sister never married Grant Dunmore. Which meant the *Chronicle of Kildare*, glimpsed for one sweet moment, was lost to her.

She didn't even want to think of the sharp twinge of disappointment that she felt over the man himself. For a few moments there in the library, she thought she glimpsed his true self, a sensitive scholar and collector, he never showed to anyone. But it had all been playacting.

Everything in their lives was always playacting. Only the world found in books was real. She couldn't forget that again.

She stepped into the drawing room and forced a smile onto her lips. It wouldn't do for anyone to see something was amiss. Anna, who played a game of piquet with Lord Melton, called out, "Caro, there you are! Hiding in the library again?"

"Yes," Caroline answered. "It was rather dull though, no interesting volumes at all."

"I'm not surprised, considering the library belongs to Sir Grant," said Melton, Anna's partner. He sounded a bit unsteady, as if he had consumed too much wine. "I doubt he reads anything but the racing papers."

"Well, I am having a very good evening," Anna said happily. "Luck is with me tonight, so I can buy you your own new book to soothe your disappointment."

"Just be careful, Anna," Caroline warned. "Luck has a way of turning, I fear."

"Not tonight!" said Anna.

Caroline smiled at her and went to sit with their mother, who talked to Lord Hartley by the fire. How she did like Hartley! He was good, kind, and a bit dull but full of the love of scholarship, with no hidden angles so sharp they could cut. They could build a content life together, she was sure of it.

And if he never made her heart pound like Grant Dunmore—well, that was all for the best. She didn't need such distractions in her life at all.

Chapter Seventeen

Anna pulled the hood of her cloak closer around her face as she hurried down the street. There was no fog that night, but the wind was biting, sweeping off the river and up the lanes like a furious ghost. She also didn't want anyone to recognize her, though there were few people out and about at that hour. She had the hackney leave her at the corner so she could walk to the Olympian Club, and thus give herself a few moments to think.

When they returned from Grant Dunmore's house, she had retired to bed as a sensible person should, yet she couldn't sleep. She lay there in the dark, her mind racing with all she *should* do, all she probably *would* do in the end—and all she really wanted deep in her heart.

She knew what her mother wanted from her. She wanted her to marry Grant Dunmore, to be mistress of his fine townhouse and his country estate, and take her place as a leader of Society. With Eliza's exile and Caroline set on marrying fusty old Lord Hartley and being a blue-stocking, Katherine deserved one daughter convention-ally settled. Anna had spent two years getting into trouble and causing gossip. Perhaps it was time that she thought of what she owed her family.

Tonight's party had shown her a glimpse of what her future life would be as Lady Dunmore: parties, chatter, an elegant home, a handsome, charming husband. A husband who had a streak of ruthlessness behind his so-handsome face. A man had to be ruthless to try and use the unjust Penal Laws to snatch the estate from his own kinsman.

But was Adair any better, any less ruthless, in going after what he wanted? He certainly had his share of secrets.

She had terrible judgment in men, it was true. Both were less than sensible choices, Adair least of all. Yet something kept pulling her back to him.

And that was why she crept out of her house in the middle of the night again. She wanted to see him once more in the wild hope that she could see clearly at last. She would know what to do, as if by magic.

Highly unlikely, of course, but here she was making her way, half-bold and half-fearful, to the Olympian Club. But the club seemed to be closed.

Anna stood by the low wrought-iron fence around the elegant gray-stone building and stared up at its darkened windows. It was silent tonight, no one coming or going at all, and the knocker was muffled.

"Blast it all," she muttered. She didn't know where Conlan might actually live and wasn't sure where to look for him now. She went up the steps and pounded on the door with her fist, to no avail.

She didn't want to just slink back home. Not yet. She drew her cloak closer around her and slipped back down the steps and to the back of the building. There was a small garden and a terrace, perfect for clandestine meetings, yet they were also deserted. Even the servant's entrance was locked.

"So much for my spy work," Anna muttered. And so much for that overwhelming desire to see Conlan tonight. Feeling quite foolish, she made her way back to the street to find another hackney and go home.

Just as she turned the corner, the door opened, and Conlan stepped out into the night. He wore a caped great-coat and wide-brimmed hat, a scarf muffling his lower face, but she knew it was him. No one else was so tall with such broad shoulders; no one else walked with such confidence. He glanced down the street, and then set off at a brisk pace.

Impulsively, Anna took off after him. Where was he going so secretly? Cursing her curiosity, she followed him at a discreet distance, keeping to the shadows.

Once or twice he glanced back, and she was sure she would be discovered, yet he always kept going on his mysterious path. He went from the quiet, elegant lanes back toward the neighborhood of McMasters's tavern. The streets narrowed and darkened, and the cobblestones were damp and slippery under her boots. Was he just going for a drink then?

He turned not to the tavern but down another street, a narrow alley between tall houses. Anna dared not follow there; he would be sure to notice her in such a confined space. She lingered at the alley's entrance and peeked around the corner as he knocked at a door. After a moment, a man answered. A flickering candle in his hand cast a glow over his face and rumpled hair as he peered out cautiously.

Anna pressed her hand hard to her mouth so she would not cry out. It was Monsieur Courtois, Caroline's gorgeous new drawing teacher! How did he, a Frenchman who made his living teaching, know Adair? Why were they meeting?

"Were you followed?" Courtois said. His voice was low and furtive, but it echoed on the alley's close-packed walls.

"No," Adair answered. "Nothing of consequence."

"Come in." The door closed, and Anna was alone again in the eerily quiet night. Once she was sure they were gone, she ran down the alley to examine the house. There was one small window by the door, but it was barred and muffled by dark curtains. She couldn't even make out a single ray of light.

She longed to rattle the bars, to pound on the door and shout at them, to demand answers! They were in some terrible conspiracy, Adair and Courtois, she was sure of it. If only she could be sure it was not something horribly dangerous to her own family.

She had the cold feeling that it was, and that she was already deeply involved in ways she couldn't even fathom. Yet.

She went back to wait at the mouth of the alley for Conlan to re-emerge. She would follow him back to the Olympian Club and make him talk to her, one way or another.

She didn't have very long to wait. After less than an hour—though to Anna it felt like a year—he came out and went on his way. He didn't go straight back to the club but turned toward the river. She followed him along the embankment, hard-pressed to keep up with his long-limbed pace.

She was so intent on him that she didn't see the other shadows until they suddenly emerged from behind an upturned fishing boat. There were two of them, and they moved like a swift mist rolling off the river. One grabbed Conlan around the neck, dragging him back as the other unsheathed a dagger. The starlight glinted along the lethal steel.

"Conlan!" Anna screamed as the dagger lunged toward his chest. She ran forward, heedless of any danger to herself in her terror. He drove his elbow hard into the belly of the man who held him, shoving him to the ground. His boot shot up toward the one with the knife, obviously aiming for his groin.

But the assailant leaped back, Conlan's kick landing on his leg. The man staggered and quickly recovered, diving toward Conlan with the dagger. In the blink of an eye, that shining steel sank into Conlan's shoulder, past wool and linen, into flesh.

"Bloody hell!" he shouted. He pressed his hand to the wound, struggling to stay upright as his attacker tried to stab him again.

Anna drove herself into the villain, hard, sending him flying back to the cobblestones. The dagger clattered to the ground, and she kicked it into the water. As she spun around to face Conlan, the man he had shoved to the ground hauled himself to his feet. He, too, held a knife, and she caught a glimpse of the raw, violent fury on his scarred face.

"Conlan, behind you!" she screamed.

Conlan drew a small pistol from inside his coat, and in one smooth motion spun around and fired. The man collapsed, silent, a dark stain spreading over his chest. His co-conspirator fled.

Anna, her blood boiling with anger, started to run after him, but a gasp from Conlan stopped her. "Anna," he muttered in a voice tight with pain. "My avenging witch."

She twirled back to him, just in time to see him fall to the ground. "Conlan!"

She knelt beside him on the cold stone and unfastened his coat with shaking hands. His shirt was torn and stained with blood, and she could smell the tang of it, wet and coppery. Her head whirled with the stench, with the terrible memories it summoned up. But his touch on her wrist drew her immediately back into the present crisis.

She tore off his cravat and wadded it up to press tightly to the wound. The blood still seeped through, faster than she could staunch it.

"We have to get you to a doctor," she said.

"No, not a doctor," he insisted. "We'll go back to the club."

"You can't walk that far!"

"Of course I can. This is just a scratch. I've walked farther with worse."

Anna remembered that ruined stable during the Uprising and the stained bandage around his leg. "You're a damnably stubborn Irishman, Conlan."

"And you're a double-damned stubborn Irishwoman. What are you doing here?"

She tore a strip from the hem of her petticoat to bind around his shoulder. The bleeding seemed to be slowing, but she didn't like how pale he looked, ashen under the brown of his skin. "I wanted to talk to you."

"So you followed me around the city in the middle of the night?"

"Yes. Didn't you know I was there?"

He shook his head. "I thought it was just those two villains."

"You knew about them? Why didn't you do something?"

"I wanted to see what they would do first. You shouldn't be here."

"If I wasn't, it would have been two against one, and they would have killed you for certain."

"True enough," he said grudgingly. "Thank you."

"You're very welcome."

"But that doesn't change the fact that it was foolish for you to be out tonight," he said.

"I'm not the only fool here, I think." Anna took his face in her hands and stared deep into his eyes. "What game do you play at, Conlan McTeer?"

He tried to turn from her, but she held firm. She was tired of always not knowing. "What do men get up to in a city on a cold winter's night, *cailleach*? Cards, whoring, drinking..."

"I am not so stupid as all that. If you wanted that, you could get it at your own club. You were up to none of those things, not tonight. You were meeting with a Frenchman."

"A friend," he said stubbornly. Yet she could see he was in pain, no matter how he tried to hide it, and she had to get him away from there.

"You do play dangerous games, Conlan, and I will find out what they are."

He grabbed her wrists, his fingers like iron. "No, Anna. Just stay away. You can't be part of this."

Except she already was, whether they liked it or not. "Come on, we have to go back to the club. It's cold out here, and you are still bleeding."

She slid her arm around his shoulders and supported him as he stood. He leaned on her for a moment, but then he twisted away. As she watched him, he knelt down by the body. Quickly, he looked through the man's pockets, which proved to be empty, then he shoved him into the river. The body made barely a splash before sinking out of sight.

"What's this?" a woman cried from the top of the Olympian Club stairs. Anna looked up to see it was the pretty faro dealer, her hair loose over her shoulders, clad in a velvet dressing gown.

She *was* very pretty and wandering around the club in dishabille. Anna had only an instant to feel jealous, though, as Conlan leaned heavily against her shoulder.

At first on their slow journey across the city, he had stubbornly refused her help. As he continued to lose blood, though, and grew paler, he had started to lean on her. She held him tightly, her arm wound around his waist.

"He was attacked on the street," Anna said honestly. "And he refused to go to a doctor."

"Attacked by whom?" Sarah ran down the stairs and took Conlan's other arm. Between them, they managed to haul him up the stairs.

"I don't know. And the villain can't introduce himself because he is dead now."

"You were there? You saw it all?" Reaching the top of the stairs, she led them toward an open doorway.

"She saved me," Conlan muttered, shaking off his stupor.

The woman's eyes met Anna's, wide with some sort of shocked realization. "Did she? How heroic."

"Heroics will be no use unless we can stop the bleeding," Anna said. "I still say we need a doctor...."

"No doctor!" Conlan yelled.

"No need to shout," said Anna, trying to stay calm. Hysterics would help no one. She tried to think of her mother, of her reassuringly serene demeanor as she nursed sick servants and tenants. "You'll make the bleeding even worse."

"I have medicines and bandages," Sarah said. They deposited Conlan on a bed, the covers still drawn neatly over the feather mattress. With no fire in the grate, the small chamber was cold, but a lamp was lit on the bedside table. "There are always silly fights and accidents in a gaming club. I'll go fetch them."

She hurried away, and Anna set about trying to make Conlan comfortable. She tugged off his wet boots and carefully peeled away his ruined coat and shirt. The makeshift bandage was soaked through, and she replaced it with the rest of her petticoat. He started to shiver, so she spread her own cloak over him.

Anna sat on the edge of the bed and took his hand in hers, holding on to it tightly. Now that the danger was past, she felt so very cold and tired. There had been no time to be afraid there by the river, but now all that fear weighed on her. He was in danger—real, terrible danger. Someone had attacked him twice now, and those were only the attempts she witnessed herself. Whatever he was doing made someone angry enough to try to kill.

She did not know Conlan McTeer very well, and what she *did* know would send any sensible woman running.

Yet she couldn't shake the feeling that in her heart she did know him, and he knew her. He knew the parts that she kept hidden from everyone else. To lose him now would be—terrible.

"Anna," he whispered. His fingers closed on hers so tightly it was almost painful.

"I'm still here," she said. She gently smoothed his hair back from his brow. He felt too warm to her touch.

"You should not be."

"Of course I should. I have to be certain you'll recover."

"I told you, it's just a scratch."

"This is the second 'scratch' I've seen you take. Remember St. Stephen's Green?"

"All too well. Anna, you have to leave, and I don't just mean this room tonight. You should go away from Dublin, go to the country, and never see me again."

Anna shook her head. She didn't want to leave him, not now. Not until she had deciphered what her strange, intense feelings meant. "I don't know what is happening here, Conlan, but I can help you. If you would just tell me..."

"No." He stared up at her with burning green eyes. Yet despite their heat, she could feel only ice. He still held onto her hands, but it seemed he was drawing further and further away from her. "I don't need help from a spoiled Ascendancy princess. Dublin isn't just all dancing and parties. It's dangerous, especially for those who don't understand."

She was *really* angry now, her exhaustion and fear burned away by utter fury. She was not a spoiled princess, useful only for shopping and planning parties and getting married! She had thought Conlan saw that, saw *her*. "I will never understand unless someone tells me! I'm involved in this whether you like it or not, Conlan. I will be far safer if you just trust me and tell me the truth."

He rolled onto his side, away from her. "I can't trust you, Anna. I'm sorry. You should go home."

"That's it then?" she said numbly as she stared at his unyielding back. There were still marks there where her nails had scratched him in the throes of passion. That all seemed so unreal now. He was sending her away.

"So I should just marry Grant Dunmore, play his perfect little wife, and pretend none of this ever happened?" she choked out. "That we never made love, and I never saw you almost killed?"

"You would be happier with him," Conlan said tightly. "He could keep you safe."

"Safe?" Anna wiped fiercely at her eyes, refusing to let a single tear fall. "I have not felt safe for a very long time."

And she doubted Grant Dunmore was the man who could do that. He held secrets, too, just as everyone did in these confusing days. Conlan, Grant, even her sister's drawing teacher—they all held secrets.

Even herself.

"I will go then, if that is what you want," she said. "I'll even leave Dublin and go to the Connemaras' Christmas party. But this isn't over. I am even more stubborn than you, remember? You have not seen the last of me."

She marched to the door and swung it open, coming face-to-face with Sarah. She was hurrying along the corridor with a valise and basin of water, a startled look on her disgustingly pretty face.

Anna swept past her as she heard Conlan shout, "I mean it, witch! Stay away from here or you'll be sorry."

"I'm already sorry!" she yelled back. "Just not for the reasons you think. You haven't seen the last of me, Conlan McTeer!"

She ran down the stairs and out into the night. The sky was turning a light pearl-gray as she dashed down the deserted street. Morning was not far off. A new day, full of new puzzles.

She was halfway home before she realized that she had left her cloak behind and she was freezing cold. But her heart felt even colder.

∂

"Such temper," Conlan heard Sarah say. "You'll make your wound bleed again."

He stayed on his side, listening as she reached for a basin and splashed a rag through the water. Every inch of his being ached to run after Anna, to grab her in his arms and hold on to her so that she could never get away. So closely that she would be safe from all the darkness of the world. She was his bright star, the only beautiful, good thing he had ever possessed.

And that was why she had to go away. She didn't belong to him. He would only destroy her in the end.

"She's a stubborn colleen," he said. "She wouldn't go."

"Of course she wouldn't." Sarah laid her hand gently on his shoulder to roll him onto his back. "She is in love with you."

In love? With him? A spark of something like hope rose up in his heart, but he shoved it back down again.

Love had no place in his life, only duty to his people and his name. She had a duty to her own family, one that was so very different from his own. The Blacknalls and the McTeers might as well live on different planets, not miles apart in Kildare.

"She's not in love with me. I'm just a bit of an adventure for her," he said. "She's practically betrothed to Grant Dunmore."

"Is she indeed?" Sarah carefully unwound his stained makeshift bandage to examine the wound. "Poor girl. That one will never be faithful to anyone but himself."

Conlan thought of his cousin with Lady Cannondale and hoped Anna would never really marry him. He was entirely unworthy of her. But then, was there a man anywhere who could be truly *worthy* of her?

"They say he's the most handsome man in Dublin," he said. He winced as she carefully cleaned the wound. "Rich, too. Some ladies would fancy that."

"Not me. Not her, either, I think. Looks fade, and I wouldn't trust whatever the source is of his riches. He would bore her in a fortnight."

"Would he?" Conlan asked, hopeful in spite of himself.

"Of course. What use is a man like that to women like us? There's no fire, no adventure, nothing to believe in." She poured whiskey over the reddened flesh, making him shout at the sting. "And no honor, either."

Conlan remembered the flash of hurt in Anna's beautiful eyes when he sent her away, his heart aching to lose her. Then he remembered her shouts of temper. "Perhaps. But I think I have lost her."

"Oh, no. She'll be back. And what's more, I think you *want* her to be back."

Of course, he wanted her back. "No, it's too dangerous. She'd be better off with Grant, despite all his faults."

Sarah sighed as she unwound a fresh bandage. "You have not listened to a word I've said. But you'll learn. She will never give up in what she believes in. She's too much like you, Conlan. Even I can see that."

She leaned down and gently kissed his cheek. "Oh, Conlan, my friend," she said. "I'm going to enjoy watching this little battle of yours so very much. I have a feeling you are going down to defeat."

Chapter Eighteen

W elcome, welcome!" Lady Connemara cried as the doors to her home swung open. "And a merry Christmas to you all. We will be such a fun party now that you have arrived."

Anna clambered down from their carriage, stiff and sore after their journey from Dublin. She had been hoping for a quiet evening, supper and a bath in her chamber, maybe an hour's reading with Caroline, but it seemed that was not to be. Over Lady Connemara's shoulder, she glimpsed a bustling blur of activity in the soaring, pale marble foyer, and she could hear laughter and carols on a pianoforte.

Christmas was already under way, the largest, most raucous holiday in celebration-loving Ireland. Even the traditional holly wreaths were hung on every door and window, a particularly Irish touch.

"We are so happy to be here, Harriet," Katherine said. She and Caroline climbed down from the carriage behind Anna as the servants leaped into action to retrieve their baggage. "Time in the country is always so restful."

"Oh, Dublin is too crowded for words," Lady Connemara said. "We are so quiet and peaceful here. But do come in, it is perishingly cold! Your rooms will soon be ready, and in the meantime, there is tea and brandy punch in the drawing room, and my daughters are entertaining everyone with some music of the season."

Caroline took Anna's arm as they hurried up the shallow marble steps into the house. She balanced a stack of books in the crook of her other arm. The foyer echoed with shouts and cries, running footsteps, shrieks, and music from the open drawing room doors.

"The wren, the wren, the king of all birds! St. Stephen's Day was caught in the furze, up with the kettle and down with the pan, and give us a penny for to bury the wren!" they sang loudly.

"Peaceful and quiet indeed," Caroline said wryly. "I doubt I will be able to think one single thought all week. They're like a flock of wrens themselves."

Anna laughed. "It is Christmas, Caro! It's meant to be noisy."

"She hasn't been sparing with the decorations, either," Caroline said. She gestured to the loops of greenery twined around the gilded staircase banisters, tied with huge red satin bows. Every painting was surmounted by sprigs of holly, and an elaborate kissing bough trailing white streamers hung in the drawing room doorway.

"It is lovely," Anna said. "Very—festive."

Despite the puzzlement and anger that she felt when Adair sent her away so abruptly, her spirits rose with the music and the bright decorations. It was Christmas! She had always loved an Irish Christmas with all the parties and dancing. Surely she could feel more like herself now.

She only wanted to be herself, to discover who that was. She studied the kissing bough over the door, made of mistletoe and white ribbons, and remembered that Christmas was a time for miracles. For new beginnings.

"Come along, Caro," she said. "I'm quite parched for some of that brandy punch."

"Anna." Caroline tugged at her arm, her expression serious. "I need to talk to you about something important."

Caroline wanted to talk to *her* about something important? Anna's high spirits chilled. That sort of thing never happened. "Whatever is the matter? Are you in some kind of trouble?"

Caroline shook her head. "No, nothing like that. I just don't want Mama to hear."

"We can walk in the garden soon, if we can escape the company," Anna said, intrigued. "Surely no one will follow us in this cold."

"Yes, of course." Caroline couldn't say more, as other guests arrived and they were all swept into the crowded drawing room. Friends quickly surrounded them, pulling them into the music and laughter. The lush marble and brocade room smelled of evergreen boughs and brandy, of woodsmoke and hothouse red roses, and drew her into the holiday company.

$\mathcal{B}$

Anna trailed behind Caroline through the winter-dormant garden, around the deserted stone summerhouse and along a pathway that led up the slope of a hill. At its crest, she could glimpse the high wall of the Connemaras' estate and over it a meadow with a large house in the distance.

Was that Adair Court? she wondered. So very near, but so far. Maybe if she could go out riding one afternoon, just to explore and look about...

"Are you quite set on marrying Grant Dunmore?" Caroline suddenly asked.

"What?" Anna said, startled. She kicked impatiently at the gravel path under her foot. "Why does everyone assume that? I don't think I ever said I *wanted* to marry Sir Grant. And he has not asked me."

Caroline shrugged. "I suppose his dinner party was something of a declaration of his intent. He wants a hostess for his fine house, and he seems to think it should be you."

"Is that all I can be?" Anna said quietly. "An ornament?"

"Certainly not! No one who has the craftiness to sneak out of the house right under Mama's nose should waste their talents on mere parties. But..."

"But what? Come on, Caro! Obviously you brought me out here, away from the brandy punch and music, to say something. Tell me."

"I just don't think you should marry him!" Caroline blurted.

Anna looked at her sister in surprise. "Why not?"

"Because he is not good enough for you. I don't—I don't think he's terribly honest. Or faithful."

"Oh, Caro," Anna said with a bitter laugh. "Are there any honest, faithful men?"

"There was our father. And Will. And—well, maybe that's it. I don't know."

"Two out of millions, then," Anna said. "I'm sure Grant Dunmore is no worse than any other man of our class. But you're correct in saying he's not right for me. I'm not sure I'm really the sort of wife he wants."

Caroline gave a relieved smile. Her tense shoulders slumped in her cloak. "Truly?"

"Truly. I would at least have to know him much better first."

"Anna, Caroline!" their mother suddenly called from the terrace. "Do come inside now, it's too cold to be out."

"We're coming, Mama," Caroline answered. She turned and hurried toward the house. Now that her duty in warning Anna was done, she seemed to retreat back to her quiet, self-contained ways.

But Anna caught up with her and grabbed her arm. "Caro, tell me—why did you feel the need to warn me about Sir Grant? Did something happen at the dinner party?"

Caroline hesitated and then shook her head firmly. "I just have a bad feeling about him, that's all. I shouldn't have said anything at all." She gently drew away her arm and dashed up the terrace steps into the house.

Anna followed slowly. She was quite sure Caroline wasn't telling her the whole story, but she couldn't press the point now. The drawing room was filled with new arrivals, including Lord Hartley, who swiftly claimed Caroline's attention.

Anna wondered if her sister knew that Hartley was not good enough for *her*. Caro was so pretty and clever, so young, yet she was determined to marry this middle-aged, balding, child-laden man. If Grant Dunmore sought an ornament, Hartley surely wanted a research assistant and a stepmother for his children. But at least he did seem to be kind—and faithful.

She glimpsed Grant standing in the doorway beneath the large kissing bough. He looked very handsome indeed, clad in his travel garb of greatcoat and doeskin breeches, with his coppery hair tousled. Yet the look in his eyes as he watched her was one she did not care for. It seemed almost—proprietary.

Or maybe it was just Caroline's cryptic warning that made her imagine things. She pushed away the disquiet and plunged into the crowd with determined gaiety. It was still Christmas, after all. She couldn't let worries over a man she didn't want—and one she very much *did* want, but couldn't have—entirely spoil her holiday.

Chapter Nineteen

Anna reined in her horse at the crest of a high hill. From that vantage point, high above the rolling fields, she could see for what seemed like miles and miles. The Connemara house, with all its convivial company and holiday cheer, was left far behind, and she was alone with the dark gray sky and the cold wind.

Yet it was not just the urge to be alone, to gallop over the fields and feel the rush of the wind in her hair, that drove her away that morning. Just past the low stone wall at the foot of the hill lay the Adair estate.

Her horse pawed the ground restively beneath her as she studied the land beyond that wall. She didn't know what she had expected to see there. Maybe something that would tell her an essential secret about Conlan McTeer, some magical shimmer in the very air. Yet it looked no different than any other land in County Kildare. There were lush fields and hills, a pale gold-green in the winter, laying like a patch-work blanket seamed with gray walls and strands of silvery ash trees. A few hardy sheep cropping the grass and a few crows in the trees were the only signs of life.

But in the distance, she could see mysterious towers and a curl of smoke that seemed to beckon her forward.

She glanced back over her shoulder. She was still alone. She had slipped away without a groom, far from the watchful eyes of her mother and sister and of Grant Dunmore. Far from everyone at that party, who so smugly waited for her to announce her future as Lady Dunmore. No one would know if she explored for a while before she went back.

She tugged on the reins, letting the horse run free. They dashed down the hill, the wind shrieking past them. Anna laughed at the joyous pleasure of speed and movement, shouting as the horse jumped the wall, and they were on Adair land.

She wasn't sure what she wanted to do now, so she turned the horse in the direction of the towers. There was a bridle path cut through the meadow, just wide enough for one horse, and she followed that wherever it would take her. The sky seemed even darker and lower now, a charcoal gray that threatened snow, but she didn't want to turn back. She couldn't, not yet. An insatiable curiosity drove her forward, a need to feel close to Conlan and start to understand him.

She came to the rise of another hill, one crowned with a moss-encrusted Celtic cross. She drew in the horse to study its faded designs, the familiar loops and curves of the knotwork pattern. But there were no words to tell her why it was there, what its significance could be. It was a beautiful marker of a fierce spirit fighting for survival in its own land. Much like Conlan himself.

She folded back the veil of her riding hat to better see into the distance. In one direction lay a clutch of whitewashed cottages, a small village with smoke curling over their thatched roofs. In the other lay the big house, Adair Court.

She studied it closely. It was older and darker than Killinan Castle. Killinan had been in her family for generations, but the only remnant of the old medieval keep was a single round tower, a crumbling shell where she and her sisters played as children. Later generations created a more comfortable and fashionable pale stone Palladian mansion.

Adair Court retained its crenellations and towers, like something in an old fairy tale. Ivy vines, brown in the winter, crowded over the walls and covered the mullioned windows. She wouldn't have been surprised to see a moat and drawbridge, knights galloping over it with swords drawn and horses' hooves clattering.

Much like the pounding hooves she heard now, thundering over the turf. She looked back to see Conlan himself galloping toward her on a fearsome black horse. He charged up the hill like one of those knights of old but Anna held her ground, even as he reined in a mere two feet from her. Dust and grass flew into the air.

Despite the way they parted in Dublin and her resolve to do her duty to her family she felt a terrible thrill to see him again. She didn't realize until she looked into those green eyes just how much she had missed him. It was as if she had been walking around with a part of herself missing, and now she was whole again.

Even in the cold, he wore no hat or neckcloth, just a tweed riding jacket over his shirt. He didn't smile at her, but she saw a sudden flare of light in his eyes that gave her hope that he was happy to see her, too.

"What are you doing here, Anna?" he asked.

Anna laughed. "And good day to you, too, Your Grace. Am I trespassing again, like when we first met in '98?"

"So you remember that day, too?"

"Of course I do. You seemed quite terrifying that day, like a dark villain from a Gothic novel."

"And now?"

"Now—now I know better. You are even more terrifying than you were then." And he was—terrifying because of the threat he posed to her resolve to be respectable. The threat that he posed to her heart.

A reluctant smile touched his lips, and she saw that in the country he did not shave as often. Dark whiskers roughened his jaw and those sensual lips, and his cropped hair had grown longer. It made him look even more medieval, her Irish warrior.

"I don't want to frighten you, colleen," he said. "But you shouldn't be out alone on a day like this. It looks like snow."

"I had to escape from all that holiday merriment at the Connemaras'," she said. "It's so loud and stuffy there, and if I heard 'Three ships came sailing' one more time I would start screaming and not be able to stop. I didn't mean to go far, but . . ."

"But?"

"I wanted to see your home. I was curious what kind of land could spawn such a man as you."

Conlan laughed reluctantly. "And what have you learned in your explorations?"

"Not a thing. You are more of a puzzle than ever."

"Am I? That's gratifying. What puzzles you here?"

"This cross, for one," Anna said, gesturing to the old Celtic cross. "What does it mean?"

He shrugged. "I have no idea. It's been there for many years, too many for anyone to remember. My mother used to say it was the grave of our ancestor, Ewan the Brave. He was a warrior who fought the Vikings."

"Really? An ancient warrior's grave?" She studied the cross again, even more intrigued. "How romantic."

"I admit I hardly even notice it now. It seems a part of the landscape."

"So you were not coming to visit your ancestor?"

"I had a much more prosaic errand," Conlan said. "I was going to call on some of my tenants, until I saw a witch on horseback trespassing on my estate."

Anna shifted the reins in her gloved hands. "Perhaps I should not have come. After the way we parted in Dublin, I should consider that I may not be welcome here."

His smile faded. "I was in pain that night and furious with myself for leading you into danger again. I shouldn't have shouted at you."

"It seems to me I led myself into danger."

"But you would not have been following me if I hadn't taken you to that tavern first, if..." If they had not made love. The unspoken words hovered between them. "I meant it when I said you should stay away from me."

"Yes, I should. But I can't seem to. Can you stay away from me?"

"It would appear not, since here you are. You do have a witchlike way of appearing everywhere I turn."

Anna laughed. "To be a pest is my own special magic."

"Since we can't be rid of each other, would you like to come with me now?"

"To visit your tenants?"

"Yes."

"Me?" She was very glad indeed that he invited her, that all seemed calm between them for the moment. But she was strangely frightened, too. What if they did not like her? What if they thought her a—a spoiled Ascendancy princess? "Really?"

"I can hardly leave you alone to wander on my property. Who knows what havoc you would wreak? I promise the McEgans are kind people. They will welcome you."

"Very well then. I will go with you. But I warn you, I am not as good at these things as my mother is."

"No one expects a witch to suddenly be an angel," he said. "You did say you wanted to see more of my home."

"I do. Thank you."

She tugged at the reins, following Conlan down the slope of the hill and along a narrow path around cottages laid out like a little village. They were small, but tidy and snug, the walls thick and sound. She could hear laughter through the windows, and there were holly wreaths on the doors.

"Some of the servants live there," Conlan said, "though most of them live in the house itself. There's also a shop or two." He led her past more widely spaced cottages and through a thicket of trees. Nestled among their bare limbs were two small brick buildings, with no windows and stout doors. One had a plain wooden cross above the door.

"The school," he said simply. "And the chapel."

With those words, Anna knew for certain that he trusted her. In '98, hidden Catholic chapels and secret "hedge schools," led by priests, were rooted out and brutally destroyed. Even now they were technically illegal, but a strong landowner like the Duke of Adair could keep them safe.

"Do you have many pupils?" she asked.

"A fair number. The tenants' and servants' children go there to learn reading and writing, a few sums, things to help them with their business or farms later."

And religion, too, Anna was sure. "What of trades? Such as sewing and cooking for the girls? Perhaps training as ladies' maids? My mother has a whole separate school for the girls at Killinan."

"That would be most welcome, if a lady could be found to teach them," he said.

They emerged from the trees to find more fields, fallow now for the winter season, but she could see that by summer they would be alive with wheat and oats and vegetables. The stone walls were sturdy and the hedges tall and neatly clipped.

"You are certainly a good landlord," Anna said. "Everything looks so well-tended and prosperous."

"Are you surprised? Did you expect neglect and weeds?"

"Not at all. I already know how much you care for your people," she answered. She had seen how he fought, how much he would sacrifice for them. A duke's existence was not merely one of lofty titles and privileges; it was duty, the care of the people and the land. She truly saw that now in these lands.

"The McEgans' farm is just this way," Conlan said as he led her down a hedge-lined lane. The house was also whitewashed with a thatched roof, but larger than the village cottages. It was two stories with a little vegetable garden enclosed by an iron fence. Chickens pecked around the doorstep, and rosebushes twined dormant around the blue door.

Conlan swung down from his horse and reached up to help Anna from her saddle. They stood there for a long moment, his hands warm at her waist, mere inches from each other. Anna leaned into him and inhaled deeply of his familiar, much-missed scent. How good it felt to be close to him again! She had a fierce longing to throw her arms about him, to kiss him and feel that lust rise within her again. Feel his body harden and know he wanted her, too.

But the door swung open behind them, and Conlan let her go. Flustered, her cheeks uncomfortably hot, Anna fussed with her gloves and the braided edge of her habit, before she turned to the door.

A man stood there, tall and raw-boned, and a little girl with adorable blond braids held on to his hand. They both smiled in greeting, warmth and the scent of fresh bread slipping from the house behind them.

"Your Grace!" the man said happily. "We didn't expect to see you here on such a cold day."

"I wanted to see how your mother fared, Patrick," Conlan said. He took Anna's arm and whispered in her ear, "His mother has been ill, and I sent the doctor to her yesterday. She's quite elderly now, I fear, but an excellent teller of tales."

"You send a doctor to your sick tenants?" Anna said in surprise. Her mother nursed the people at Killinan herself and sent a doctor in more difficult cases, but most landowners would not take such care. She should have known Conlan was different.

"Of course," he said. "There is a midwife, too."

"Your Grace!" the little girl cried, and to Anna's shock came skipping up the cobbled walkway to tug at Conlan's coattails. "I'm getting a new doll for Christmas!"

Conlan laughed and swung the girl up high into his arms until she shrieked with giggles. "Are you indeed, Molly girl? What a fine Christmas gift!"

"Aye, but Papa doesn't know I know, so it is a secret." She turned curious blue eyes onto Anna. "Who is this?"

"This is my friend Lady Anna," Conlan said. "Anna, this little charmer is Miss Molly McEgan."

"How do you do, Miss McEgan?" Anna said. "I am so very pleased to meet you."

Molly shyly popped a finger into her mouth and whispered around it, "She is pretty, Your Grace."

"Yes, indeed she is," Conlan said. He smiled at Anna over Molly's golden head.

Anna thought Molly would be a perfect pupil for that girls' school, and she resolved to find a proper teacher for it. "I should very much like to see your doll, Miss McEgan, once she is no longer a great secret. I once had a beautiful doll myself, named Eleanor, but I'm sure she is nothing compared to yours."

Molly's eyes widened. "You won't tell Papa I know, will you, Lady Anna? He might not give it to me then."

"I promise I will not tell," Anna solemnly whispered. "It is our secret."

"Molly, me girl, quit nattering on at the duke and let them come in where it's warm," called Mr. McEgan.

Conlan set Molly on her feet, and they followed her into the house. "Patrick, this is Lady Anna Blacknall from Killinan Castle."

"Lady Killinan's second daughter, of course," Patrick

said with a bow. "It's an honor to see you here, my lady, but I'm sorry the house is in no proper state."

Anna glanced around at the neatly swept stone floor, the dried herbs hung from the smoke-darkened rafters to perfume the air, and the comfortable chairs and pictures on the walls. "It is lovely," she said. "And so comfortable. It's kind of you to receive me so close to Christmas."

A woman in a brown dress and long apron appeared with a baby on her hip and was introduced as Mrs. McEgan. She seemed flustered to have such guests suddenly on her doorstep, but Anna hastened to give her a smile and a bright compliment, which appeared to put her at ease.

"You must have some tea," Mrs. McEgan insisted. "And some Christmas cake. It's just warm from the stove."

"I helped make the cakes," Molly said.

"Then they must be quite fine," Anna answered. "I do hope your mother-in-law is feeling better, Mrs. McEgan. I would not want to disturb her or be in your way."

"She is sitting by the fire," Patrick said. "The medicine the doctor left has done wonders for her spirits. She'll be happy to see you."

He led Anna and Conlan into the main room of the house, a cozy space with a large fireplace and cushioned chairs. A painting of the Virgin Mary hung on the wall, watching over the scene with gentle blue eyes. A small, gray-haired woman sat by the fire wrapped up in a thick quilt.

It was a scene Anna saw often when she went visiting at Killinan, but she was always with Katherine then. She tried to think of her mother's example, of her way of being helpful and kind while not being obtrusive. It was harder than it appeared.

"Mother," Patrick said loudly, "here is His Grace and Lady Anna Blacknall to see you and wish you happy Christmas."

"A lady?" the elder Mrs. McEgan cried, turning rheumy eyes toward them. "I did not know the duke had married. About time, I must say. This place has been too long without a mistress."

Anna laughed and knelt down beside the woman's chair, the purple skirts of her riding habit spreading around her. "I fear I am only the duke's friend, Mrs. McEgan, not his wife. Though any lady would be honored to be mistress here."

"He hasn't married you?" She studied Anna carefully, touching her cheek with a wrinkled hand. "Then he is a bloody great fool. This estate needs a lady's touch."

Anna glanced up to see that Conlan's color had risen suspiciously. Was he *blushing*? That made her laugh even more, and suddenly she was quite at ease. "Does it indeed? I should be most interested to hear what improvements you would suggest, Mrs. McEgan, if there was a duchess to put them into place."

"Sit here with me, my lady, and I'll tell you," Mrs. McEgan said. "Maybe my daughter-in-law will bring us some tea. And you men go off to look at the new calf or some such. We women have important matters to discuss."

Anna settled herself in the chair next to the old lady's, and Molly scrambled up onto her lap. Suddenly, Anna felt quite wondrously at home.

☙

Conlan had thought that he knew all the facets of Anna now: Society lady, the temptress in red, the brave warrior who charged in to fight by his side with no thought to her own safety. But he realized now that he had never really seen the essence of her.

For he saw that now, as he stood in the doorway of the cottage and watched her listening intently to an old lady's ramblings. She nodded and smiled as she cuddled little Molly on her lap. The girl reached up to play with the amethyst beads of Anna's necklace, leaving cake-sticky fingerprints on it, and Anna didn't even seem to notice. There was no grand lady there at all, nothing of the careless, gambling coquette she showed to the world. Just a calm-eyed, caring woman at ease in even a humble farmhouse. A true lady of the manor.

The younger Mrs. McEgan, passing from the kitchen to the sitting room with a teapot in her hands, paused as she saw Conlan lurking there. "Your Grace? Is something amiss?"

Conlan turned to her, startled. He was too wrapped up in this new, disquieting aspect of Anna Blacknall to notice anything else. "Not at all, Mary. Patrick will be in directly. He's just seeing to your fine new calf."

"Won't you come in by the fire? There's fresh tea and plenty of Mother's advice to be had."

"My boots are muddy."

She laughed. "That is nothing new here, Your Grace! But I do fear Mother has been telling all her old tales to her ladyship for this half-hour at least. I don't want to frighten Lady Anna away." She peered past him into the sitting room to study that cozy, firelit scene. "She must be bored to tears, bless her, but she doesn't show it. She's let Molly pester her, too. She's a lovely lady, so much like her mother."

"Yes," Conlan murmured. "She is very lovely."

Mary hesitated, then said softly, "I don't like to talk out of turn, Your Grace, but it's past time Adair Court had a fine mistress like that. It is a large responsibility, and you've carried it alone so long. Someone like Lady Anna could help you a great deal."

"Why, Mary," Conlan said with a grin, "I didn't realize everyone was trying to marry me off."

"Well, there wasn't a lady like her on the estate before. She even asked me what I thought about the idea of a special girls' school here! And she cares about you, Your Grace. I can see that plain in the way she looks at you. You shouldn't let her get away."

Conlan looked back at Anna. She was laughing at a joke of old Mrs. McEgan's as she smoothed back Molly's hair. The girl now wore the amethyst necklace. "I doubt a Blacknall would have me, Mary. Not with the way things are here."

"They're Protestant over at Killinan, you mean? Well—maybe we need *that* here, too, Your Grace. Just in case another uprising comes along. Now, come in and have some tea with your lady before you go out into the cold again."

Perhaps Mary McEgan was right there, Conlan thought. A Protestant duchess from an old Anglo family might be a benefit to Adair Court, one more protection. But would he not then be just like Grant, seeking to use Anna's connections for his own ends? That was not something he could solve at the moment, though, so he went and joined Anna and the McEgans for tea and Christmas cake.

By the time they left the farmhouse, the threatened snow had begun to fall, cold white flakes drifting from the dark gray sky. They caught on Anna's lashes, sparkling like diamonds as she laughed in delight.

"Now it really feels like Christmas!" she cried, galloping down the lane with Conlan chasing close behind her. It seemed like she had gone from lady of the manor to winter goddess of nature in one instant.

"We should get you back to the Connemaras' before the storm begins in earnest," he called to her.

"Oh, no, not yet! I had such a fine time at the McEgans' home. They were so kind and welcoming. I don't want to listen to silly gossip over the card table just yet." She looked back at him over her shoulder, a mischievous smile on her lips. "Take me to see your castle, Conlan."

There was nothing he wanted more at that moment than to take her home with him. To see her in his house, his bed, and hold her there until they were sated with each other at last. Until this obsession burned away, and good sense and duty reigned again.

Only he feared that he could *never* be sated with her. Her brightness would always draw him in.

"Won't they miss you there?" he said.

She shook her head. "Not until dinner, and that's hours away. They're too busy planning some sort of amateur theatricals."

"And you don't want to join in? A play seems just your sort of thing, Anna."

She tugged at her horse's reins, slowing to a walk so she could face him squarely. "I'm tired of playacting, Conlan. That's why I'm so glad you took me to see your tenants, why I want to see your house. I want to be in something real."

Something real. That was what he sought, what he fought for, all his life. Adair Court was real. His people and their needs were real. Could his golden witch possibly be real, too? Or would she just vanish like those snowflakes, spinning away in yet another incarnation of herself that he could not follow?

He shook his head, but she reached out and covered his hand with her own. Her gaze was steady and dark blue. "Please, Conlan," she said quietly. "Please show me your house before I have to go back. We should get out of this snow before we catch cold."

It fell thickly around them now, a cold mass that blanketed everything in concealing, purifying white.

"For an hour or two," he said. "Until the weather clears."

Then they would both have to wake from their winter dreams.

Chapter Twenty

"You have a holly wreath on your door," Anna said as Conlan lifted her down from her horse. "My nanny used to say fairies would hide under the leaves to get away from the winter cold."

"You know the old tales then?" His hands lingered at her waist, only sliding away as a groom appeared to lead the horses away.

Anna felt a sharp pang of regret at his lost touch. She had missed being near him so much. She had to enjoy it while she could. "Of course," she said, following him up the rough stone steps to the stout, iron-bound doors. "My parents always had a holly wreath at Christmas, and my nanny always told us the story as it was hung, as well as the reason we left a candle in the window, to show the Holy Family the way. Christmas was always so wonderful at Killinan."

"Then I hope you won't be disappointed by the lack of festive greenery here," he said as he swung open the doors. "Most of the servants have gone to stay with their own families until Boxing Day, and it's bare and cold."

"Oh!" Anna cried at the sight of the grand foyer. "It is like something from King Arthur."

The interior matched the exterior of the house, just as she had hoped. The foyer soared upward, bisected by a wide stone staircase lined with an ornate wrought-iron balustrade. An enormous iron chandelier hung overhead, looking down on ancient pennants, shields, and swords hanging on the walls, speaking of times past for the McTeer family. A thick, plush green carpet muffled their footsteps and warmed the cold stone floor. Anna saw a faded gold knotwork pattern woven along its edges.

"It's not very fashionable," Conlan said ruefully. "No fine plasterwork or brocade French furniture."

"Everyone has those things. This is ever so much better." Anna took off her hat and gloves and tossed them onto a mosaic-topped table before she dashed to the nearest door. She threw it open to reveal a drawing room, but not just any drawing room. It was more like the great hall of a feudal king with a long, polished wooden table that ran the length of the chamber.

Tapestries covered the walls with scenes of Irish mythology, and at the far end of the room, a woman's portrait hung over the enormous fireplace. A dark-haired lady clad in a yellow satin gown and pearls looked out at the world with Conlan's green eyes. She sat before that very same fireplace, a book open in her hand, smiling proudly as if to welcome guests into her home.

"Is that your mother?" Anna asked.

"Yes. She loved this room."

"I can see why. It's wonderful." Anna made her way along the table, studying the tapestries as she went. They were all woven in rich, glowing colors, telling wondrous tales of gods and heroes from ancient Ireland. She paused before the last one, an image of Deirdre and her doomed husband, Naoise, embracing on the rocky shore. "Deirdre of the Sorrows?"

"Ah, so you know not only the legend of the holly wreath but also the Sorrowful Tales of Erin?" Conlan said teasingly. "How shocking, Lady Anna. Anyone would think you were *Irish*. Maybe even a member of that horrid Hibernian Society."

"I've told you before, Conlan McTeer—I *am* Irish," she answered. She studied Deirdre's sad, beautiful face, the tragedy of impending, profound loss in her eyes. "My family has been at Killinan for generations."

"It's not possession of the land that makes a person truly Irish."

"No. It's belonging to the people, isn't it? Caring about them, being one of them. That's what my sister Eliza always said." She thought of Eliza, so far away in her exile, and how she gave up so much to be Irish. Anna had always envied her.

But now she understood how such a passion could drive a person. She had begun to feel it herself.

"You are cold," Conlan said. "I'm afraid it can be rather drafty here."

"No, I'm fine," Anna protested, but he took off his coat and laid it over her shoulders. Its soft, tweed folds smelled of him, of lemons and starch and clean air, and it still held the heat of his body. She clutched it tightly around herself, snuggling deeper into its warmth.

"I'll build us a fire," he said. He took her arm in a gentle clasp and led her to one of the large, green velvet armchairs by the hearth. "I may be a duke, but I'm not completely useless."

"No," Anna murmured. "Not completely." She sat back, wrapped in his coat, and watched as he built a fire in that huge grate, large enough to roast a boar for a feast. The long, lean muscles of his back and shoulders shifted and flexed against his shirt, and she remembered how his bare skin felt under her touch. The heat and strength of him. How she felt so safe with him; how she trusted him.

She was not the only one he kept safe.

"You belong to the people, Conlan," she said.

He glanced back at her, his brow creased. The kindling in the hearth caught into flames. "Do I?"

"I saw that today at the McEgans' house." She couldn't meet his green, steady gaze. Instead she watched the growing fire. "I've seen how the workers on other estates live, with barely enough to eat and no sturdy roof over their children's heads. Dirty, cold—it is shameful. There's nothing like that here. It's like this is its own little country."

He sat back on his heels. "Of course, there is no starvation here. I would never allow anyone at Adair Court to starve. It is the duty I was born with."

"And because you care about them. They are like your family, and they see you that way, too. I could see that so clearly. You are part of this land, really part of it."

"So are you, Anna." He took her hands as he knelt at her feet. How handsome he was, she thought, outlined by that fire, his dark hair windswept. He belonged in this room, just like that, an ancient chieftain.

She gave him a gentle smile. "An Ascendancy princess?"

"Ah, Anna, you know I did not mean that. You're one of the least spoiled women I have ever encountered."

"The least spoiled Anglo-Protestant woman?"

"I thought you said you were Irish, and so you are. You have that spirit in you, that fire. This is your home, too, if you want it. You're Irish—if you want to be."

"That is what my sister Eliza said. Look where her Irish passion got her—sent to Switzerland." Anna slid her hands from his and framed his face in her palms. "Where will it get you, Conlan, and all the people of this estate? What would they do without you?"

He turned his face to kiss the inside of her wrist. His breath was so warm and vital on her skin. If only *she* could hold *him* safe, keep him with her always. Help him.

"I do what I must to protect them," he said.

And who protected him? She feared she wasn't strong enough to do that. No one was.

She slid down to sit beside him on the hearth rug as the fire blazed away to heat the cold room. Outside the high, narrow old windows, the snow fell in white earnest, enclosing them in their own small world.

She couldn't warn him or beg him for answers or promises. She knew he wouldn't give them. She could only be with him now, while she had the chance.

"Remember the Three Sorrowful Tales?" she said, thinking of that beautiful tapestry and Deirdre's sad eyes.

"Tell me." He stretched his tall body out on the rug, resting his head on her lap.

She smoothed her fingers softly through his hair, feeling the rough slide of it on her skin.

"Long ago," she began, "the five kings of Ireland met to decide who would be crowned the head king, and King

Lir of the White Field expected to be elected. But Dearg, son of Daghda, was chosen. Lir left, angry, and the others would have cut him down for his disobedience. But Dearg said instead, 'Let us bind him to us by the bonds of kinship, so that peace may always dwell in the land.' And he was given Dearg's kinswoman Aoibh, the fairest maiden in the land, for his wife. She gave him four children, a daughter Fionnuala and three sons, Aodh, Fiachra, and Conn.

"But Aoibh died, and Lir was overcome with terrible grief. The king, who feared Lir would die of this grief, sent him Aoibh's sister Aife to be his new wife. At first all seemed well, but Aife grew bitterly jealous of Lir's love for his children, and she used a Druid's magic to turn them into swans, bound together by silver chains. In punishment, she became a demon of the air for all eternity. But that did not help the children of Lir. For nine hundred years they lived as swans, cursed to remain so until 'the woman from the south and the man from the north' came together. And so it came to pass after hundreds of years that the prince of Connaught was to wed the daughter of the king of Munster, and she had a desire to possess the beautiful swans, which had come under the protection of St. Mac Howg of Glory Isle. When the prince went to seize the birds, their feathery coats fell away, and they were revealed as humans again.

"And thus was the fate of the children of Lir," she finished. "After nine hundred years of suffering, they were free."

Conlan was silent as her words faded. The tale was done, yet it seemed those enchanted swans lingered in the room with them, their gleaming white wings enfolding them. The children of Lir found their freedom at long last, but could she?

Conlan reached up to toy with the black braid trim of her bodice. His touch was light, but to Anna it burned. She craved that touch so very much after being apart from him. Perhaps those magical chains bound them as well, and when they tried to break them they only wounded themselves.

"I try to send you away, try to do what is right for us both, and you keep returning," he said. His hand trailed along her rib cage, his fingers spreading over her waist. His touch was gentle through the wool of her riding habit, but it made her want so much more. She wanted his bare skin on hers, wanted to feel that connection again and know she was not alone.

She covered his hand with hers and pressed him closer. "I was never much concerned with doing what was prudent or careful, Conlan."

He laughed and reached up with his other hand to caress her cheek. She nuzzled into his touch, kissing his palm. He smelled of lemons, smoke, and snow. "I have certainly learned that much about you, Anna. No one could ever accuse you of being *careful*. You're like a warrior goddess."

"A warrior goddess and a witch?" Anna said lightly, though inside she was terribly pleased. "La, how busy I must be!"

"Every time I think I know you, you change. You show me a different side of you, and I'm baffled all over again."

"But you know me better than anyone else ever has. You actually *look* at me; you see me." She leaned closer to him, their lips hovering mere inches apart. She felt those silver chains tighten, and she knew that even if he sent her away again and forever, she would still be bound to him. "And I see you, Conlan. As much as you fight to deny it, you are a good man. A Celtic warrior king."

He shook his head, but he did not turn from her. He didn't even look away, and in his green eyes, she saw her own turmoil and desire reflected back to her.

"You know I am a liar and a killer," he said.

"So am I. You do not condemn me for my sins, so I certainly won't do the same to you. You do what you must to take care of your people. I know that." She closed the space between them and brushed her lips softly over his. She felt their breath mingle and the damp heat of their kiss. "But who takes care of *you*?"

Before he could answer, she pressed her lips to his again, harder, letting him feel all her desperate desire. She needed him so much, and she wanted him to need her, too. She felt his hands close around her hips, and he shifted his body so that she lay on top of him. His tongue traced the curve of her lower lip, lightly, teasingly, before he slid inside. She opened her mouth in welcome, tasting, feeling him intimately.

And, like the swans, she soared free.

"Anna," he growled. Through the blurry heat of her desire, she felt his touch tighten over the curve of her backside, dragging her against him. She arched her hips into his erection, spreading her legs to cradle him with her body.

He groaned deeply, and their kiss slid into wild, frantic need. She tore at the lacings of his shirt until she could touch his bare skin at last. She pressed her palms hard to his chest, reveling in the hot, smooth satin of skin over those hard muscles, the roughness of his hair on her

hands. His breath, his heartbeat, his life, his strength—
she craved all of it. Needed all of him.

But there were too many blasted clothes in the way!

Anna sat up, her knees braced to either side of his hips,
and unfastened the tiny jet buttons along the front of her
habit. He watched very closely as she released each button, parting the bodice inch by inch to reveal her sheer
chemise and the naked skin beneath.

She eased her arms from the long, tight sleeves and let
the garment fall away. Never taking her gaze from his,
she slid the ribbon straps down, too, leaving her breasts
bare. The purple and white fabric pooled around them.

She shoved away a pang of shyness and forced herself
to hold her head high, her shoulders back. "Do you like
what you see, Conlan?" she whispered.

He braced himself up on his elbows beneath her. "You
know I do. I've never seen anything as beautiful as you."

"I like what I see, too." She trailed her fingertips down
his chest. Lightly, teasingly, she traced the sharp curve
of his hip, the line of his thigh—and pressed against his
penis, iron-hard through his breeches.

"Anna," he growled, his hips flexing. In one swift
move, he knelt before her, his hands hard around her waist
as if he would push her away. Instead he dragged her tight
against him. Not a single breath was between them.

He kissed her fiercely, her head pressed back as he
tasted her deeply. There was no artifice or deception to
that kiss, only pure, raw need. Passion that overcame all
else. There was no refuge in respectability, no prudence
or caution, not for people like them. Those chains tightened, and they had to be together.

She felt his touch on her naked breast, his rough palm

sliding beneath to cradle it. His long fingers teased at her hardened nipple, tracing one light, fleeting caress over the very tip, barely touching. He teased her until she arched her back and pressed herself hard against him, insisting on what she wanted. He gave her what she longed for, plucking at the sensitive nipple, rolling it hard between his fingers.

The sensations raced through her, lightning along her nerves. Her desire burned even higher. She held tightly to his shoulders, blindly shoving at his shirt until the intrusive fabric fell away, leaving his chest and shoulders bare to her. She dug her fingers deep into his skin, holding him with her.

He leaned away, and she cried out in wordless protest. But he merely stripped out of his shirt and tossed it away before grabbing her in his arms again. His mouth closed hard on her nipple, sucking deeply as he covered her other breast with his hand.

Anna's head fell back weakly, and she murmured incoherently, begging for what she only half-understood in the haze of her need. His open mouth trailed along her rib cage to her stomach, his tongue circling her navel, then down to that freckle just below her waist.

He pushed her skirts out of his way, discarding them near his shirt, and licked a fiery ribbon over her hip. His hand curved hard around the back of her thigh and tugged her closer to him. He pressed a kiss to the inside of her leg, just above the black silk edge of her stocking. One finger eased along the seam of her womanhood and slid into her.

"Conlan," she panted. She closed her eyes tightly to concentrate on every feeling, every touch. His fingers spread her wider, and she felt his tongue touch her *there*. "Conlan!"

"Shh, let me," he whispered, and she gave herself completely over to him. He kissed her deeply, tasting her so intimately she could have no secrets from him at all. She was completely vulnerable to him. Waves of hot pleasure washed over her, and she was drowning in them, tugged down deeper and deeper.

She drove her fingers into his hair and held him against her. The air was filled with the scent of musky desire and woodsmoke, and she only wanted more and more of what he gave her. She wanted everything, all of him.

Her climax took hold of her, low at the very core of her, a building, burning pressure. She let it expand over her whole body until every thought vanished and there was only the feeling. As he pressed his tongue deep, thrusting one last time, his hands hard on her thighs, she exploded.

"Conlan," she sighed, sinking to the floor. She rested on the soft carpet, shivering, her legs spread as he knelt between them. He stared down at her, his eyes so dark they almost seemed black, his lips damp with her own essence. His chest gleamed with sweat, heaving with the force of his breath. It was an almost unbearably erotic sight.

Anna reached out to unfasten his breeches and push them away from his hips. His penis, hard and thickly veined with his own unfulfilled desire, velvet over hot iron, beckoned for her touch, and she gave in to the temptation. She ran her hand slowly up his length and down again, catching the tiny drop of pearly moisture there on the tip of her finger. He trembled at her caress, his erection straining against her hand, but he held very, very still.

Anna slid her fingertip between her lips to taste him. As she sucked at the salty wetness, he moaned deeply and closed his eyes. A muscle ticked along his jaw as if he reined himself in hard.

"*Diolain*," he muttered.

She sat up and pushed him down in her place, flat on his back on the carpet. She stripped away his breeches until she could see his naked body at last, nothing in her way. The firelight turned him to molten gold, and she thought he must be some sort of Celtic god in truth. She touched every inch of him, exploring, wondering at his beauty and strength.

On his left upper arm he had a tattoo, a small, purple-black mark of an elaborate Celtic cross. She traced over the pattern with her fingertip.

"Did this hurt?" she whispered.

"Aye," he answered tightly. "Like the very devil."

"And this?" She touched a puckered, pale pink knife scar over one rib.

"I don't remember."

"You don't remember being stabbed?" she said. Her heart ached to think anyone could ever hurt him. That he had suffered so much.

"I was a foolish youth, brawling in a tavern."

"Well, surely you remember this one." She touched a scar on his thigh, larger than the knife wound, puckered and faded red. She remembered that night during the rebellion, when she found him in that ruined stable. His leg had been hurt then, bound with stained rags. "From '98?"

"Yes," he said shortly.

"And this . . ." She turned to the half-healed wound on his shoulder. "I remember this one all too well."

"Then you must remember why I told you to stay away from me, colleen."

Anna laughed. "I fear I have a terrible memory. And I never obey."

"So I've noticed."

She bent her head to press an openmouthed kiss just below that shoulder wound. Slowly, taking her time to fully enjoy him, learn him, she kissed his flat brown nipple, biting at it lightly. He cursed and tried to catch her by her hair, but she slid away from him. She trailed the tip of her tongue down the taut line of his torso, over his abdomen. The muscles tightened under her lips.

She kissed the old wound on his leg. One day, she would get him to tell her that story. But not now. Now she wanted him to think only of her, of the two of them in that moment, and not of the past or the future.

Gently, she kissed the inside of his thigh, as he had with her. His skin was hot, damp, and he smelled of that dark, clean essence she loved about him. Slowly, carefully, she touched her tongue to the tip of his penis.

"Anna!" he shouted.

"Shh—let me," she whispered, echoing his words to her. He lay back, but she could feel the taut wariness of his body. She licked along his length, tasting his salty sweetness, feeling that hard, velvety heat under her tongue. Then she took him fully into her mouth.

"Anna, nay." He tugged at her hair, drawing her away from him. His eyes burned into her as she sat back on her heels to look at him. "You'll kill me."

"I hope not. I have plans for you, Conlan McTeer, and they will take a very long time to carry out."

"And I have plans for *you, cailleach*," he growled. He

seized her by the hips and bore her down to the carpet as he rose up over her.

He buried his face in the curve of her neck and shoulder, kissing her skin as she laughed happily. "Do you promise?"

"If I could, I would lock you up in this house for weeks and weeks," he muttered against her. "I would tie you to my bed and never let you go."

Anna shivered at the images that his words summoned. "That sounds delicious. And what would you do then, when I was at your mercy?"

"I would kiss you here . . ." He lightly licked at her hardened, ultra-sensitive nipple. "And here." He slid lower, kissing the damp curls between her legs, the soft inside of her thigh. His tongue trailed down her leg as he slowly removed her stocking, until he bit gently at her toe. Then he did the same to her other leg, until she was completely naked. His willing captive.

"I would kiss every single inch of you until you begged me to stop," he said.

"I never would," she whispered. "So we would be here forever."

"Even better." He gently spread her legs wider, kneeling between them. "Do you want me, Anna? Do you want me inside of you?"

"Yes!" she cried. She opened herself to him, and he drove deeply home.

This time there was no pain, only that delicious fullness, the press and friction of being joined together at last. She wrapped her legs around his waist, urging him deeper, faster.

He drew back only to drive forward again and again,

that friction rougher and hotter. She closed her eyes and listened to the harsh, uneven rhythm of his breath as they moved together. He was part of her now, but she wanted even more of him. She wanted everything he could give— and she wanted to give him everything in return.

Faster and faster they moved, their cries and gasps mingling. She rose up and caught his lips with hers as she felt her climax build again. She cried out at the release; a shower of sparks fell over her. His back tightened under her touch, taut as a drawn bowstring, as he shouted out his own release.

He fell heavily to the floor beside her, facedown as he trembled. Anna was shaking, too, exhausted and exalted by that wondrous, unbelievable pleasure. By the joy of being with him. She opened her eyes to stare up at the ceiling beams, breathing slowly and deeply until she could feel herself slowly float back down to earth. She heard the crackle of the fire, the soft brush of snow against the window, and Conlan's breath against her ear. The pounding of her own blood in her veins.

She smiled, feeling so wonderfully decadent, so free, so perfectly where she should be.

Conlan sat up beside her and gently took her face between his hands as he stared down at her. He looked so solemn that she felt suddenly chilled.

"What is it?" she said. "Is something wrong? Did I—did I do something wrong?"

"I'm so sorry, Anna," he said hoarsely. "I wasn't able to pull away."

"What?" she said, completely confused.

"I couldn't stop in time."

"I don't—oh. Oh!" And she felt so deeply foolish. In

all her wild pleasure, her heedless desire, she had not stopped to consider the possibility of a child.

For one small, wonderful instant, she thought of a tiny, green-eyed baby, a fierce little Irish boy or girl. Then she remembered she was not Conlan's duchess. She was...

Well, she did not know what she was, or even what she really wanted to be. She only saw his remorseful face.

"I—I think it is all right," she said. She sat up and reached for her chemise to cover her nakedness. Frantically, she tried to remember all her mother and Eliza had told her about marital matters. "I just had my courses."

"If there is..."

"There will not be!"

"Anna, colleen." He took her hand, forcing her to look at him. "If there is, you will tell me at once, won't you?"

So he would be forced to marry her? She did not want that, not at all. She *did* want him, but only if he wanted her just as much. Wanted a life with her because of *her*, not because they had to. "It won't come to that. Now, please, can we talk about something else? Or better yet, not talk at all."

He hesitated, and she could see he wanted to argue and press the issue. But at last he nodded. "Very well. If you will promise to tell me."

"I promise."

"Should I take you back to the Connemaras' now? I don't want to."

Anna glanced at the clock on the stone mantel. "We have a little more time," she said. She lay back down on the floor, tugging him down beside her. She wrapped her arms around him as he rested his head on her shoulder. The clock ticked ominously, as if to remind her how brief and precious their time really was.

"I love being here," she murmured. "I love this house. It's like a fairy tale."

"You don't think it is terribly outdated and unfashionable?" he said with a laugh.

"It's romantic and dignified. Why do you never have parties here?"

"Who would come? I'm not the best-liked man in Society, you know."

"Everyone would come, of course." She smoothed her fingers through his hair as she studied the ceiling and the great fireplace. "You are the duke. Plus, they would be perishing of curiosity to see what it looks like in here. It could be of great use to you."

"How so?"

"Just like the Olympian Club. When people are having fun, drinking and gossiping, they say things they ordinarily would not. And they make alliances with those who share their amusements. Such alliances strengthen a family's position and helps them do what they want to improve their lands without hindrance. A really good party is so much more than amusement and so much stronger than anything they do in Parliament."

Conlan propped himself on his elbow to stare down at her. "Is this Lady Anna Blacknall speaking? The girl they say only cares to dance and gamble at cards? I knew there was more to you."

Anna laughed. "I am glad you think so. But every lady who grows up as I do learns these things. I saw it with my own parents, and with their friends like the Leinsters, the Conollys, and the Shannons. Glittering displays are exceedingly useful. I was taught to be a hostess when I was in leading strings." She paused, staring into the fire as visions whirled in her head. "You could have a wonderful ball in here. A masquerade with a medieval theme. Perhaps even an entire house party weekend with a joust and a grand feast! You could have actors from Dublin to do the joust, and..."

"Anna!" Conlan laughed and stopped her words with a kiss. "Such vast plans. A girls' school, a medieval feast."

"Oh." Feeling foolish, her cheeks hot, she rolled onto her side and sat up. This was not her house, nor was it likely to be. She was carried away by daydreams, as usual. "Of course. It is your house. You have a perfect right to keep it to yourself. But fine entertaining could help your cause, if you would let it."

She heard him sit up behind her, the rustle of cloth as he reached for his breeches. "My cause?"

"Yes." She looked at him over her shoulder. His face was carefully expressionless. "I know you have one. It's what the Olympian Club is all about, yes? Why people try to kill you. Is it the Union?"

He hesitated and shook his head. "You should not be involved, Anna."

"I am already involved," she cried. She was so angry at the way he let her in, let her close to him, then pushed her away again. All for her own good, he said. Yet she was tired of being sheltered. "I was there twice when someone tried to kill you. I am your lover, Conlan, and I want to help you if I can. I am not entirely without resources of my own."

"I know," he said roughly. "You're brave, and you have a gift for knowing people. Caring about them—even if you want people to think you're careless."

He thought she was brave. No one had ever thought

that before. She smiled, despite the lingering anger and frustration. "I also have connections in Society. Now tell me, Conlan—is it the Union that puts you in danger?"

"Yes," he said. He reached for his discarded coat and took a cheroot from the pocket. He lit it with a stick from the fire and took a long drag from it before he went on. "I work with those who oppose it, and there are many who would stop us. They have much at stake if the Union does not happen, money and estates that were bribes from the English government. They would do anything to hold on to them."

Anna frowned as his words sank in, the confirmation of all her suspicions. "Does that not put you with Ascendancy men like Foster and Parnell? And they say many Catholics are *for* the measure."

Conlan exhaled a plume of gray-blue smoke, studying the glowing tip as if it held the answers in its fire. "Some of them expect Prime Minister Pitt to pass Catholic emancipation in exchange for their support, but they are fools. He might do it on his own, but Parliament and the British nobility would never allow it. But there are anti-Union Catholics, just as there are pro-Union anti-Catholics, and everything in between. Everyone has their own motives. And through the Olympian Club I can find what they are."

Anna leaned back against the edge of the chair and hugged her knees to her chest. "But why are *you* anti-Union? Why do you ally yourself with those men at all?"

"I only ally with Ascendancy men for my own ends, as they do with me. They think they can make us English just by calling us so, that by taking away the Dublin Parliament but leaving the Viceroy at the Castle, they can control us. Pitt says it will lessen our receptivity to—French ideas."

"French ideas. Hmm," Anna said, remembering Monsieur Courtois and Conlan's meeting with him.

He went on. "But the power of the County landowners would be diminished with no Dublin Parliament. *My* power would be diminished, and that is how I keep my title and how I keep my people safe. This property protects them."

Anna thought of little Molly and her family, snug and warm in their comfortable house. She thought of Killinan Castle's own people, the care her parents always had for them. And of the poor, hungry people of other estates, where no one fought for them. She thought of Eliza and her work, of all it meant to belong to Ireland.

"I cannot sit in Parliament myself since I'm Catholic," he said. "Being a landowner is my power, and I will always fight to hold on to it, against any who would take it away."

"Like your cousin?"

Conlan gave a humorless chuckle. "Grant was always a greedy bastard. He wanted to be the duke, to have this land with its fertile fields for himself. He would have used it up and discarded it."

As Grant would with her, if she let him? "Is that the only reason you fight?"

"No." He tossed the end of the cheroot into the fire and reached for her. She fell into his arms, snuggling close to him. "We are Irish. And we must fight every chain England would use to bind us to them. The Parliament in Dublin is a corrupt and poor one, but at least it is composed of those who have property here. In Westminster, we would have no voice at all."

"My sister Eliza would say that we can never stop fighting," Anna said.

"Your sister is a wise woman."

"Has she helped you with the Union?"

"She may have written a pamphlet or two," Conlan said.

"And does anyone else I know help you?"

Conlan paused. "That is their own secret to tell. But there is a network that uses the Olympian Club as their headquarters."

"Then I can help you, too!" She wound her arms around his neck, staring deeply into his eyes. She wouldn't let him reject her now. "I know there are many guests at the Christmas party who have been bribed to be pro-Union. They all think I am a silly featherbrain, so they will not be careful with what they say to me."

"Anna, no." He took her firmly by the shoulders, but she would not be discouraged.

"It's not like getting into a knife fight by the river, Conlan. It is just listening. You can't stop me from listening, can you?" She gave him her brightest smile. "Besides, I have you to protect me."

He scowled darkly, but she was not frightened. How could she be, when she could be useful at last? "I'm here, not at the Connemaras'," he said.

"But you are invited to their Christmas Eve ball, aren't you? Lady Connemara said you were, though she was sure you would not come. You will just have to surprise her."

She kissed his lips softly, once, twice. Then again, deeper. His lips parted under hers, and he tasted of mint and smoke and himself. She felt her body stir to life again, the kindling of desire deep in her heart.

"Say you will come to the ball," she whispered. "Say you will dance with me and meet me under the kissing bough."

"With an incentive like that, how can I refuse?" he muttered. His hands closed around her hips and dragged her against him again. His mouth closed hard over hers, his tongue sliding inside.

Anna closed her eyes and let herself fall deeply into him, into her feelings for him. Union vanished, everything vanished, and she wanted just him and this moment. It was where she belonged, with him and with Ireland.

If only he could see that, too.

Chapter Twenty-one

Katherine peered into the shop window, holding on to her hat as a cold gust of wind threatened to carry it away. It was Christmas Eve, and she had slipped away from the party to do a little shopping in the village.

Gifts for Caroline were easy enough—books. The selection in the bookshop here was not as great as in Dublin, but she found a fine set of Plato for her. Caroline liked the Greeks and Romans as well as the Irish. What to get for Anna, though? Katherine carefully examined a length of pale green silk that could make a fine ballgown, but it didn't seem to be exactly what she was looking for.

She was quite worried about her Anna. Her second daughter, always her most sensitive child, was so quiet lately. She always seemed to be thinking of things very far away, things no one else could see and which she didn't share. And Katherine didn't know how to reach her.

How could she get Anna to share secrets when she herself held one of her own?

Katherine sighed as she examined a pair of pearl

earrings. She had hoped that by coming to the country, distracting herself with Christmas festivities, she would forget Nicolas Courtois. That was not so. Among all her old friends, people who had known her so long that they no longer really saw her, she thought of him more than ever.

There in her library he saw her. And she knew him, too, deep down inside. It seemed she knew nothing of him really—he was young, handsome, talented, reserved—and so entirely unsuitable for her. Yet that night, she glimpsed the sensitive soul within, and she longed to know him even better.

"You are being ridiculous," she muttered to herself. Anyone would think she was just a silly schoolgirl, sighing over a handsome face. Not a woman with three grown daughters.

She stared at her reflection in the window. Her hair, untidy in the wind, was still blond, her skin white and smooth. But was that a new line between her brows? Horrors!

Perhaps it was time to give up, to retire to the dower house at Killinan and take up knitting. She could start wearing lace widow's caps, especially once Anna was married and Caroline's Season launched.

But her daughters needed her, even as she feared Anna had misunderstood her words about security and marriage and Grant Dunmore. She had to try and talk to her again. Maybe when she gave her the perfect Christmas gift.

Reflected in the glass behind her were the bustling Christmas crowds, shoppers flocking in from the countryside to find gifts and delicacies for their holiday tables. A man emerged from the bakery across the street, and the watery sunlight caught on his golden hair.

Katherine's heart leaped, and suddenly she couldn't breathe. Nicolas!

Even as she told herself not to be even sillier than she already was, that he was far away in Dublin, she turned to look.

It *was* him, Nicolas. Here in the village. She had the frantic urge to run and hide in the shop until he was gone. But there was the other, equally strong urge to call out, to run to him.

The decision was taken out of her hands when he saw her standing there. A brilliant smile lit his face, quickly fading into wary uncertainty. Did he, too, feel torn between running forward and fleeing?

She waved to him, and he made his way across the crowded street between the wagons and carriages. She straightened her hat, trying to compose herself and put her social mask into place before he reached her. They managed to be coolly polite in Dublin. Why should they not be here?

"Lady Killinan," he said with a bow. "What a pleasant surprise."

"Monsieur Courtois," she answered. Yes, she *could* smile politely. "I did not know you planned to spend the holiday in Kildare."

"I did not, but I received a commission to paint a portrait of Lord Napier's daughters after you recommended me to him in Dublin. He was most insistent I begin at once, so I am here to do as much as I can before I have to return to the city."

"What a great opportunity for you, monsieur! But rather sad you must work at Christmas."

"I do not mind. Christmas in the country is charming, *n'est-ce pas?* I love the green wreaths everywhere."

"It is very pretty, yes. It reminds me of holidays when I was a girl."

"Are you at Killinan Castle to celebrate?" he asked.

"Not this year. My daughters and I are staying with the Connemaras until the new year. I just came to do a bit of shopping."

"And I came to fetch supper," he said, holding up a paper parcel. "*Le pain calendeau,* traditional French bread for Christmas. The baker here kindly made it for me. Cheese, wine, and it is a fine holiday."

Katherine laughed. She strolled slowly down the walkway, and Nicolas kept pace with her. "What else is done in France for Christmas?"

"Oh, there is *la buche de Noel,* the Yule log brought in on Christmas Eve, and *le Reveillon,* the great feast. The usual sort of things."

"And are you lodging with Lord Napier?"

"No, I have rooms here in the village. Just over there, above the bookstore. There is room for my work, and it is very quiet at night, much more so than in Dublin."

Katherine hesitated, torn again between the urge to flee and the even crazier urge to dash forward and fling herself over the cliff.

"I should like to see your work," she said.

He looked down at her, his brow raised. "You would?"

"Oh, yes. I did love those sketches you showed me in Dublin. They seemed full of a rare talent."

"Then I am happy to show my work to you. I warn you it is in rather a rough stage."

"I don't mind that."

"Very well, then. When would you like to see them?"

"Why not now? I do not have to return to the party until teatime."

He nodded and held out his arm to her. Katherine slid her gloved hand over his sleeve, feeling his lean muscles tighten under her touch. For an artist, a man who worked with paintbrushes in his studio all day, he was surprisingly hard and strong.

He led her to a back door of the shop which opened onto a narrow back staircase. The door swung shut behind them, enclosing them in sudden quiet. The bustling Christmas world, the real world, was left outside. Katherine followed him up the stairs to his room.

It was a fairly large chamber, with a tall window looking down on the street and letting in whatever meager light there was. His easel was set up there, along with a table littered with sketchbooks, paints, and charcoal pencils. The only other furniture was a narrow bed, a battered dresser, and one threadbare armchair by the tiny fireplace.

Katherine removed her hat and gloves as she went to examine the half-finished portrait. Nicolas leaned back against the closed door, watching her in silence.

She tried to forget he was there, his beautiful brown eyes on her, and just look at the work. She did know the Napiers and their daughters, two rather plain but sweet girls. In Nicolas's painting, they sat, clad in matching ruffled blue gowns, at a round table, hard at work on their embroidery, surrounded by books, dogs, and parrots. He had managed to make them look like themselves yet better, glowing with health and good spirits, young ladies ready to be wives.

"I fear that once this portrait is seen Caroline will lose you as her teacher," she said. "You will be much in demand as a Society portraitist. Everyone will want you to paint their children." She studied the smiles on the girls' faces and wondered if the sight of the handsome artist had put them there.

Nicolas laughed. He left the door to come stand beside her, studying the portrait with her. "It does pay well, but I should not like to spend all my time in such scenes. There is no—how do you say?—challenge in it. No fire."

No fire. She knew how that felt, the bland, dutiful sameness of days with no passion. "If you could paint whatever you liked, what would it be?"

"I don't know. The outdoors maybe, nature: light, storms, water."

She glanced out the window at the gray sky. Always gray. "There doesn't seem much scope for that here, monsieur. Do you ever think of Italy perhaps? Or Lausanne? My daughter Eliza is there, and she says there is a great community of artists."

"Of course, I think of such places. But I have work to finish here first."

"Like this portrait?"

He hesitated. "Among other things."

Other things? Katherine longed to know what they might be. What preoccupied him. But he said nothing else, and she turned to look at the sketches scattered on the table. Studies of Napier's daughters, images of their dogs and parrots. But also trees and streams, and fields bisected by stone walls. Nature in all its wonder.

Plein air painting was not held in the same esteem as history and mythology scenes, not seen much at the

Academy, but she could see his great skill at such images. There was such passion in every pencil stroke.

"You should go to Italy, monsieur," she said. "The air there is so clear it makes the light shimmer. And it's so warm, so full of life."

He leaned his elegant artist's hands on the table beside her, so near she could feel the heat of his body. "It sounds as if *you* should go to Italy as well, my lady. That you should seek the sun."

"I would love that," she said. Then she said something she had never admitted, even to herself. "I dream sometimes of escaping, of running to Tuscany or Capri and spending all day walking in the light. But I have other duties here."

"What of your duty to yourself?"

"Myself? No, I have to think of Killinan, the girls..."

"Lady Killinan—Katherine," he said fiercely. He reached for her, clasping her arms to spin her toward him. He wouldn't let her go, and the look in his eyes was as warm as that dream of Italian skies. "You are so beautiful, so full of life and warmth. Why do you hide it so? Why do you deny it?"

She shook her head, balancing on the edge of something like panic. For so long she held herself in check, ferociously suppressing any hint of emotions or needs. Now all those tightly leashed feelings were slipping free, and she was powerless to imprison them again.

"I deny nothing," she insisted. "I am content in my life."

"Then why do you dream of escaping it? Why do you hide your true beauty?" He released her arms only to catch her face between his hands. He stared deeply into her eyes and would not let her turn her face away. "Katherine, *ma belle*, don't hide from me now. I beg you. I can't bear it any longer."

A sob escaped her lips, and she knew she could not hide. Not from him or herself, not now.

He kissed her, and she had never been kissed like that before. Nicolas kissed her as if she was precious and beautiful, as if he had waited all his life for someone just like her and was filled with awe to find it. She, too, had been waiting, though she hadn't realized it until this very moment. Waiting and hoping.

His tongue lightly traced the curve of her lips, and she opened for him, meeting his kiss with her own. She wound her arms around his shoulders, holding on to him tightly so he could not vanish from her. He tasted warm and sweet, like springtime, and she felt her long-cold heart melt.

"You're trembling," he whispered, his lips trailing over her cheek.

"I—I thought such things could never be mine," she said. "I thought they could only belong to the young."

He laughed and held out his hand. "I'm trembling, too. Oh, Katherine, I never thought I would find you, but here you are."

"Find me?"

He pulled her close, and she felt him rest his cheek on top of her head. She heard his deep, ragged breath as he inhaled the scent of her hair. She closed her eyes and curled her hands tightly into his coat. How she wished she could stay like that forever. Just him and her, and no one to judge them.

"I used to dream of a woman like you," he said. "Beautiful, kind, wise. A muse. An angel."

"Angel?" She laughed harshly. "Everyone is so very wrong about that."

"*Non*, Katherine." He pressed a fevered kiss to her temple. "You are an extraordinary woman. You have made me see life in a new, glorious way. Not just art but everything. I was in despair before, angry, drifting, always searching for some purpose. Some reason. Then I saw you. . . ."

Katherine tilted her head back to study his face, amazed at his passionate words. "I did all of that?"

"And more. I have never known anyone like you, Katherine. You are—amazing."

She dropped her head to his shoulder. How she wished she could believe him! His words filled her with such joy and hope. All her life she lived for others—her parents, her husband, her children, the people of Killinan. When Nicolas looked at her she felt beautiful, and young, and whole, with a world of possibility before her.

But those were only feelings, wild hopes. She could give him nothing. She was older than him and bound by her duties. He surely was caught in some infatuation, just as she was.

It was very sweet while it lasted, though. And why should she not have a little, secret moment for herself?

She slid her hands up his neck, into his hair, holding on to him so that she could look deeply into his eyes. She read no artifice there, no flash of hesitation or doubt. He looked at her as if she were indeed an angel.

"Kiss me again, Nicolas," she whispered.

He smiled at her. "With the greatest pleasure, Katherine." And he did, his lips covering hers hard, as if he would not ever let her go.

Chapter Twenty-two

Anna stood in the shadows of the little minstrels' gallery high above the Connemaras' ballroom. She rested her elbows on the railing and stared down at the brilliant whirl of activity far below. Usually she adored such gatherings, loved being a part of the music and dancing, especially at Christmas. Tonight, though, she felt strangely reluctant to join in.

The elaborate pattern of the polished parquet floor was covered by a kaleidoscope of blues, greens, whites, and purples, in shimmering satins, lustrous velvets, and soft, floaty muslins. Jewels flashed and sparkled in the glow of hundreds of candles. The air was thick with the scents of evergreen, red roses, and holly. Wreaths and loops of red ribbon were draped along the white walls.

The orchestra played a lively rendition of that omnipresent "Wren Song" as the dancers twirled and skipped over the floor. Everyone who did not dance crowded around its edges, the laughter growing louder and rowdier as the punch flowed.

Anna didn't know where Lady Connemara had found

so many people on Christmas Eve or how she had lured them out into the cold night from their own holiday hearths. Along with the house party guests, there was all the Kildare gentry and more from even farther afield. She saw Caroline sitting in the corner with Lord Hartley, the two of them actually ignoring the dance to study a book. Her mother talked with the local vicar and his wife by one of the large holly wreaths. Jane danced with Lord Connemara, clad in another enviable gown of amber-colored silk.

But there was no Duke of Adair.

Anna carefully studied every newcomer who crowded through the doors and down the stairs to the ballroom, and none was ever him. She was quite disappointed.

She tugged at the Christmas-green sash of her white silk gown, fiddling with the corsage of artificial holly tucked into its satin folds. She had taken even greater care with her appearance than usual, filled with dreamy visions of dancing with him in front of everyone. Of celebrating Christmas with him, forgetting their troubles for one night, just being with him. Pretending they belonged together.

She couldn't do that if he did not even show up.

The door behind her clicked open, and she spun around in a flare of wild hope. But it was not Conlan. It was Grant Dunmore.

Her heart sinking again, Anna leaned back on the marble balustrade as he shut the door behind him. She could see why all the ladies loved him so much. He was so perfectly handsome, like a hero from a book, so impeccably stylish, so admired and well-connected. Everything she herself should want, had once thought she *did* want.

Yet she felt nothing when she looked at him or when he smiled at her. She could no longer summon up even a halfhearted desire for him and the glittering life they could have together. Not even for duty and expectations.

He gave her a dazzling smile. "So this is where you are hiding, Lady Anna."

"I was not hiding, Sir Grant," she said, taken aback by his sudden appearance and by a certain quality to that smile she had not noticed before. A certain smugness, as if she was a pretty child that he meant to indulge. "I merely did not feel like dancing."

"You? The finest dancer in all Kildare? I find that hard to believe." He joined her at the balustrade to peer down at the party.

"I cannot rival Lady Cannondale for dancing." She gestured to Jane, dancing so beautifully in the patterns of the reel, full of vivid life. "Or our hostess."

"Nonsense. You are famous for your grace and beauty, Lady Anna, and everyone knows it." He leaned his elbows on the railing, as she had done. Even in that, he looked like casual perfection. "Perhaps you are imagining what your own Christmas ball would be like, if you were the hostess."

"I doubt I would have a house as grand as this," Anna said carefully.

"You would make any house grand. And attract the cream of Society to all your gatherings."

She laughed, suddenly uncomfortable in his presence as she never had been before. She couldn't explain it, but the gallery felt too small and close. "I have no such ambitions, Sir Grant."

"Do you not? You could rule this world if you wanted.

You could have anything at all you desired." He caught her hand in his, startling her. She tried to pull away, but he held on tightly. "I could give you that, Anna. Together we would be the most sought-after, most powerful couple in Dublin. Maybe in all Ireland. London, too, if that was what you wanted."

"I—I don't think..." she stammered, confused. She had refused proposals before, but she had never been caught so off her guard. "I don't think so."

Grant, usually so smooth and charming, so correct, scowled at her. His hand flexed on hers. "What do you mean? I am asking you to be my wife," he said. "Surely you have been aware of my intentions toward you. Our situations in life are so suited to each other, by fortune and connection. You must know that."

Their situations—not themselves. Not their hearts. He did not even seem to *see* her, and she remembered Caroline's warning in the garden, and her own fears. He wanted her for an ornament, a piece in his puzzle of social advancement and ambition.

"I'm sorry, Sir Grant, but I had no idea you had a—a regard for me," she said. She carefully tried to tug her wrist away, but he held on to her. "I thought you were only polite to me, as to any lady."

"Of course I was not being polite!" he said, his silken charm turning rough. "There is no lady better suited to be my wife. You are beautiful, of good family. I can give you a home where you can shine."

Anna shook her head. "Where I can be an ornament?"

"A diamond."

"I don't want that, though," she said. "I want to be useful, to have a real purpose."

"Useful? You would be useful to *me*," he said impatiently. "I have ambitions in politics, as I'm sure you know, and I need a suitable wife and hostess to help me in that."

"Many ladies could be that for you," Anna said. Grant had many feminine admirers, and he admired them in return. Surely one of them would be most happy to grace his table, as well as his bed, lead his political salon. She could not. Even to make her family happy, she could not. She would wither and die.

"But there is no one as beautiful as you," he said.

"Of course there is! I am very honored at your proposal, Sir Grant, but I fear we would not suit. I am sorry." She twisted her wrist again, hard, and at last he let her go. His golden eyes darkened, like thunderclouds, and she whirled around to hurry to the door.

"Is it because there is someone you prefer?" he called to her.

Her hand froze on the door handle. There was such fury in his voice, tightly leashed anger that she could not have imagined he possessed under his perfect surface. But she knew she shouldn't be surprised, not after seeing the way he confronted Conlan on St. Stephen's Green. A man who would try to steal his own cousin's ancestral estate was not a man to be thwarted.

"I am not ready to marry anyone," she answered.

He laughed harshly. "I cannot believe that, Lady Anna."

"It doesn't matter what you believe, Sir Grant, it is the truth. Now I must return to the party." She rushed out the door, slamming it behind her. She had the strongest urge to pick up her skirts and run, but there were people strolling in the corridor, so she made herself slowly walk to the staircase. He didn't follow her to press his suit, thankfully, and when she slipped back into the ballroom, it seemed more crowded than ever. Surely there was safety in such a press.

The reel was ending, and she made her way through the laughing throng in search of her mother or sister. Her head ached; some of the brightness of the holiday dimming as her fear lingered. She had closed the door on one path, the path everyone expected her to take, and she didn't know what to do now. She hadn't expected Grant's anger, and the chill of that lingered, too.

She couldn't find her mother, but she glimpsed Caroline walking toward the dance floor with Lord Hartley. So the two of them *could* abandon their books sometimes. As Anna glanced back, she saw the ballroom doors open again, and Conlan appeared there at last. He stood still for a moment, at the top of the steps, and everything else faded to a blur around him.

Anna realized that she had only rarely seen him as the Duke, and when she had it did not go very well, but here he fulfilled his position entirely. Tall, powerful, and dressed in stark, perfectly tailored black and white, he surveyed the company with casual confidence as Lady Connemara hurried to greet him. He didn't even seem to notice all the curious stares and the whispers that turned his way. *The reclusive duke, here!*

But he did notice her. He gave her a quiet and intimate smile and then disappeared into the crowd. Still in a daze where everything seemed slow and silent, Anna pushed her way past the laughing, tipsy people, searching for him.

She found him standing beneath one of the kissing boughs.

"So you came after all," she said breathlessly.

"You did say I should cultivate connections with my neighbors," he answered. "That I should not hide away like an angry bear on my estate, an old recluse."

Anna laughed. "I did not exactly say that, Your Grace. Angry and reclusive you may be, but a bear—well, yes, you can be that as well."

"Now that I am here, though, I scarcely know what to do next. You must help me."

Anna could hear the orchestra tuning up for a scandalous Viennese waltz, just like at the Olympian Club. There was the great rustle of silk, footsteps, and laughter as couples hurried to take their places. "I think you should begin by dancing with me."

"Dancing?"

"Of course. You cannot pretend you don't know how, for we have danced together before. Now you have to show everyone here your graceful, refined side."

He snorted. "Grace and refinement will always be beyond me, I fear. Yet I would never turn down the chance to dance with the prettiest lady in the room."

He offered her his arm with a bow, and she let him lead her onto the dance floor. This time there were no concealing masks. They were only themselves, together in full sight of everyone.

And everyone certainly did watch. A place was made for them at the center of the floor, right next to Caroline and her Lord Hartley. Anna's sister looked mischievously delighted, but Anna ignored everyone. She watched only Conlan as he slid one arm about her waist and took her hand in his. She rested her other hand lightly on his shoulder. Even though they stood the proscribed, correct distance apart, she couldn't help the rush of excitement that shivered through her.

"They say the waltz is still terribly scandalous in London," she said. "All the high sticklers say it incites improper lust."

He grinned down at her. "No wonder it's so popular in Dublin then."

Anna laughed as the musicians swung into the lilting tune, and Conlan whirled her in a circle. He *was* a good dancer, even without the wild freedom of the Olympian Club. Their steps were perfectly matched, their movements as one as they turned and dipped and twirled. The giddy patterns made her want to laugh in delight, to whirl on and on with him just like this forever.

But the song ended too soon. All the couples spun to a stop as the last strains of the violins died away. Anna curtsied low to Conlan one more time, still laughing helplessly.

As she rose to take his arm again, she glanced up at the minstrels' gallery. Grant Dunmore still stood there, his fists braced on the balustrade. Even from that distance, she could feel the burn of his angry stare. He whirled around and stalked out of the gallery.

Anna shivered, and Conlan asked, "Are you all right, Lady Anna? Are you chilled?"

She made herself shake away the cold touch of that fury and smiled up at him. She wanted nothing to ruin this moment, this Christmas night. Cold morning would come soon enough. "I think I am in need of some refreshment, Your Grace. Would you escort me into the dining room? Lady Connemara has laid out a fine buffet."

"Of course."

"And then maybe you will dance with me again?" she said. She noticed Caroline standing in the dining room doorway with Lord Hartley, watching them with avid interest. Her little sister was far too observant. "But first, I fear you will have to meet my sister Caroline. Don't let her quiz you too much about the history of Adair Court, and you may not want to mention your ancestor Ewan the Brave. She adores things like that and would question you about it incessantly."

Conlan laughed, as if he was completely undaunted by the prospect of being quizzed about his Irish ancestors by a young bluestocking. "She sounds like a most unusual colleen."

Anna sighed. "Yes, she is that. But that's our family for you—unusual."

He leaned close and whispered in her ear, "Lucky for me I am highly appreciative of the—unusual."

Chapter Twenty-three

"Are you sure we should be going to Parliament today of all days?" Caroline said.

Anna leaned back on the carriage seat, watching the crowded Dublin streets flash by outside the window. It was a gray, wet day, and the pretty white Christmas snow had turned to black mush as they moved into the new year of 1800. Even though it was barely January, the bright holiday seemed long past.

"Of course, we should be going, today above all," she said. "It is the last debate before the Union vote."

"That's what I mean. It's sure to be a terrible crush in the gallery, and someone is bound to start a fight."

"I do hope so."

"And you'll be fortunate not to get slapped or have your hair pulled, wearing that ribbon."

Anna toyed with the ribbon pinned to her fur-edged spencer. Its blue satin length was embroidered with the words "British Connection, Irish Independence, No Union." "Jane gave it to me. If someone quarrels with us, you could hit them over the head with that book you insist on lugging about."

The carriage jolted to a sudden stop, and Anna could hear curses and shrieks out on the street. She peered from the window to see that they were trapped in a terrible traffic snarl on Hoggen Green, far down from the Parliament building. They were blocked in on all sides, and it was obvious they wouldn't be moving anytime soon.

"Come on, Caro, we'll have to walk the rest of the way," Anna said as she reached for the door latch. When it swung open, the shouts grew louder, and the pungent smell of rotted vegetables was noxious in the cold wind.

"Anna, maybe we should just go home, or maybe to the milliner…" Caroline began, always the voice of prudence.

"Nonsense! The fate of our homeland is being decided in there today, and we don't want to miss it." Anna took her sister by the hand and tugged her out of the carriage. They pushed their way past the crowds until they found the gray stone steps and the colonnade of soaring Ionic columns that led into the Parliament building.

And there, they also found the main attraction, just at the foot of those steps. One of the Honorable Members, a man notorious for taking English bribes, attempted to alight from his fine new carriage, but his path was blocked by shrieking market women. They pelted him with old cabbages whenever he stuck out a silk-clad leg, much to the merriment of the onlookers.

"English dog!" they shouted. "Castlereagh's pig! Just try and sell *us* out, you fancy turd."

The guards stationed along the columns just laughed, and the crowd waiting to press inside acted as if they were watching a particularly amusing Christmas pantomime. Still holding on to Caroline's hand, Anna shoved past them, ducking the flying vegetables. They hurried beneath the portico, lined with the grand statues of Hibernia, Fidelity, and Commerce. Their stone eyes stared down at the chaos without much interest, but the royal coat of arms above hadn't fared very well. It was splattered with cabbage.

The guards let Anna and Caroline go by into the marble foyer with its glittering crystal chandeliers. There was no quiet dignity there today, though, if there ever was. The hordes of people trying to get into the octagonal Parliament chamber were thickly pressed together, a tangle of pro-Union orange ribbons and anti-Union blue. There was just as much shouting as outside, shoving and pushing, and just as Caroline had warned, there was hair-pulling. No one was safe, whether man or woman, peasant or princess.

Anna held on to Caroline with one hand and her blue-feathered hat with the other and went up the stairs to the observers' gallery. The galleries surrounded the chamber on all eight sides, with widely spaced columns and tiered seating so that all the action below could be observed. She had been there a few times with friends, and it was always full of interested onlookers, heckling the speakers and eating sugared almonds and coffee. But it was never like today. People were jammed into every available space, opera glasses at the ready.

"Anna!" she heard Jane call. "Here, I've saved you a seat."

Jane had somehow snared a prime place, at the end of one of the benches on the front row, and she was hotly defending it. Anna managed to slide onto the wooden seat beside her, dragging Caroline with her. Caro beat off an attempted poacher with her book.

"Modern politics is no fun at all," Caroline muttered. She dragged her battered bonnet from her head and straightened her spectacles. "They should try hand-to-hand combat to settle questions, like the ancient Celts."

"I think it might come to that," said Jane with a laugh. She, too, wore a blue ribbon and blue feathers in her hat.

"Have we missed anything?" Anna asked. She pulled her opera glasses from her reticule and trained them on the floor below, but she could only see a tangle of black coats down there.

"Not at all. The Speaker is reading the Resolutions—or he would if he could keep from being shouted down," said Jane.

Anna's glasses found Mr. Foster, the Speaker, where he stood on a platform. He waved a clutch of papers wildly, shouting, "We cannot begin until the Resolutions are called!" No one paid attention, except for the booing women in the gallery. All the Members were arguing amongst themselves, overturning benches and scattering more papers.

Anna swung her glasses across the way to see who listened in the other galleries. The boos and cheers, orange and blue, seemed evenly divided, with no one getting the upper hand.

"There is your rejected suitor," Jane said wryly. "Keeping an eye on his pet delegate, I suppose."

"Rejected suitor?" said Anna, still caught up in the action.

"Grant Dunmore, of course." Jane moved Anna's hand so the glasses pointed to another gallery. "Obviously he prefers behind-the-scenes work to—what did you call it, Lady Caroline? Hand-to-hand combat?"

"I suppose you would know, Lady Cannondale," Caroline murmured under her breath. "You seem expert at that sort of thing."

It *was* Grant Dunmore, coolly watching the debate boil below. Anna hadn't seen him since the Christmas Eve ball because he had departed from the Connemaras' the next morning, not even waiting for the Boxing Day theatricals. He wore a somber black greatcoat and stark white cravat, his coppery hair trimmed shorter and brushed back. The look on his face was utterly inscrutable.

"Is he really pro-Union, then?" Anna asked. "I thought so, but he is not one to let his convictions show."

"Convictions?" Jane laughed. "Some men have convictions; others have fortunes to protect or acquire. Scores to settle. Why else would he commandeer the by-election in Queen's County last year, when he never cared about it before?"

Anna lowered her glasses. "So he thinks Union, and a cozy relationship with Westminster, will open Adair Court to him again?"

Jane didn't answer as the roar from below grew even louder. Anna didn't need an answer, though; she was already sure. And she felt like a fool for not seeing it before.

The clang of a giant bell, hurriedly wheeled in from some unknown church, established a measure of order. The members fell back to their seats just long enough for Mr. Foster to take his seat on the Woolsack and the resolutions finally to be read. Then the debates commenced in full earnest, for and against, amidst even more boos and shouts. Finally came the moment everyone waited for, when the charismatic Mr. Grattan, an outspoken opponent of the Union, took the speaker's podium, and the chamber fell silent at last.

"This Union is not an identification of two nations," he began. "It is merely a merger of the parliament of one nation into that of the other. One nation—England—retains her full proportion, while Ireland strikes off two-thirds; she does so without any regard to either her present number, or to comparative physical strength. She is more than one-third in population, in territory, and less than one-sixth in representation! Her tax coin, her products of wool and linen and crops, are taken without regard to the good of this land and its people."

As he went on with this litany of injustice, the murmurs of the crowd grew steadily into a low roar, and his voice rose as he hammered his fist on the podium. "It follows that the two nations are not identified, though the Irish legislature be absorbed, and by that act of absorption, the feeling of one of the nations is not identified but alienated! I say British connection, Irish independence, no Union!"

The throngs on the floor surged forward again, Grattan carried from his platform on the shoulders of anti-Union members as blue ribbons rained down from the galleries. It seemed his passionate eloquence had carried the day, but the jeers were just as loud.

Anna caught a glimpse between the columns of black hair and broad shoulders, and she swung her glasses up just in time to see Conlan turning down the stairs. Grant Dunmore was several paces behind him.

She knew that he couldn't hear her shout above the din, but she had the terrible feeling that she had to warn him somehow. Of what, she didn't know, but that sense was very strong. Amid all the shouting and bell-ringing, and the shower of ribbons and torn paper, something was bound to happen.

She jumped to her feet and pushed past the crowds in the gallery. Everyone stood atop the benches now, shoving each other amid the clamor. She made it to the stairs and dashed down them to the foyer, but she didn't see Conlan or Grant anywhere.

She ran down the corridors, much quieter than the chaotic chamber but still crowded with people rushing in to be part of the madhouse. She burst out onto the steps next to Commerce, and there at last she glimpsed Conlan standing on the walkway below. The market women were gone, leaving only piles of old cabbage, and there were just a few wise souls who departed the building around him. He calmly lit a cheroot, perfectly composed, as if he had not just escaped from Bedlam.

"Conlan!" she cried and hurried down the steps. Her shoe slid on a bit of cabbage, and she collided with his shoulder just as he turned to her.

"Well, *cailleach,* this is quite a greeting," he said, his arm coming around her waist to keep her from falling.

Despite her rush of panic, she was very happy to see him again. His teasing smile and the glint in his green eyes were as gorgeous as ever. "Are you—well?" she asked.

"As well as a man can be who just escaped a wild menagerie," he answered, tossing aside the cheroot. "And you? I'm surprised you wanted to come to this pandemonium."

"How could I not? After everything we talked about. I thought I could..."

Suddenly, she felt a hard push to her shoulders, and she

fell hard to the stone steps. Pain flashed through her side, and all the breath was knocked from her lungs. She heard a woman scream, it sounded like Caroline, and the violent pounding of skin on skin and the crack of bone.

She managed to push herself up, her head spinning, just in time to see Grant punch Conlan in the face.

For an instant, Anna could only stare, stunned. It was so entirely unreal that she was sure it must be a hallucination brought on by her fall. But it was all too real.

All Grant's calm inscrutability in the chamber had vanished in a raw, primitive fury. As Anna scrambled to her feet, Grant and Conlan went tumbling down the steps locked in combat.

"Stop this right now!" Anna shouted, struggling to be heard over Caroline's screams and the shouts of the crowd gathering around them. Dublin was always a rowdy city, but a duke, a baronet, and an earl's daughter in a brawl was not seen every day. The tale would be known everywhere by sunset, but Anna couldn't worry about that now.

She had to keep the two stupid men from killing each other.

"*Diolain!*" Conlan shouted. He had the upper hand, holding Grant's arm pinned behind his back. But a livid bruise bloomed on his jaw where Grant had punched him, and Grant seemed to be possessed by some demon of fury. He drove his elbow back into Conlan's ribs and called out hoarse, incoherent words that no lady should hear.

The onlookers were no help. They only kept shouting encouragement of more violence. A few fights even broke out amongst *them*.

Anna snatched the book from under Caroline's arm and cried, "Help me, Caro!"

Caroline nodded numbly and followed Anna into the fray.

Dodging flying fists, Anna cracked Grant over the head with the book. She rained down blows on him until he fell back. Caroline seized him by the arm and dragged him down the steps with a burst of strength as Anna fell to her knees by Conlan.

His eyes were nearly black with fury, and he lunged after his retreating cousin as if to finish Grant off, once and for all. Anna threw her arms around his shoulders, using all her strength to hold him back.

"No more, Conlan!" she cried. On the steps below them, Caroline had twisted her fist hard into Grant's cravat and seemed to be lecturing him. He, like Conlan, looked mutinously angry, but he stayed where he was. The crowd, sensing the drama was over, slowly dispersed in search of other diversions.

Anna felt out of breath and exhausted. The fight had lasted only minutes, a sudden firestorm of murderous temper, but she felt as if she had been battling for hours.

"Please, Conlan, no more," she begged. "No more."

He tore out of her grasp and spun around, as if he would shout at her, too. But something in her appearance—her hat lost, hair pulled from its pins, and face dirty from rolling around on the steps—made him freeze.

"You're hurt," he said hoarsely. He reached out and gently touched her lip. His finger came away smeared with blood.

She swiped her hand over the spot and found a cut. She hadn't even felt it in the furor of the fight. "Blast," she whispered. Then she caught sight of her blue velvet sleeve, smeared with cabbage. "Double blast! This was my favorite jacket."

"*Diolain!*" Conlan shouted as he spun back toward Grant. He stood up straight, his arms spread wide. "You've been scheming to get me for years, Dunmore. Well, here I am. Face me like a man. Don't involve innocent women in your villainy."

"You stole everything from me," Grant called back. He shook away Caroline's grasp to face Conlan squarely. His handsome face was twisted with rage. "Everything that should have been mine. But you had best beware, cousin. Your day of reckoning is coming fast. Your time is ending."

"And you're lurking in the wings, waiting to swoop in and claim what is *yours*?" Conlan said with a sneer. "The estate you couldn't get by treachery? My fortune? Maybe even my woman."

Grant's stare raked over Anna with palpable contempt. "After your dirty Irish hands have touched her? I don't think so."

With a roar, Conlan lunged toward Grant. Anna seized his coat and yanked him back just in time, almost sending them both toppling to the ground.

"Heed my words, *cousin*," Grant said. "Your time is over. This time I will win." He stalked off down the street, disappearing into the rushing crowds as Caroline stared after him angrily.

Anna suddenly felt every bump and bruise, every touch of the cold wind. The sudden violence made her think too much of '98, the nearness of rape and death. She wrapped her arms around herself, trembling.

"Anna, don't cry, colleen," Conlan said. He gently touched her arm, but she shook him away. "It is over."

"Of course it's not over," she whispered. "You heard him."

"Grant? He's nothing. I fought him before. I'll win again."

Anna shook her head. "It isn't just him, though, is it?"

"Your Grace?" someone called. "What happened here? They said in the gallery there was a fight."

Anna turned to see Monsieur Courtois, Caroline's drawing teacher, hurrying down the steps toward them. Jane was right behind him, her usual expression of fashionably cynical amusement replaced by tense concern.

"Grant Dunmore thought he would start something with me here," Conlan answered. "But he's gone now."

"Monsieur Courtois," Anna said. She was amazed that her voice sounded steady at all. "I didn't know you were interested in politics." She did remember that the Frenchman knew Conlan, though. They had met the night that Conlan was attacked next to the river.

Had Grant sent those men, too? Her head was spinning, and she swayed dizzily. She didn't fall, though, because Caroline rushed to catch her arm.

"Lady Caroline," Monsieur Courtois said in surprise. "I didn't know you and Lady Anna planned to attend Parliament today. Is your mother here?"

"She's not interested in politics, monsieur," said Caroline. "Now I see she was quite wise. Politics are perilous to one's health."

Jane took a handkerchief from her reticule and pressed it gently to Anna's lip. "Politics are a necessary evil, Lady Caroline," she said. "It is *politicians* one must be wary of. Did Grant do this?"

"I was merely a bystander who got in the way," Anna said. "He ran into me on his way to Conlan. He wanted to kill Conlan. I could see it in his eyes."

"Let me take you home," said Jane. "My carriage is right here."

Anna glanced at Conlan. She had so many questions. It seemed wrong to let him out of her sight. But he gave her a decisive nod. "Go with Lady Cannondale, colleen. You and your sister should be at home."

"And stay there with the doors locked and pistols at the ready?" Caroline said wryly.

"If you are so inclined," Conlan answered. "I have a feeling you would be a formidable shot, Lady Caroline."

"But what of you?" Anna protested. "You shouldn't be alone."

"Monsieur Courtois will walk with me," said Conlan.

Anna uncertainly examined the elegant drawing teacher. "Monsieur Courtois?"

"I assure you, Lady Anna, I am armed with more than a paintbrush," he said.

"Come with me now, Anna," Jane said, tugging at Anna's sleeve. "We should be out of the cold. Plus, you rather reek of old cabbage."

Anna lifted her sleeve to her nose for a careful sniff. She did indeed stink, one more indignity to add to the day. She nodded and let Jane lead her and Caroline down the street to her carriage. Conlan and Monsieur Courtois set off in the opposite direction, talking together intently.

Anna wanted so much to know what they said, to know all of what was going on here. But she was also suddenly very weary. She slumped back onto the fine silk cushions as Jane's carriage jolted into motion.

"I'm sorry I'm getting your pretty carriage dirty," Anna murmured.

Jane waved her apology away. "I'm just glad you are not hurt. Whatever happened out there?"

Caroline answered. "Grant Dunmore attacked the duke and knocked him down on the steps. Then Anna hit him, Dunmore that is, over the head with my book and drove him away like a rabid dog. By the way, I seem to have lost that book. And my spectacles. But it was worth it. It was actually rather exciting."

Jane laughed as Anna protested, "It wasn't quite as simple as that. I was shocked by Sir Grant's sudden rage."

"I wouldn't be surprised," Jane said. "He is a man full of hidden darkness. I just fear we have only glimpsed the beginning of it all. You should be on your guard, Anna."

"Should I take to carrying a pistol?"

"It couldn't hurt." Jane opened her reticule to display a tiny, pearl-handled firearm. "You never know what can happen in these dangerous days."

"Is that real?" Caroline asked in avid curiosity.

"Of course," Jane said. She took out the gun and pressed it into Anna's hand. "You should keep it. I have others at home."

Anna tested its dainty weight on her palm. It was almost as light as a fan, yet was somehow reassuring. As Jane said—these were dangerous days.

"That was quite a scene, Sir Grant."

Grant, stalking past an open carriage door on Fishamble Street, was brought up short by the slurred words. The anger that overcame him when he saw Adair put his arm around Anna Blacknall had died down to simmering embers, but they still sizzled with the old, old injustices. He couldn't even think straight anymore, and it made him foolishly lose his temper and show his hand too soon. Now word of his breach would spread over the whole city.

Scowling, he peered into the dark depths of the carriage. George Hayes sat there, a silver flask in his hand as usual. The ridiculous sot was so lost in debt that he would do any dirty deed for money, yet he laughed at Grant.

"It was an unfortunate lapse," Grant said coldly. "It won't happen again."

"I should say not," said George. He took another swig from his flask. "Here, get in. I'll drive you home."

"I would rather walk."

George's bloated face turned from tipsily genial to furious in a flash. "After what you just did, Sir Grant, brawling like a common prizefighter in the street, you have no cause to look down on *me*! Now get in. We have to talk about what action to take now."

"Did Lord Ross send you?"

"Just get in."

Grant glanced down the street. Everyone seemed to be scurrying on their own errands, paying him no attention even with his bruised face and dirty coat. But a carriage turned the corner, one with the Cannondale crest on the shiny black door. Jane—his former lover, and, as he had just discovered from one of his spies in Parliament—a traitorous bitch. He climbed into George's carriage before she could see him and slammed the door behind him.

George offered him the flask, and Grant shook his head in disgust. George shrugged and gulped down the last of it. The interior of the carriage reeked of old upholstery, brandy, and rotten cabbage.

"It doesn't matter who sent me. We have to act now," George said. "The final vote on Union is very soon. We have the numbers on our side now, but that could change too easily. Adair has been a thorn in our side too long."

All my life, Grant thought. Adair had been his nemesis all his life. But that would end soon. Even if he had to ally with scoundrels like George Hayes to achieve it. "What are you saying?"

"Adair seems to know everything we're doing before we do. He frightens men off so even bribes don't work on them. And every time someone is sent to finish him off, he walks away unscathed. It has to stop. Too bad you didn't finish that fight by bashing his ugly Fenian head on the marble steps."

Grant flexed his bruised hand. He had wanted to do that with a ferocity that shocked him. "He doesn't have to be dead for me to get what I want."

"A man like that? Of course he has to be dead. Come, Dunmore. You want Adair Court; I want Killinan Castle. My lovely cousin has been unlucky in her children. Eliza and her damned United Irishman, and now Anna wasting her considerable charms on the likes of Adair. Caroline is just a useless bluestocking. But poor Katherine seems to love them. Emotions can be useful. They can be used against people when it's most needed."

Grant stared down at his bloody knuckles and thought of Caroline Blacknall. She was small, slender, so young, but she had been so fierce as she dragged him out of the fight. Like Athena, riding into war.

Yet her brown eyes were so soft as she looked at the *Chronicle of Kildare;* as if she understood its significance.

"I won't involve ladies in this," Grant muttered.

"Even a lady like Anna Blacknall, who threw you over for an Irishman?" George said with a drunken laugh. "She's already involved up to her beautiful neck. Now, do you want to defeat Adair or not?"

Grant slammed his fist down on the seat, blotting out the image of Caroline Blacknall's dark eyes and pretty smile. "I want to take him down."

Chapter Twenty-four

"Is my mother home, Smythe?" Anna asked as the butler opened the door for them. She leaned lightly on Caroline's arm as they stepped into the foyer, still a bit unsteady after the day's adventures.

"No, Lady Anna. She is still at her Ladies' Charitable Committee meeting, and I must go to the market for her before she arrives home. She wanted veal chops for dinner and cook has run out, and it seems the kitchen maid has a cold," Smythe said with a suffering sigh. His eyes widened as he took in their disheveled state. "Shall I send up some hot water before I go, my lady?"

"Yes, please, Smythe. A great quantity. And some tea," said Anna.

"Of course, my lady," Smythe said. "Right away. Oh, and this letter arrived today from Switzerland. I thought you might like to read it immediately."

"News from Eliza!" Caroline cried, taking up the thick letter. "At last. It has been ever so long since we have heard from her."

"That is something cheerful, at least," Anna said.

"Come, Caro, you can read it to me while I change my clothes. We can certainly use the distraction."

Deeply grateful that her mother was not home to see the state of her daughters, Anna hurried to her chamber and tore off her ruined jacket. The sight that greeted her in the mirror almost made her shriek—wild, tangled hair, red cheeks, and her eyes glittering with nervous excitement. No wonder Conlan called her a witch.

As soon as the maids delivered the hot water and tea tray, she splashed great handfuls on her face and scrubbed with her scented soap. But it couldn't erase the violence of the fight or the fact that, despite her resolve to be respectable from now on and not embarrass her family, she had brought gossip onto them yet again.

"That was quite an adventure," Caroline said after the servants departed and they were alone again. "Should we talk about it?"

Anna shook her head. She reached for her brush and yanked the bristles hard through her tangled hair. "Not yet. I'm not sure I could be quite coherent. Read me Eliza's letter."

Caroline looked as if she very much wanted to argue. But she just nodded, poured out some tea, and opened the letter. Anna closed her eyes as she listened to her faraway sister's words, trying to lose herself in Eliza's accounts of walking in the beautiful, sparkling white snow, skating on frozen lakes, and Swiss Christmas festivities. It sounded like a magical, unreal world.

"Even though I don't much care for sweets, I have had such cravings for the *stollen*, a sort of Christmas cake they seem to adore here, because..." Caroline suddenly broke off with a squeal. "Because I am to have a baby in the summer! Oh, Anna, we will be *aunts*."

"A baby!" Anna's eyes flew open, and she snatched the letter away to read it herself.

"Mama will be so happy when she hears!" Caroline said.

"Indeed she will. A grandchild at last," said Anna. "And it should also distract Mama from my brawling in the streets of Dublin like a market woman."

"Oh, Anna, she won't be angry," Caroline protested. "You had to come to the duke's aid when he was attacked."

Anna laughed ruefully. "I hardly think someone like Adair needs *my* assistance in combat."

"If I was in trouble, I would definitely want you at my back. You were quite fearless, the way you hit Grant Dunmore over the head with my book."

"Speaking of that, I will be sure and buy you a new volume tomorrow."

Caroline shrugged. "It was only Herodotus. I have more of his work somewhere around here. Have you definitely decided against Dunmore then?"

Anna remembered the raw, burning fury in his eyes. "I would say assuredly yes. He is not the man for me. He never was."

"But Adair is the man for you?"

"He hasn't asked me to marry him."

"He will, I'm sure. Especially after today. And you always did say you wanted to marry a duke."

"He is not quite the duke I imagined when I used to say that!"

Caroline propped her chin on her hands, steadily

watching Anna with her solemn brown eyes. "What did you imagine? Pomp at Court in London? Coronets of strawberry leaves while everyone bows to you?"

"Something like that, I suppose. Something grand and—and purposeful."

"And what do you imagine with Adair?"

With Adair she had, or could have, everything. Everything she had never realized she needed so much. Love, belonging, a place where she could be really useful. Passion like she had never imagined, but danger, too.

"Caro," she said slowly, "how do you know so decidedly that Lord Hartley is what you want?"

Caroline shrugged. "I just knew, the first time we talked together. We have so many mutual interests, and we understand each other. I know he is not much to look at, but he is kind and intelligent. He will never expect me to be something I'm not. We could have a comfortable and content life together."

Comfortable and content—those were certainly two things Adair was *not*. "But what do you feel when he kisses you? Does it feel as if you'll explode, burst into flames, when he touches you?"

Caroline looked at her in bewilderment. "I've never kissed him. But I doubt it would be like that. I'm not even sure that would be—required. Is it that way with you and Adair?"

"Yes," Anna said simply. "I forget everything when I'm with him. He makes me feel completely alive."

"Well," said Caroline. "I think you had better marry him, then. You should have no problem getting Mama's permission now. Once she hears Eliza's news, she'll want more grandchildren."

"Won't she have Lord Hartley's brood, once you become their stepmother?"

"Yes," Caroline said. For the first time a note of doubt crept into her voice. "I suppose she will. But they are not children."

"I don't think we can solve all our romantic dilemmas right now," said Anna with a yawn. "I'm so tired I can hardly think at all. Maybe I should just lie down until Mama returns."

"I'm tired, too." Caroline rubbed at her spectacle-less eyes. Without them, she looked younger, prettier, and more vulnerable. Anna hoped her too-smart-for-her-own-good sister was not making a terrible mistake with Hartley.

She hoped *she* didn't make a mistake with Adair, either. She couldn't afford any more mistakes.

They both curled up on Anna's bed as the day slid into evening, and Anna drifted into a troubled sleep.

Crash!

Anna sat straight up, bewildered, still caught in the sticky cobweb of sleep and dreams and startled by the sound of breaking glass. Was it only part of her dream? But then she heard another pane shatter, and she knew it was no dream. In the hazy half-light, she saw a large gloved hand reach through the broken window to unlatch the casement and swing it open.

"Caro, run!" she whispered frantically, pushing at her sleeping sister's shoulder. She tried to jump off the bed, but her numb legs refused to work. Her panicked brain couldn't seem to command her body.

"Wha . . ." Caroline said as she sat up groggily. She, too, saw the man climbing in the window, and she screamed and rolled off the bed, landing with a thud on the floor.

The haze vanished from Anna's mind in a sinking, cold rush of terror, and she screamed. But it was too late. One of the intruders, a large, burly man in rough wool, grabbed her hard around the waist and clamped his gloved hand hard over her mouth. She could hardly breathe, yet the fear made her fight like a wild beast. Anna kicked at him through her skirts, ruing the fact that she took off her boots before going to sleep. She twisted her head to bite his hand.

"Crazy bitch!" the man muttered. He didn't sound Irish, or even English. He forced his palm harder over her face and pushed her to the floor on her stomach. "How is yours?"

"Just as wild," another man said. Then Anna heard Caroline drive her elbow into his belly, and the sickening crack as he slapped her. "I thought these fine ladies were supposed to faint as soon as you look at 'em."

"Well, I thought there was only supposed to be one. That's what they told me when they said to use this window," Anna's captor said. She struggled to roll over and gouge his eyes out, but he wrangled her arms back and bound them tightly together. Sharp pain shot from her right shoulder as it was wrenched. "We'll just have to take 'em both, let the toffs sort it out."

Through the pain, Anna could hear her sister struggling. "I vote we just kill them and leave them here, troublesome sluts," one of the men said.

"Then we wouldn't get paid. Here, tie this around yours and lower her out the window to Jim. I'll follow with this one," said the other captor.

They meant to carry her and Caroline away to some horrible fate! Anna was an avid reader of Gothic novels; she knew just what happened when fair ladies were kidnapped by villains. Terrified, she summoned up every bit of her strength and threw her head back. It smacked into his jaw with a satisfying crack, but her head pounded.

"Bitch!" the man cried. "No more trouble from *you*." Something landed hard at the base of her skull, and everything went black.

Chapter Twenty-five

A re my daughters home, Smythe?" Katherine said. She deposited her parcels with the butler and stripped off her gloves and cloak. Sparkling bits of ice clung to the velvet folds. "I hope they haven't ventured out. It's terribly cold."

"They've been resting upstairs for a while now, my lady," Smythe answered. "I only just returned from the market with the veal you wanted for dinner."

"Yes, the meeting ran long, I'm afraid. And then I had to purchase some new paints for Lady Caroline's lessons." Lessons with Nicolas. Just thinking his name made Katherine smile. It had been thus ever since they met at Christmas—and again, secretly, once they returned to Dublin. She felt quite ridiculously ebullient these days, like she might burst out laughing at any moment.

"I will just go look in on my daughters," she said. "I'm anxious to hear how it went at Parliament today."

"Oh, I gather it was quite lively, my lady."

Katherine laughed and climbed the stairs to the quiet corridor that housed the family bedchambers. At Anna's door, she could hear no voices or laughter. Parliament *must* have been tiring, then, if they were actually resting.

"Girls," she called as she knocked on the door. "Are you awake? It's nearly time for dinner."

There was no answer. She turned the unlocked door handle and pushed it open. A rush of cold air greeted her, and the first hint of disquiet touched her heart. The chamber was dark and silent.

"Anna? Caroline?" she cried anxiously. She stepped into the room and heard the grind of broken glass under her shoe.

In one frantic instant, she took in the terrible scene. The shattered, open window. The empty, rumpled bed. And, in the middle of the mattress, a dagger hilt standing straight up.

Katherine stumbled forward to find the blade pinned to a note. By the moonlight from the open window, she read the scrawled words.

If Adair wants his whore back, tell him to come get her. The Dowling wool warehouse by the river, midnight. Alone. Or she dies.

$\mathcal{B}\mathcal{I}$

"How long have they been gone?" Conlan said as he stared down at the torn note. He kept his voice quiet and his demeanor still and calm for the sake of Lady Killinan. For his own sake, too—the heat of his fury would surely blind him and make him reckless when he most needed to be calculating to get Anna back.

But someone would pay for this. Painfully.

Lady Killinan shook her head. She sat at the end of

Anna's bed, cradling one of her daughter's shawls in her arms. She looked white and stricken. Her face, so much like Anna's, was streaked with tears. "I'm not sure. I returned from my charity meeting less than an hour ago, and the butler said they had been in here perhaps two hours."

Three hours. It was possible Anna had been gone for three whole hours. Conlan glanced at the clock on the fireplace mantel. It was almost three hours until midnight.

Anna's maid stood in the doorway wailing, pressing her apron to her face. It was the only sound beyond the ticking of the clock and the lashing of the freezing rain outside. Someone had tacked muslin over the broken panes, but it did nothing to keep out the biting cold.

"And no one saw anything?" he said.

"Nothing," Lady Killinan answered. "The butler was at the market, and everyone else was below stairs. This house is large, and there was no one to hear when—when the villains broke the window and took them."

"They came up the ivy vines over the portico?"

"Yes. I did intend to order them cut back, but I kept forgetting, and..." Her words broke on a raw sob, and she clutched at the shawl. "It was my fault. I am their mother, and I was not here to protect them. I knew something was wrong, that Anna was hiding something from me, and I did nothing. I waited for her to come to me."

"No, Lady Killinan, no," Conlan protested. He knelt beside her and took her trembling hand in his. "If anyone is at fault, it is me. I should have sent her away, forgotten her."

She raised her reddened eyes to his face. "How could you have done so? You're in love with her."

"Yes," he said, shocked by the way the stark truth of those words hit him. Of course, he loved Anna, beautiful, fiery, softhearted Anna. He had loved her since she knocked him unconscious in that ruined stable.

And look where his love got her. Kidnapped from her own home and in terrible danger.

"I will find them, Lady Killinan," he said. "I will find them and bring them back to you, and whoever did this will pay." He would die himself rather than let any more harm come to her or her family.

Lady Killinan stared into his eyes for a long moment. He had never seen anguish like that before. "I know you will. And I will help you."

There was the sound of running footsteps on the stairs. Nicolas Courtois burst past the sobbing maid as the butler shouted, "You can't go in there! Come back this minute, Mr. Courtois! Oh, what is this world coming to?"

Nicolas ignored all of that and ignored Conlan, too. His attention was all on Lady Killinan.

"Katherine," he said hoarsely. He held out his arms, and much to Conlan's shock, she ran into them and buried her face in his coat. Their golden heads bent close together. "*Ma belle,* I'm so sorry."

"They're gone, Nicolas," she said, and the racking sobs she had held back came pouring forth. "I wasn't watching them, and they're gone."

"I know, I heard," Nicolas said. He held Lady Killinan tightly and smoothed her hair with unbearable tenderness. "But we will find them. They will be safe in your arms before sunrise."

He kissed the top of her head, and Conlan feared his old friend looked at Lady Killinan as he himself looked at Anna—as if the world began and ended in her eyes.

But there was no time to worry about that now. First

they had to find the Blacknall women and destroy whoever dared take them.

Lady Killinan stepped back from Nicolas, wiping at her eyes. "But—how did you know, Nicolas? How did you get here so quickly?"

Nicolas's gaze met Conlan's over her blond head, and Conlan said, "I sent for him."

Lady Killinan looked back at him, her expression puzzled. She did look so much like Anna. "You sent for Nicolas?"

"Yes, *ma belle*," said Nicolas. "You see, we are old friends, the duke and I. My mother worked as a seamstress for his mother when we came here from Paris, and they became friends. Conlan and I did, too."

"And now he sometimes helps me," said Conlan.

Lady Killinan frowned. "Helps you how? I do not understand."

"There isn't much time to explain," said Conlan. "I have been working to see that the Act of Union is not passed."

"Yes," she said wryly. "I *have* noticed something of that."

"Nicolas sometimes hears information of interest in his work," Conlan said. "That's all."

She swung around to glare at Nicolas. "And were you spying on us, too?"

"Of course not, Katherine," Nicolas protested.

"I suppose we never did anything of interest. But you are right, Adair—there is no time for explanations now." She snatched the ransom note from his hands. "It is growing late. We need a plan."

"I already have one, such as it is." Conlan firmly shut

the door on the sobbing maid. "Listen to me closely, for time grows short...."

⟋⟍

The warehouse looked dark and abandoned under the thick, cold clouds. The icy wind off the river lashed at the small, blank windows.

Conlan studied the building carefully, watching for any hint of movement or noise, searching for vulnerable points. The owner was clearly more careful than Lord Ross, whose house had burned in the riot. The lower level windows were bricked up and the doors were bound in iron and closed off with gates. A fence surrounded it, with one of those gates opening to the river in the back where the boats would be loaded.

But suddenly, there was a flash of light in one of the upper windows, a flare as if from a candle, then it was gone.

Conlan crept away from his watching post, back to where Nicolas waited behind one of the other riverbank warehouses. Two other men were with him.

"They are there?" Nicolas asked quietly.

"I think so. They have certainly chosen a secure prison."

"What should we do now?"

"What the note said—wait until midnight and then go in."

"You cannot go in alone!" Nicolas protested again.

"I have to give the convincing appearance of being alone, or they will kill Anna and her sister," Conlan reminded him. "So you must go back to Henrietta Street and keep an eye on matters there. I set McMann to watch the house, and Lady Killinan will send word through him if anything occurs. It seems as if she might need *you* right now, though."

Nicolas's jaw tightened. "Not now. She thinks I spied on her and her daughters."

Conlan remembered how she clung to Nicolas. "No. She needs you. And I need you to look after her until we bring Anna and Caroline to her." He didn't know what state they would be in when that happened. Lady Killinan would need all her strength—and so would he.

Nicolas nodded and hurried off into the night. Conlan sent the other two men to their posts and crept around to the back of the massive warehouse. The brief light had vanished, and all was dark again. He scaled the fence by the light of the faint stars, leaping over it to land on the other side. Stout crates full of processed wool were ready to ship and stacked against the brick walls, perfect to use as a ladder to the upper windows.

Conlan started climbing in grim, focused determination.

Chapter Twenty-six

"Anna? Anna, wake up! Please, please, wake up."

Anna slowly crawled up through a dark, thick cloud. It pressed down on her, as if to drag her back to the depths of unconsciousness, but she struggled against it. It was comfortable there in the blackness, soothing, yet she felt that there was something urgent she had to find. Something just beyond her weak grasp. That voice pulled her upward.

Painfully, she pried open her eyes. Candlelight pierced her brain, so faint yet so bright. Her head pounded.

"What is happening?" she said. Her voice sounded rough and raspy.

"Oh, thank God! You're alive." Caroline's face slowly swam into view above her. Her dark hair fell in tangles over her shoulders, and her cheeks were smeared with dirt. A purple bruise marred one cheekbone. "I was so frightened."

Anna found that her head rested on Caroline's lap, and they were on a hardwood floor. It was very cold, and they wore only their muslin gowns, no shawls or shoes. And the only light was one candle stub, propped on a crate next to Caroline.

Then everything came flooding back in her mind. The men breaking into her chamber, the shattered glass, the screams and ropes. They had been kidnapped, right from their own home.

Anna sat up too fast, wincing as more pain rushed through her head like tiny, stabbing blades. "Where are we? Are you hurt, Caro? Did they..."

"No, no," Caroline said quickly. "Nothing like that. They just tied me up and gagged me, muffled me in an old, smelly blanket, and brought us here in a closed carriage." She shivered. "I wish they had left us that blanket."

"Where is here?"

"A warehouse of some sort. Near the river, I think. I could hear water as they lifted me out of the carriage."

"Did they say what they wanted?"

"No, nothing. They just shoved us in here, untied us, and left. It feels as if it's been hours, but I know it can't be." A rough sob escaped her lips. "Oh, Anna, I thought you would die, and there was nothing I could do about it!"

"Shh, it's all right. I'm perfectly fine." Anna gathered her sister close and kissed her unbruised cheek. The sight of that wound filled her with so much horror and anger that she couldn't bear it. "I'm sure it's just some clumsy attempt at ransom. Have you looked for an escape route?"

Caroline shook her head. "I was too worried about you."

Anna pushed herself to her feet, swaying as a dizzy nausea flowed down from the bump on her head. She shoved that away and carefully examined their prison.

It was a big, stark room filled with crates, all piled up to the bare rafters. The only windows were long, narrow slits set up high, too small to squeeze through, even for someone as thin as Caroline.

She pried open one of the crates and peeked inside. Bundles of raw wool. Not very helpful for effecting an escape. At least they could sit on them while they waited.

Waited for what she didn't even want to contemplate.

"I wish I still had that pistol Jane gave me," she murmured as she heaved out the greasy bundles.

"You can't shoot them if they don't come back," Caroline said.

"They'll be back."

"Do you think all they want is money? Or is there more to it than that?"

"I don't know," Anna said. They rolled the wool closer to their one precious candle and sat down on the bundles, close together to stay warm and find courage. "I suppose it could have been something to do with the Union or politics, but I don't know what exactly."

"Maybe it's the duke they're after."

"Yes," Anna said. "Well, if it is, I hope he stays far away."

"I seriously doubt he would do that when you are in danger."

Anna feared Caroline was right. Surely by now their disappearance was discovered. If their mother sent for Conlan...

She shook her head hard, trying to keep fear at bay. She looked around for a door and found it in one corner, a large double entrance big enough for carrying out crates. There was also a smaller door that seemed to lead to a chute. When she and Caroline tested them, they found them predictably locked, and no amount of pounding could dislodge them.

"Perhaps we shouldn't make so much noise," Caroline said as she hammered at the thick wood with a crate lid. "They might come back and be even more angry."

"You're quite right. It's not working, anyway." Anna collapsed to the floor, staring up at their prison door. "If they were to come back, they would have to come through here, right?"

"I suppose."

"Then I have an idea."

Caroline peered at Anna warily through her tangled hair. "What sort of idea?"

"Well, surely anything is better than just sitting here waiting for our fate like a pair of ninnys! Help me unroll that wool and bring it over here."

"Oh!" Caroline's eyes widened with sudden excitement. "I see."

They ran over to drag the spools of wool back to the doors and spun the cobweb-like fibers across the threshold. "If we can bind them up in it, we'll have an instant to hit them over the heads with the crates and then run," Anna said.

And if it did not work—the scoundrels would probably kill them. But maybe at least Caroline could get away, if Anna created enough theatrics. She was good at that.

Once they were finished with their task, Caroline crouched by the wall with her crate lid, and Anna started pounding on the door again. She had nearly bloodied her hands by the time they finally heard footsteps, and the metallic grind of a lock sliding back. As she stumbled backward, the door flew open, and a burly man in a rough brown coat appeared there.

He did not look happy as he stalked into the room, closer to the wool. From the smell, Anna deduced they interrupted him drinking gin and eating onions.

"Here, wot's going on?" he said. "You two had best quiet down!"

"Now!" Anna shouted. Caroline brought the lid crashing over his head, and he collapsed heavily to the floor, entangled in their web of wool.

Anna grabbed Caroline's hand, and they ran out of the room. They were halfway down the stairs when a man appeared at the bottom. She couldn't see his face, as he was illuminated from behind by a lamp, but he was no rough bully. He was tall and lean, clad in a finely tailored dark coat and well-tied cravat.

In two steps, the tall man was upon them, catching Caroline around the waist and lifting her from her feet. Her hand was torn from Anna's.

Anna screamed as Caroline kicked and twisted. The man just tossed her over his shoulder as if she were another bundle of wool and threw out his arm to block Anna's way.

"Why did you take them both?" he said, his voice filled with cold fury.

And Anna heard with shock that it was Grant Dunmore. Elegant, gorgeous, charming Grant, now a street brawler and a kidnapper?

"You," she gasped. He just stared down at her in the shadows, holding on to the wriggling Caroline.

Another man appeared behind him. He held the lamp in one hand and a bottle in the other. It was George Hayes, their mother's cousin.

"They were both there when the hired men broke in," George said. "What else could they do? Leave Caroline to sound the alarm? Kill her?"

"Maybe if you hadn't hired such incompetents, this wouldn't have happened," Grant said tightly. He slapped Caroline across the bottom. "Be still!"

"How dare you!" Caroline shouted. She pulled at Grant's hair.

"Those men worked cheap. That's the important thing," George said, sounding infuriatingly amused. "Once Adair takes the bait, we can let them go with no harm done. Except to your pretty hair, it seems, Dunmore."

With a shriek of fury, Anna lunged at Grant. "You bastard! I won't let you hurt Conlan."

Grant caught her with his free arm and pushed her down the stairs toward George. "Blast it, George, take this one. I can't handle them both."

George dropped the bottle, which didn't break but scattered drops of wine everywhere, and grabbed Anna before she could fall. Like the ruffian upstairs, he stank of liquor and onions, and his teeth were stained wine-red as he leered at her.

"I told you the Blacknall girls were little hellions," he said with an unpleasant laugh. "I've had my eye on this one for a long time."

Anna spit at him, and he slapped her across the face. Her head snapped back, stars whirling in her brain, but he had to let go of her for that blow. She ran, yet only got two steps before he caught her again.

"That was not a good idea, lovely Anna," he said.

"Lock her in that closet," Grant said. "I'll take care of Lady Caroline."

"Gladly," George said, dragging Anna against his body. Disgustingly, she could feel his erection pressed to her hip. Rather than filling her with fear, making her remember that would-be rapist solider, it made her even more angry. She was consumed with fury; it blotted out all else.

"And leave her alone," Grant said. His voice rang with unmistakable authority. "Adair is the goal here, remember."

George scowled, but he nodded. He was a weak man at base, used to taking instructions from those who were stronger. He took her arm in a bruising clasp and hauled her along a narrow corridor. "You spilled my wine, you little bitch," he muttered in her ear. "You'll pay for that."

He shoved her into a cupboard set in the wall and slammed the door after her, turning the key in the lock. She was utterly alone, closed in darkness and silence except for a small, steady drip of water. And the pattering of what sounded horribly like rats' feet.

Anna leaned back against the damp wall and wrapped her arms tightly around herself to ward off panic. She did hate the dark, but even worse was the worry about Conlan and her sister. Above her head, she heard a scraping noise, a crash, then all was quiet again.

She closed her eyes and remembered the night that Conlan took her to the tavern. She thought of the music, the dancing, and the light, and held them to her heart fiercely.

"Under dark and moonless sky, he rode into the night," she sang hoarsely, hoping it would help keep the fear away. She licked her cracked, dry lips and went on louder, bolder. "To see his love o'er the way. The smell of flowers in the air, he passed not a care, across a bridge o'that sad day...."

ℬ

Caroline landed hard on the pile of wool as Grant dropped her. She immediately ran as far from him as she could, pressing herself against a stack of crates. She watched in numb horror as he pushed the groaning, half-conscious ruffian out the door and closed it behind him. Grant braced his fists on the wooden panels, his shoulders heaving as if he struggled to hold on to control.

"*You* are the one behind all this," she said. "How could you?"

How could any man who showed such pride and tenderness over *The Chronicle of Kildare* be so cruel? That made no sense, of course. Plenty of men who loved art and literature had been cruel despots. But she had never imagined that of Grant Dunmore.

Philanderer, maybe. User of women, of course. Not kidnapper.

"You weren't supposed to be involved in this," he said.

Caroline gave a bitter laugh. "And that is supposed to make it better? The fact that you intended to snatch away only Anna?"

"I did not intend for anything like this to happen at all." He pushed back from the door and turned to look at her. His handsome face was drawn and haunted-looking. "I only wanted what should have been mine."

Caroline was utterly confused. "What should have been yours? How will kidnapping my sister and me correct that?"

"You can't understand. You have always been sheltered and secure."

"You don't know anything about me," Caroline said.

She slid down until she sat on the wooden floor and drew her knees up to her chest as she wrapped her arms around them. "Tell me."

He leaned back against the door and crossed his arms. At first, she thought he would just ignore her, but he said, "When I was a child, my father died, and soon after, my mother discovered his fortune was lost to gambling and ridiculous moneymaking schemes. It's a pathetically common tale, but my mother was very proud. She sold everything she could to hide her situation from her friends. In the end, she had to do what she most dreaded."

Caroline, pulled in by this rare glimpse of a strange and enigmatic man, straightened her legs out on the floor in front of her. "What was that?" she whispered.

"She went to her family."

"Isn't that what families are for?"

"Your family, perhaps," he said with a rueful laugh. He sat down on the floor near her, but not so near that she could kick him. "When my mother married, she broke with her old Irish Catholic family. She took me with her to Adair Court to try and reconcile with her brother, Conlan's father. She cried and begged, but it was no use. He told her that she had betrayed her family and her homeland, and he sent us away. As we left, I saw Conlan coming up the drive on his pony. That was *his* home, his place. His father who betrayed my mother and left us humiliated."

Caroline could not fathom how that would feel. He was quite right—she was sheltered, despite all her reading, despite all she had seen in the Uprising. Her parents had loved her and her sisters, and she couldn't imagine anything that would make her mother cast her out of Killinan. Despite all Grant had done, all he was still doing as he held her in this freezing warehouse, she felt a twinge of something like pity.

But she knew that he would not want her pity. He was proud, like his mother. "What happened then?" she asked.

"My uncle did relent somewhat and gave my mother money to go abroad where she could live more cheaply. We went to Italy, and she died there when I was thirteen. My uncle then agreed to pay for my schooling, when he was pressed by some of my mother's old friends. I went to Trinity and managed to make my way from there. But he refused to ever see me, to let me be part of Adair at all."

"Until you tried to take it from his son," Caroline said quietly.

Grant leaned his head back against the crate with his eyes closed. She had never seen such pain on anyone's face, carved deep in bitter lines on his beautiful face. "Adair *belonged* there, he was part of it. Part of Ireland, of its people. I wanted it. That was all."

"It was his by right!"

"And I was a coldhearted English bastard to try and take it," he said. "So I've been told. All I could think about was the way my mother cried as we left Adair that day, the way they turned their backs on her, and we had nothing. We belonged nowhere."

And he still did not. Caroline could see that, feel it as cold as that winter wind on her skin. Despite his place in Society and all the ladies in love with him, he belonged to nothing. Maybe that was why he loved the *Chronicle of Kildare* so much—for what those ancient pages represented.

She couldn't help herself. She reached over and gently took his hand.

His eyes flew open, and he stared at her in astonishment. She thought he might fling her away and turn back to that fearsome harshness. Then, slowly, he laid his other hand atop hers.

"It doesn't have to be that way," she said. "You don't have to go on as you have. You don't need Dublin Society. Take your books and go and study them. Find Ireland in those pages, and you will see that you are truly a part of it, too."

"Caroline," he said. He gave her a gentle smile, heartbreaking in its sweet sadness. "You think scholarship is the answer to everything, don't you?"

"No, not everything. But so much that we seek can be found in the pages of books, if we take the time to look."

"Time is the one thing I don't have. My cousin will kill me for hurting your sister, and quite rightly. I've made too many mistakes."

"We all make mistakes. Yours have just been more spectacular than most."

Grant laughed. "What would you suggest I do to atone then?"

"Well," Caroline said, "the first thing you should do is let Anna and me go. And push George into the Liffey. He's caused my family problems for years. He's no fit ally for anyone."

"And then?"

"And then—I don't know. Perhaps you should find a sensible wife and take her to your country estate. You could study, write books, and run your farm there."

"Is that what you would do? If you could have any life you wanted?"

She had never really thought about it, and it gave her

pause. What would she do, if she could do anything? If she was not bound by the strictures of being a woman. If she had not already set her course with Lord Hartley. "Yes. I would live somewhere quiet and pretty, where I could read and raise a family. Where I could just be—me."

"Ah, but you know who you are," he said. "I think I haven't even started learning who I might be, except for my evils."

Caroline reached up to gently touch his cheek, tracing her fingertips over the angles of his face and the sad hollows under his eyes. "I think there is more to you than that."

Grant's eyes narrowed as he studied her. Slowly, as if he fought against something inside himself, he leaned toward her, and his lips touched hers, lightly, tenderly. A sudden feeling of bizarre *rightness* shivered through Caroline, as if this was what she had been waiting for forever.

Then the world exploded. The door burst in, its stout wood and iron locks splintered. Grant shoved Caroline away and blocked her body with his. She glimpsed Adair, who looked like an enraged bear. His face was dark, his eyes burning.

"Take your hands off her!" he roared. Before Caroline could scream, run, or even think, he grabbed Grant by the front of his coat and hurled him across the room. Caroline leaped to her feet, her throat paralyzed.

"For God's sake, girl, run!" Adair shouted at her, and she ran. She couldn't help Grant as he and Adair crashed around the room in a brutal bare-knuckle fight. She had to find her sister.

"Where is Anna?" Adair demanded. "What have you done with her, *diolain*?"

"She's downstairs!" Caroline cried as Grant's face turned white under Adair's hold on his neck. "In a—a closet, I think." She whirled around and ran down the stairs, but her path was blocked by a sudden cloud of white smoke in the corridor.

In a day of terrifying moments, she was sure this was the worst. The smoke wrapped around her throat, thick and acrid, choking her. Blocking her way to Anna.

She heard the crackle of flames, licking through greasy wool and old wood. Beyond the smoke, she could see its first incandescent flicker.

"Fire!" Caroline shouted. "Fire!"

Chapter Twenty-seven

O'er the bridge that sad day…" Anna couldn't sing anymore. Her throat was tight and her chest ached as if it was caving inward. How long had she been singing? Hours? Days? In the darkness it was all the same.

"I'll come back to you, Conlan," she whispered. "I swear it."

She choked on the words, something sharp and pungent seeping into her nostrils. Her eyes flew open, and she saw smoke curling under the door and around her feet.

"*Fuilleach,*" she whispered. She reached out until she could feel the door. It was warm.

"Let me out!" she screamed, pounding on the wood. The smoke was thicker now, and she pressed her sleeve to her face as she coughed. "Let me out!"

Was this the end then? Had she survived the Uprising only to die in this tiny cupboard? She thought of her mother and sisters, of Eliza's baby to come, of Conlan and how much she loved him. She thought of the green, cool meadows of Killinan. Would she never see them again?

"No!" she cried. No, her life would not end here. She

had too much to do, too much to live for. She threw her whole body against the door. Pain shot through her shoulder, but she pushed it away and threw herself forward again and again.

The door was suddenly flung open, and she stumbled forward. She would have fallen if a pair of strong arms hadn't closed around her and lifted her high.

"Anna," Conlan shouted. "Are you hurt?"

She shook her head, sobbing. It *was* him! Her warrior, her Celtic god. He had never looked more a lord of the Underworld than he did now, with his face blackened with smoke and his hair standing on end. She had never seen anyone so beautiful.

"I'm not hurt," she managed to say. The smoke was a miasma out here, great billowing clouds, and she could hear the snap of flames. Somewhere in the building, timbers crashed down.

"We have to get out of here," Grant Dunmore shouted. Anna glimpsed him over Conlan's shoulder, half-hidden in the poisonous clouds. His coat was gone, his shirt torn and face bloodied.

"Where is Caroline?" she screamed at him. She twisted in Conlan's arms but he wouldn't let her go. "What have you done with her?"

"She ran outside to sound the alarm," said Conlan. "She's safe, which is more than I can say for us."

"Go!" Grant called. He pushed them ahead of him, and Conlan hoisted Anna higher as he ran. The heat and smoke were almost unbearable, and Anna's head swam as if she would faint. Conlan kept running, though, his strength never flagging.

Through a doorway, Anna glimpsed George's crumpled

body next to the broken glass of a lamp. But he soon vanished, consumed by flames, and Anna could feel Conlan's lungs heaving in his chest. She buried her face against his shoulder.

At last, they fell out into the night, the icy wind a blessing on her singed skin. Just as Conlan stumbled through the gate to the river, lowering her to the ground, part of the roof collapsed with an explosive roar.

Anna slumped over, retching. The fresh, icy air blew away the smoke from her throat, but she still felt sick. She couldn't stop shaking with the memory of how close they had all come to death.

"But we didn't die," she whispered. "We're still alive." And that thought made even the cold, hard stone beneath her and the ice pelting her skin feel glorious.

"Anna, my love, are you hurt?" Conlan said roughly. He knelt beside her, his hands gentle and careful as he touched her shoulders. His face was illuminated in the garish light of the flames, and his clothes were torn and stained.

She threw herself against him, wrapping her arms hard around him. "I'm not hurt," she sobbed. "I just—I thought I might never see you again."

He held her close and kissed the top of her head, her cheek, her nose. "I'll always come for you, my witch. Always, no matter what."

"Anna!" she heard Caroline cry. She twisted around to see her sister racing along the embankment. She wore Grant's black coat over her rumpled dress, but her head and feet were bare. Caroline threw herself at Anna, and Anna held on to both her and Conlan, laughing and crying all at the same time. Caroline was safe; they were all safe.

It felt like awakening from a nightmare into a clear, bright new morning.

"What happened when they separated us?" Caroline said, her voice tight as if she gasped for breath.

"Nothing happened except I was locked in a smelly cupboard," Anna said. She carefully examined her sister for any injury, but Caroline seemed unhurt, blessedly free of blood or new bruises. "George is dead. And Grant..."

Anna had forgotten about Grant in the excitement. She glanced along the embankment. Curious onlookers had begun to gather, but there was no Grant. The other ruffians were gone, too. "I thought he was right behind us."

A crashing noise echoed from the warehouse as another section of roof collapsed. Windows shattered. Anna spun around to the fire just in time to glimpse a tall silhouette in one of the lower windows. He was quickly engulfed in a cloud of smoke.

"There he is!" Anna screamed, pointing at the terrible sight.

"No," Caroline whispered. She lurched to her feet, her eyes wide and glassy with shock. She took a stumbling step toward the inferno, but Anna grabbed at her skirt and pulled her back.

"Stay here, both of you," Conlan commanded. As Anna watched, horrified, he ran back to the warehouse. It happened so swiftly she couldn't even cry out in protest before he was gone.

She clung to Caroline, both of them staring numbly as the fire grew and grew in strength, consuming the whole structure. The crowd around them grew, and a bucket brigade formed to try and save the nearby warehouses, but Anna hardly noticed any of it. She could only see that doorway to hell where Conlan and Grant disappeared.

She had just got him back. How could he be gone now?

"They'll come out of there," she whispered.

"They have to," said Caroline.

And then at last, she glimpsed a shadow behind the flames. Conlan staggered out with Grant slung over his shoulder. Conlan fell to his knees just beyond the reach of the smoke, coughing fiercely. Grant slid to the ground and lay there, perfectly still.

Anna ran to them with Caroline right behind her. Conlan seemed unhurt, just gasping for a breath of fresh air.

"Is he…" Anna said as she knelt beside Conlan. She saw that Grant still breathed, though the rise of his chest was shallow under his singed shirt. But his neck and the left half of his famously handsome face were raw with blistering burns. Once he was conscious, the pain would be terrible. Despite all he had put her through, the terrible things he had done and bad choices he had made, Anna's heart ached.

Caroline slowly fell to her knees beside Grant. Her shaking hand touched his hair, easing the smoke-darkened strands back from those livid red wounds.

"He's not dead," Conlan said. "But he needs a doctor and to get in out of this cold. We all do."

Anna nodded. She felt so numb, so weary. And her feet were freezing. "Why did you go in after him?"

Conlan closed his eyes for a moment, his face creased with pain. "Because—he is my cousin."

"Yes," Anna said. "Family is important in the end, no matter what."

Chapter Twenty-eight

Katherine gently tucked the bedclothes around Anna's sleeping figure. The sunlight streamed through the repaired window, turning her daughter's hair to pure spun gold. She had tried to draw the curtains closed, but Anna stopped her before she fell asleep.

"No," she had murmured hazily, under the effects of the doctor's laudanum. "I want the light." So the curtains stayed open. Katherine would have given her the sun itself if she wanted it.

She didn't know what exactly happened in that warehouse. Anna and Caroline gave only jumbled accounts of locked rooms, escape attempts, and fire. Her imaginings were terrible enough, though the doctor assured her they were unhurt. Just cold and tired.

Unlike Grant Dunmore, who was badly burned and had been taken off to the country, not expected to recover. She could pity him, but she could not find it in her heart to forgive him.

She gently kissed Anna's cheek. The bruises would fade, yet she feared the memories would take longer to go away.

She tiptoed from the chamber and peered into Caroline's room next door. Caroline slept, too, her books scattered around her on the bed as if she had sought forgetfulness in their pages. Katherine closed them and piled them on the floor before tucking the blankets around Caroline and leaving her to her dreams.

She went down to the drawing room, feeling restless and unfocused. There was nothing more she could do for her daughters now. They slept as peacefully as they could. The house was quiet, the servants going about their tasks in silent efficiency. No doubt Smythe had instructed them not to disturb her today.

She wished they *would* disturb her, though! Some minor household crisis would distract her from her restless thoughts. They were too well-trained, and there was nothing for her to do.

She drifted into the library, which was also perfectly tidy. A fire burned in the grate, and the settee where she had kissed Nicolas, sat before it. She turned away from those memories and went to the desk.

Caroline's sketchbook sat there, open to a drawing of Anna. It was a fine, assured work, one that not only showed how Anna looked but the spirit in her eyes, the mischief in the curve of her smile. In the short time Nicolas had been teaching Caroline drawing, she had made great progress.

Nicolas was everywhere Katherine turned. She couldn't escape him. What was worse, she didn't even want to.

She firmly closed the sketchbook. She shouldn't want Nicolas, not any longer. He had a life that was hidden from her. He worked with Adair, and she was sure he had many other secrets as well.

But his kisses had awakened something in her, shown her a part of herself she didn't even know existed. He brought out a passionate woman she hardly recognized as herself.

How could she retreat from that, from him? How could she forget she ever knew him, ever kissed him? But how could she be with him?

She reached absently for the post, sifting through the invitations and tradesmen's bills in some vague hope that there would be distraction there. At the bottom of the stack was a rumpled, thick letter, already opened as if Anna or Caroline had read it. The address was in Eliza's handwriting.

"At last!" Katherine cried. It had been a while since the last news from Eliza. She sat down behind the desk to read the precious letter with the news of an expected baby.

Katherine felt tears prickle at her eyes, but now they were tears of happiness and not fear. She had missed Eliza desperately in her time of exile, worried about her. Now Eliza would be a mother herself. Her girls would all be safe, and soon, God willing, happy.

And what would she have? What would she choose to do now?

The butler knocked at the half-open library door. Katherine quickly wiped away her tears and refolded the letter. "Yes, Smythe?" she called.

"Mr. Courtois is here to see you, my lady," said Smythe, a faint disapproval in his very proper voice.

Nicolas, here? Now? She had not seen him since her daughters returned home after the fire, but he had stayed with her in silent vigil while they waited to find out what happened. She had not had the courage to speak to him then. Maybe she could now. Confused and excited, Katherine nodded. "Send him in, please."

She hurried to the mirror and tried to smooth her hair and arrange her expression in a serene pattern. Sadly, she thought there was nothing she could do about those tiny lines around her eyes. Nothing she could do to turn back the years.

She just had to grab onto the time still left.

She sat down on the chaise and carefully arranged her silk skirts around her. She folded her hands in her lap, feeling as nervous as a schoolgirl to see him again. How could she possibly be about to become a grandmother?

When he came into the room and shut the door softly behind him, he watched her in cautious silence for a long moment.

"Hello, Nicolas," she said quietly.

"How are your daughters?" he asked.

"Better, I think. At least they are sleeping."

"And you?"

Katherine laughed. "I fear I have not slept at all. I have such dreams, and then I lie awake going over and over what happened. But then I go look at them, see they are safe, and I am well again."

"I'm glad to hear it." He fell quiet again, just watching her as if he hoped to read something in her face. Katherine was struck again by how very handsome he was, like a young, golden prince in a fairy story. Like a dream.

"I never spied on you, Katherine," he said. "I could not. I'm an artist—that is my world. I try to find beauty and truth, and such a sordid thing..."

"I know," Katherine said. "You don't have it in you to be treacherous, Nicolas. You would be a terrible spy."

"Yes. Perfectly useless." He suddenly laughed. "Though I don't know if I should be flattered or insulted by your words. Am I so very easy to read that I could never keep a secret?"

"Not at all. I think you hold too many secrets, hide too many horrors in your past." As they all did. But she was very tired of secrets, of living as someone not entirely herself.

Nicolas came to her and knelt at her feet. He took her hands in his and kissed them as if they were precious.

"I never want to keep a secret from you again, Katherine," he said, pressing her palm to his cheek. "I only helped Conlan because he has been my friend for a long time. I would never have betrayed anything I heard here."

"I know." Katherine gently caressed his face, memorizing every angle, every texture. The smooth, warm satin of his skin, the roughness of his whiskers, the sharp turn of his jaw. "I don't want to have secrets from you, either. I'm tired of hiding things."

He gazed up at her with his dark blue eyes. They were like a night sky, the deepest part of the ocean. She could happily drown in them.

"I can no longer hide, *ma belle,*" he said. "No matter what the consequences, even if you send me away, I must speak. I love you, Katherine. I love you with everything in my heart, in a way I didn't think could ever exist outside a painting. I can't give you what you deserve, a life of riches and beauty. I can only give you my love, but it will always be yours entirely, to do with as you will."

Katherine's throat tightened with hot, unshed tears. Could a person die of happiness, burst into flames and disappear because the joy of it was too much?

"I have had riches all my life," she said. "And they are nothing, *nothing,* to the gift you have given me, Nicolas. Love is the greatest thing of all, no matter where it is found. I love you, too."

She had never said that to a man, or ever heard it from one. Between her and her husband there had been affection, a mutual care for their family and duty, but not love like this. He had never said he loved her. She, too, had thought it couldn't exist except for poets and the mad.

She was definitely one of the mad.

"*Ma belle,*" he said. His smile was like the sudden appearance of the sun on a bleak winter day.

"I do," she said again, her heart expanding and growing until she was sure it would burst forth. "I love you, Nicolas. I don't know what to do now, what comes after, but I love you."

He kissed her, passionately, wildly, and she answered with all the love she had found. No, she did not know what to do next, but this felt right. To be in Nicolas's arms felt like coming home at long, long last.

Chapter Twenty-nine

"Cook says she made these cakes especially for you, Anna, and if you don't eat them she will be quite upset," Caroline said.

Anna watched as her sister set the heavily laden tray on a table by her chaise. She laughed as she studied the vast array of delicacies. "Cook has done nothing for the last few days but try to stuff food in my mouth. You shall have to widen the doorways to get me out of the house."

"I very much doubt that. If you don't eat some cake soon, you will fade away to nothing. At least have some tea."

"Very well. A cup of tea. I doubt I am in any danger of fading away, though."

"Are you sure?" Caroline carefully poured out the dark Indian tea and laid out lemon and milk. Her movements were careful and precise, but her face still had that sad shadow that she had worn since they escaped the fire. "You have hardly left this room since we—well, since we came home. That's not like you."

Anna set aside the book on her lap. "Maybe you have

finally convinced me of the joys of study. Irish mythology is quite fascinating."

"I told you it was," Caroline said. She handed Anna her cup and sat down beside her. "But Psyche needs exercise in the park, and so do you. You have a mountain of invitations all piled up, and your friends keep calling and leaving flowers. Smythe can't go on turning them away forever."

"I see them arrive out the window," Anna said. She nodded toward the clear view of the street. The windows were repaired, and the tangle of vines were cut down at last. "There's been no one I want to see. Not since Grant tried to use me to kill Conlan."

"You mean Adair hasn't called."

"Not yet." Conlan had written to inquire after her health, to tell her he was well and he was working on closing down the Olympian Club, but he had not come to her. She spent far too much time wondering, agonizing over, why that could be.

"You should go to him," Caroline said.

"I couldn't do that."

"Are you so proper and cautious all of a sudden, Anna? It never stopped you before."

"It's not propriety. It's just…"

"Just what?"

Anna shook her head. "I don't want to talk about him right now. I've thought about him quite enough. Tell me about Lord Hartley instead. I saw him arrive this morning, all dressed up in a new coat and hat."

"Yes, he came to ask Mama for my hand."

"And what happened?" Anna asked eagerly. She might not think Hartley was quite right for Caroline, but at least here was a courtship with a straightforward trajectory, a definite ending. Unlike her and Conlan, which had never been straightforward at all. And Caroline deserved some happiness. She had been so quiet and solitary since they came home.

"She said we could be engaged, but we couldn't marry until I am at least seventeen," Caroline said. "Even though *she* was married when she was younger than me."

"That sounds quite sensible."

"Yes, I suppose. I just so wanted things to be settled at last. I wanted to move forward and not make any more mistakes."

"I do, too." The problem was, what could she move forward to, after all that had happened? She couldn't go back to where she was, but she couldn't go forward, either.

"I do have some news, though," said Caroline.

"Tell me! I love news, especially now."

"George's poor wife, or widow I should say, is to marry again. Only days after his death. It's quite scandalous."

"No!" Anna thought of pale, cowed Mrs. Hayes. At least something good had come of their ordeal. George had brought himself down and set his abused wife free. "Who is she to marry?"

"A man named Mr. Wise, who it seems is in trade and one of the richest men in Belfast. They say he courted her before her parents made her marry George and has been in love with her all this time."

"Well, I do hope he will be good to her. She certainly deserves it."

"And she is not the only one to be married."

"Who else?"

"Your friend Lady Cannondale, of course."

"Oh, yes," Anna said with a laugh. "She wrote to me yesterday. She has run off to Rome with her Gianni. I would never have guessed she was serious about him. I thought he just escorted her to the opera and dinners and such."

"I would not have thought them serious, either," Caroline said musingly. "She always seemed to have—other interests."

"She says she is going to write a novel set in ancient Ireland while she's in Italy, and she has asked me to visit once she is settled."

"And will you?"

"Perhaps. Maybe I could find a handsome Italian gentleman of my own, since I seem to have no luck here."

"Oh, I would not be so hasty to decide, sister."

"What do you mean?"

"Look who has come to call at last." Caroline pointed out the window.

Anna peeked outside to see a glossy black carriage at their portico. A footman in green-and-gold livery opened the door, and Conlan stepped out, clad in a fine, fashionable blue greatcoat. No hat, though, as usual.

"It's the duke," Caroline cried happily. "And in such grand state, too. Could he possibly be trying to impress someone?"

"He has no need to impress anyone here," Anna murmured. She watched as he climbed their front steps, her heart pounding. He had come to her finally! She knew she should be angry at what he put her through, but the rush of happiness at seeing him again overcame all of that.

She pushed back her blanket and leaped to her feet. "Help me change clothes, Caro, quickly!"

ᘓ)

The drawing room door was open when Anna tiptoed down the stairs from her chamber. With Caroline's help, she had speedily changed from her dressing gown to a proper dress of pretty blue muslin and brushed and pinned her hair. She assuredly looked better than she had the last time he saw her, all dirty and battered, but she wished she still had something alluring and eye-catching like Jane's red gown.

Anna peeked into the drawing room. Conlan sat across the tea table from her mother. He, too, looked better than the last time they met, his black hair neatly trimmed, clean-shaven, well-dressed, but he looked very solemn as he listened to her mother.

Anna thought it was quite ridiculous to be so nervous about meeting with Conlan after all that had happened. He had rescued her from a fire, fought over her—kissed every inch of her naked skin. But she was very anxious, unaccountably so.

She took a deep breath, smoothed her skirt, and stepped into the drawing room.

"Ah, Anna, there you are," Katherine said. "His Grace has come to inquire in person after your health."

"I am quite well, thank you, and so is my sister," Anna said. She sat down beside her mother, still feeling that strange, stiff formality. "I fear we would not be, though, if it were not for you."

"We are planning to return to Killinan soon," Katherine said. She calmly poured out a cup of tea and passed it to Anna, as if she hosted such awkward little gatherings every day. "This has been a most—interesting social season. I think we need the quiet of the country for a while."

"Very wise of you, Lady Killinan," said Conlan. "I must return to my duties at Adair Court as well."

"Indeed?" said Katherine. "I hope you will call on us at Killinan then. It's not a far distance for an energetic rider."

Conlan watched Anna closely. "I am not entirely certain Lady Anna would welcome me there."

"Are you not?" Katherine glanced between them, her eyes narrowed. "Well, perhaps the two of you would like to walk in the garden for a bit. The sun is out at last, and I'm sure a bit of exercise would do Anna some good."

Before Anna knew what was happening, she found herself wrapped in her cloak and pushed out the doors into the little garden with Conlan. The icy rain had frozen on the tree branches and shrubbery, and that rare winter sunlight turned them to sparkling cut glass. Shards of it lay over the pathways, crunching under her shoes.

She broke off one of the diamond-like leaves and twirled it between her fingers. She still felt shy with him. "I suppose here, at least, we need have no fear of being shot at or stabbed."

"Just spied on?"

Anna glanced back at the drawing room windows and saw one of the satin draperies twitch. "Oh, Mama is quite used to male callers by now. Lord Hartley came seeking Caroline's hand this morning."

"Did he now?"

"Yes." She held up the leaf to study its crystalline facets. "Why have we not seen you here earlier, Your Grace?"

He reached out to take the leaf, his strong, rough, warm fingers closing over hers. "I thought you might not want to see me. Not yet."

She stared up at him in astonishment. How could he think such a thing? She had contemplated nothing but him for days, going over every moment they spent together, every word said between them, every kiss and caress. "Why would you think that?"

"You said it yourself—whenever we're together there is a shooting or a stabbing. You and your sister were kidnapped because of me."

"Not because of you!" she protested. "Because of cruel, greedy men who hate you and what you stand for. You can go on with your work, and I want to help you."

Conlan gave a humorless laugh. "You think they are the only ones who hate me? Anna, I will always have enemies. There will always be men who, as you say, hate what I stand for. Who I am."

"All the more reason why you need someone to stand with you."

"Anna." Conlan caught her face in his hands, his thumbs gently tracing the curve of her lips, holding her close. She swayed into him. How she had missed being close to him, just like this. "There is nothing I want more than to be with you. But I also want you to be safe and happy. To have all that you deserve in life."

Anna gathered up all her courage to finally say what was in her heart. "I was never truly happy until I found *you*. You see me for who I am, who I want to be, and not just a silly, pretty ornament. You are strong and brave, and you make me want to be those things, too. You make me see a purpose in life—to help the people of Ireland, to be one of them. I love you, Conlan, and I know I could make you love me, too, if you would just let me. Please, let me show you how strong I can be."

"Oh, my beautiful *cailleach*," he said. His voice was heavily accented, as if he tried to keep from laughing or crying. He pulled her closer until there was nothing between them, nothing to hold them apart. "You don't have to make me do anything. I love you with everything I am. That's why I tried to stay away, though obviously I couldn't."

Anna looped her arms around his neck. If he tried to leave her now, she would just have to hold on tighter and tighter. "What do you mean? Why would you leave me if you loved me?"

"You've been raised to an easy, glittering life," he said. "One with a man like my cousin. Adair Court is not an easy demesne."

"And you would be no easy husband, Conlan McTeer," she said with a laugh. "But my mother taught me well how to run an estate, how to help people. I will never be called Angel as she is, but I can do the work. I want a husband who will be my partner, who will let me work with him and will see me as myself. As I see you, my fierce Celtic warrior."

Conlan laughed and bent his head to kiss her. She parted her lips under his, welcoming him eagerly. He tasted of mint and tea and cold winter wind—he tasted of the future, and of home and life.

"Ah, Anna my girl," he said as he rested his forehead against hers. "I see I shall have to seize you before you think better of this bargain."

"I never shall. You're everything I ever wanted, Conlan."

"Then there is just one more thing to say."

"What is that?"

"Lady Anna Blacknall, will you marry me and be my duchess?"

Anna closed her eyes and held those words close to her heart. Their Graces the Duke and Duchess of Adair, the most loving couple in all of Ireland. "Yes. I most certainly will."

Epilogue

Adair Court, August 1800

Where is he? He should be home by now!" Anna
stood on the front steps of Adair Court, peering
along the sweep of the drive as if she could will her husband's carriage to appear there. But there was nothing
at all, just the hot summer sun beating down on the lush
green fields.

The child in her womb kicked hard, as if it could sense
her worries. She pressed her hand to the swell of her belly
and felt the imprint of a tiny foot on her palm. She wasn't
the only one anxious for Conlan to come home.

"Soon, little one," she whispered. "Your father will be
home very soon."

Conlan had been in Dublin for weeks now, ever since
word came of the Act of Parliament in London last month.
That meant a vote for the Union in the Dublin Parliament
was imminent, and Conlan had gone to Dublin to join his
anti-Union allies in a final push to stop it. Anna couldn't

go, as she had grown so slow and ungainly with the baby, so tired in the summer's heat, and so she was forced to stay home and do what she most hated—wait.

Aside from hasty messages saying he was safe, she had heard nothing more for weeks. Until yesterday, when word came that the vote for Union had passed amid protests and violent riots. There were deaths and arrests, and news was maddeningly slow to reach Adair Court.

"You should come in the house, Your Grace," she heard Mrs. McEgan say behind her. "It's much too hot for you to be standing about outside."

Anna glanced over her shoulder to smile at the woman who stood in the doorway. Mary McEgan had been very kind to come and sit with Anna every afternoon, to talk to her and distract her, even though she worried for her own husband. Mr. McEgan had gone to Dublin with Conlan, along with several other men of the Adair estate. Anna and Mary worked on plans for the new girls' school at Adair Court, sewed baby clothes, played card games— and sat and waited.

"I'm not tired, Mary," Anna said.

"Maybe not, but I would wager the wee one is, Your Grace! Come sit down and have some lemonade. They probably won't be home today, and if they are, we'll hear their arrival just as well from the sitting room."

Anna glanced once more down the empty drive and nodded. She didn't have just herself to think about now; there was the baby. The future of Adair Court, and all of Ireland, no matter what happened in Dublin.

She went back into the house and shut the door against the bright day. "If they were hurt or locked up in

Kilmainham Gaol, we would have heard by now," she said.

Mary nodded. "Of course we would have. I'm sure they're on their way home now."

They went back upstairs to Anna's own little sitting room, a cool, pretty chamber decorated in shades of rose and cream, that looked out over the drive and the fields and road beyond. When Conlan arrived she would be able to see it from her window.

Little Molly McEgan played with her dolls on the carpet under the gaze of Anna's sisters from their portraits on the wall. Listening to Molly's sweet, girlish murmurs and being surrounded by her familiar piles of books, estate ledgers, and pictures helped Anna feel a bit calmer. But she still kept a close watch out the window.

"Perhaps you could read the letter again, Your Grace," Mary suggested as she poured out glasses of lemonade from the refreshment tray. "That always makes you smile."

Anna laughed as she took the well-worn letter from her sewing basket. She kept them all in there where she could bring them out whenever she needed a bit of comfort. "I have memorized it entirely! I don't really need to read it any longer."

She balanced the precious missive carefully in her hands. The thick packet was worn soft from reading, but she kept it close. It was three letters in one, from her mother and both her sisters in Lausanne. The pages were filled with wonderful accounts of their life in the pretty, lakeside town, news of Eliza's new son and Caroline's studies and her future wedding plans with Lord Hartley.

After the two weddings at Killinan last winter—Anna's

grand affair filled with tiaras, lace, and roses, and Katherine's small family-only ceremony—there had been weeks of celebrations and family parties. Then Katherine, now Madame Courtois, and her new husband departed to join Eliza and Will in Switzerland for a long honeymoon, taking Caroline with them to give her time to consider carefully the match with Hartley. Killinan was left in Anna's care.

They would probably still be there for months to come, and Anna missed them terribly. But the letters brought them close to her, and they were always in her heart.

"I want to hear about Switzerland again!" Molly said eagerly. "About the ice skating. It sounds like so much fun."

Anna laughed. "I am sure they can't be ice skating in August, even in Switzerland!" She pulled out an older letter from the winter and re-read it for Molly and Rose, distracting them all with tales of snow and ice, sledding and skating, until the sun began to set outside.

"I should probably be getting home to see about Mother's dinner," Mary said. "And you need to eat, too, Your Grace. You need to keep your strength up for the baby. I'm sure the men will return tomorrow."

"Yes, I know you're right, Rose. I fear we're going to need all our strength very soon," Anna said, thinking of the impending Union and all it would mean for their country. "Won't you and Molly come back..."

Suddenly, she heard a clamor from outside. She pushed herself from the chair and hurried to the window, with Molly and Mary close behind her. From along the drive came a sight she had been praying to see for days—Conlan coming home.

And he was not alone. It looked as if the entire estate accompanied him in a triumphal parade. Tenants walked alongside the carriage bearing torches, while some of them had even unhitched the horses from their traces and drew the vehicle themselves.

Anna pushed the window open to hear the crowd singing the old Irish song *The Cliffs of Doneen*. She felt the sting of tears in her eyes, and her heart pounded with pride for her husband and her country. Even now, with the last illusion of Irish freedom gone, they were all united. They would not give up.

As the carriage drew to a halt at the front steps of the castle, Anna turned and hurried from the room and down the stairs. As she pulled open the door, the baby stirred again as if to join in the excitement.

Amid the singing and cheers, Conlan climbed down from the carriage. He looked tired, his eyes circled in purple shadows, but he was unbowed. He looked up at her, smiling but somber. He would go on fighting, and so would she. They were truly as one now, dedicated to each other, their family, and their people.

Anna ran down the steps and into his welcoming arms. He held her very close. "You're home at last," she cried.

"Home at last," he answered. He kissed her forehead, her lips. They were together again at last. "But I come in defeat. The final vote for the Union has passed."

Anna shook her head and gestured toward the crowd behind them, still singing and cheering, welcoming their chieftain home. "*They* do not see it as defeat, Conlan! They see that you fought for them, that you will always fight for them. *We* will fight for them."

Conlan laughed and kissed her again. "My fierce *cailleach*."

"I *am* fierce, because you have shown me how to be," she answered. "Together, here, we can do anything."

"Anna," he said. "*Is tu mo ghra*." *I love you.*

"*Is tu mo ghra*," she whispered. "Always."

AUTHOR'S NOTE

I was so excited to revisit the Blacknall sisters in *Duchess of Sin* and discover exactly what happened to Anna. I never had any sisters of my own, though I always wanted one, and this family is my way of living out that fantasy. It makes it even more fun that they live in my very favorite place on earth, Ireland, in a time of great excitement and change. And their story isn't quite finished! We get to see Caroline in book three, *Lady of Seduction*.

Here's some of the history behind the story: The Act of Union was actually two acts, the first passed as an Act of the Parliament of Great Britain on July 2, 1800, and the second an Act of the Parliament of Ireland on August 1, 1800. The two acts united the Kingdom of Great Britain and the Kingdom of Ireland to create the United Kingdom of Great Britain and Ireland, which came into effect on January 1, 1801. In the Republic of Ireland, the first Act was not repealed until the passing of the Republic's Statute Law Revision Act in 1983.

Before these Acts, Ireland had been in personal union with England since 1541 when the Irish Parliament passed the Crown of Ireland Act proclaiming Henry VIII as King of Ireland. England and Scotland were united into a single kingdom in 1603.

The Parliament in Dublin had gained a measure of independence by the Constitution of 1782, and many of its members guarded this hard-won freedom fiercely (the most notable being Henry Grattan, the hero of the anti-Unionists and a minor character in this story). They rejected a motion for Union in 1790 by 109 votes versus 104. Not that the Irish Parliament was open to all Irishmen—only Anglicans of a certain class could become Members of Parliament.

By the late 1790s, with the French Revolution of 1789 and the Irish Rebellion of 1798 (the background of the first Daughters of Erin book, *Countess of Scandal*), Britain was scared and determined to make those wild Irish settle down. The final passage of the Act in the Irish Parliament was achieved in part by bribery, such as awarding peerages, estates, and money to get votes. The measure passed 158 to 115.

A good source to learn more about the politics of the time is Alan J. Ward's *The Irish Constitutional Tradition: Responsible Government and Modern Ireland, 1782–1992* and W. J. McCormack's *The Pamphlet Debate on the Union of Great Britain and Ireland*. (Grattan's speech in Parliament, which I had Anna witness, can be found here in its entirety.) You can visit my website, http://laurelmckee.net, for more sources and historical info, as well as pictures of the sites seen in these books.

And as for the Children of Lir, a statue of them can

be seen in the Garden of Remembrance at Parnell Square in Dublin. It is said to symbolize the rebirth of the Irish nation following 900 years of struggle for independence, just as the swans were reborn after 900 years. It's a very moving sight, and one I'm grateful to have seen!

Don't miss the final book in

Laurel McKee's

Daughters of Erin trilogy!

Please turn this page
for a preview of

Lady of Seduction

Available in June 2011.

Chapter One

Off the Coast of Ireland, 1804

This was not how Caroline Blacknall expected to die.
Not that she had ever thought about it very much.
Living took up too much time and energy to think about
dying. But she would have thought it would be quietly,
in her bed, after a long life of scholarship and travel and
family. Not drowning at the age of twenty-one on a crazy,
ill-advised pursuit.

Caroline clung to the slippery mast as a cold wave
washed over her and lightning pierced the black sky over
her head. The little fishing boat rocked and twisted under
the force of the howling wind. Waves crashed over its
hull, higher and stronger every time, nearly swamping
them completely.

She couldn't hear the shouts of the crew any longer, or
even her own screams. All she could hear was deafening
thunder and the crash of those encroaching waves.

She squeezed her eyes shut and held even tighter to the

mast. She dug her ragged, broken nails into the sodden wood. A splinter pierced her skin, but she didn't mind the pain, or the bitter cold wind that tore through her wet cloak. It told her she was still alive, although probably not for much longer.

Behind her closed eyes, she saw the faces of her sisters, Eliza and Anna, saw her mother's gentle smile. She felt the tiny hands of her nieces and nephews wrapped around her shoulders, heard her stepdaughter Mary's laughter. Were they all lost to her forever?

No! She had just begun to live again after her husband's death a year ago. She had just begun to find her own purpose in the world. That was what this voyage was about, putting the past to rest and moving into the future. She couldn't give up now. Blacknalls did *not* surrender!

She opened her eyes and twisted her head around to see the crew of the little boat scurrying and sliding over the deck as they desperately tried to save the vessel and themselves. They hadn't wanted to take on a passenger, especially a woman, but she had begged and bribed until they gave in. No one but fishermen ever went to the distant, forbidding Muirin Inish.

She wagered they would never take a "cursed" woman aboard again, if they all made it through this.

Caroline tilted her head back to stare up into the boiling sky. It couldn't be much past noon, but that sky was black as pitch, black as midnight. Only jagged flashes of lightning broke through the gloom, lighting up the thick clouds and the turbulent sea.

When they set out from the coast of Donegal that morning, it was gray and misty. One of the sailors muttered about the absence of seabirds, the silence of the water, but despite these supposed ill omens they set sail. Birds couldn't stand in the way of commerce, and Caroline refused to be left behind. She had traveled too far to turn away now, when her destination was at last within her grasp.

She had even glimpsed the famous pink granite cliffs of Muirin Inish, so close yet still so far, when those black clouds closed in. It was all much too fast.

Was he there somewhere? she wondered. Did he watch the storm from those very cliffs?

A crack sounded above her, loud as a whiplash, and she looked up to find that the mast, her one lifeline, cracked. Horrified, she watched it slowly, oh so slowly, topple toward the deck.

Caroline felt paralyzed, captured, and she couldn't move. But somehow she managed to throw herself backward, unpeeling her numb hands from the wood.

She moved just in time. The broken mast drove down into the beleaguered deck, cutting a wound in the boat that swiftly bled more salt water. It twisted onto its side, and Caroline was thrown into the waiting sea.

She had thought it was cold before, but it was not. *This* was cold, a freezing knife thrust into her very heart that stole her breath away. The waves closed over her head, dragging her down.

Somehow she ripped away the ties of her cloak and kicked free of its suffocating folds. She had learned to swim as a child, lovely summer days with her sisters at the lake near their home at Killinan Castle. She blessed those days now as she summoned all her strength, pushed away the numb cold, and swam hard for the surface.

Her head broke through the water and she sucked in a

deep breath of air. The hulk of the floundering boat was far away, a pale slash in the inky sea. The rocky cliffs of shore beckoned through the darkness, seemingly very far away.

Caroline kicked toward it, anyway, moving painfully slowly through the waves. Her arms were sore and terribly weak; it took every ounce of her will to keep lifting them, to not give in to the restful allure of the deep. She knew if she couldn't keep moving she would be lost, and she couldn't give up.

A piece of wood drifted past her, a section of the broken mast. She grabbed onto it and hauled herself up onto its support. It floated toward shore, taking her with it, and all she could do was hang on tightly.

Once it had been fire that separated her from him. Burning, scarring fire and the acrid sear of smoke. Now it was water, cold and just as burning. It felt like the primal wrath of the ancient Irish gods she loved studying so much.

Caroline pressed her cheek to the wood of her little raft and closed her eyes. "This shouldn't be happening to me," she whispered. It was utterly absurd. She was a respectable widow, a bluestocking who preferred quiet hours in the library to anything else. She was not adventurous and bold like her sisters. How did she find herself caught in a perilous adventure straight out of one of Anna's beloved romantic novels?

But she knew how it was she came here. Because of *him,* Grant Dunmore. A man she should have been happy to never see again. They seemed fated to brave the elements together through their own folly.

Caroline felt something brush against her legs, something

surprisingly solid. She opened her eyes to find she was not far from the rocky shore of Muirin Inish. She tried to kick toward it, but her legs had become totally numb and refused to work.

She sobbed in terrible frustration. The tide was catching at her, trying to drag her back out to sea, even as land was so tantalizingly near!

Above the wind, she heard a humanlike shout. Now she was surely hallucinating. But it came again, a rough call. "Hold on, miss! I've got you."

Someone grabbed her aching arm and dragged her up and off the mast. She cried out at the loss of her one solid reality and tried to cling to it, yet her rescuer was relentless. He wrapped a hard, muscled arm around her waist and pulled her with him as he swam for the shore.

Caroline's chest ached, as if a great weight pressed down on her, and dark spots danced before her eyes. She couldn't lose consciousness, not now so close to redemption! She struggled to stay awake, to hold on.

Her rescuer carried them to shore at last. He held her in his arms, tight against his chest, as he ran over the rough, stony beach. Caroline was vaguely aware that she was pressed to naked skin, warm on her cold cheek, like hot satin over iron strength. His heartbeat pounded in her ear, quick and powerful, alive. It made *her* feel alive, too, her heart stirring back into being.

He laid her down on a patch of wet sand, gently rolling her onto her side. "*Diolain,* don't be dead," he shouted. "Don't you dare be dead!"

His voice was hoarse from the salt water, but she could hear the aristocratic English accent under that roughness. What was an Englishman doing on an isolated rock like

Muirin Inish? What was *she* doing there? She couldn't even remember, not now.

He yanked at the tangled drawstring of her plain muslin gown, ripping it free to ease the ruined fabric from her shoulders. Through her chemise he pounded his fist between her shoulder blades, and she choked out the seawater that clogged her lungs. The pain in her chest eased and she dragged in a deep breath.

"Thank God," her rescuer muttered.

Caroline turned slowly onto her back as she reached up to rub the water from her aching eyes. The man knelt beside her, and the first things she noticed were the stark blue-black tattoos etched on his sun-browned skin. A circle of twisted Celtic knotwork around his upper arm, a small Irish cross on his chest. Dark, wet hair lay heavy on his lean shoulders.

Dazed and fascinated, she reached up to trace that Celtic cross with her fingertip. The elaborate design blurred before her eyes.

He suddenly caught her hand tightly in his. "Caroline?" he said. "What the devil are you doing here?"

She slowly raised her gaze to his face, focusing on those extraordinary golden-brown eyes. She had seen those eyes in her dreams for four long years.

And now she remembered exactly why she had come to Muirin Inish.

"I'm here to see you, of course, Grant," she said. Then the world turned black.

THE DISH

Where authors give you the inside scoop!

♥ ♥ ♥ ♥ ♥ ♥ ♥ ♥ ♥ ♥ ♥ ♥ ♥ ♥ ♥

From the desk of Kate Perry

Dear Reader,

In going through my desk, I found personal case notes from Rick Ramirez, the hero of TEMPTED BY FATE, Book Three in the Guardians of Destiny series...

From the files of Rick Ramirez,
Homicide Inspector,
San Francisco Police Department

There's something in the air, and it's not good.

In fact, its been stinking up the city for over a year—just about the time I first met Gabrielle Sansouci Chin, in fact. Although I was investigating a homicide at the time, so maybe I was inclined to be suspicious.

Gabrielle struck me odd, and it didn't help my image of her when she took up with Rhys Llewellyn. He may be an internationally respected businessman, but I can tell he has secrets—dark ones. So does Gabrielle, although as hard as I try I can't seem to uncover them.

As if that wasn't bad enough, my close

friend Carrie Woods got in over her head with the wrong people several months ago. Fortunately, she had her muscle-bound boyfriend Max Prescott to watch over her. That didn't stop her from getting mixed up in one of the strangest deaths I'd ever seen in my career as a homicide inspector for the SFPD.

And now this. Two dead bodies on a park bench.

It should be routine. It should be easy. But something is off—again—and I can't figure out what that is.

I hate that I can't work it out.

Worse: at the scene, I noticed a woman walking away. Or more correctly, I saw the gleam of her white-blond hair as she slipped into the night. The murderer? Highly likely. Which makes the feeling in my gut way more complicated.

Complicated? Right. Screwed up is more like it. Because I want to chase her down, and not to question her about the homicide. Let's just say when I picture putting cuffs on her, it's in less than a professional capacity.

A homicide inspector and the chief suspect in more than one murder. A match made in hell...

RR

I hope you enjoy Ramirez and TEMPTED BY FATE! Don't forget to check out the equally engaging (and hot) heroes in the other Guardians of Destiny books. And drop by www.kateperry.com to say hi—I'd love to hear from you.

Kate Perry

♥ ♥ ♥ ♥ ♥ ♥ ♥ ♥ ♥ ♥ ♥ ♥ ♥ ♥

From the desk of Laurel McKee

Dear Reader,

A while back, I read a book by Paul Collins called *Sixpence House: Lost in a Town of Books*, that stated that a writer's characters can no more take over a story than an eggplant can take over a kitchen. I had to laugh at the image of a bossy eggplant marching into my kitchen (and I sort of wish it *could* take over in there, because I'm a terrible cook), but I have to disagree about the characters.

Sometimes we're lucky enough to meet a character who comes so vividly to life in our imagination that their story *must* be told—and they insist it has to be told *their* way! One such character for me was Lady Anna Blacknall.

Anna was the sister of Eliza Blacknall, the heroine of my first "Daughters of Erin" book, COUNTESS OF SCANDAL. When I started writing that first novel, I knew Anna would have her own story, but I wasn't sure yet what it would be. Then I really "met" her, and she was so many things that I wish I could be: blond, tall, extroverted, a good card player. Even worse—she was really *nice*. She practically sat down by my desk and told me what her story would be. I just had to find the right hero for her, and he presented himself as the dark, strong, mysterious Duke of Adair. A good match for the passionate and rebellious Anna, and the two of them were more than a match for me. She told me their love story, and I just had to keep up and write it all down just as she wanted.

Writing DUCHESS OF SIN was a wild ride, and I was so sorry to say good-bye to Anna and Conlan at the end! (Luckily we'll see them again in the third book, LADY OF SEDUCTION. You can also find excerpts and historical background on the books at my website http://laurelmckee.net.)

I never could have kept up with Anna and her Duke without lots of tea and sugary desserts to see me through. Since these books are set in Ireland, writing them and picturing that country made me crave some of my grandmother's old recipes. This is one of my favorites: Sticky Toffee Pudding. It's a great inspiration!

Ingredients:

- 1 cup plus 1 tbsp all-purpose flour
- 1 tsp baking powder
- ¾ cup pitted dates
- 1 ¼ cups boiling water
- 1 tsp baking soda
- ¼ cup unsalted butter, softened
- ¾ cup sugar
- 1 large egg, lightly beaten
- 1 tsp vanilla

Toffee Sauce:

- ½ cup unsalted butter
- ½ cup heavy cream
- 1 cup packed light brown sugar
- 1 cup heavy cream, whipped

Preheat oven to 350 degrees. Butter a 10-inch round or square baking dish. Sift flour and baking powder onto a sheet of waxed paper. Chop the dates fine. Place in a small bowl and add boiling water and baking soda; set aside. Beat the butter and sugar until light and fluffy. Add egg and vanilla; beat until blended. Gradually beat in the flour mixture. Add date mixture to the batter and fold until blended with a rubber spatula. Pour into the prepared baking dish. Bake until pudding is set and firm on top, about 35 minutes. Remove from oven to a wire rack.

Sauce: Combine butter, cream, and brown sugar in a small, heavy saucepan; heat to boiling, stirring constantly. Boil gently over medium low heat until mixture is thickened, about 8 minutes. Preheat broiler. Spoon about 1/3 cup of the sauce over the pudding. Spread evenly on top. Place pudding under the broiler until the topping is bubbly, about 1 minute. Serve immediately, spooned into dessert bowls. Drizzle with remaining toffee sauce and top with a spoonful of whipped cream.

Enjoy!

Laurel McKee

Want to know more about romances at
Grand Central Publishing and Forever?
Get the scoop online!

GRAND CENTRAL PUBLISHING'S ROMANCE HOMEPAGE

Visit us at www.hachettebookgroup.com/romance
for all the latest news, reviews, and chapter excerpts!

NEW AND UPCOMING TITLES

Each month we feature our new titles
and reader favorites.

CONTESTS AND GIVEAWAYS

We give away galleys, autographed copies,
and all kinds of fun stuff.

AUTHOR INFO

You'll find bios, articles, and links to personal
websites for all your favorite authors—and
so much more!

THE BUZZ

Sign up for our monthly romance newsletter,
and be the first to read all about it!